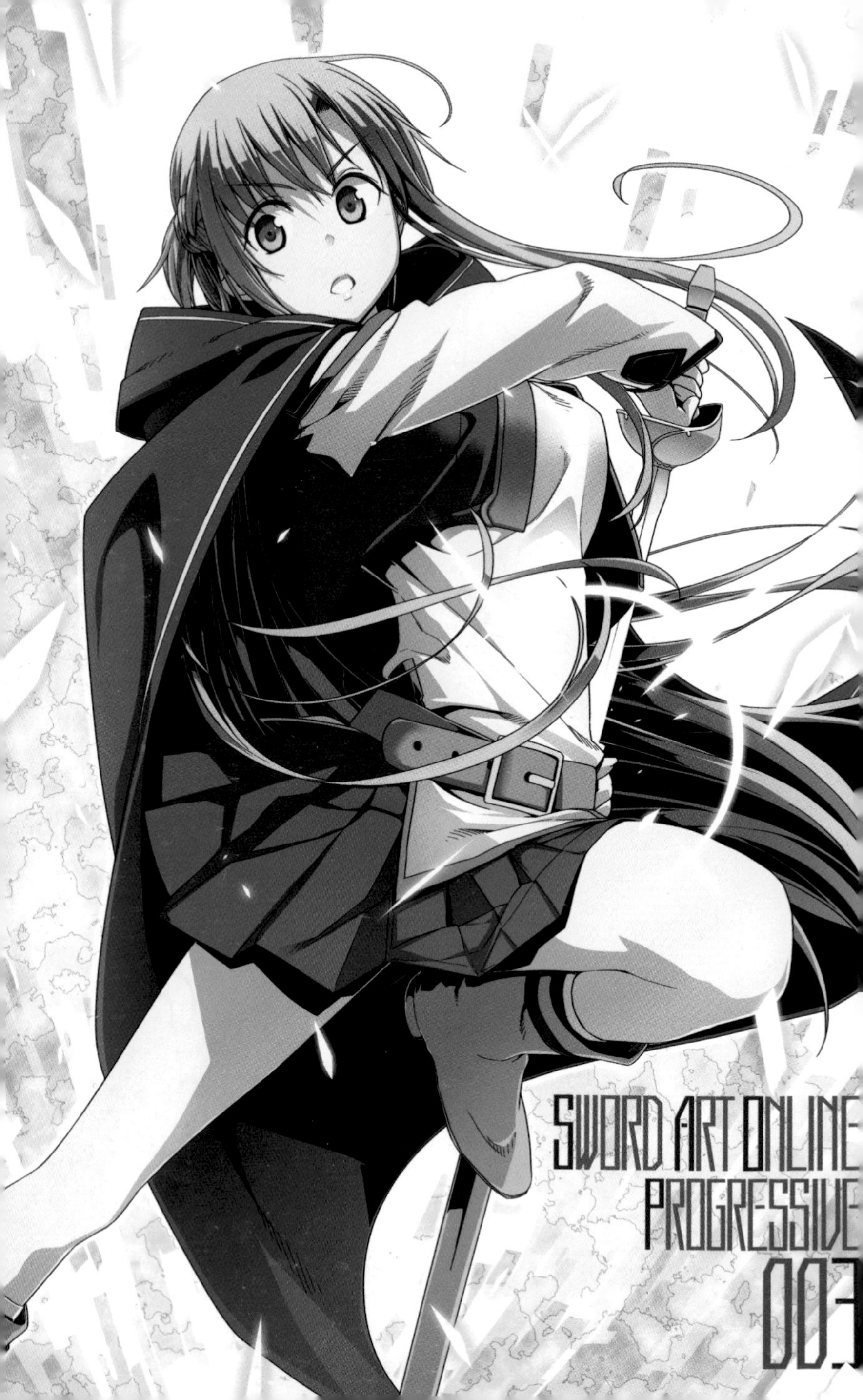
SWORD ART ONLINE
PROGRESSIVE
003

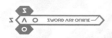

SWORD ART ONLINE PROGRESSIVE 003

CONTENTS.

ART: KISEKI HIMURA
ORIGINAL STORY: REKI KAWAHARA
CHARACTER DESIGN: abec

#010.5: Loss

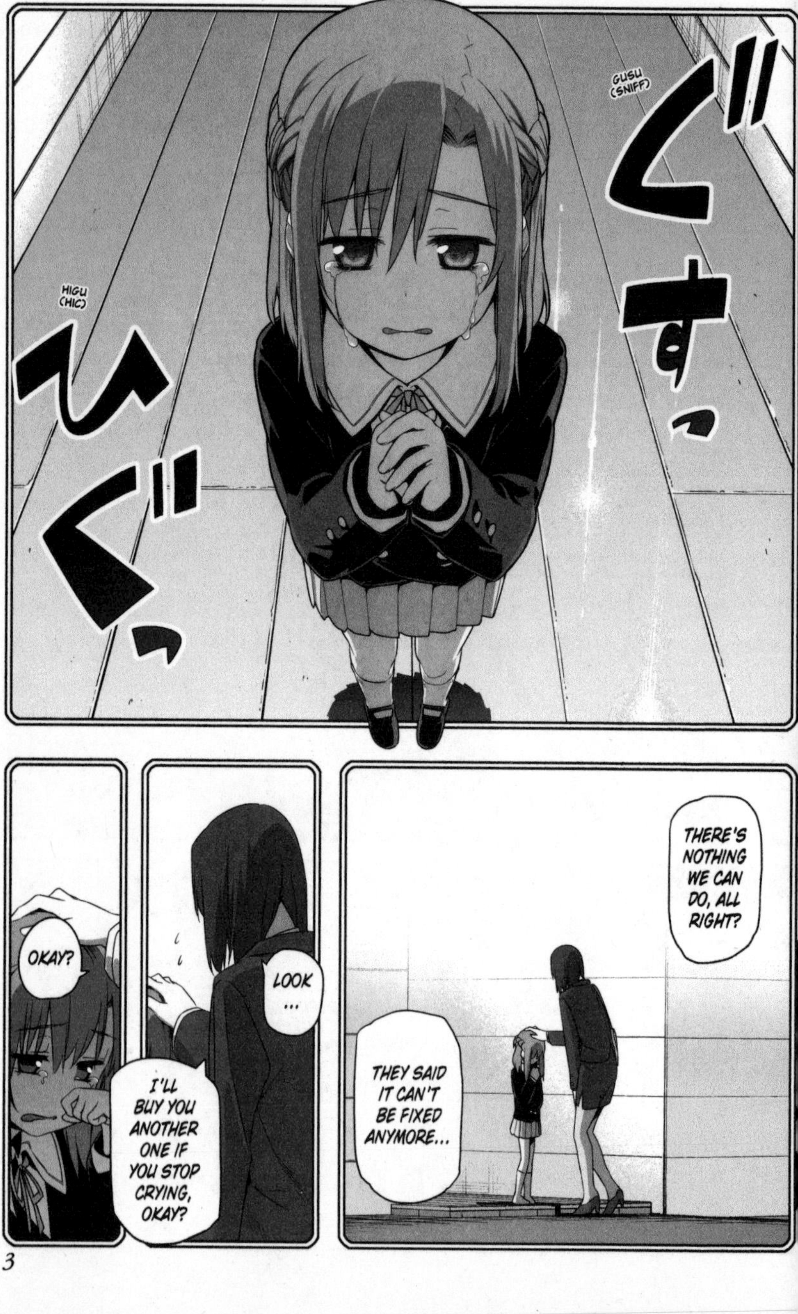
GUSU (SNIFF)
ぐすっ
HIGU (HIC)
ひぐっ
THERE'S NOTHING WE CAN DO, ALL RIGHT?
THEY SAID IT CAN'T BE FIXED ANYMORE...
LOOK ...
I'LL BUY YOU ANOTHER ONE IF YOU STOP CRYING, OKAY?
OKAY?

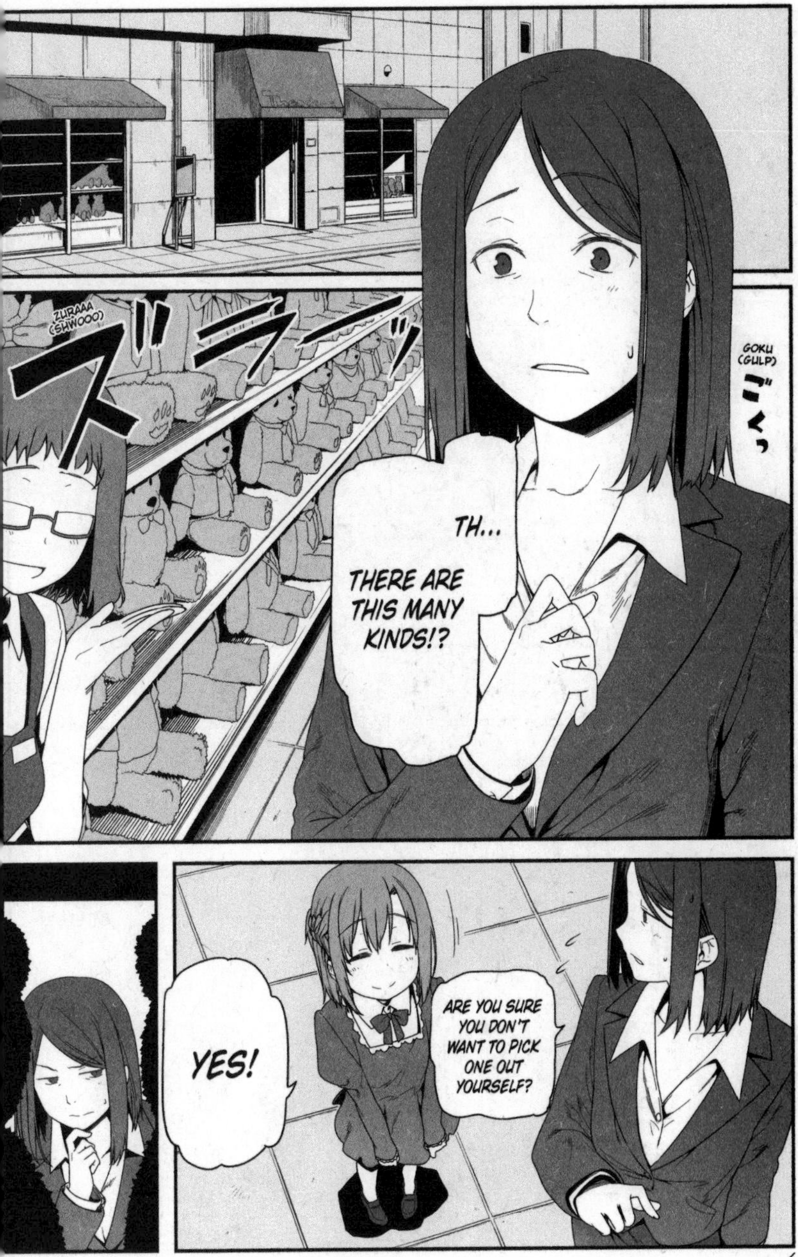
GOKU (GULP)
ごくっ
TH...
THERE ARE THIS MANY KINDS!?
ZURAAA (SHWOOO)
ズラーーッ
ARE YOU SURE YOU DON'T WANT TO PICK ONE OUT YOURSELF?
YES!

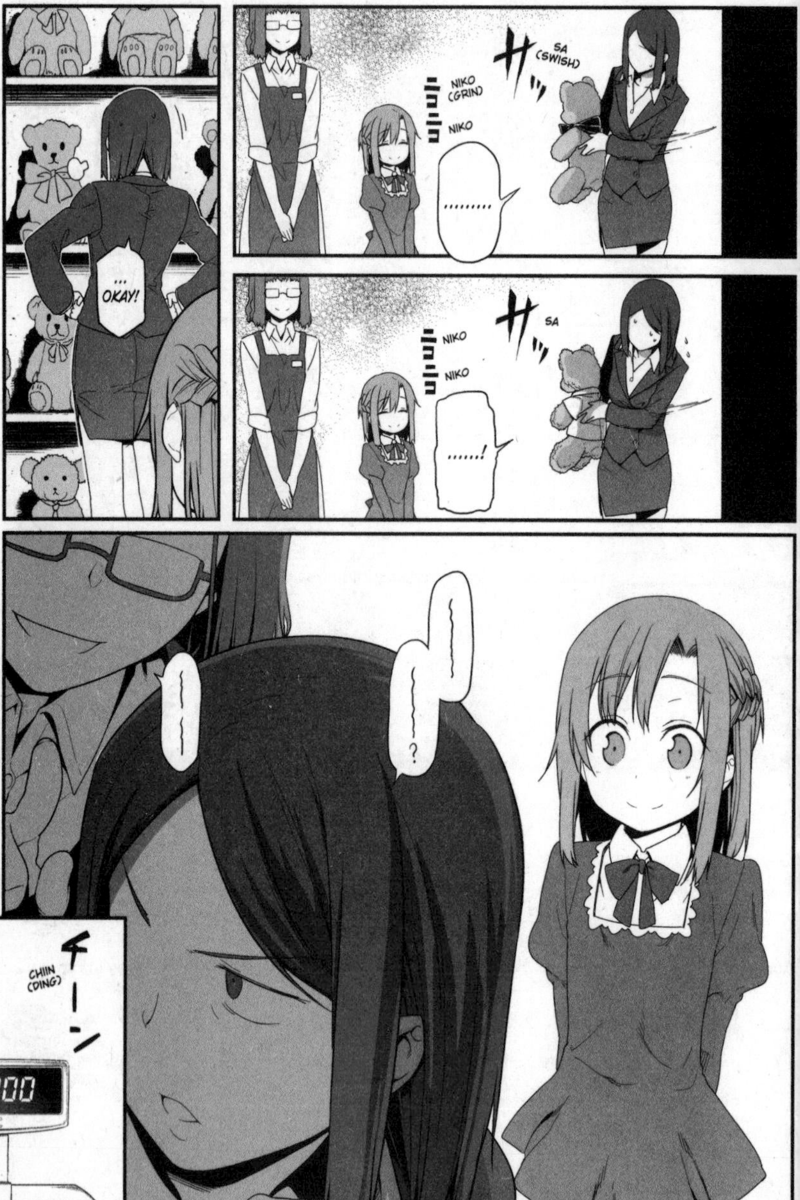
SA (SWISH)
NIKO (GRIN)
NIKO
....
SA
NIKO
NIKO
......!
... OKAY!
......?
......
CHIIN (DING)
900

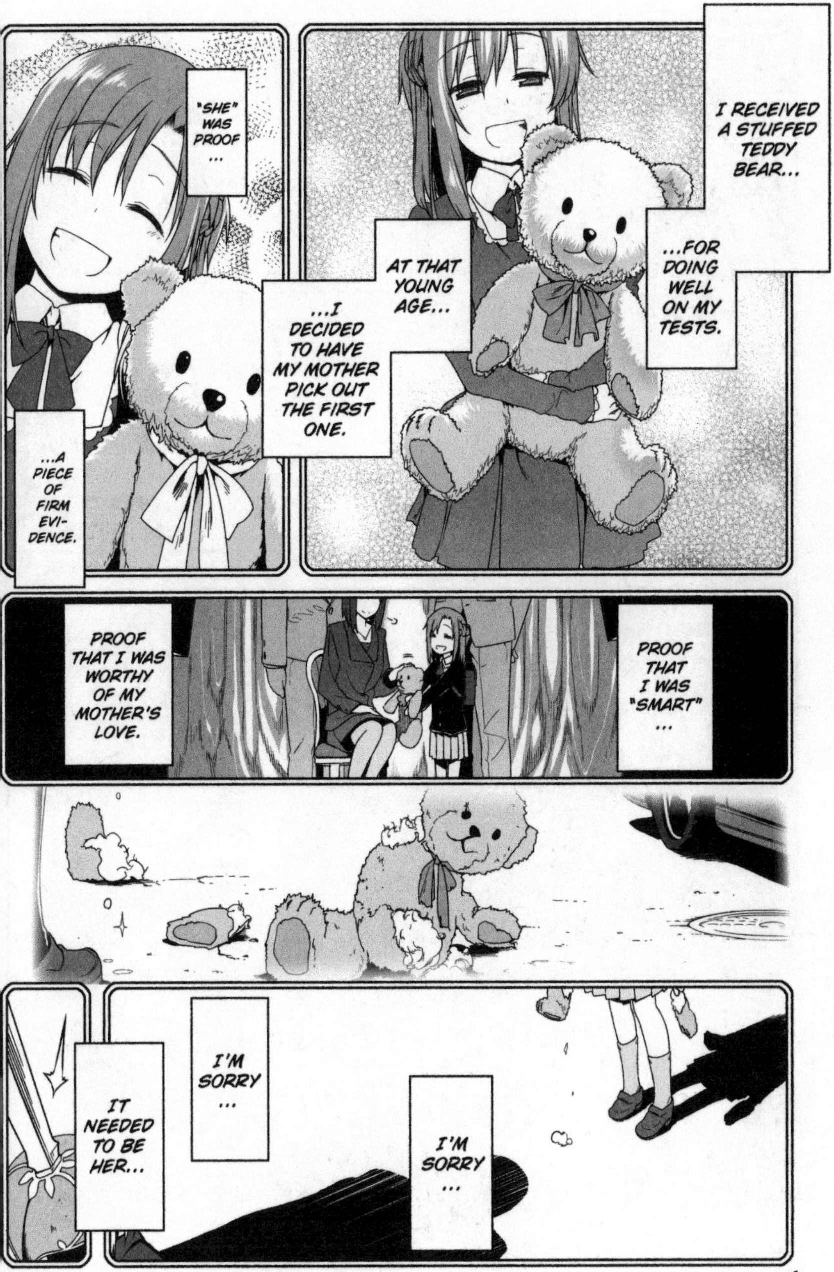
I RECEIVED A STUFFED TEDDY BEAR...
...FOR DOING WELL ON MY TESTS.
AT THAT YOUNG AGE...
...I DECIDED TO HAVE MY MOTHER PICK OUT THE FIRST ONE.
"SHE" WAS PROOF ...
...A PIECE OF FIRM EVI-DENCE.
PROOF THAT I WAS "SMART" ...
PROOF THAT I WAS WORTHY OF MY MOTHER'S LOVE.
I'M SORRY ...
I'M SORRY ...
IT NEEDED TO BE HER...

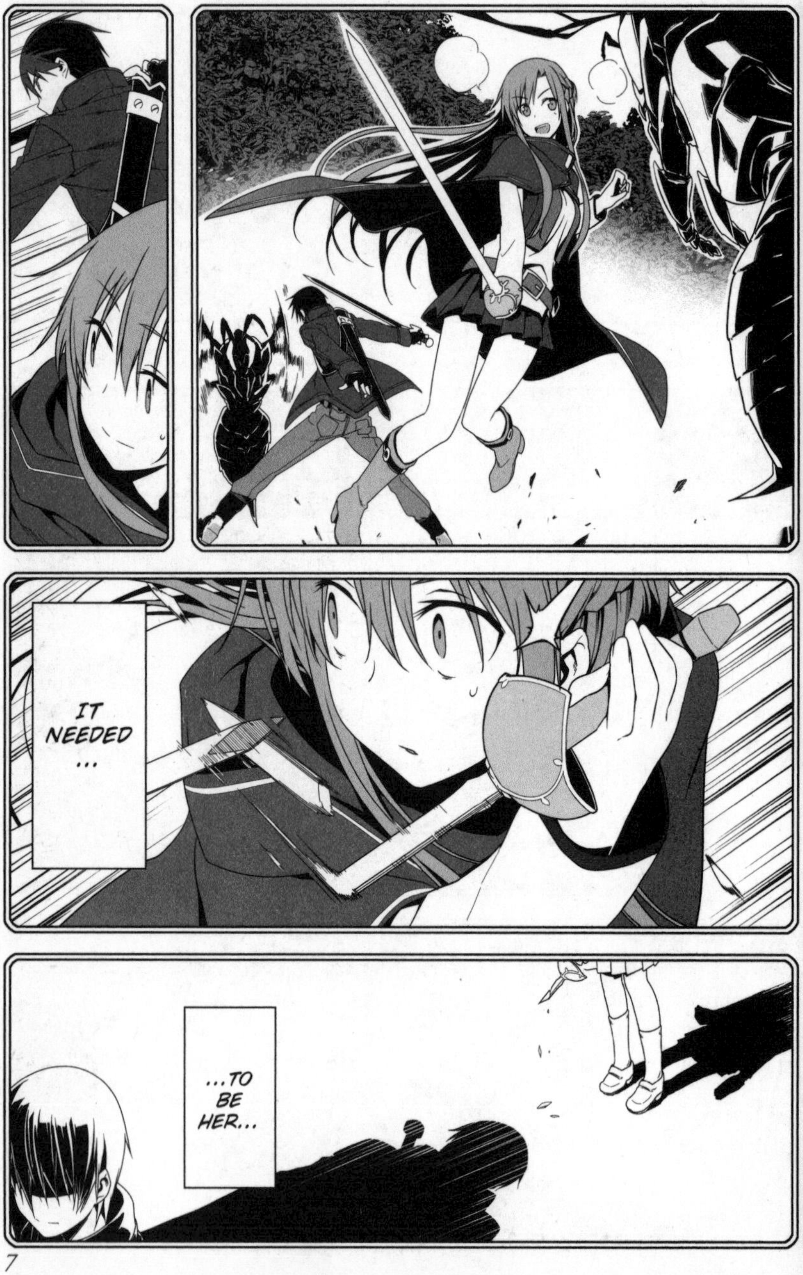
IT NEEDED ...
...TO BE HER...

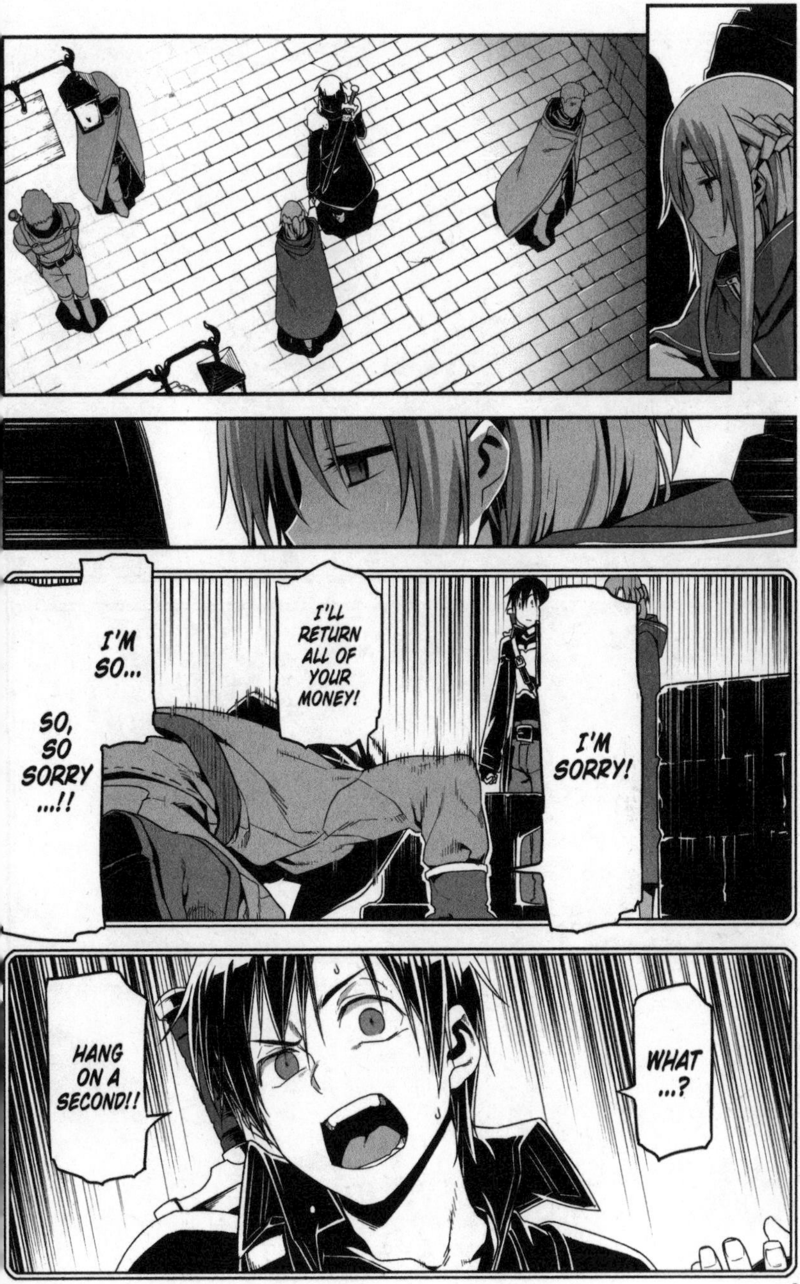
I'M SORRY!
I'LL RETURN ALL OF YOUR MONEY!
I'M SO...
SO, SO SORRY ...!!
WHAT ...?
HANG ON A SECOND!!

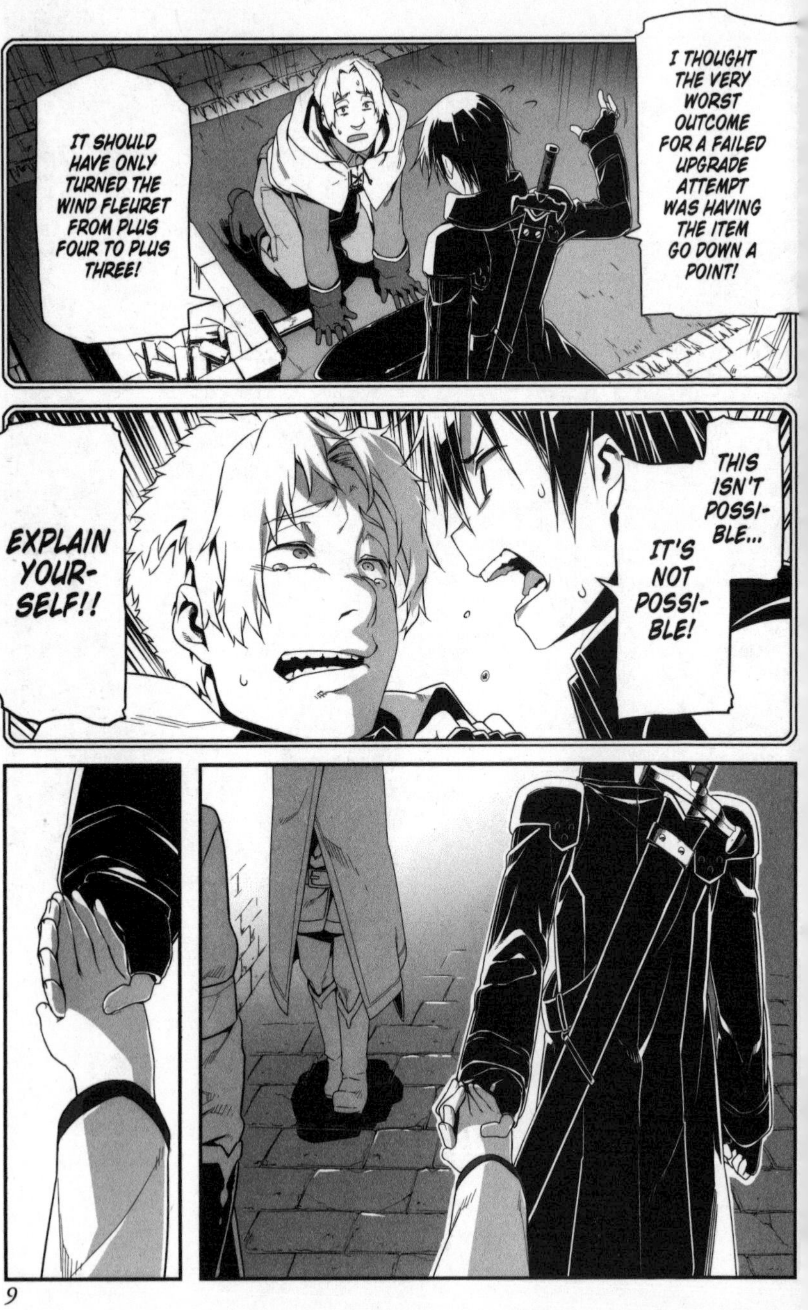
I THOUGHT THE VERY WORST OUTCOME FOR A FAILED UPGRADE ATTEMPT WAS HAVING THE ITEM GO DOWN A POINT!
IT SHOULD HAVE ONLY TURNED THE WIND FLEURET FROM PLUS FOUR TO PLUS THREE!
THIS ISN'T POSSIBLE...
IT'S NOT POSSIBLE!
EXPLAIN YOURSELF!!

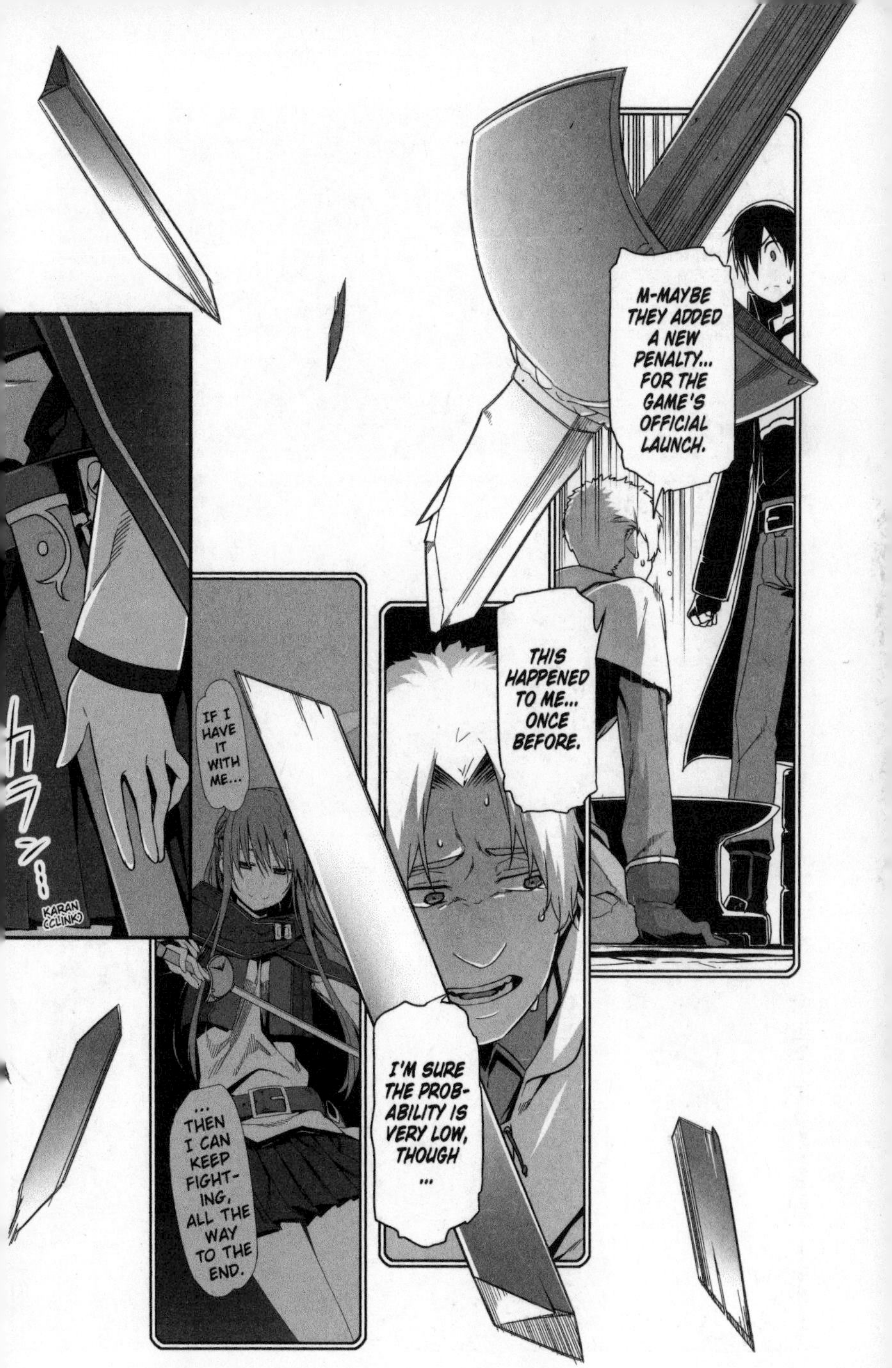
M-MAYBE THEY ADDED A NEW PENALTY... FOR THE GAME'S OFFICIAL LAUNCH.
THIS HAPPENED TO ME... ONCE BEFORE.
I'M SURE THE PROB-ABILITY IS VERY LOW, THOUGH ...
カラン
KARAN (CLINK)
IF I HAVE IT WITH ME...
... THEN I CAN KEEP FIGHT-ING, ALL THE WAY TO THE END.

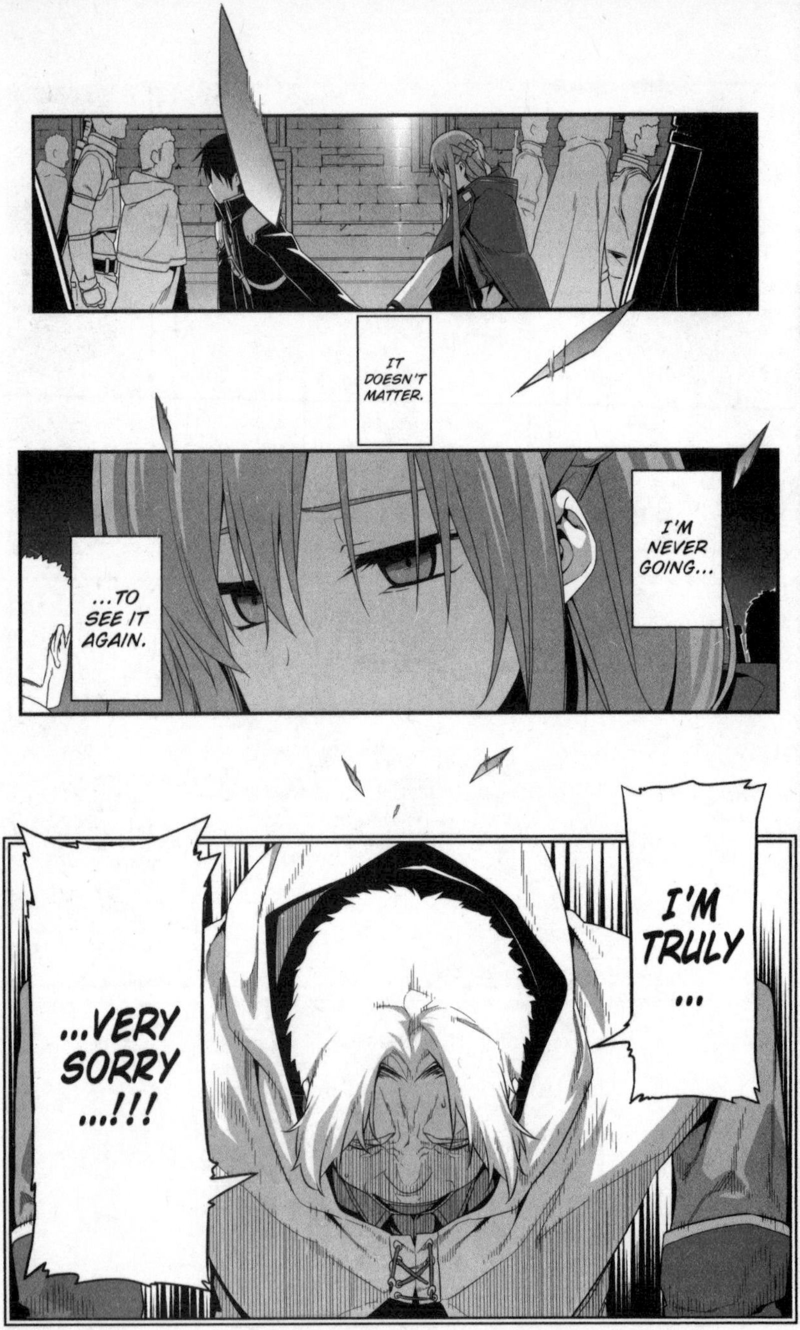
IT DOESN'T MATTER.
I'M NEVER GOING...
...TO SEE IT AGAIN.
I'M TRULY ...
...VERY SORRY ...!!!

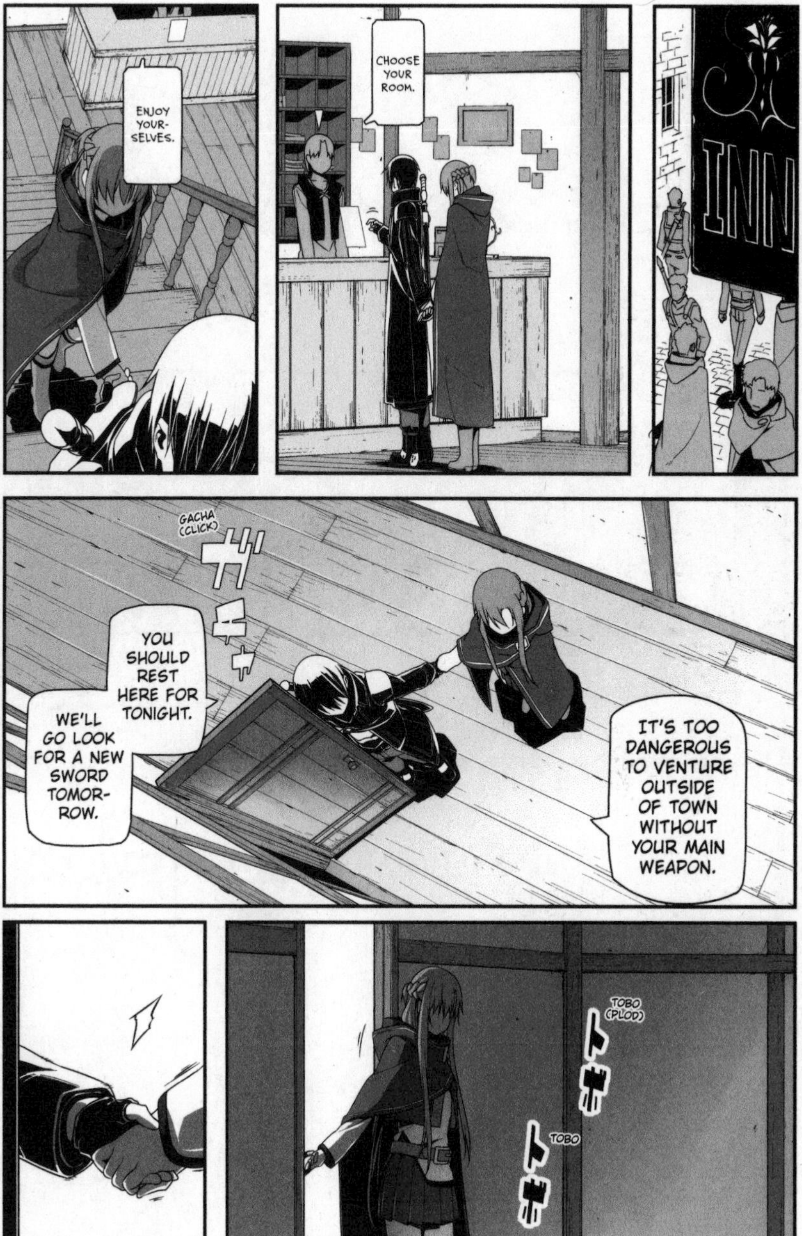
INN
CHOOSE YOUR ROOM.
ENJOY YOUR-SELVES.
GACHA (CLICK)
IT'S TOO DANGEROUS TO VENTURE OUTSIDE OF TOWN WITHOUT YOUR MAIN WEAPON.
YOU SHOULD REST HERE FOR TONIGHT.
WE'LL GO LOOK FOR A NEW SWORD TOMOR-ROW.
TOBO (PLOD)
TOBO

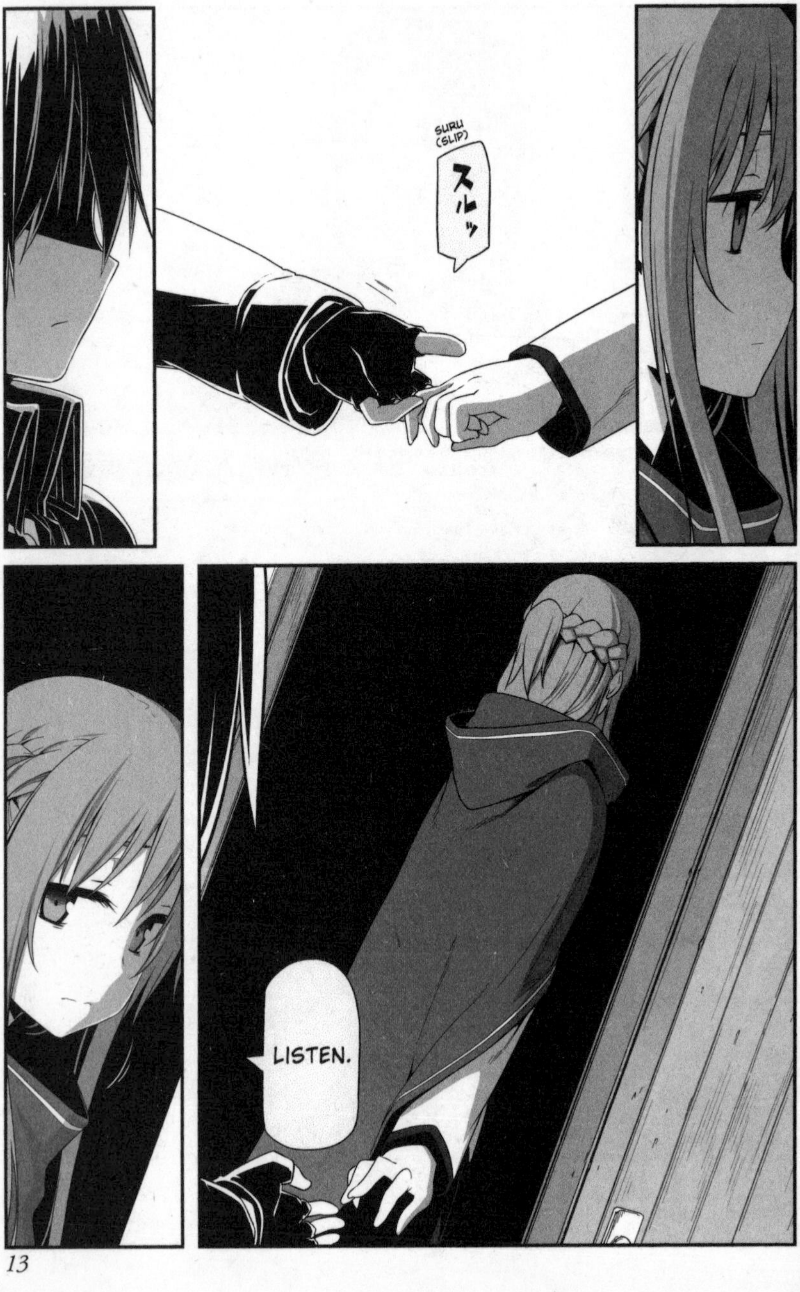
SURU (SLIP)
スルッ
LISTEN.

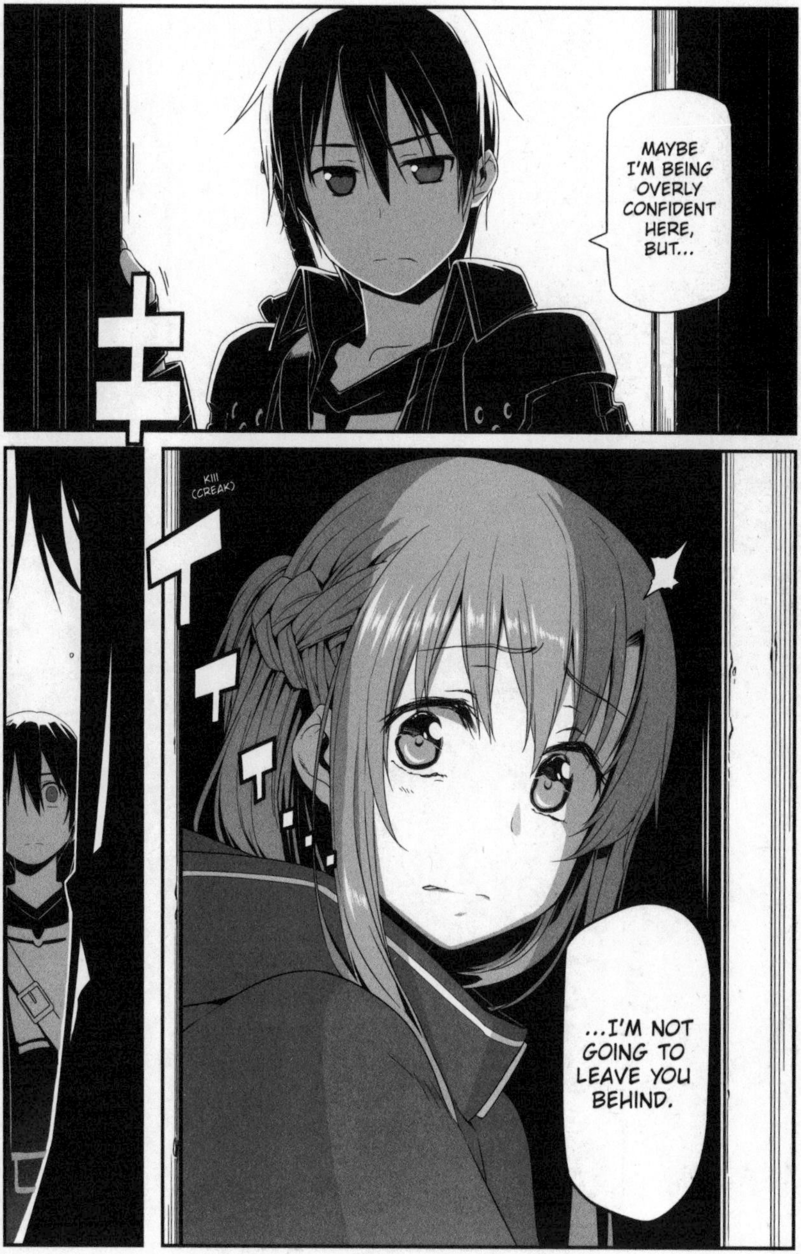
MAYBE I'M BEING OVERLY CONFIDENT HERE, BUT...
KIII (CREAK)
...I'M NOT GOING TO LEAVE YOU BEHIND.

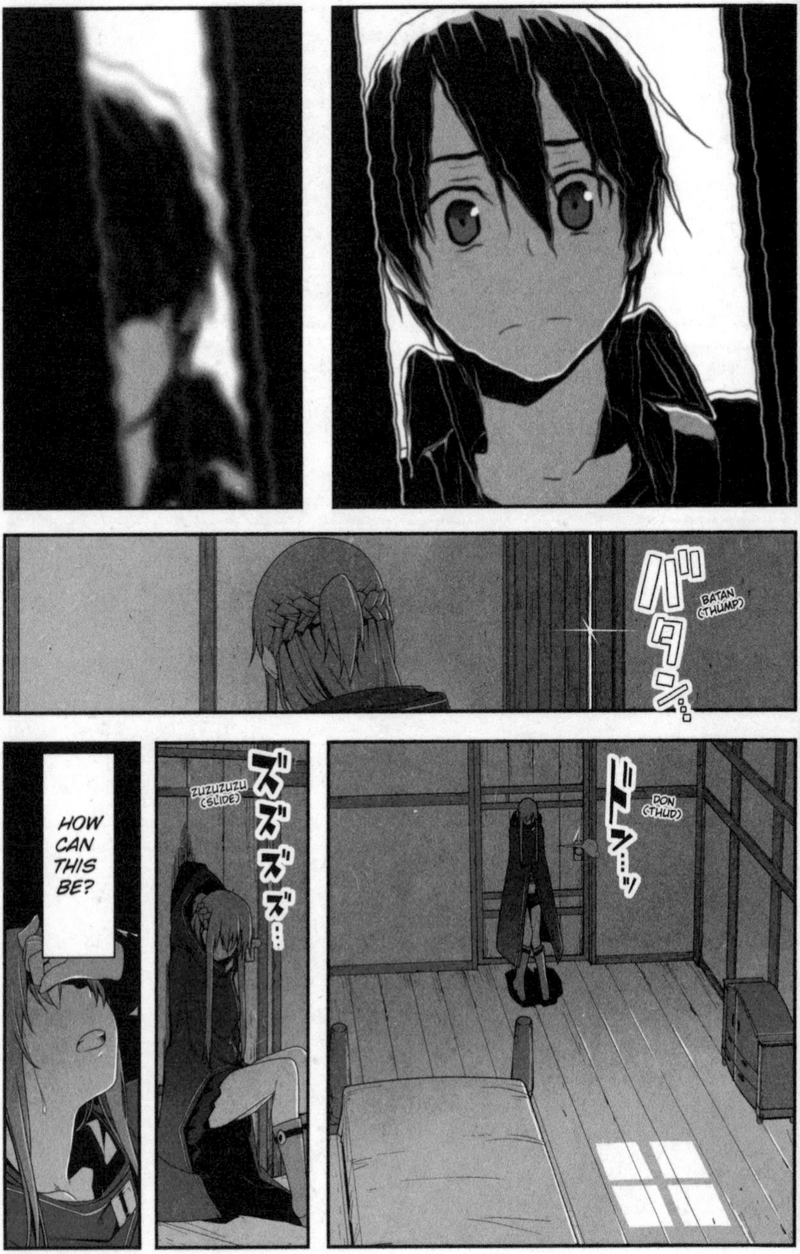

バタン
BATAN (THUMP)
ドンッ
DON (THUD)
ズズズズ…
ZUZUZUZU (SLIDE)
HOW CAN THIS BE?

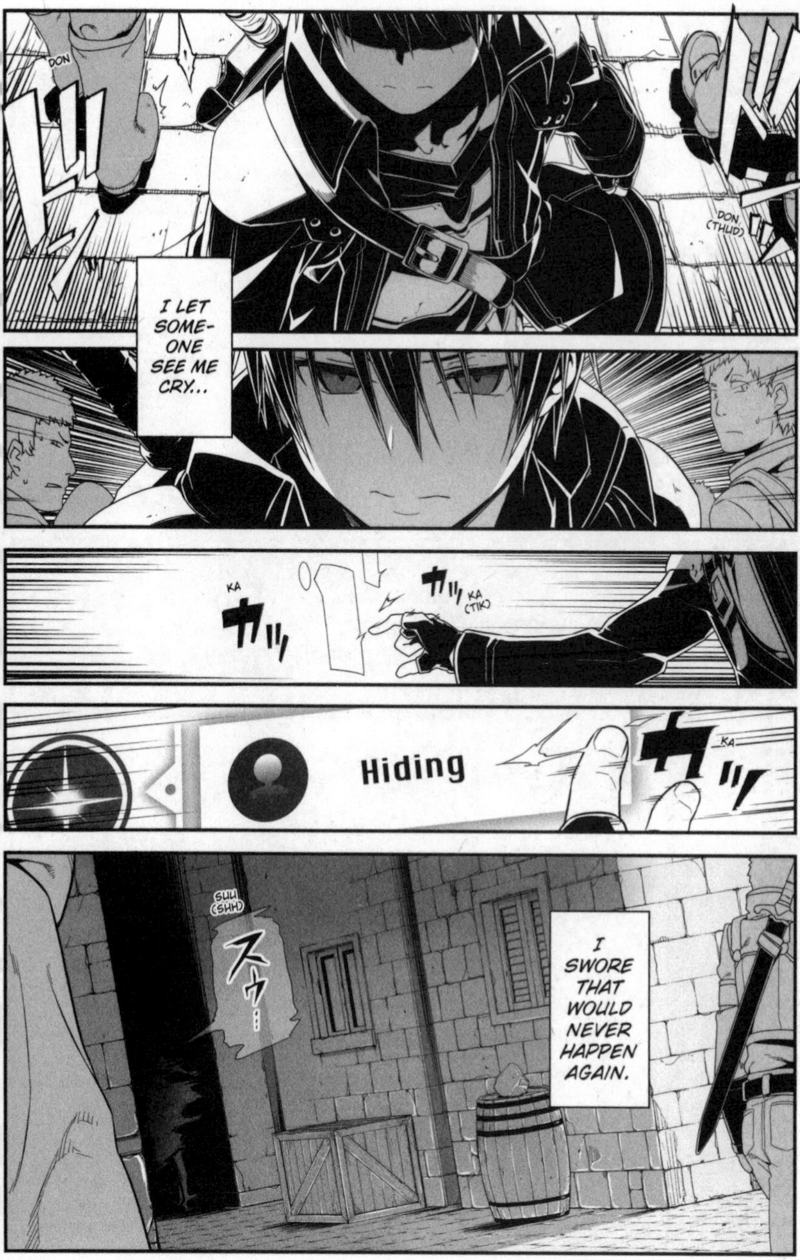
DON (THUD)
DON
I LET SOME-ONE SEE ME CRY...
KA (TIK)
KA
KA
Hiding
SUU (SHH)
I SWORE THAT WOULD NEVER HAPPEN AGAIN.

#011: Return

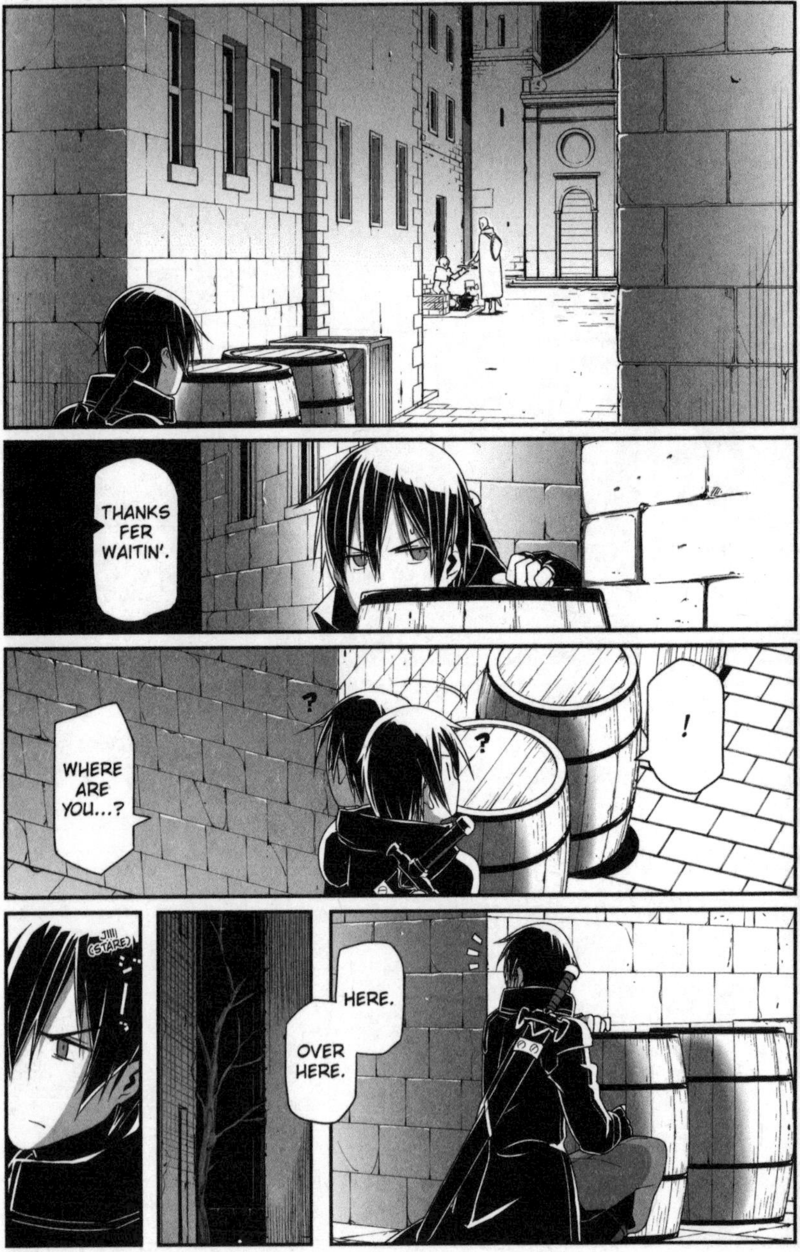
THANKS FER WAITIN'.
!
?
?
WHERE ARE YOU...?
HERE.
OVER HERE.
JIIII (STARE)

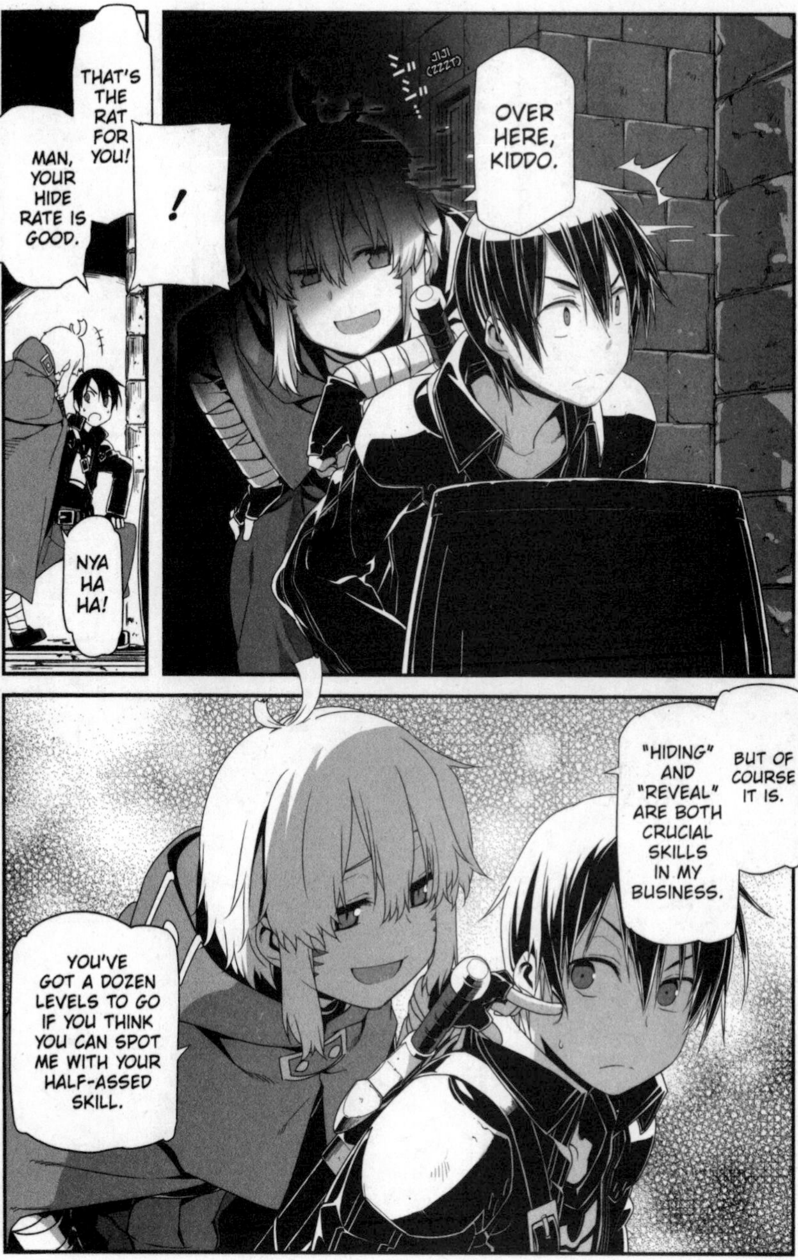
OVER HERE, KIDDO.
JIJI (ZZZT)
!
THAT'S THE RAT FOR YOU!
MAN, YOUR HIDE RATE IS GOOD.
NYA HA HA!
BUT OF COURSE IT IS.
"HIDING" AND "REVEAL" ARE BOTH CRUCIAL SKILLS IN MY BUSINESS.
YOU'VE GOT A DOZEN LEVELS TO GO IF YOU THINK YOU CAN SPOT ME WITH YOUR HALF-ASSED SKILL.

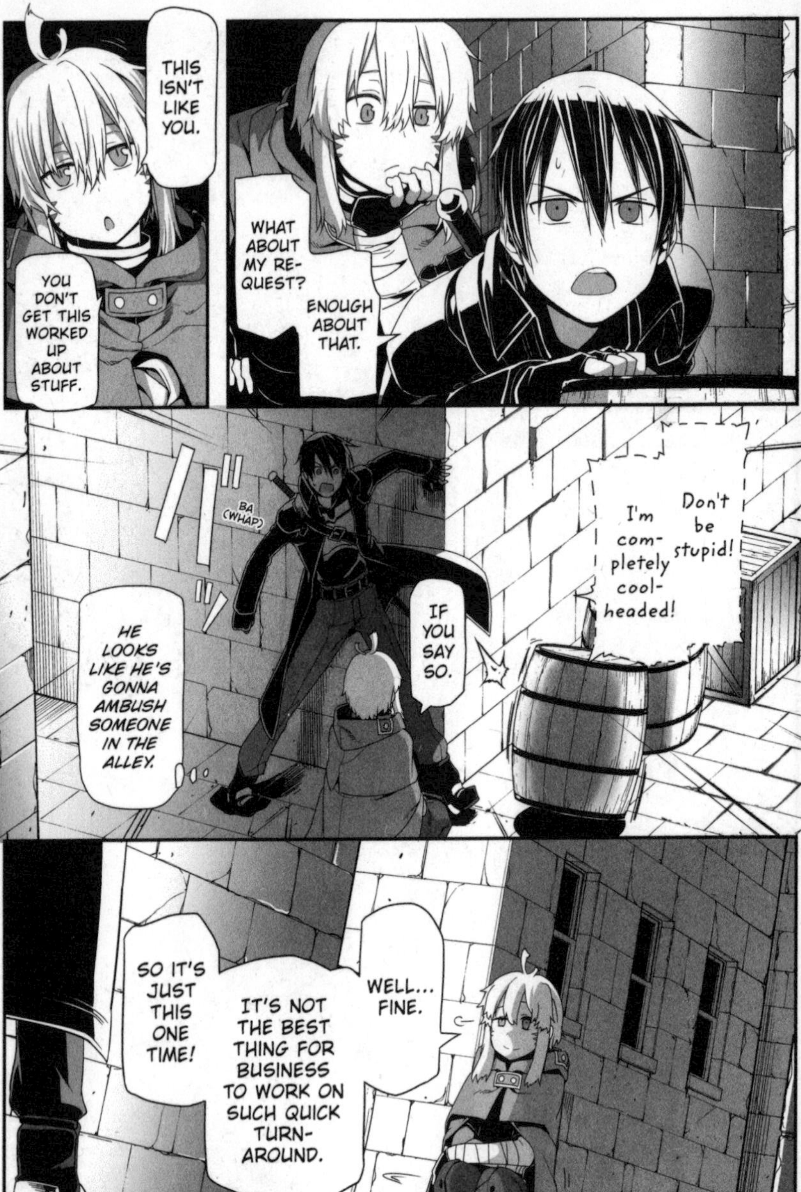
WHAT ABOUT MY RE-QUEST?
ENOUGH ABOUT THAT.
THIS ISN'T LIKE YOU.
YOU DON'T GET THIS WORKED UP ABOUT STUFF.
Don't be stupid!
I'm com-pletely cool-headed!
BA (WHAP)
IF YOU SAY SO.
HE LOOKS LIKE HE'S GONNA AMBUSH SOMEONE IN THE ALLEY.
WELL... FINE.
IT'S NOT THE BEST THING FOR BUSINESS TO WORK ON SUCH QUICK TURN-AROUND.
SO IT'S JUST THIS ONE TIME!

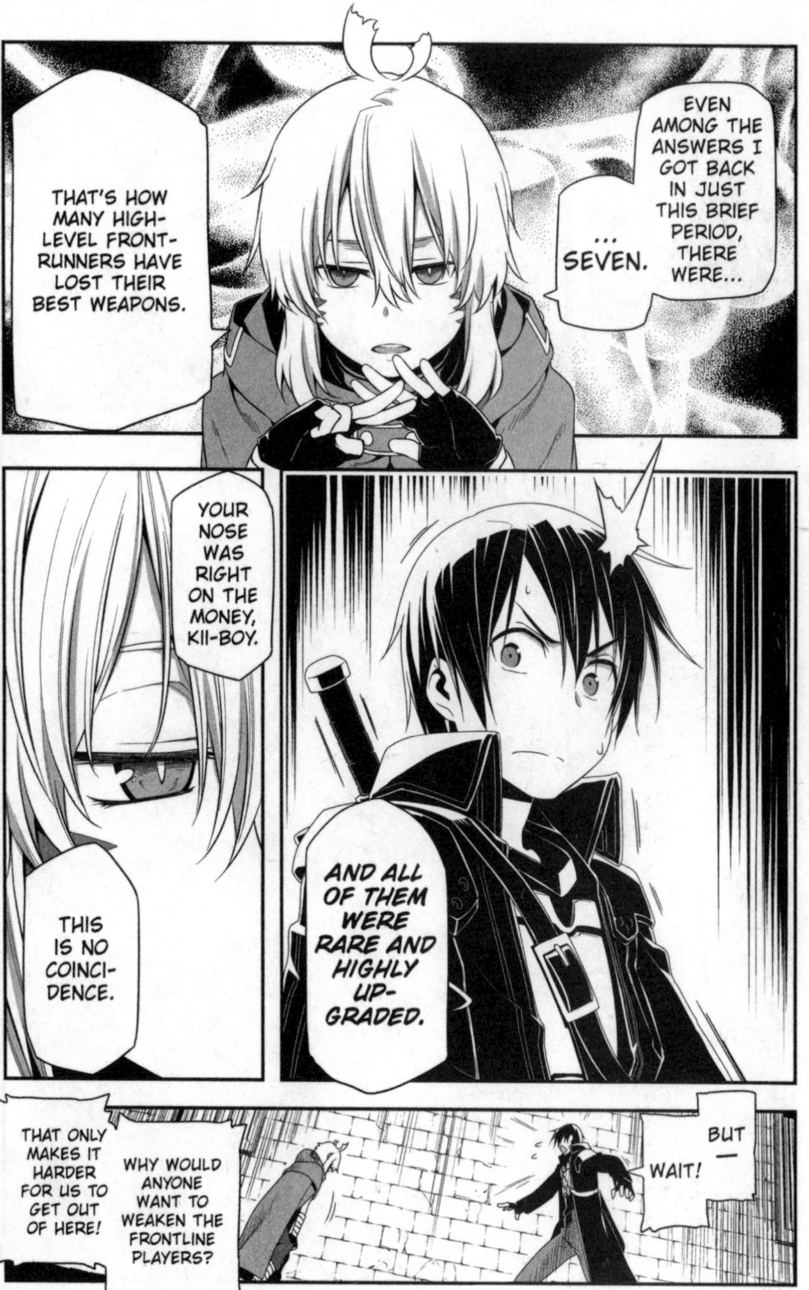
EVEN AMONG THE ANSWERS I GOT BACK IN JUST THIS BRIEF PERIOD, THERE WERE...
... SEVEN.
THAT'S HOW MANY HIGH-LEVEL FRONT-RUNNERS HAVE LOST THEIR BEST WEAPONS.
AND ALL OF THEM WERE RARE AND HIGHLY UP-GRADED.
YOUR NOSE WAS RIGHT ON THE MONEY, KII-BOY.
THIS IS NO COINCI-DENCE.
BUT —
WAIT!
WHY WOULD ANYONE WANT TO WEAKEN THE FRONTLINE PLAYERS?
THAT ONLY MAKES IT HARDER FOR US TO GET OUT OF HERE!

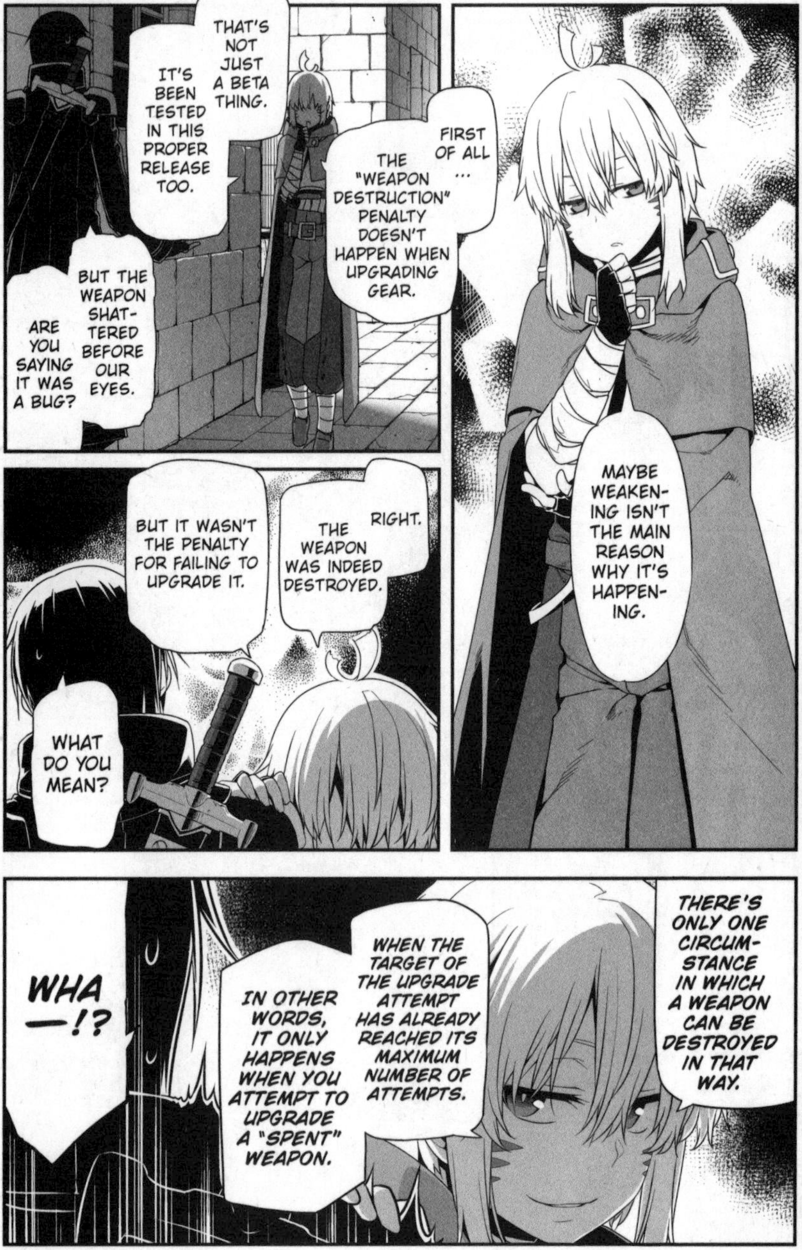
MAYBE WEAKENING ISN'T THE MAIN REASON WHY IT'S HAPPENING.
THAT'S NOT JUST A BETA THING.
IT'S BEEN TESTED IN THIS PROPER RELEASE TOO.
FIRST OF ALL ... THE "WEAPON DESTRUCTION" PENALTY DOESN'T HAPPEN WHEN UPGRADING GEAR.
BUT THE WEAPON SHATTERED BEFORE OUR EYES.
ARE YOU SAYING IT WAS A BUG?
RIGHT. THE WEAPON WAS INDEED DESTROYED.
BUT IT WASN'T THE PENALTY FOR FAILING TO UPGRADE IT.
WHAT DO YOU MEAN?
THERE'S ONLY ONE CIRCUMSTANCE IN WHICH A WEAPON CAN BE DESTROYED IN THAT WAY.
WHEN THE TARGET OF THE UPGRADE ATTEMPT HAS ALREADY REACHED ITS MAXIMUM NUMBER OF ATTEMPTS.
IN OTHER WORDS, IT ONLY HAPPENS WHEN YOU ATTEMPT TO UPGRADE A "SPENT" WEAPON.
WHA—!?

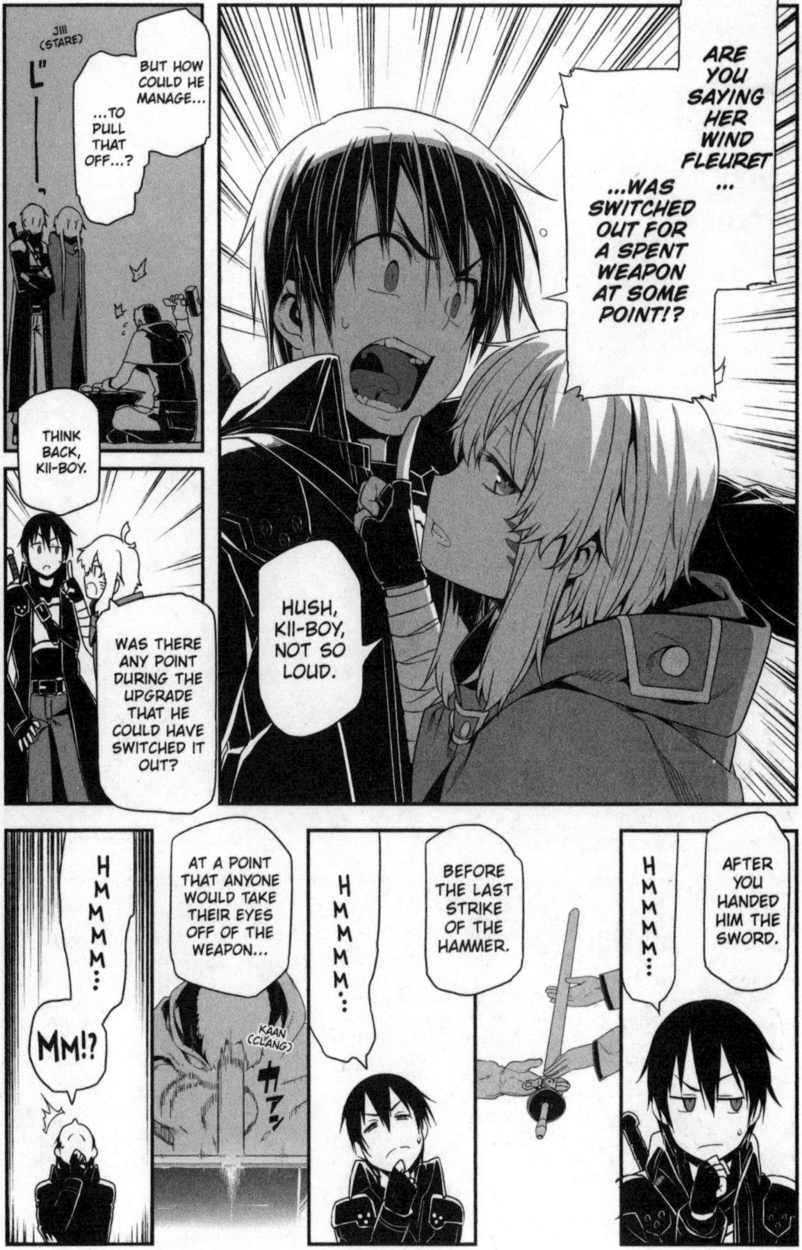
ARE YOU SAYING HER WIND FLEURET...
...WAS SWITCHED OUT FOR A SPENT WEAPON AT SOME POINT!?
HUSH, KII-BOY, NOT SO LOUD.
JIII (STARE)
BUT HOW COULD HE MANAGE...
...TO PULL THAT OFF...?
THINK BACK, KII-BOY.
WAS THERE ANY POINT DURING THE UPGRADE THAT HE COULD HAVE SWITCHED IT OUT?
AFTER YOU HANDED HIM THE SWORD.
HMMMM...
BEFORE THE LAST STRIKE OF THE HAMMER.
HMMMM...
KAAN (CLANG)
AT A POINT THAT ANYONE WOULD TAKE THEIR EYES OFF OF THE WEAPON...
HMMMM...
MM!?

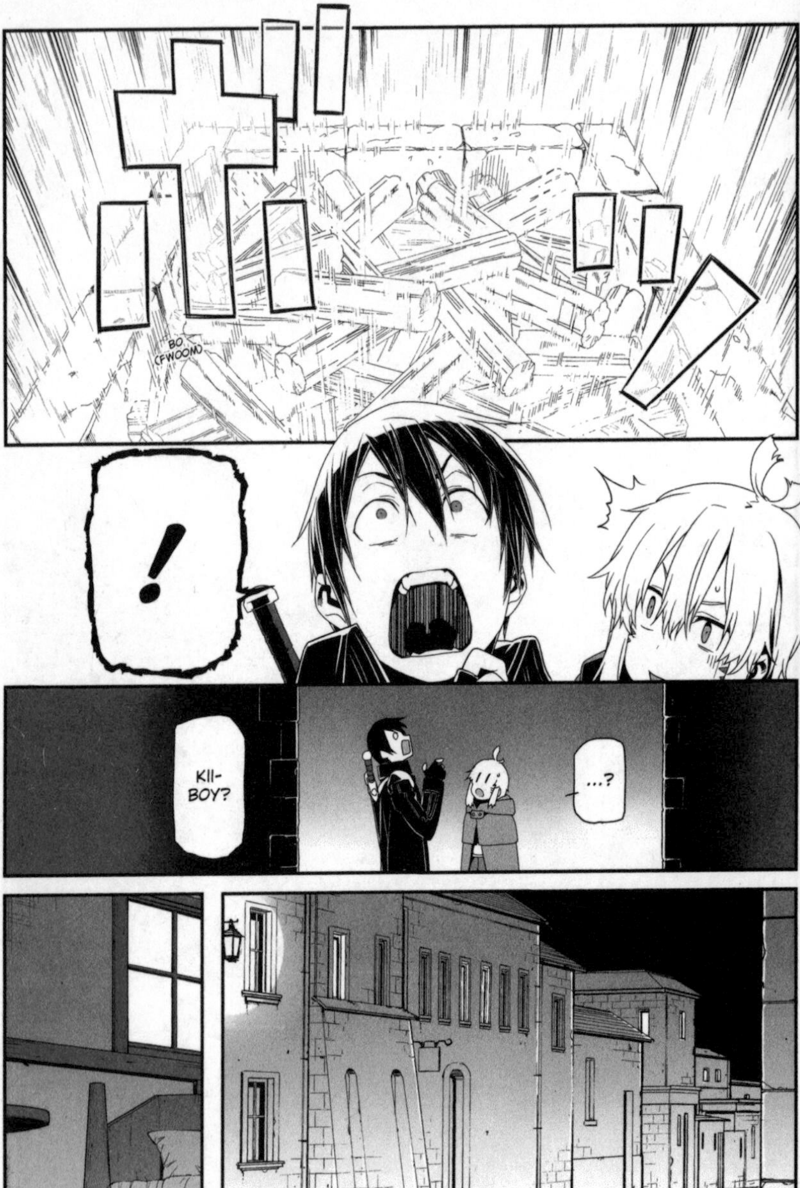
BO (FWOOM)
!
...?
KII-BOY?

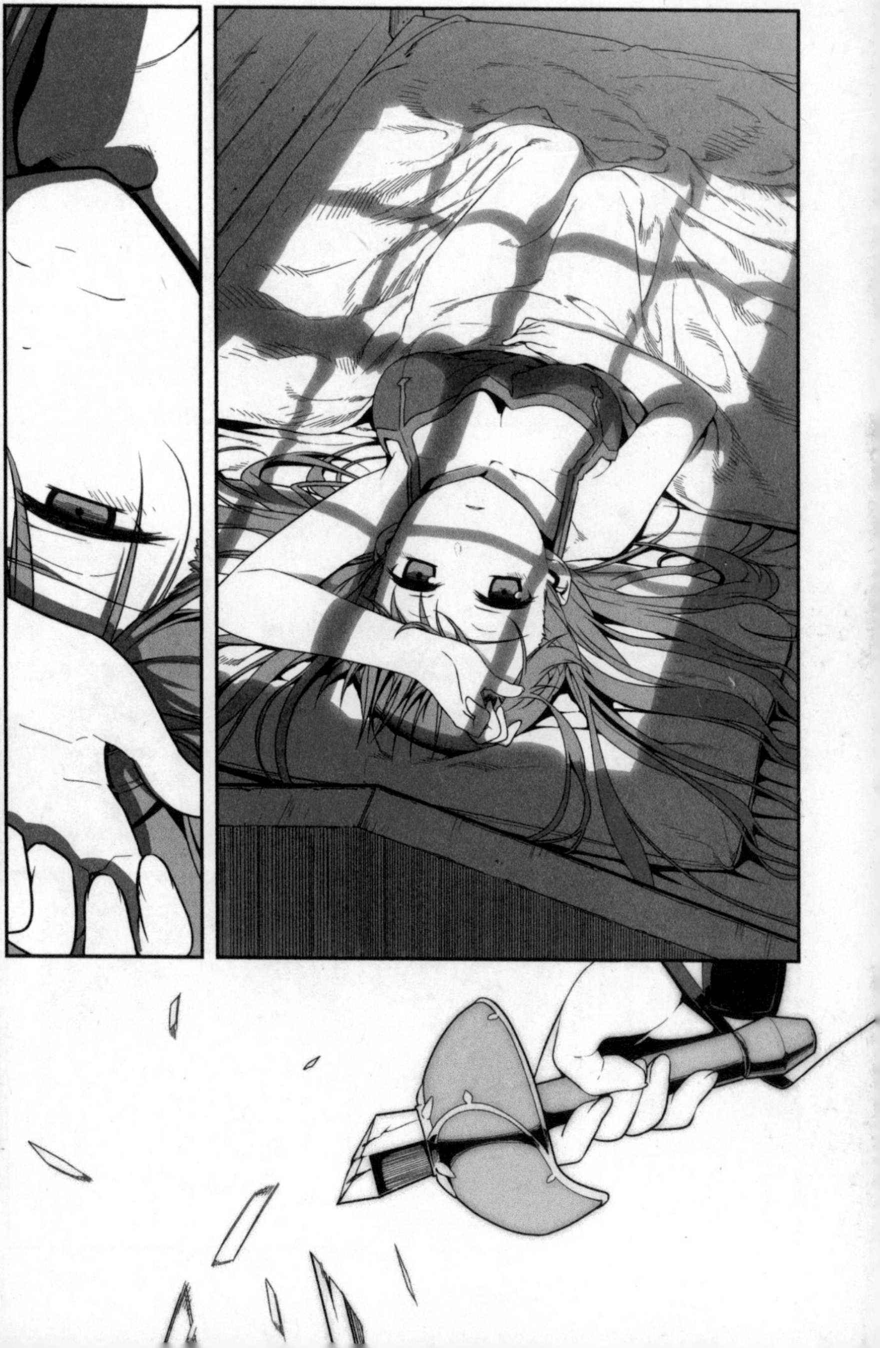

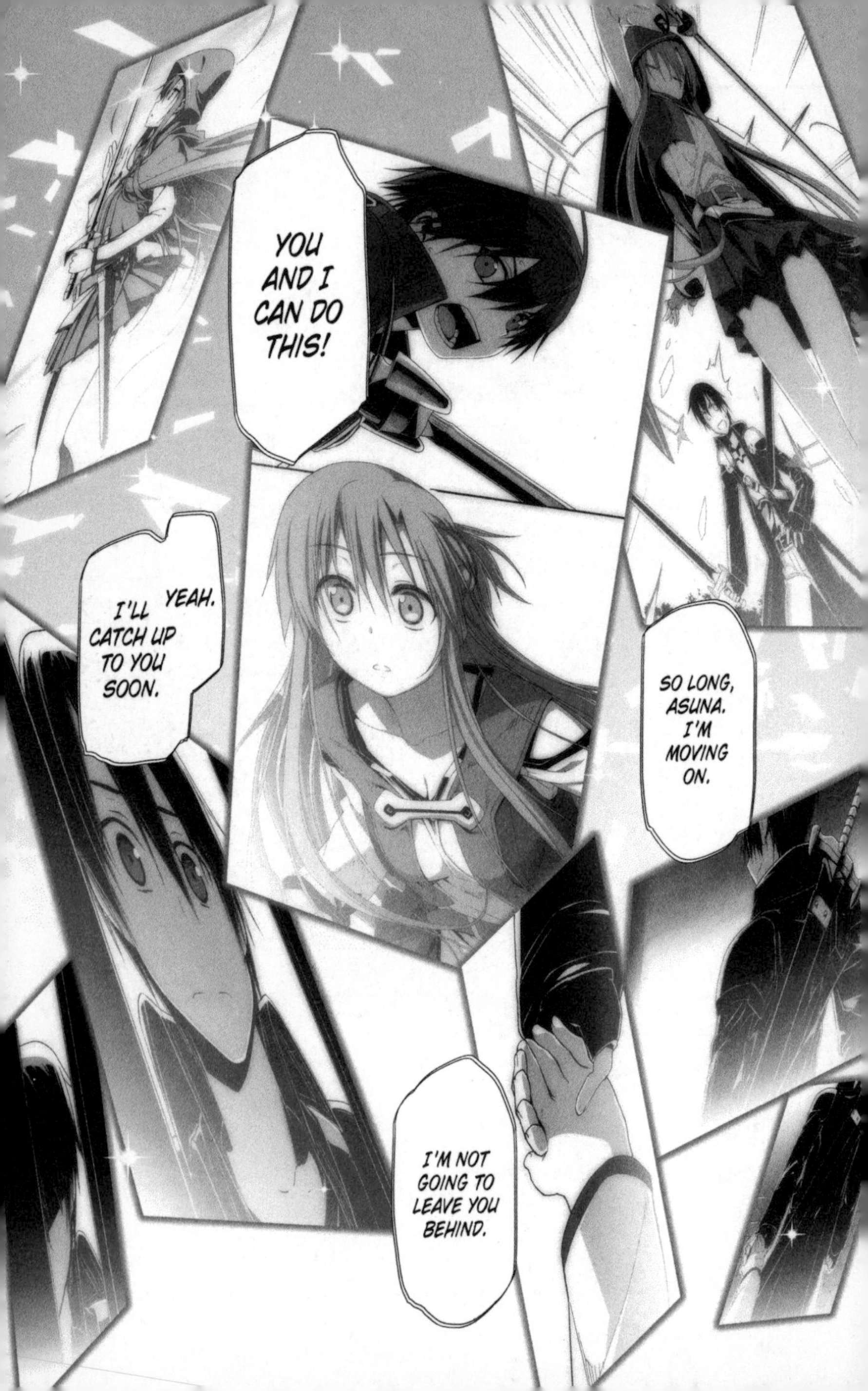
YOU AND I CAN DO THIS!
SO LONG, ASUNA. I'M MOVING ON.
YEAH. I'LL CATCH UP TO YOU SOON.
I'M NOT GOING TO LEAVE YOU BEHIND.

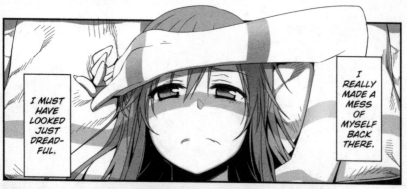

I REALLY MADE A MESS OF MYSELF BACK THERE.
I MUST HAVE LOOKED JUST DREAD-FUL.
~~~...!
バ
BA (KICK)
ギ
GI (CREAK)
NOT GOOD.
GOTTA SWITCH GEARS...
WHEN YOUR HEART WILTS OVER SOME-THING SAD...
...THAT JUST DRAWS IN FRESH MISFOR-TUNE.
GOTTA GET BACK ON MY FEET...
...BEFORE THE NEXT DISAS-TER.
THE NEXT —
~~~

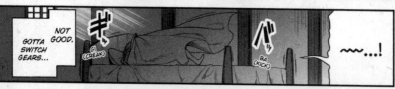

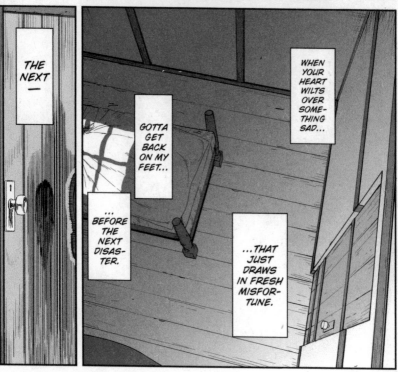

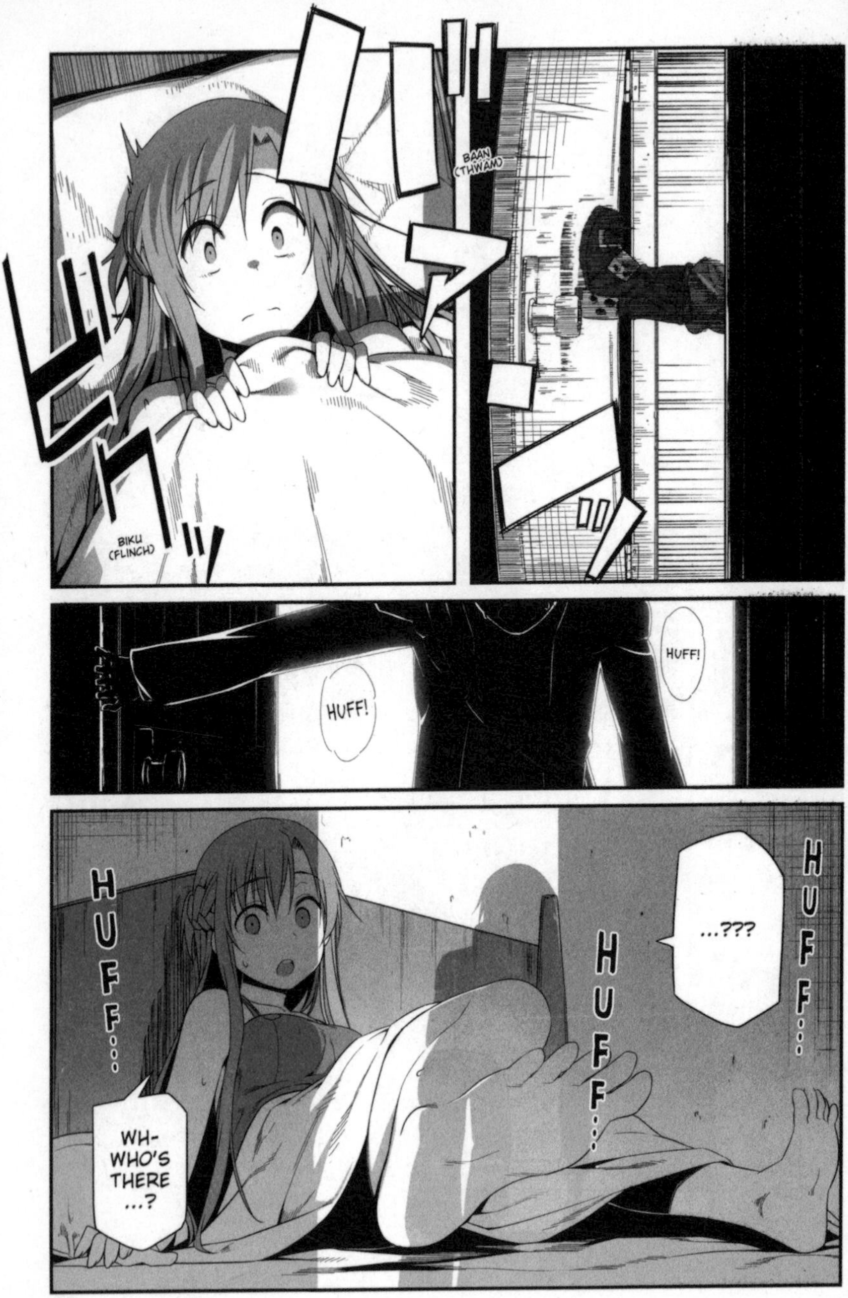
BAAN (THWAM)
BIKU (FLINCH)
HUFF!
HUFF!
HUFF...
HUFF...
...???
HUFF...
WH-WHO'S THERE ...?

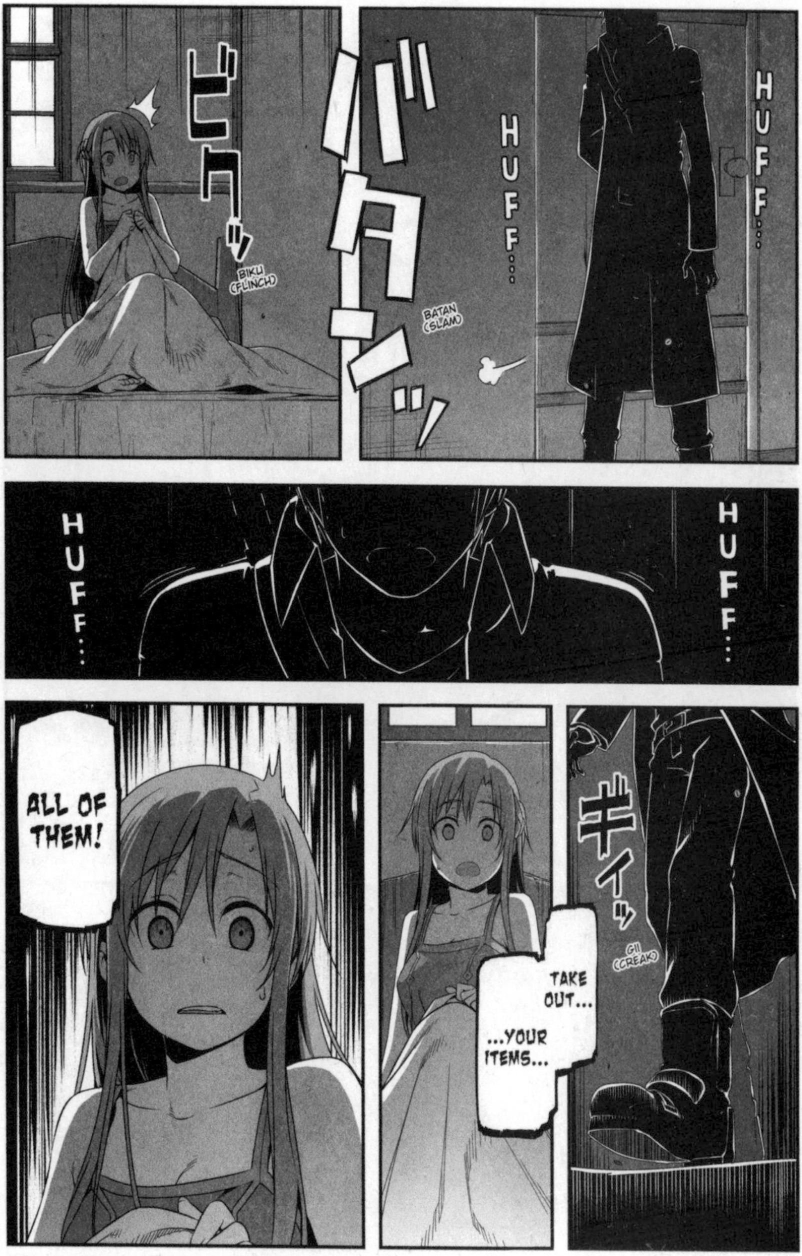
HUFF...
HUFF...
バタン
BATAN (SLAM)
ビクッ
BIKU (FLINCH)
HUFF...
HUFF...
ギイッ
GII (CREAK)
TAKE OUT...
...YOUR ITEMS...
ALL OF THEM!

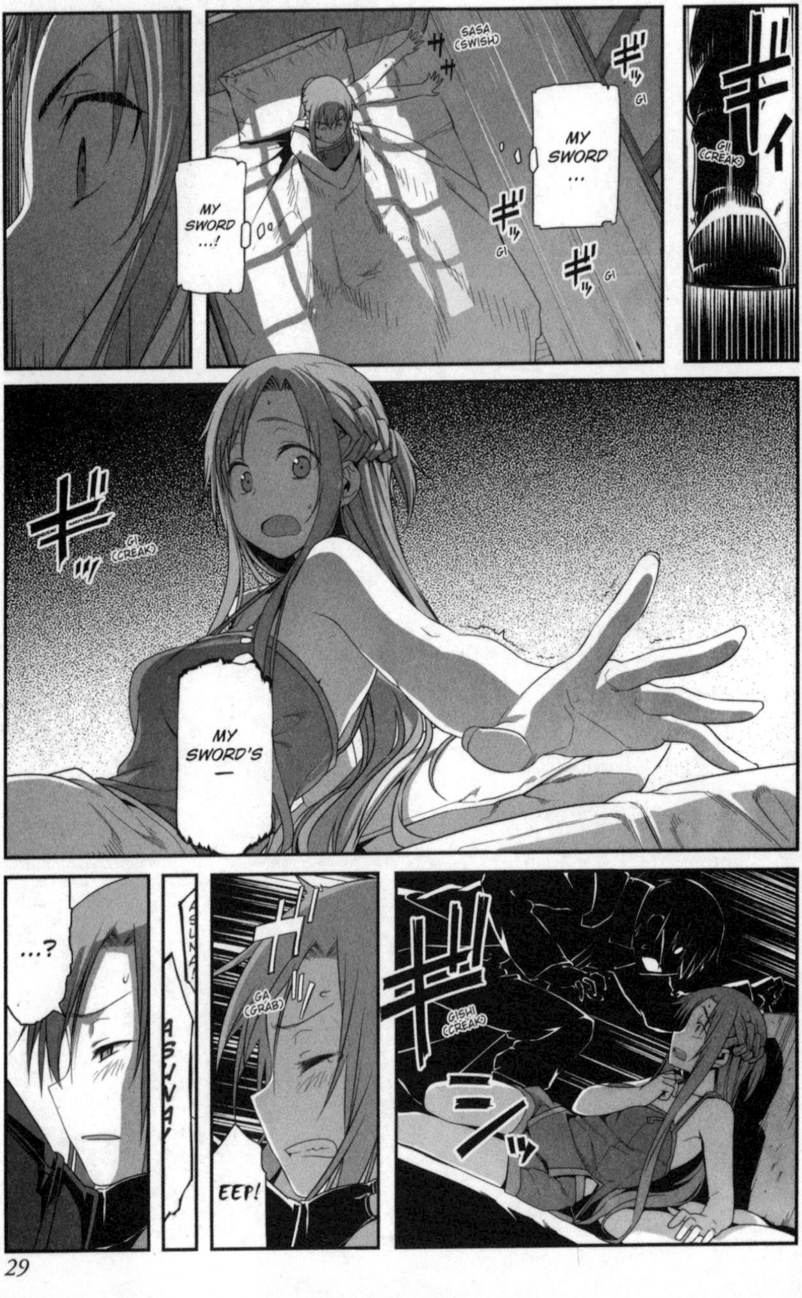
GII (CREAK)
GI
SASA (SWISH)
MY SWORD ...
GI
GI
MY SWORD ...!
GI (CREAK)
MY SWORD'S —
GISHI (CREAK)
GA (GRAB)
EEP!
ASUNA!
ASUNA!
...?

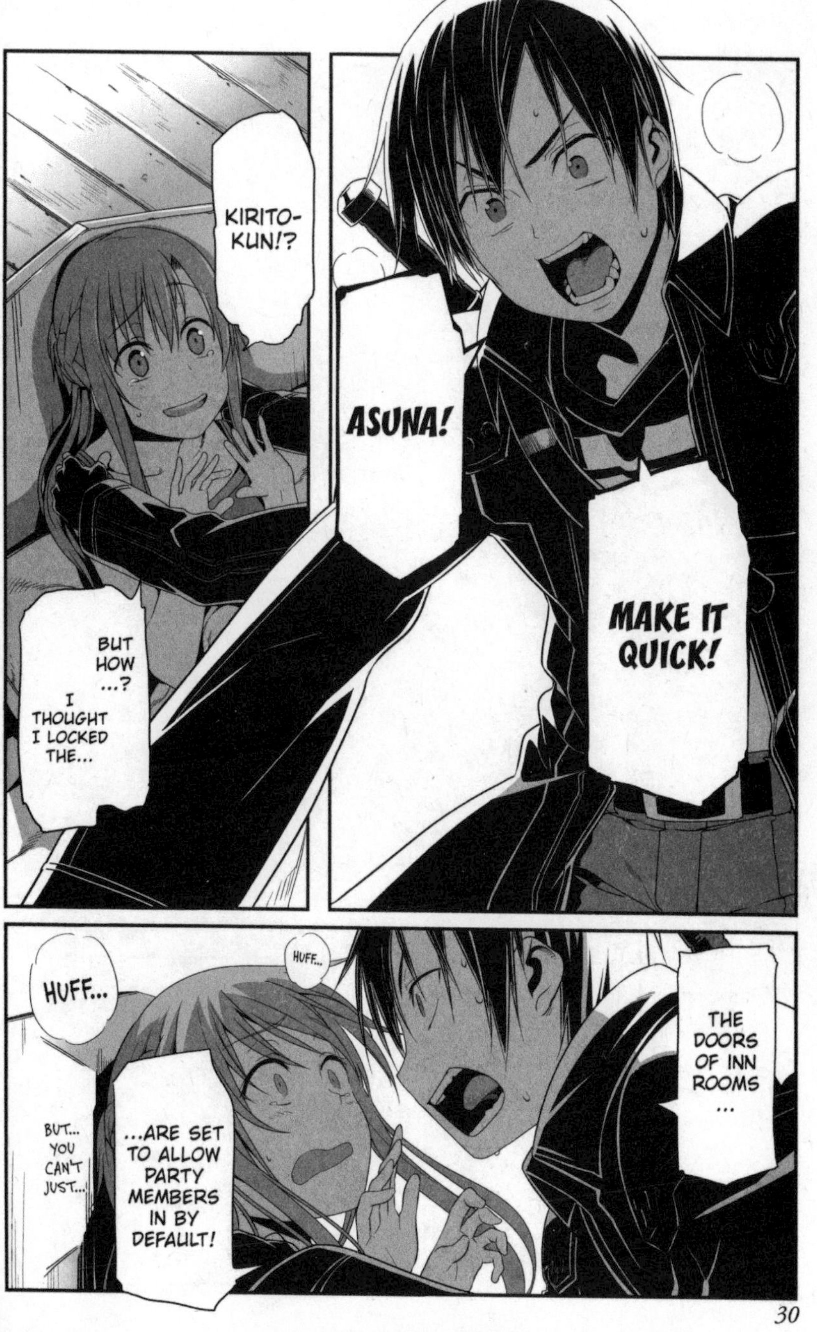
ASUNA!
MAKE IT QUICK!
KIRITO-KUN!?
BUT HOW ...? I THOUGHT I LOCKED THE...
THE DOORS OF INN ROOMS ...
HUFF...
HUFF...
...ARE SET TO ALLOW PARTY MEMBERS IN BY DEFAULT!
BUT... YOU CAN'T JUST...

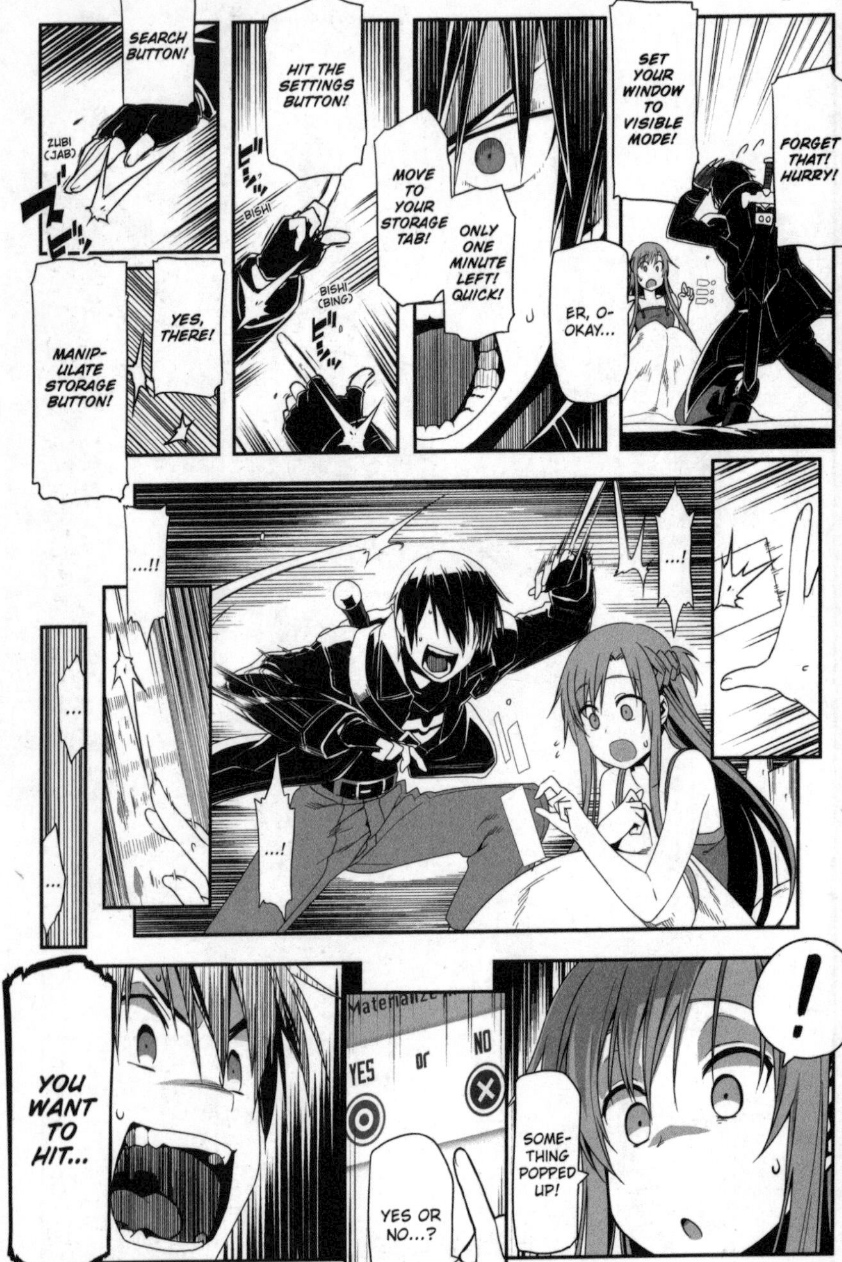
SET YOUR WINDOW TO VISIBLE MODE!
FORGET THAT! HURRY!
ER, O-OKAY...
MOVE TO YOUR STORAGE TAB!
ONLY ONE MINUTE LEFT! QUICK!
HIT THE SETTINGS BUTTON!
BISHI
BISHI (BING)
SEARCH BUTTON!
ZUBI (JAB)
YES, THERE!
MANIP-ULATE STORAGE BUTTON!
...!
...!!
...!
...
...
!
SOME-THING POPPED UP!
YES or NO
YES OR NO...?
YOU WANT TO HIT...

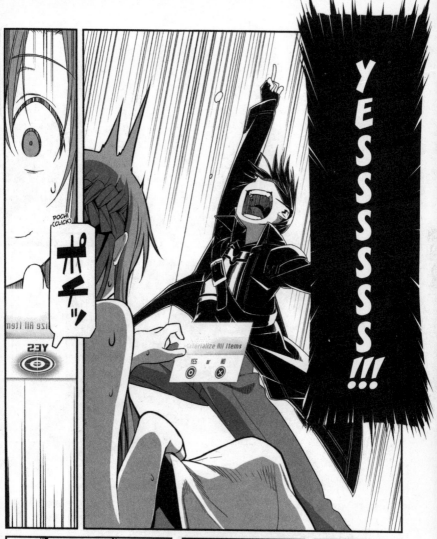

YESSSSS!!!

POCHI (CLICK)

Materialize All Items

YES or NO

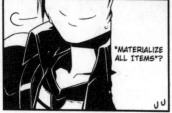

"MATERIALIZE ALL ITEMS"?

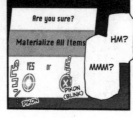

Are you sure?

Materialize All Items

HM?

YES or NO

MMM?

PIKON

PIKON (BLINK)

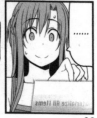

......

Materialize All Items

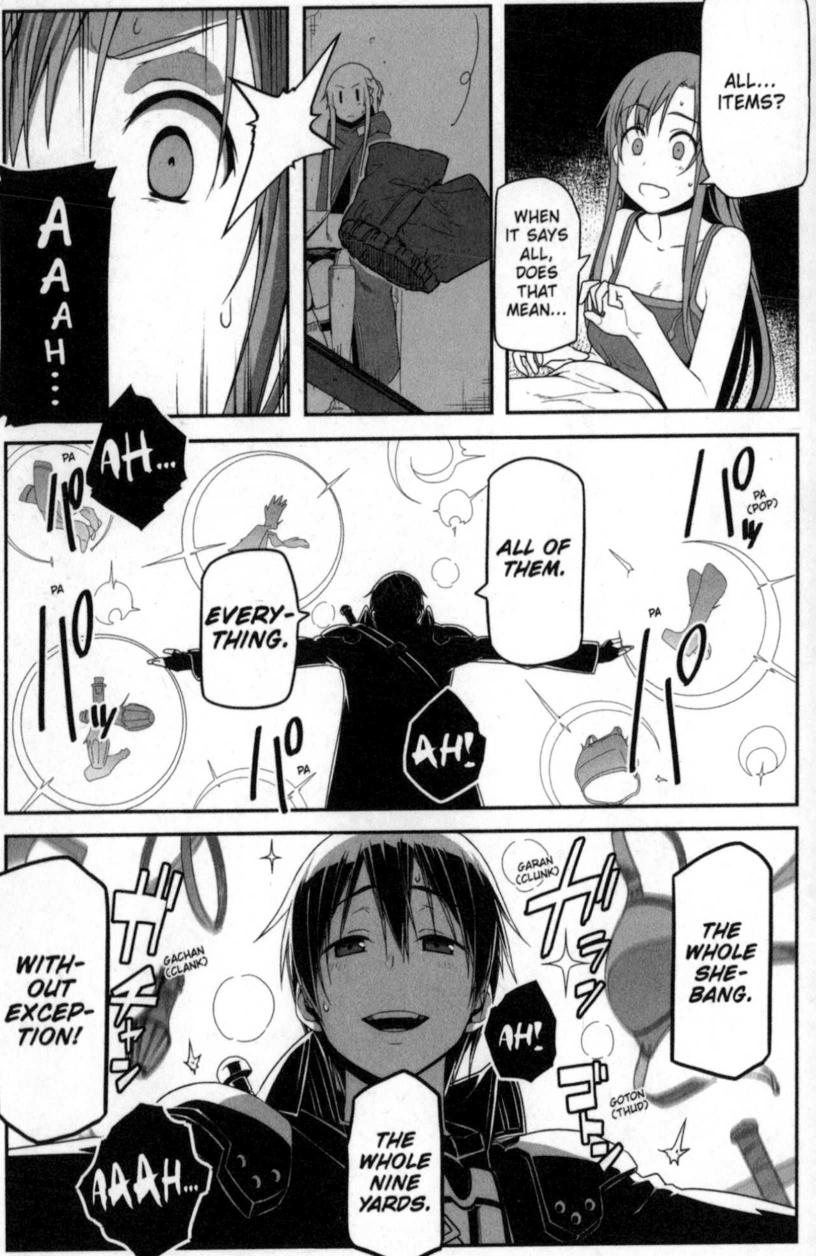
ALL... ITEMS?
WHEN IT SAYS ALL, DOES THAT MEAN...
AAAAH...
AH...
PA (POP)
ALL OF THEM.
EVERY-THING.
PA
PA
PA
AH!
PA
THE WHOLE SHE-BANG.
GARAN (CLUNK)
WITH-OUT EXCEP-TION!
GACHAN (CLANK)
AH!
GOTON (THUD)
THE WHOLE NINE YARDS.
AAAH...

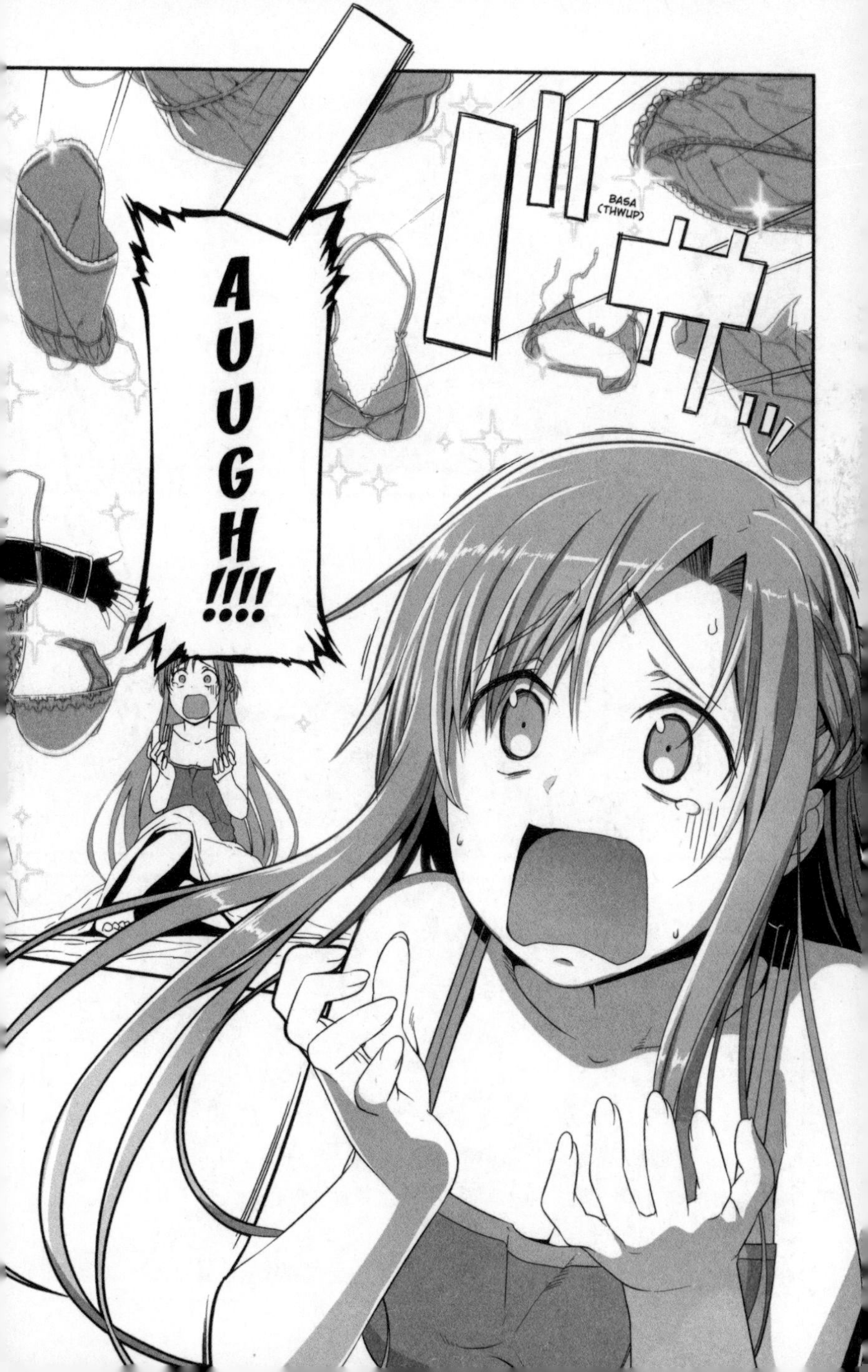
AUUGH!!!!
BASA (THWUP)

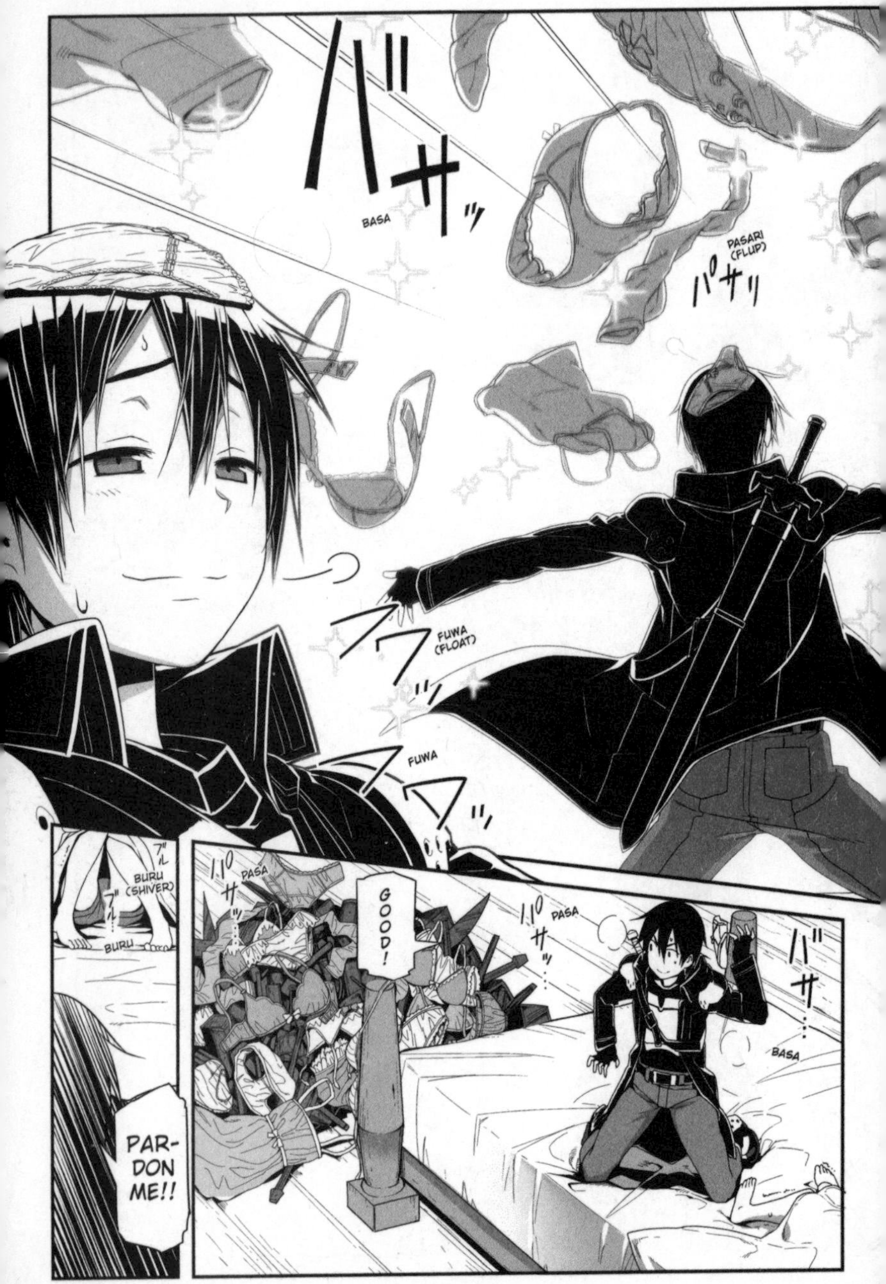

バサッ
BASA
パサリ
PASARI (FLUP)
フワッ
FUWA (FLOAT)
フワッ
FUWA
バサ…
BASA
パサッ…
PASA
GOOD!
パサッ…
PASA
ブル
BURU (SHIVER)
ブル…
BURU
PARDON ME!!

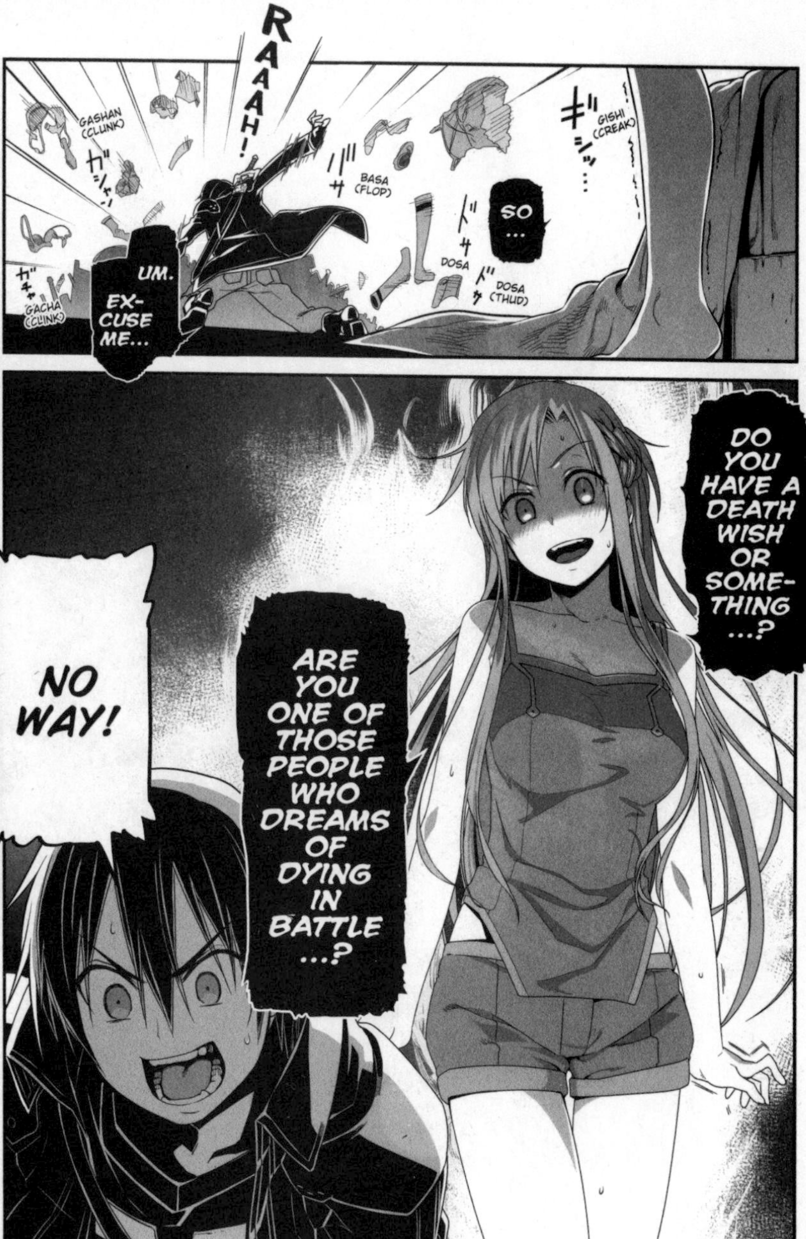
ギシッ…
GISHI (CREAK)
SO…
ドサ
DOSA
ドサッ
DOSA (THUD)
バサ
BASA (FLOP)
RAAAH!
GASHAN (CLUNK)
ガシャン
UM. EX-CUSE ME…
ガチャ
GACHA (CLINK)
DO YOU HAVE A DEATH WISH OR SOME-THING…?
ARE YOU ONE OF THOSE PEOPLE WHO DREAMS OF DYING IN BATTLE…?
NO WAY!

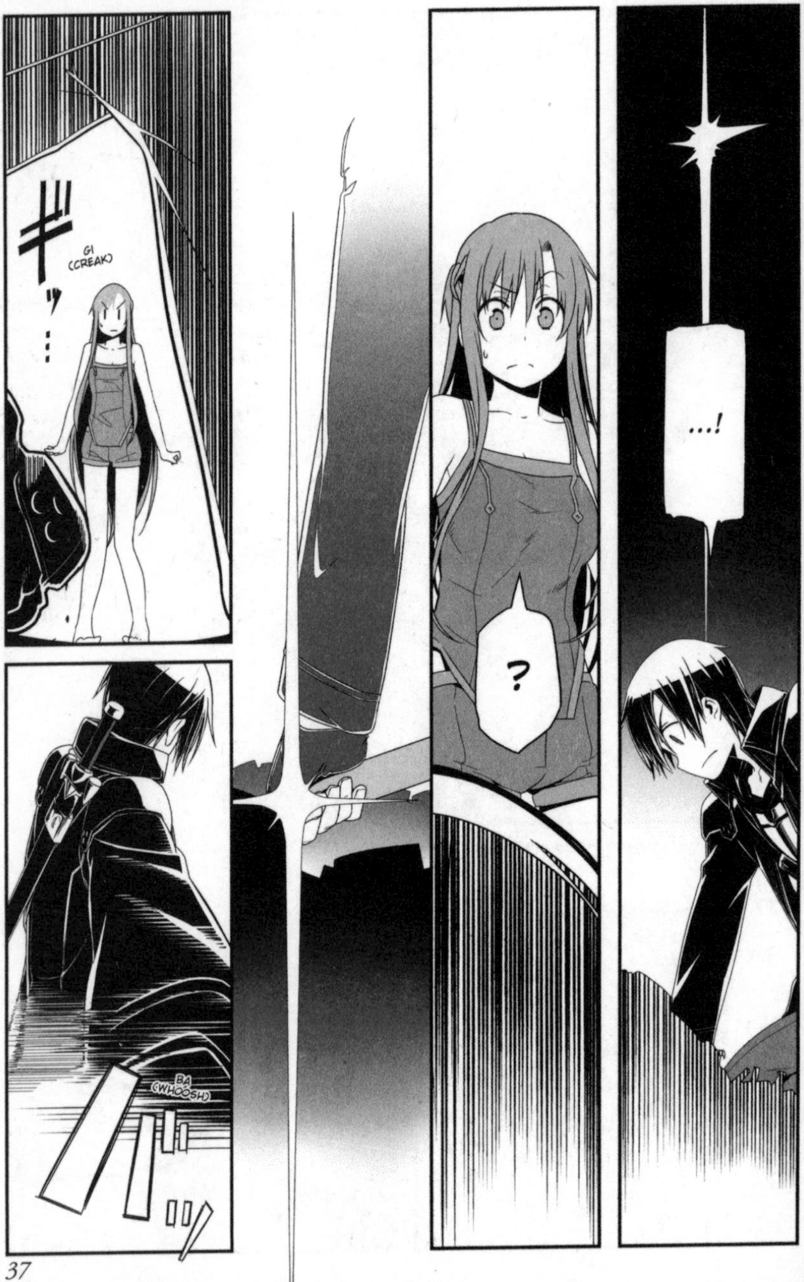
...!
?
ギッ…
GI (CREAK)
BA (WHOOSH)

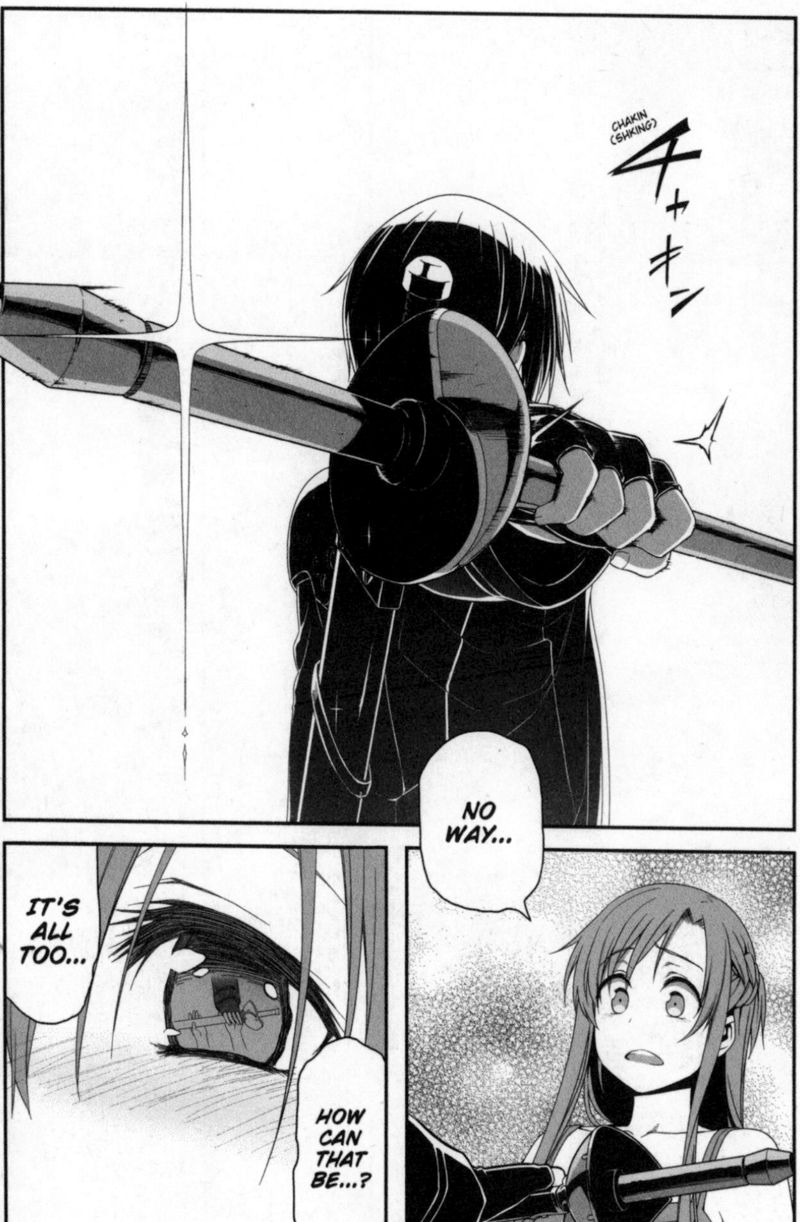
CHAKIN (SHKING)
チャキン
NO WAY...
IT'S ALL TOO...
HOW CAN THAT BE...?

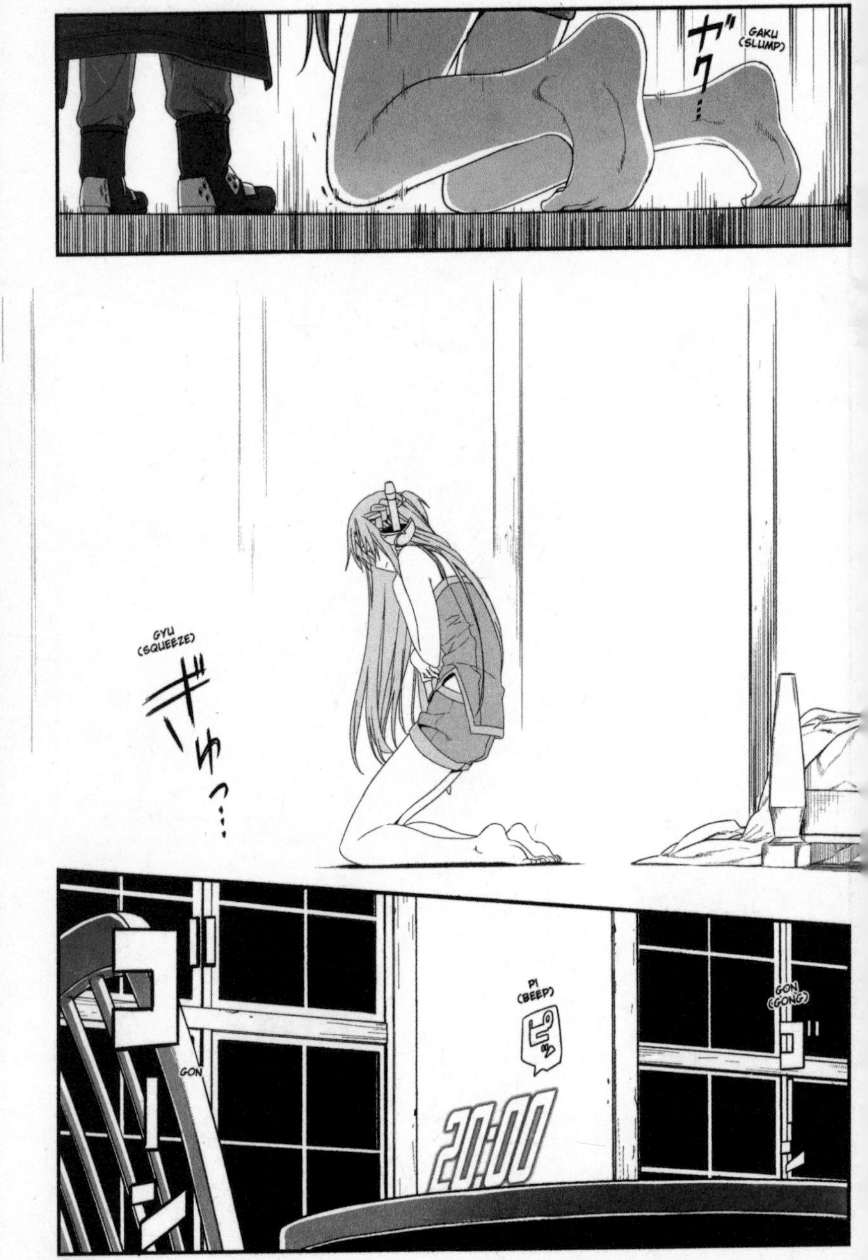
ガク…
GAKU (SLUMP)
ぎゅっ…
GYU (SQUEEZE)
ゴ
GON (GONG)
ピッ
PI (BEEP)
GON

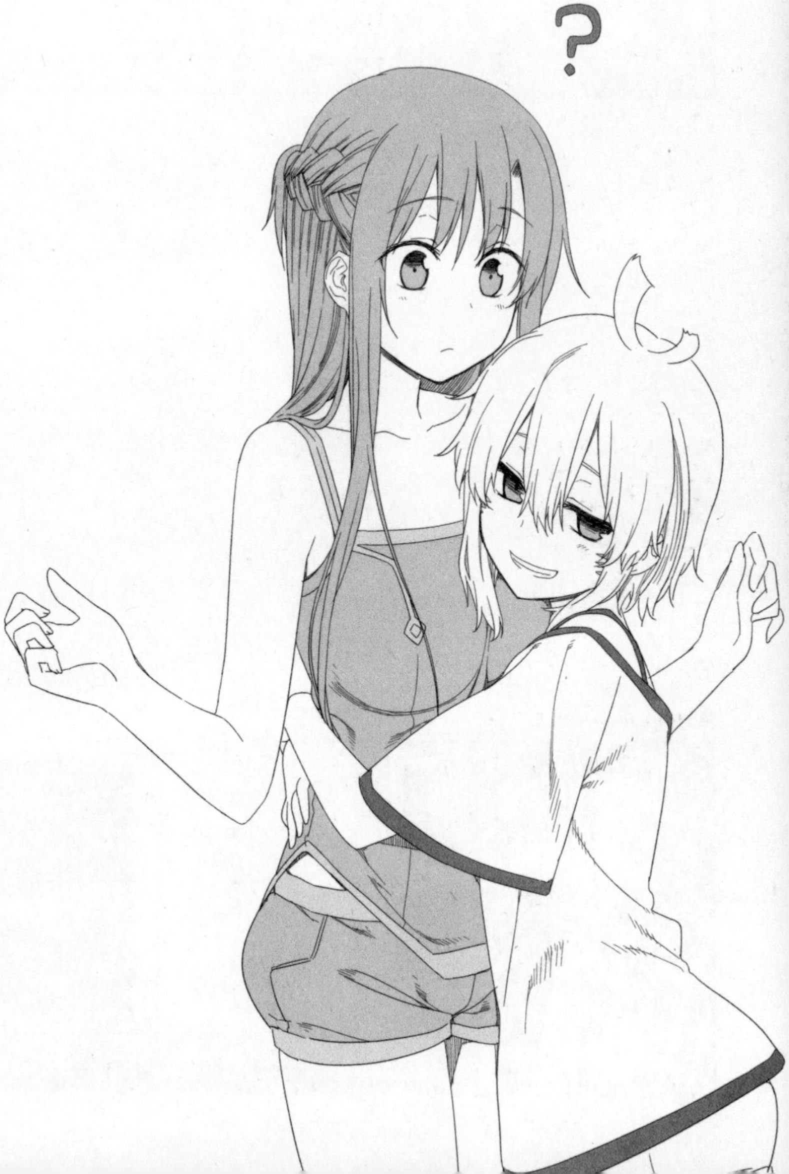
?

#012: Debuff

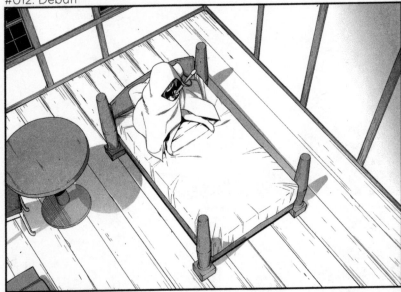

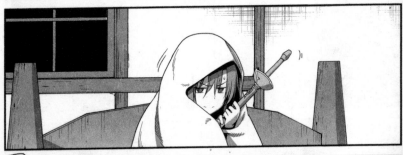

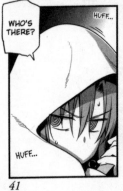

WHO'S THERE?

HUFF...

HUFF...

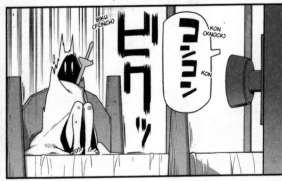

BIKU (FLINCH)

KON (KNOCK)

KON

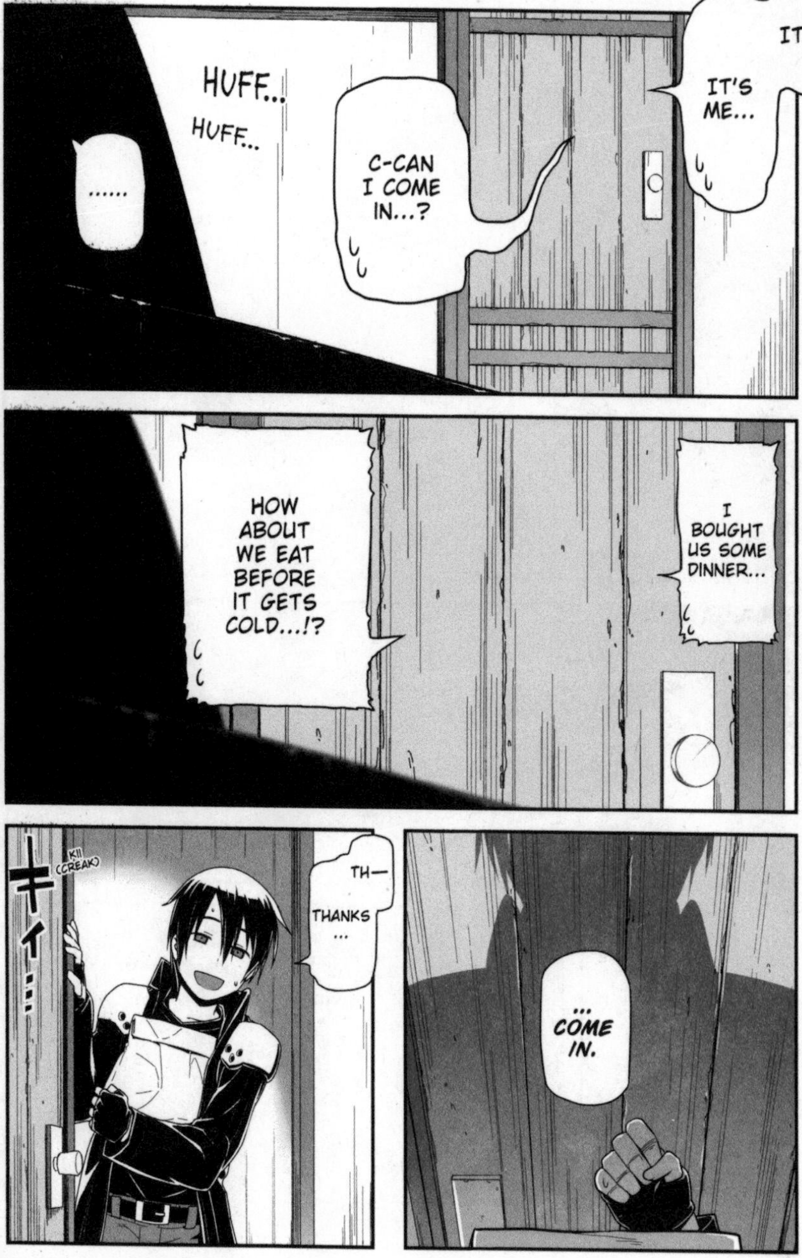
IT...
IT'S ME...
C-CAN I COME IN...?
HUFF... HUFF...
......
I BOUGHT US SOME DINNER...
HOW ABOUT WE EAT BEFORE IT GETS COLD...!?
... COME IN.
KII (CREAK)
TH— THANKS ...

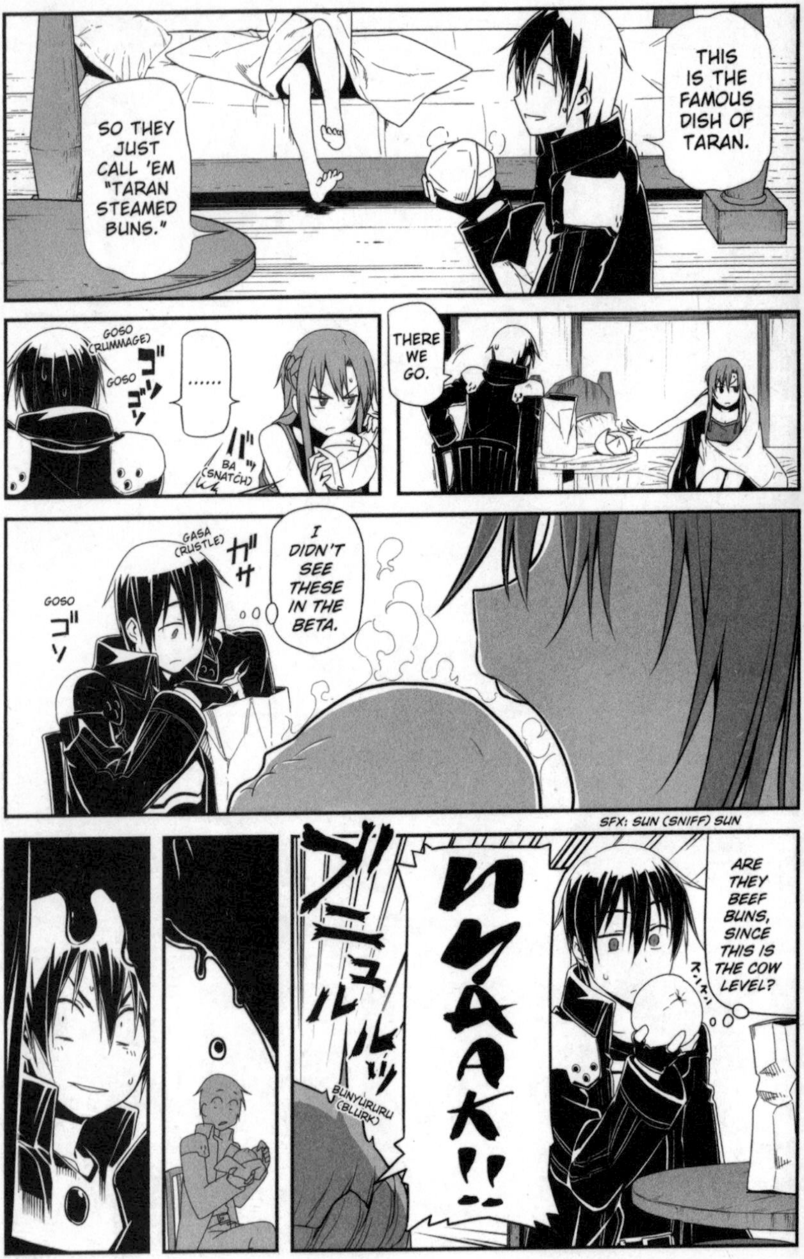

THIS IS THE FAMOUS DISH OF TARAN.
SO THEY JUST CALL 'EM "TARAN STEAMED BUNS."
THERE WE GO.
GOSO (RUMMAGE) GOSO
......
BA (SNATCH)
I DIDN'T SEE THESE IN THE BETA.
GASA (RUSTLE)
GOSO
SFX: SUN (SNIFF) SUN
ARE THEY BEEF BUNS, SINCE THIS IS THE COW LEVEL?
UMAK!!
BUNYURURU (BLURK)

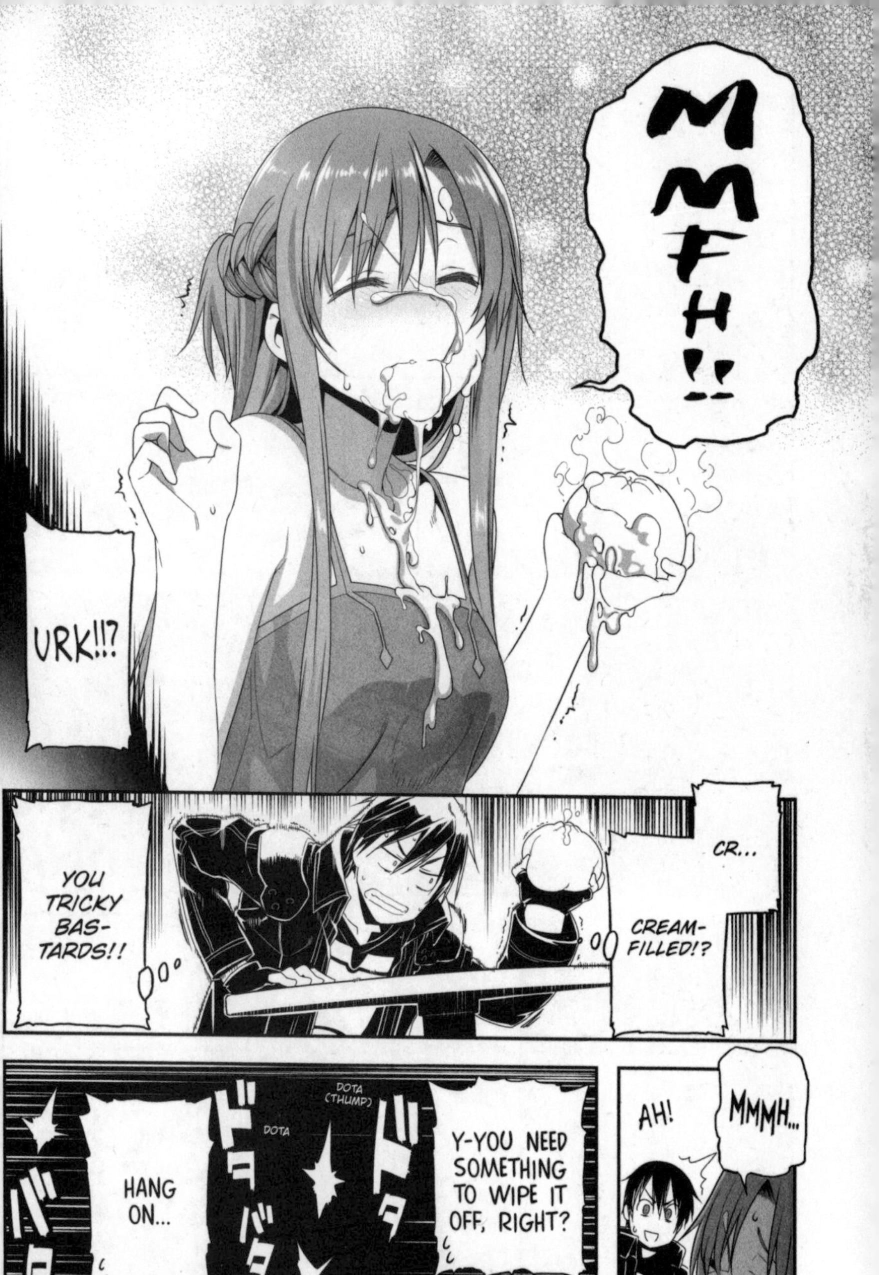
MMFH!!
URK!!?
CR... CREAM-FILLED!?
YOU TRICKY BAS-TARDS!!
MMMH...
AH!
Y-YOU NEED SOMETHING TO WIPE IT OFF, RIGHT?
DOTA (THUMP)
DOTA
HANG ON...
BATA (THUMP)
BATA

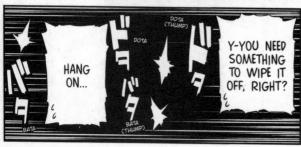

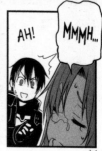

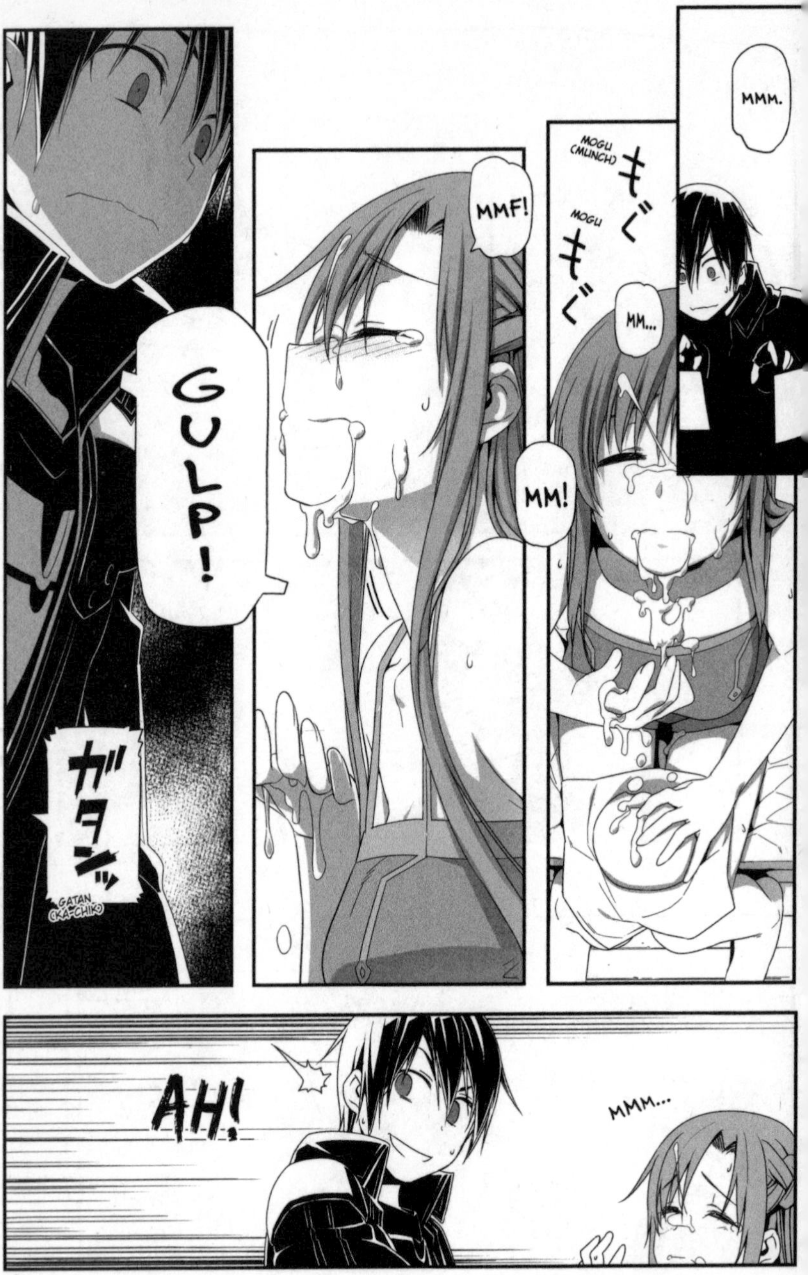
MMM.
MOGU (MUNCH)
もぐ
MOGU
もぐ
MM...
MM!
MMF!
GULP!
ガタンッ
GATAN (KA-CHIK)
MMM...
AH!

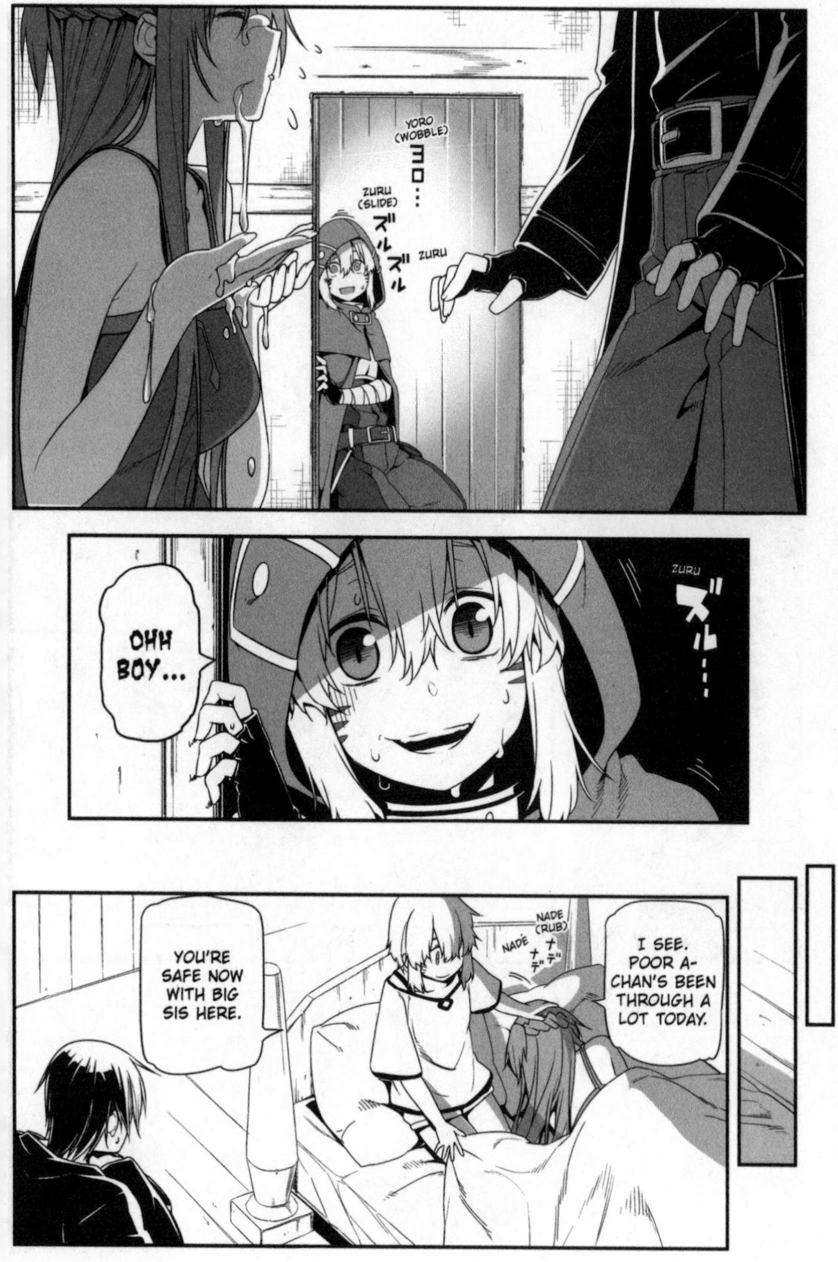

YORO (WOBBLE)
ヨロ…
ZURU (SLIDE)
ズル
ZURU
ズル
ZURU
ズル…
OHH BOY...
I SEE. POOR A-CHAN'S BEEN THROUGH A LOT TODAY.
NADE (RUB)
ナデ
NADE
ナデ
YOU'RE SAFE NOW WITH BIG SIS HERE.

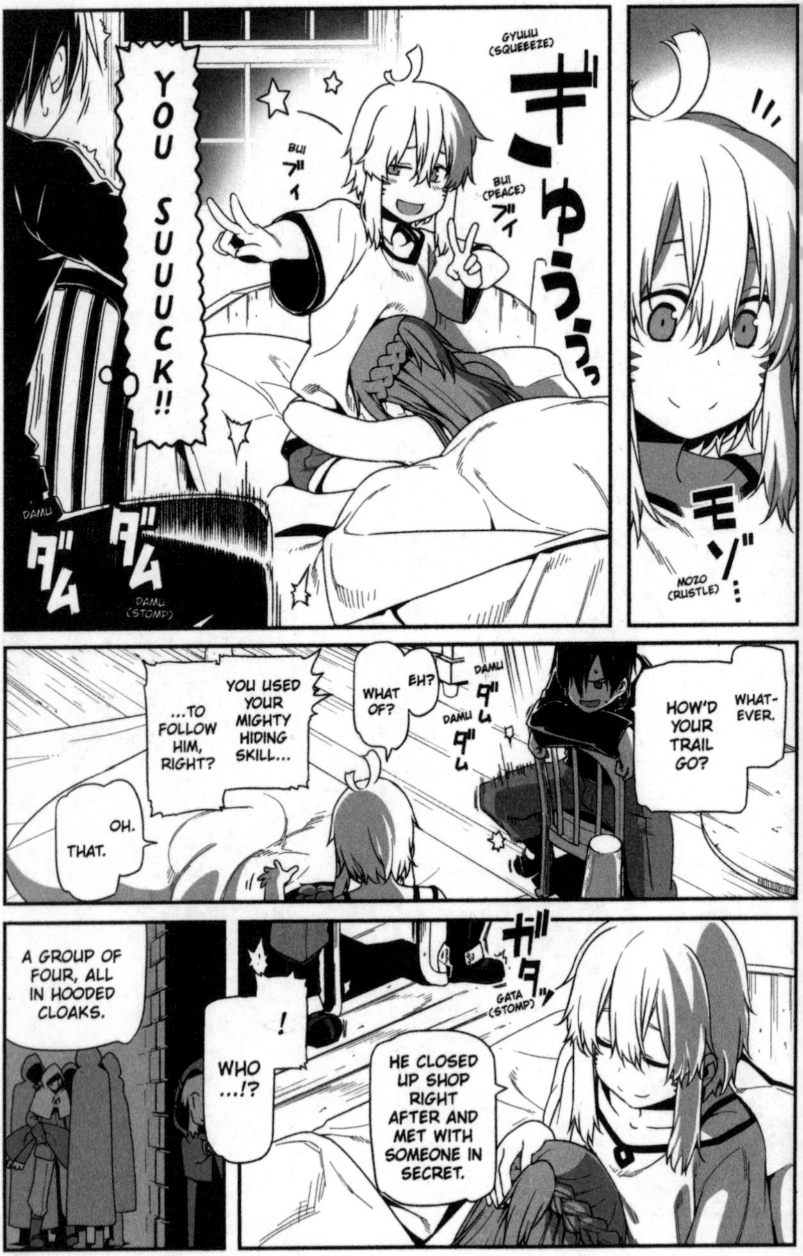

MOZO (RUSTLE)
モゾ…
GYUUU (SQUEEEZE)
ぎゅううっ
BUI (PEACE)
ブィ
BUI
ブィ
YOU SUUUUCK!!
DAMU (STOMP)
ダム
DAMU
ダム
WHATEVER.
HOW'D YOUR TRAIL GO?
DAMU
ダム
DAMU
ダム
EH?
WHAT OF?
YOU USED YOUR MIGHTY HIDING SKILL...
...TO FOLLOW HIM, RIGHT?
OH.
THAT.
ガタッ
GATA (STOMP)
!
WHO ...!?
HE CLOSED UP SHOP RIGHT AFTER AND MET WITH SOMEONE IN SECRET.
A GROUP OF FOUR, ALL IN HOODED CLOAKS.

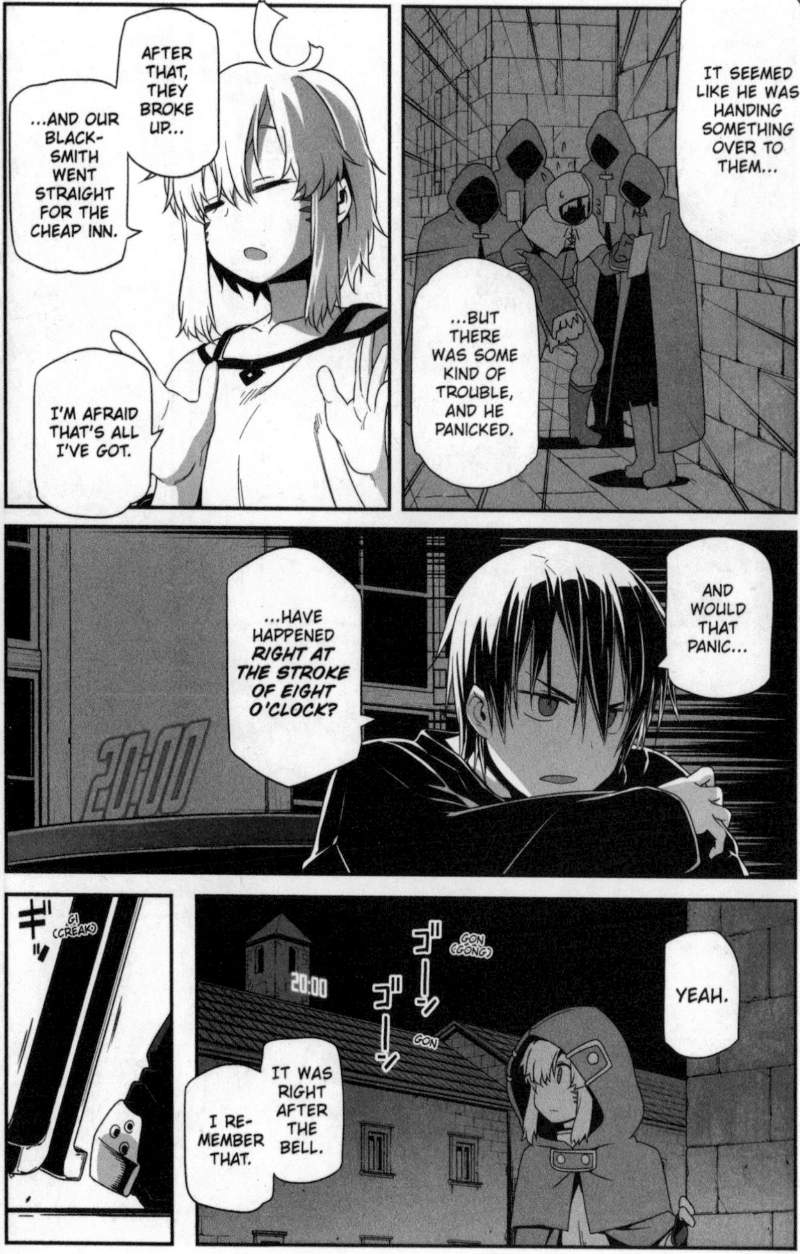
IT SEEMED LIKE HE WAS HANDING SOMETHING OVER TO THEM...
...BUT THERE WAS SOME KIND OF TROUBLE, AND HE PANICKED.
AFTER THAT, THEY BROKE UP...
...AND OUR BLACKSMITH WENT STRAIGHT FOR THE CHEAP INN.
I'M AFRAID THAT'S ALL I'VE GOT.
AND WOULD THAT PANIC...
...HAVE HAPPENED *RIGHT AT THE STROKE OF EIGHT O'CLOCK?*
20:00
YEAH.
GON (GONG)
20:00
GON
IT WAS RIGHT AFTER THE BELL.
I REMEMBER THAT.
GI (CREAK)

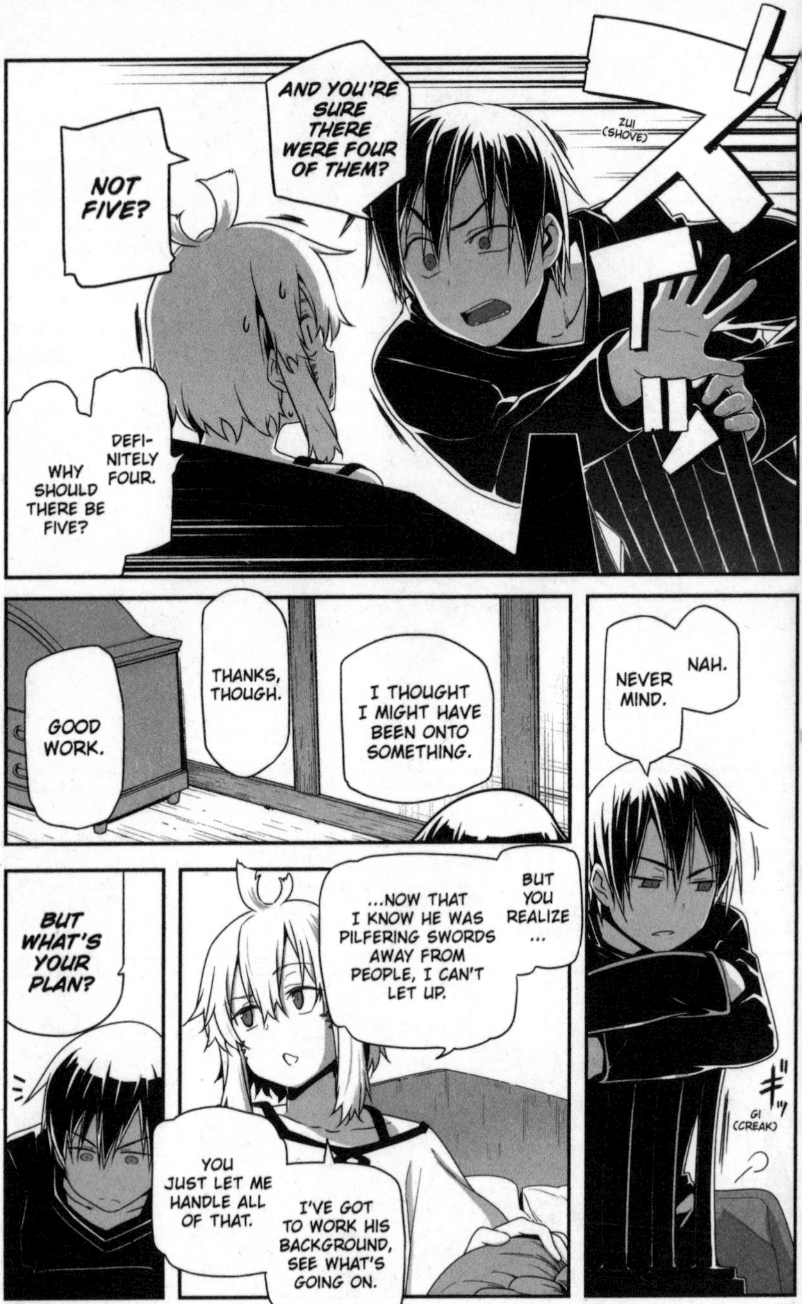
ZUI (SHOVE)
AND YOU'RE SURE THERE WERE FOUR OF THEM?
NOT FIVE?
DEFINITELY FOUR.
WHY SHOULD THERE BE FIVE?
NAH.
NEVER MIND.
GI (CREAK)
I THOUGHT I MIGHT HAVE BEEN ONTO SOMETHING.
THANKS, THOUGH.
GOOD WORK.
BUT YOU REALIZE ...
...NOW THAT I KNOW HE WAS PILFERING SWORDS AWAY FROM PEOPLE, I CAN'T LET UP.
I'VE GOT TO WORK HIS BACKGROUND, SEE WHAT'S GOING ON.
YOU JUST LET ME HANDLE ALL OF THAT.
BUT WHAT'S YOUR PLAN?

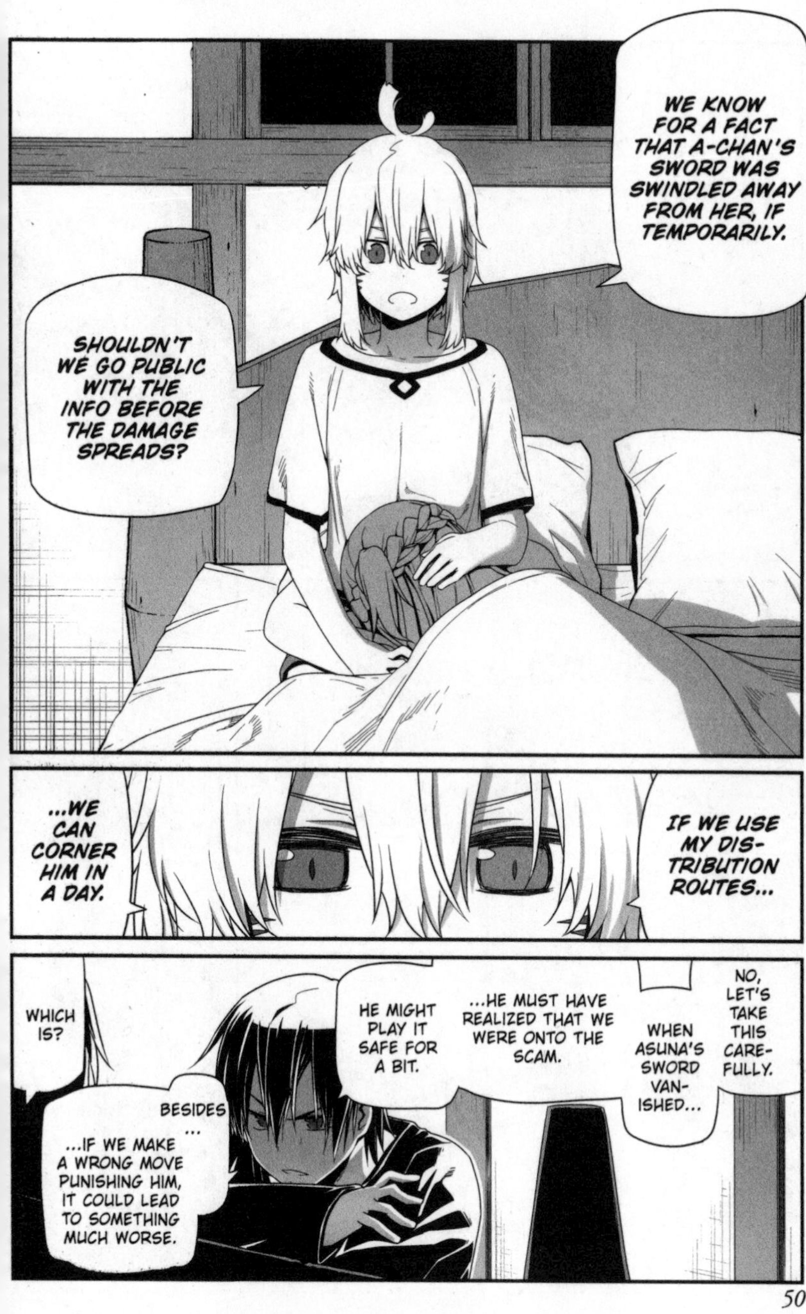
WE KNOW FOR A FACT THAT A-CHAN'S SWORD WAS SWINDLED AWAY FROM HER, IF TEMPORARILY.
SHOULDN'T WE GO PUBLIC WITH THE INFO BEFORE THE DAMAGE SPREADS?
IF WE USE MY DISTRIBUTION ROUTES...
...WE CAN CORNER HIM IN A DAY.
NO, LET'S TAKE THIS CAREFULLY.
WHEN ASUNA'S SWORD VANISHED...
...HE MUST HAVE REALIZED THAT WE WERE ONTO THE SCAM.
HE MIGHT PLAY IT SAFE FOR A BIT.
WHICH IS?
BESIDES...
...IF WE MAKE A WRONG MOVE PUNISHING HIM, IT COULD LEAD TO SOMETHING MUCH WORSE.

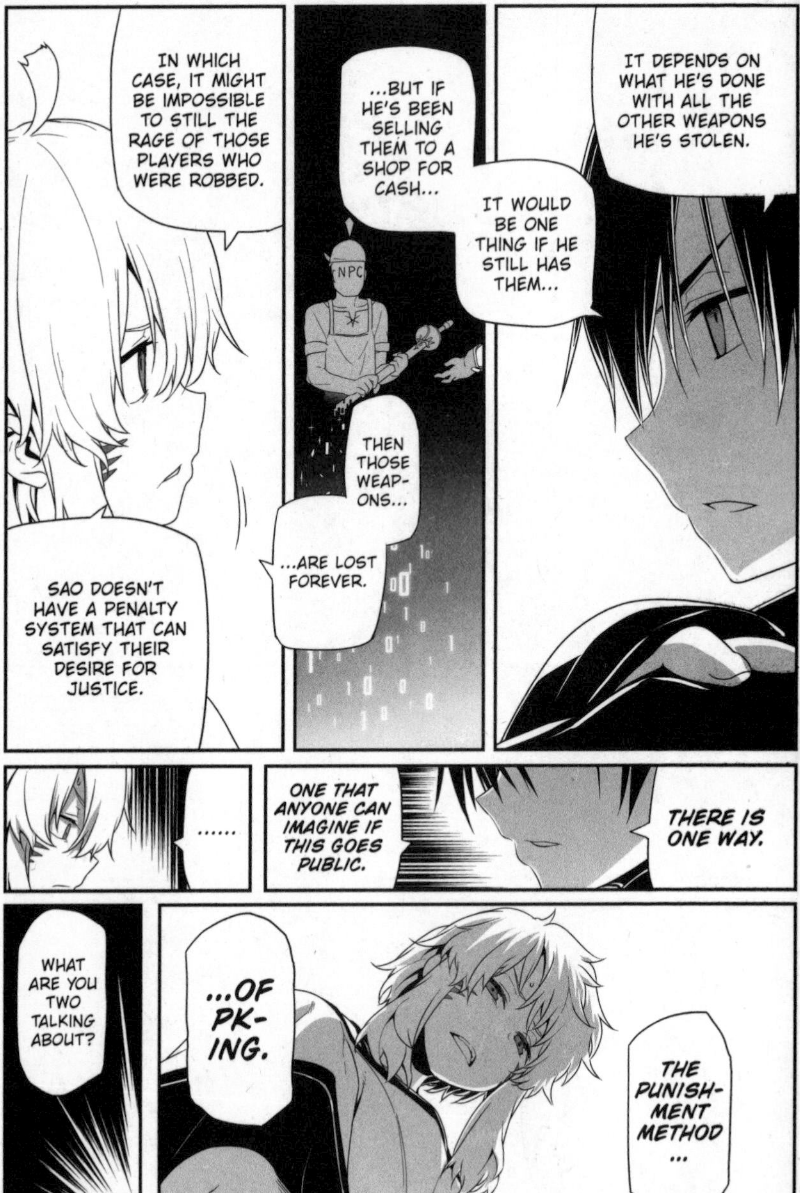
IT DEPENDS ON WHAT HE'S DONE WITH ALL THE OTHER WEAPONS HE'S STOLEN.
IT WOULD BE ONE THING IF HE STILL HAS THEM...
...BUT IF HE'S BEEN SELLING THEM TO A SHOP FOR CASH...
NPC
THEN THOSE WEAPONS...
...ARE LOST FOREVER.
IN WHICH CASE, IT MIGHT BE IMPOSSIBLE TO STILL THE RAGE OF THOSE PLAYERS WHO WERE ROBBED.
SAO DOESN'T HAVE A PENALTY SYSTEM THAT CAN SATISFY THEIR DESIRE FOR JUSTICE.
THERE IS ONE WAY.
ONE THAT ANYONE CAN IMAGINE IF THIS GOES PUBLIC.
......
THE PUNISHMENT METHOD...
...OF PK-ING.
WHAT ARE YOU TWO TALKING ABOUT?

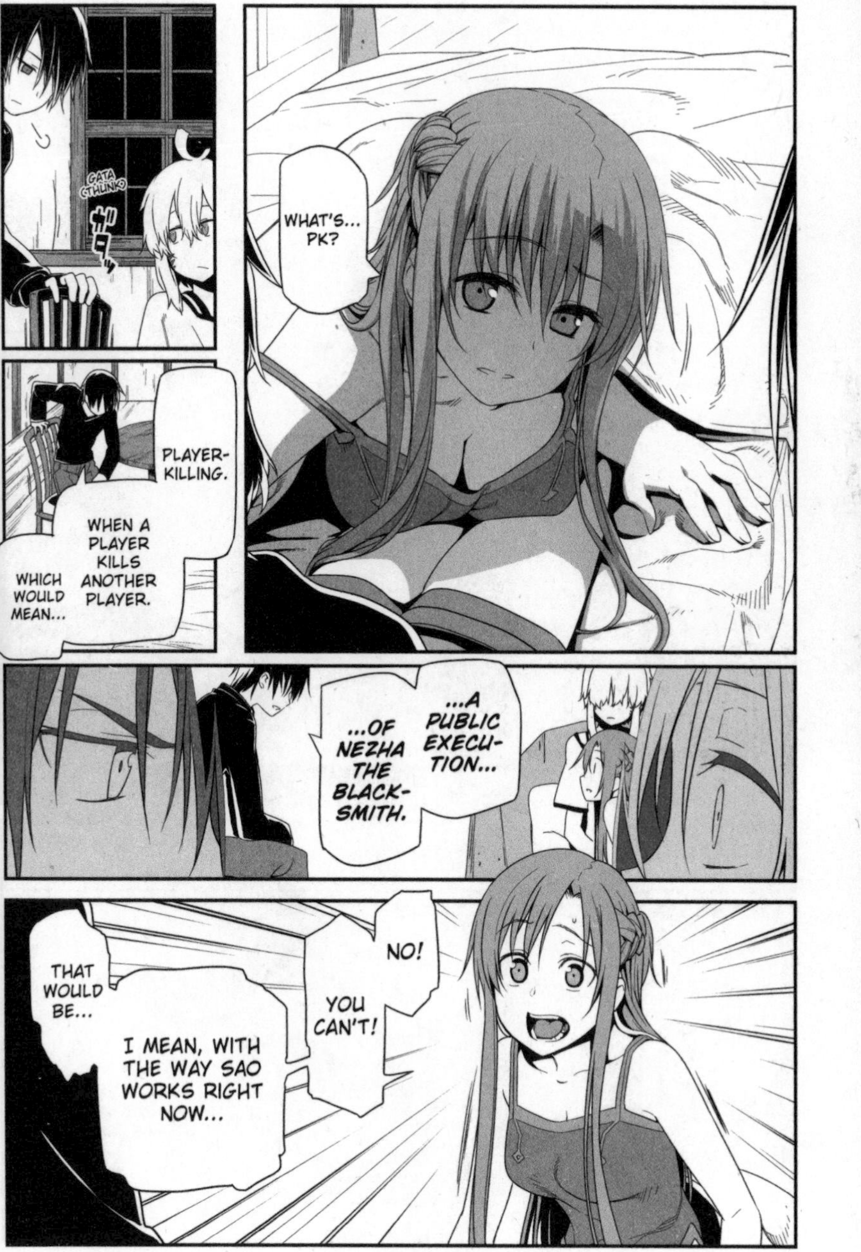
WHAT'S... PK?
GATA (THUNK)
PLAYER-KILLING.
WHEN A PLAYER KILLS ANOTHER PLAYER.
WHICH WOULD MEAN...
...A PUBLIC EXECUTION...
...OF NEZHA THE BLACKSMITH.
NO!
YOU CAN'T!
THAT WOULD BE...
I MEAN, WITH THE WAY SAO WORKS RIGHT NOW...

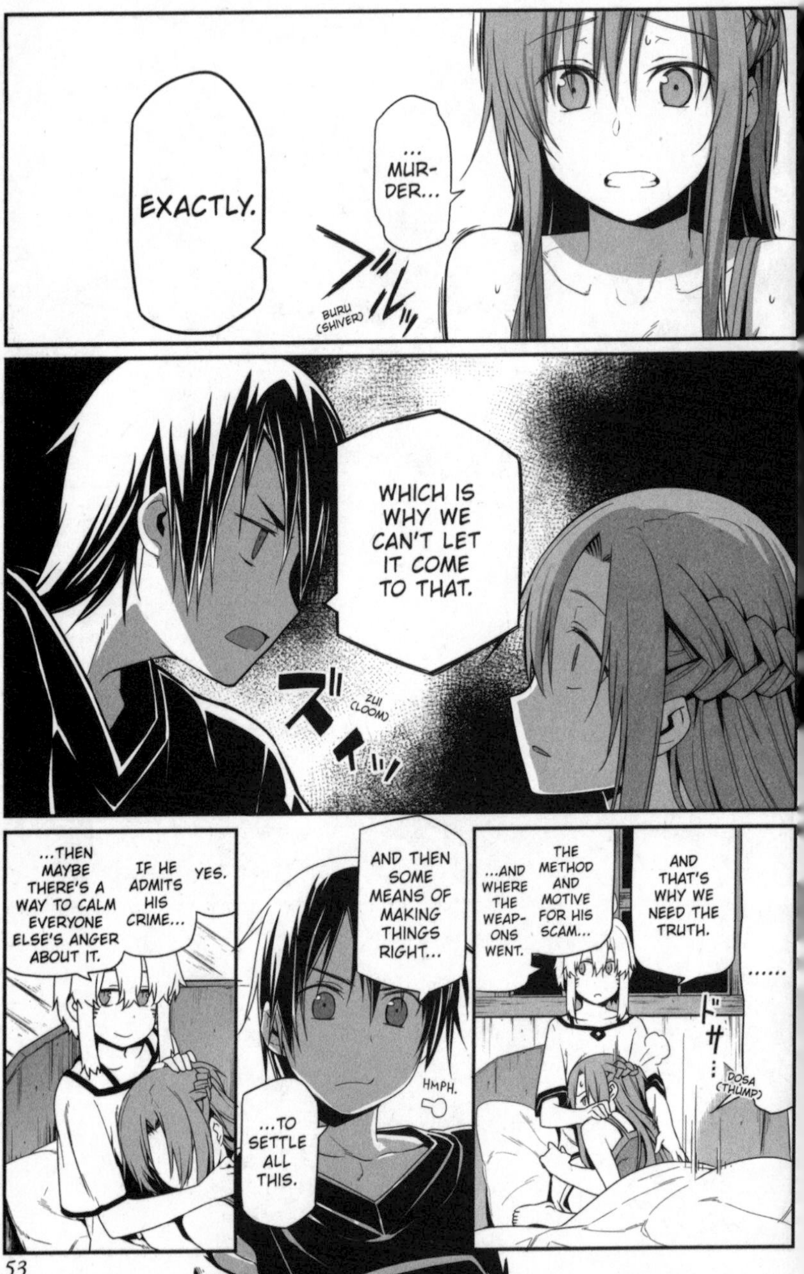

... MURDER...
BURU (SHIVER)
EXACTLY.
WHICH IS WHY WE CAN'T LET IT COME TO THAT.
ZUI (LOOM)
AND THAT'S WHY WE NEED THE TRUTH.
......
THE METHOD AND MOTIVE FOR HIS SCAM...
...AND WHERE THE WEAPONS WENT.
DOSA (THUMP)
AND THEN SOME MEANS OF MAKING THINGS RIGHT...
HMPH.
...TO SETTLE ALL THIS.
YES.
IF HE ADMITS HIS CRIME...
...THEN MAYBE THERE'S A WAY TO CALM EVERYONE ELSE'S ANGER ABOUT IT.

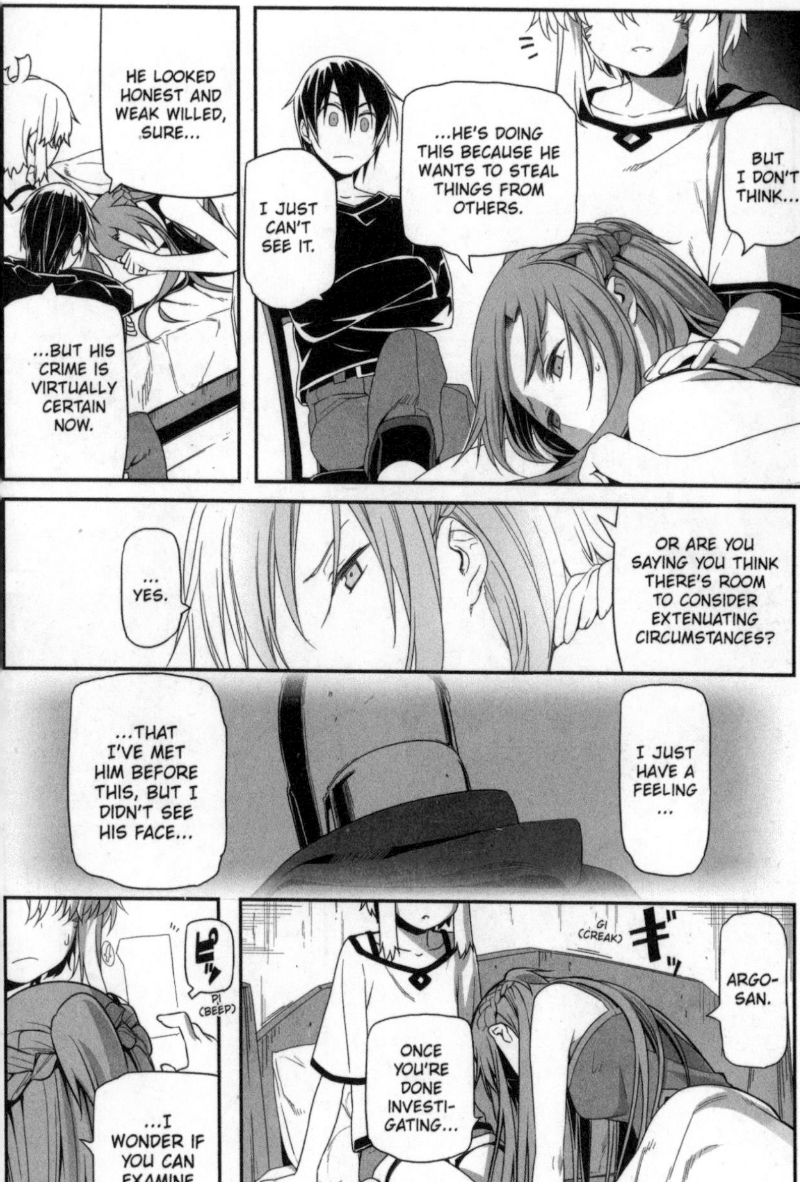
BUT I DON'T THINK...
...HE'S DOING THIS BECAUSE HE WANTS TO STEAL THINGS FROM OTHERS.
I JUST CAN'T SEE IT.
HE LOOKED HONEST AND WEAK WILLED, SURE...
...BUT HIS CRIME IS VIRTUALLY CERTAIN NOW.
OR ARE YOU SAYING YOU THINK THERE'S ROOM TO CONSIDER EXTENUATING CIRCUMSTANCES?
... YES.
I JUST HAVE A FEELING ...
...THAT I'VE MET HIM BEFORE THIS, BUT I DIDN'T SEE HIS FACE...
ギッ
GI (CREAK)
ARGO-SAN.
ONCE YOU'RE DONE INVESTIGATING...
ピッ
PI (BEEP)
...I WONDER IF YOU CAN EXAMINE THIS.

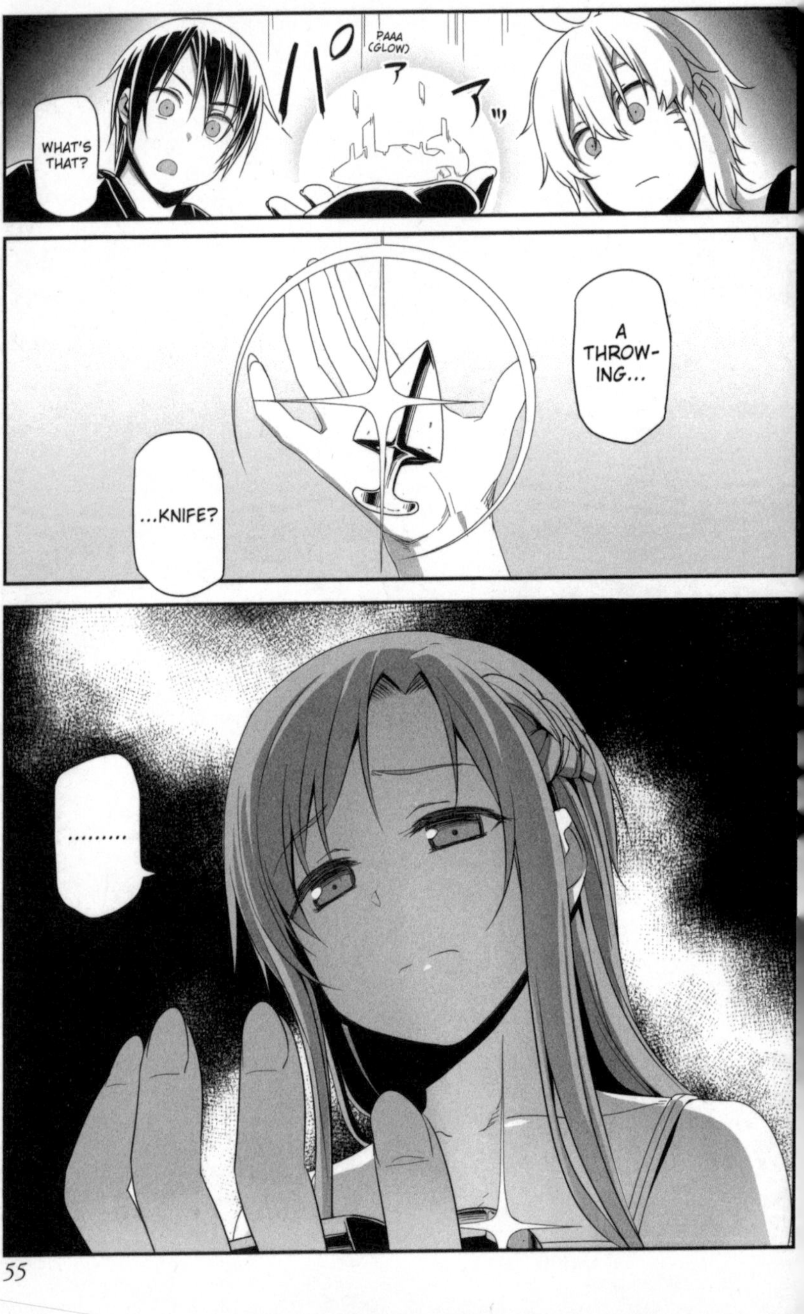
PAAA (GLOW)
WHAT'S THAT?
A THROWING...
...KNIFE?
....

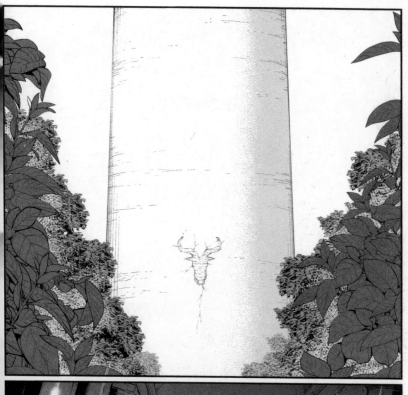

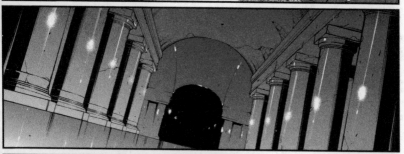

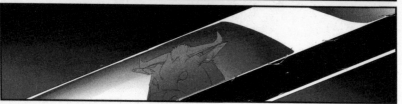

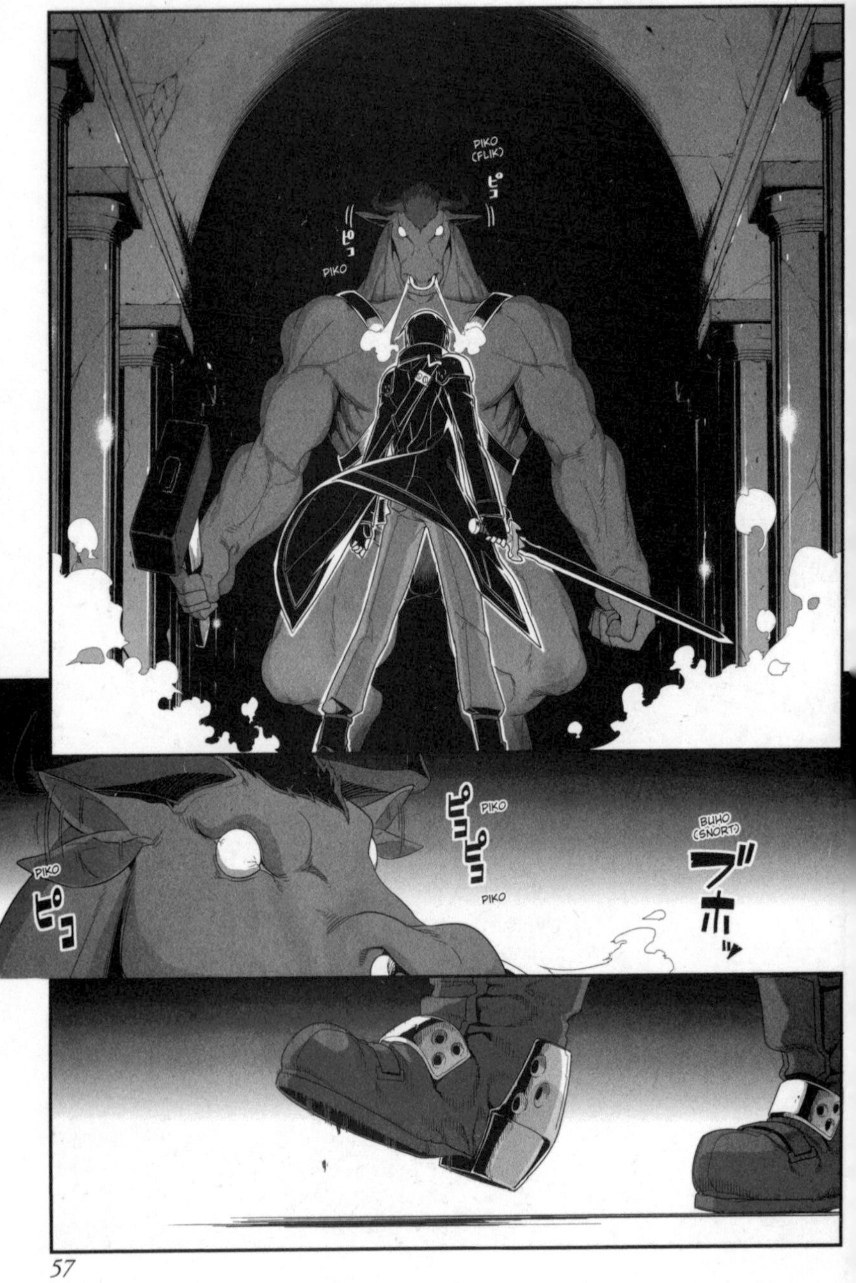
PIKO (FLIK)
ピコ
ピコ
PIKO
BUHO (SNORT)
ブホッ
ピコピコ
PIKO
PIKO
PIKO
ピコ

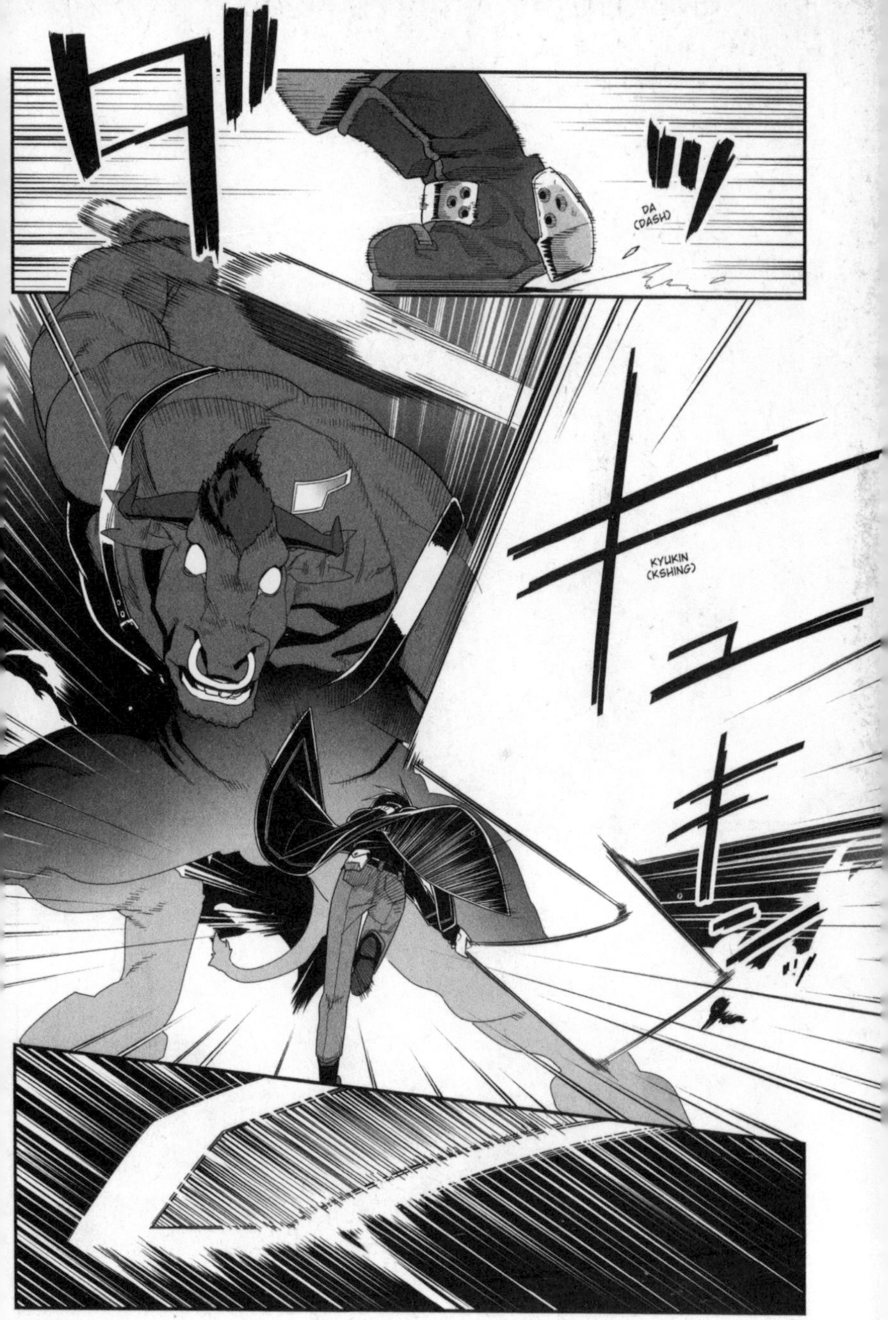
DA
(DASH)
KYUKIN
(KSHING)

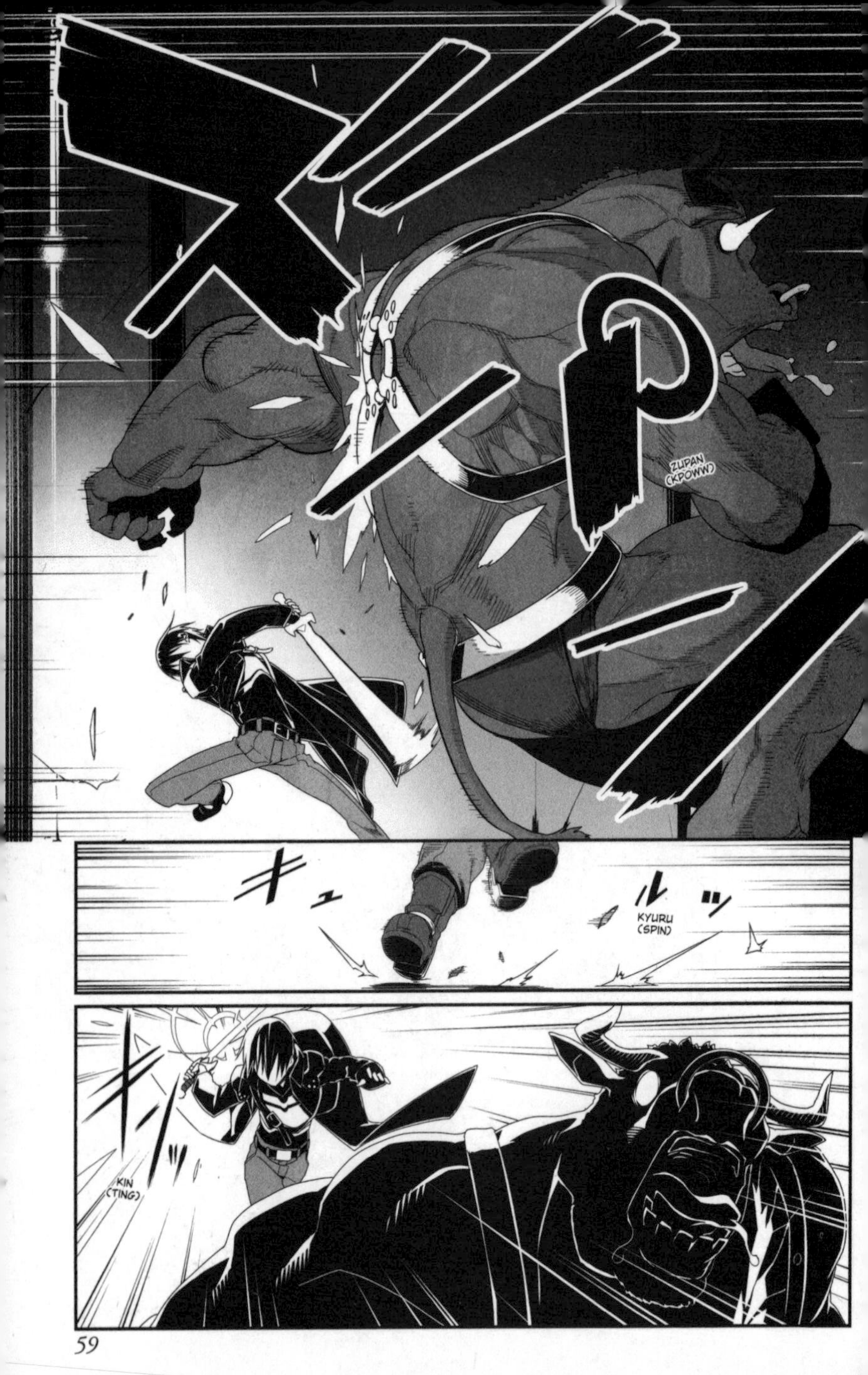
ズパン
ZUPAN (KPOWW)
キュルッ
KYURU (SPIN)
KIN (TING)

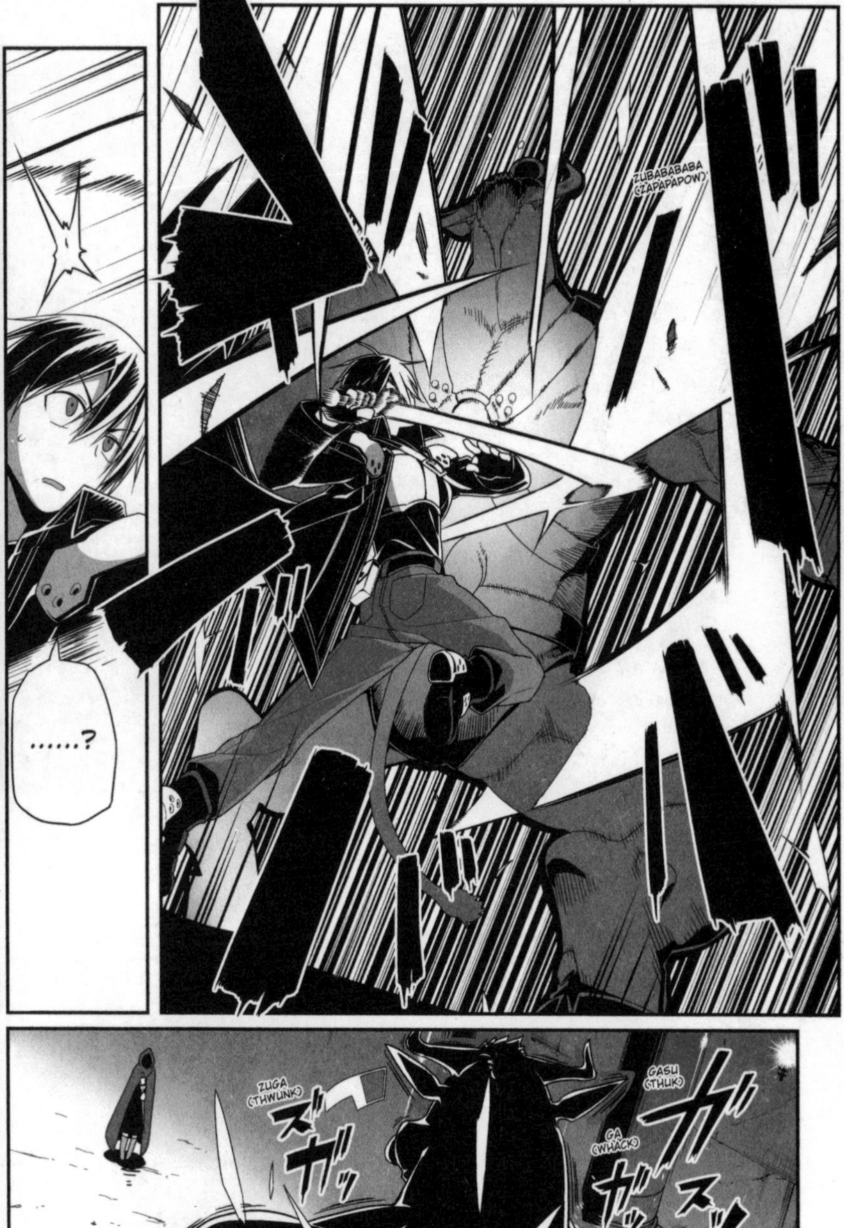
ZUBABABABA (ZAPAPAPOW)
......?
GASU (THUK)
GA (WHACK)
ZUGA (THWUNK)

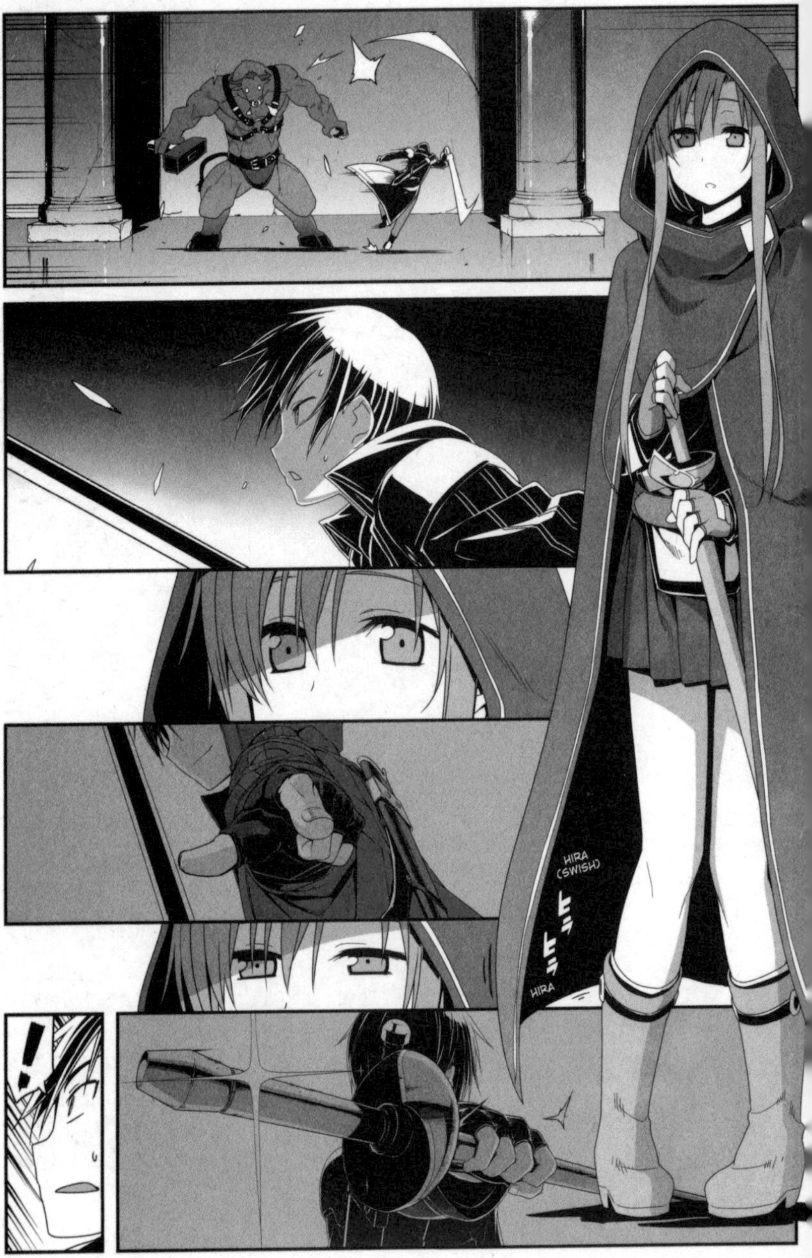
HIRA (SWISH)
HIRA
!

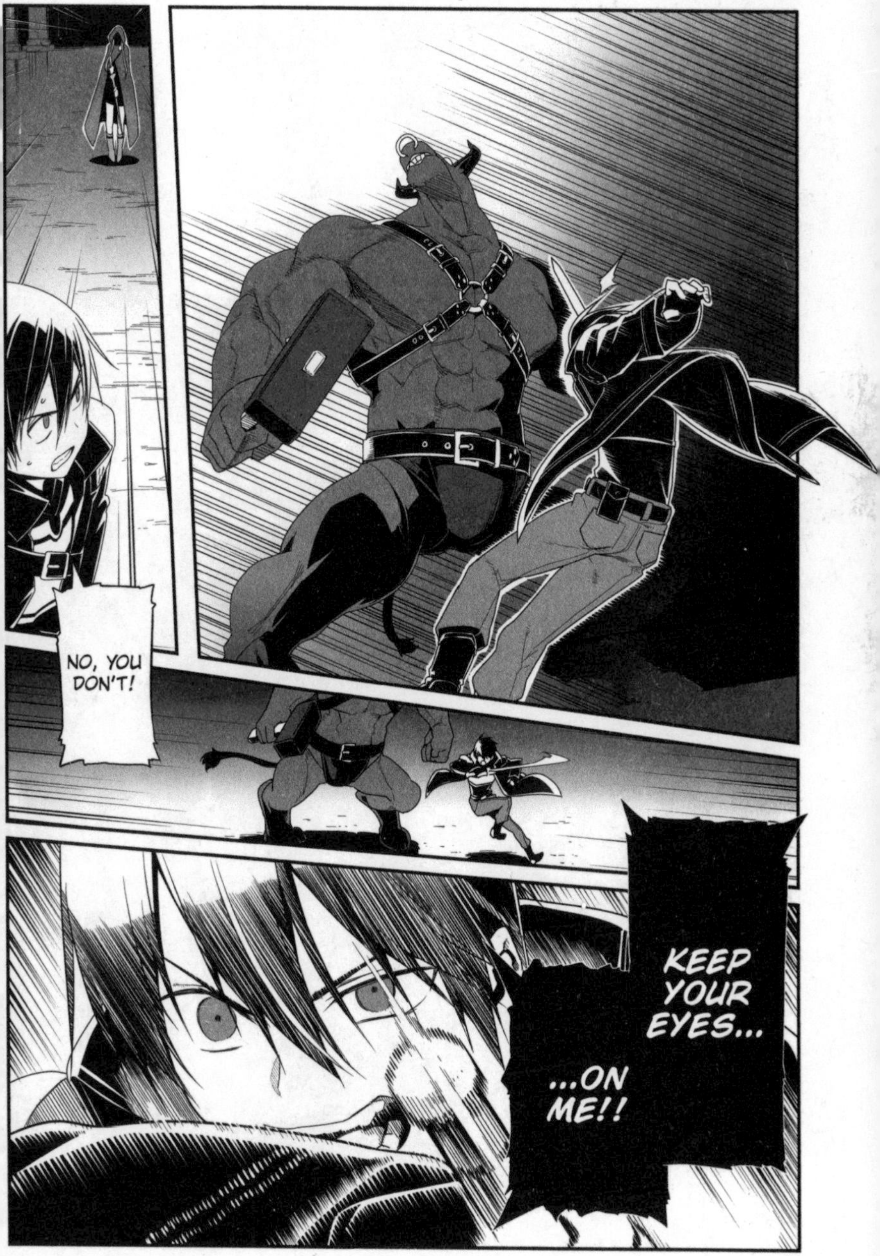
NO, YOU DON'T!
KEEP YOUR EYES...
...ON ME!!

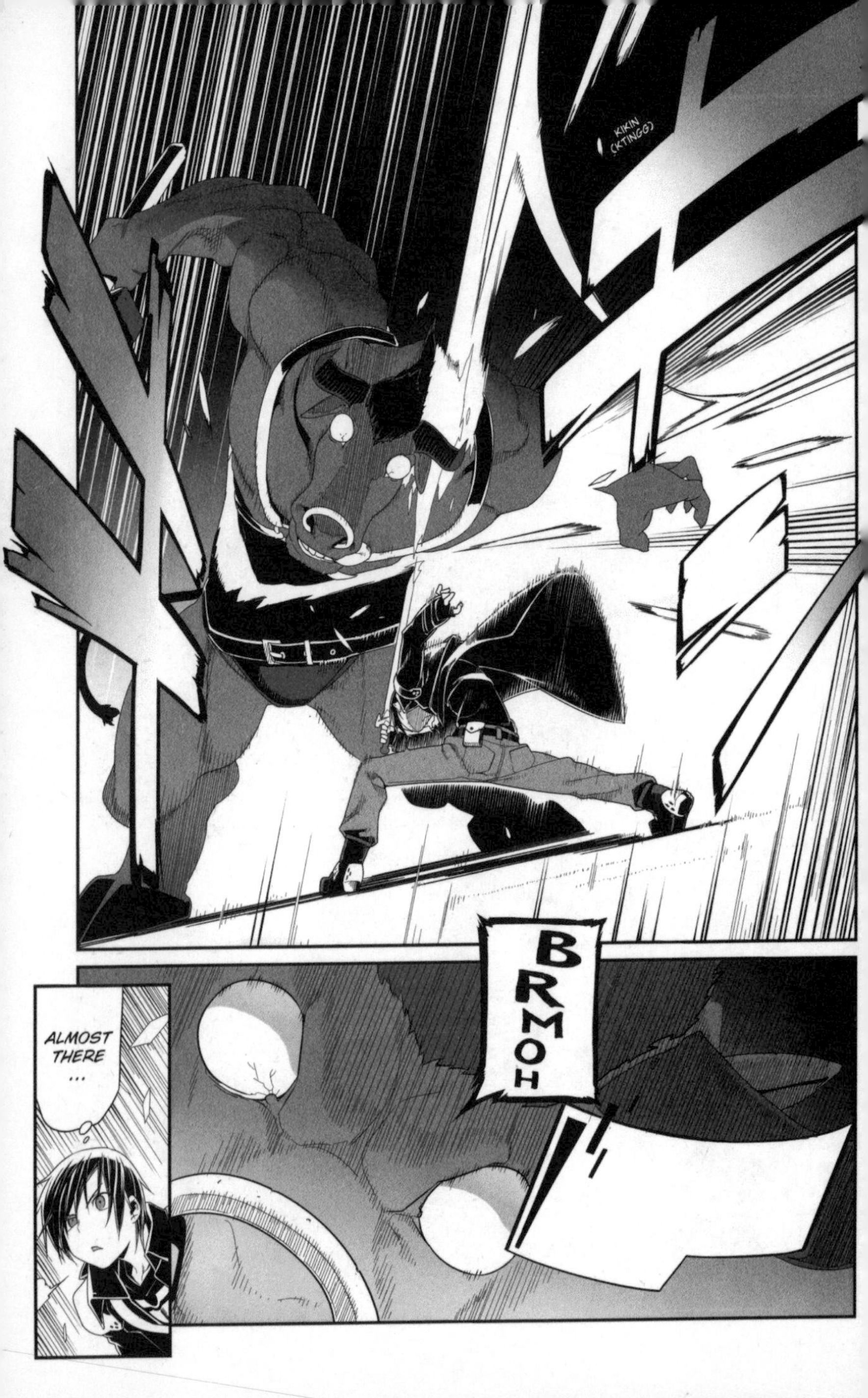
KIKIN (KTINGG)
BRMOH
ALMOST THERE ...

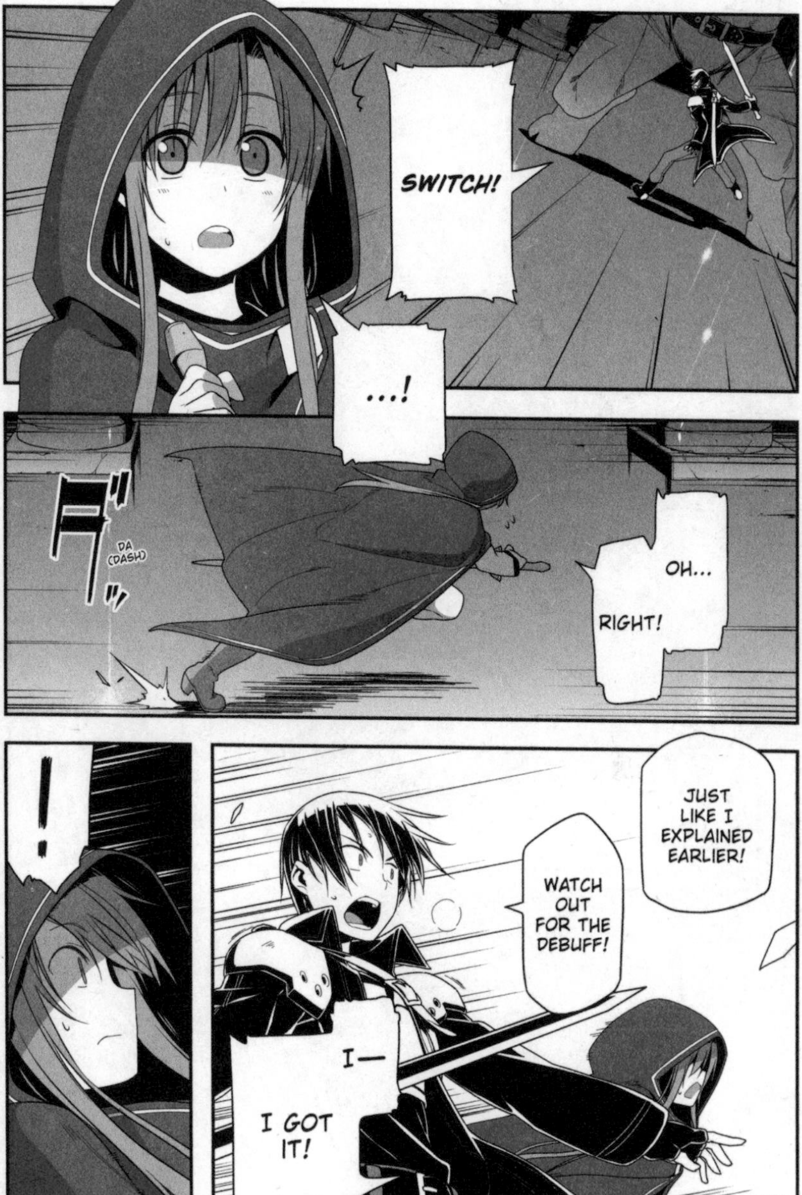
SWITCH!
...!
OH... RIGHT!
DA (DASH)
JUST LIKE I EXPLAINED EARLIER!
WATCH OUT FOR THE DEBUFF!
I— I GOT IT!
!

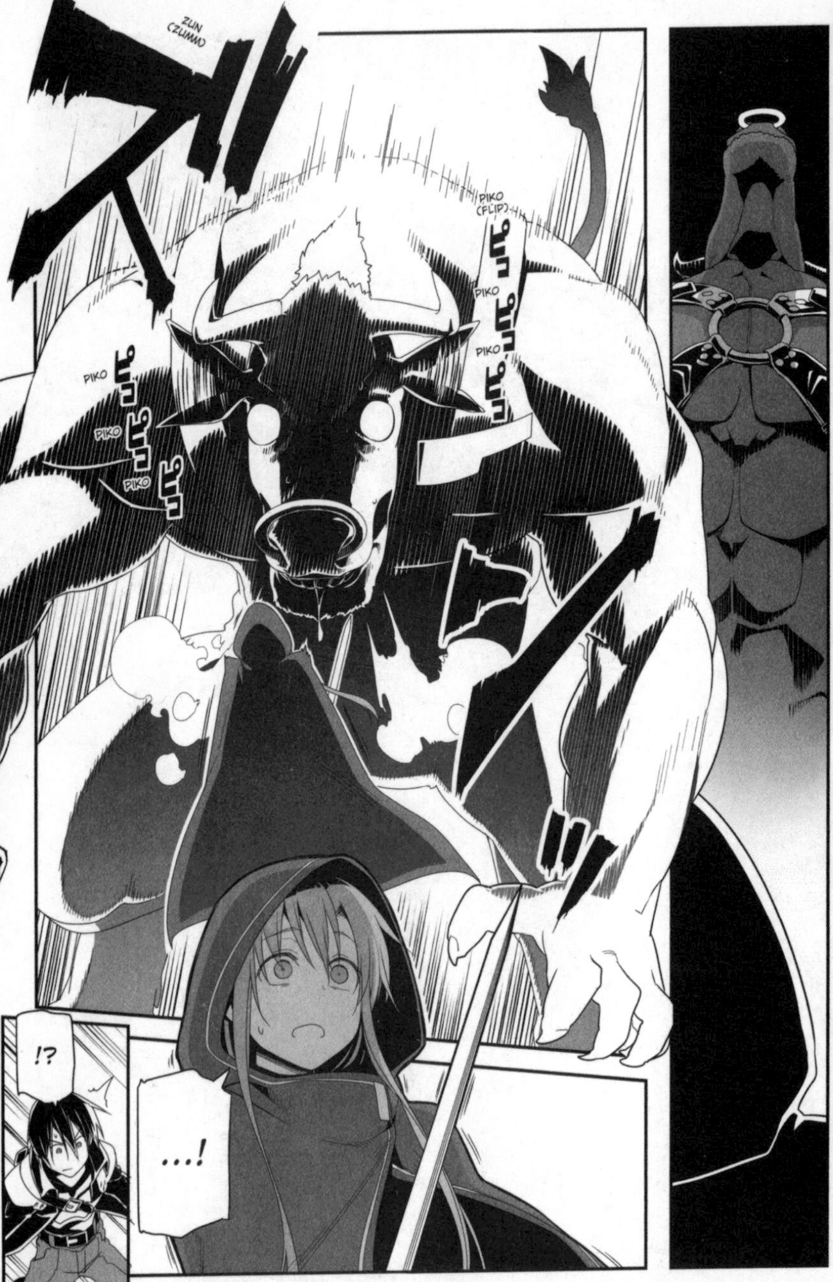
ZUN (ZUMM)
PIKO (FLIP)
PIKO
PIKO
PIKO
PIKO
PIKO
...!
!?

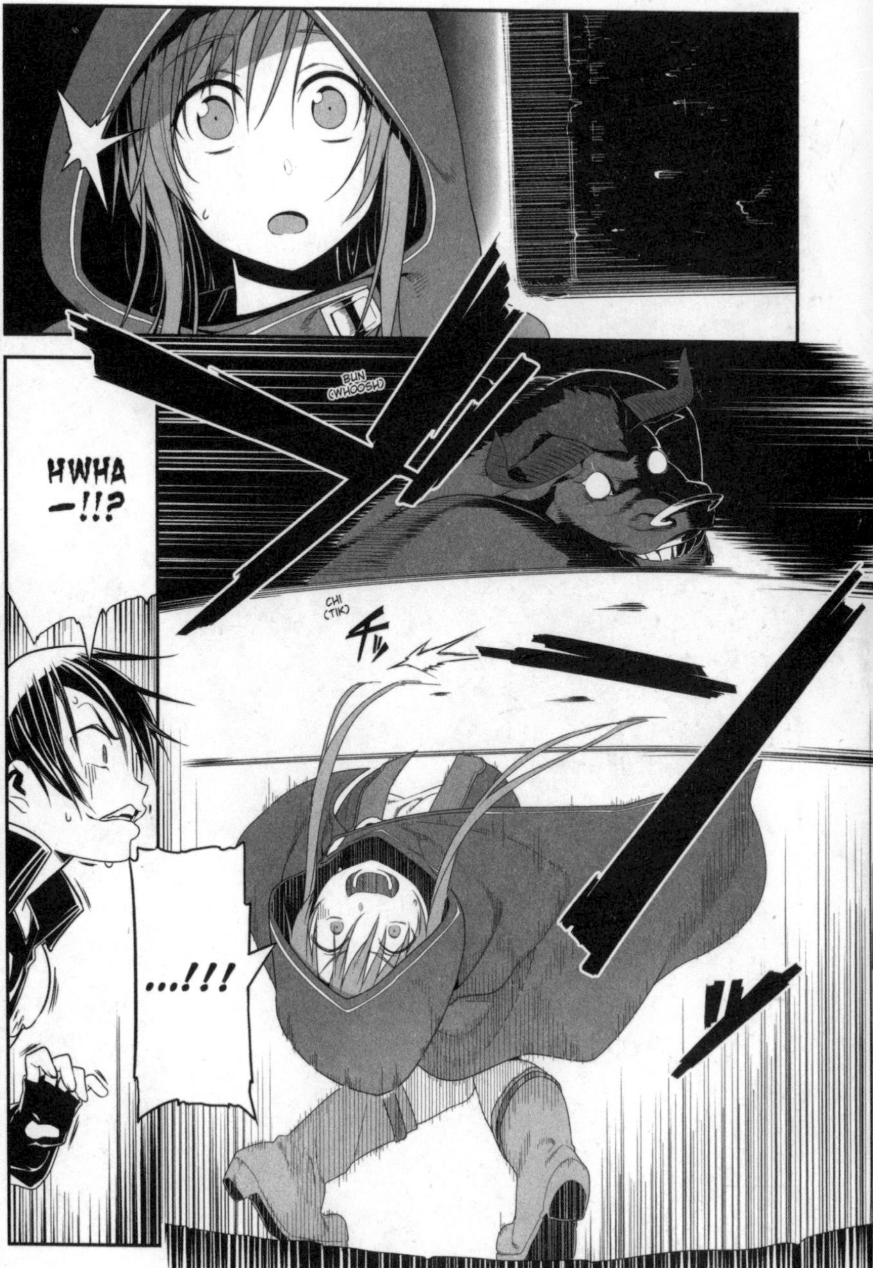

BUN (WHOOSH)
CHI (TIK)
HWHA—!!?
...!!!

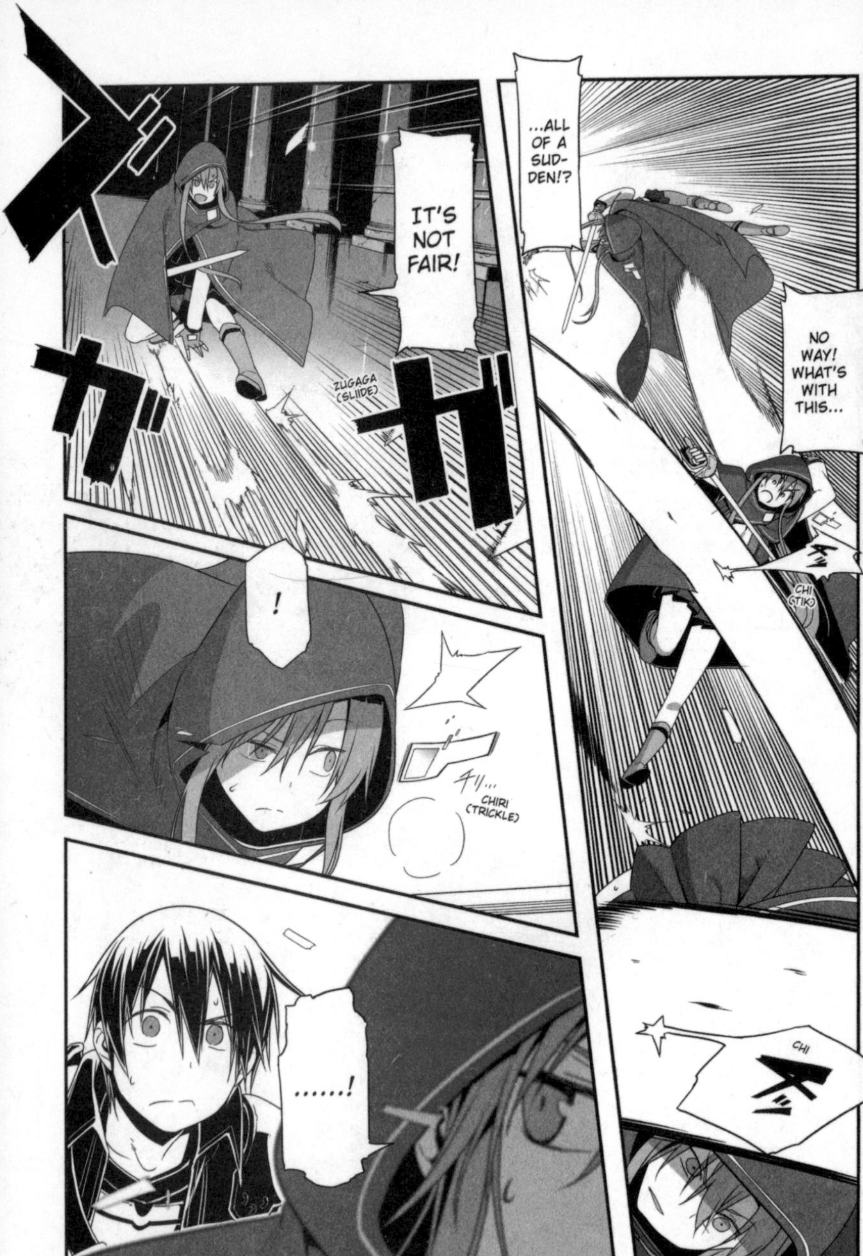
...ALL OF A SUD-DEN!?
NO WAY! WHAT'S WITH THIS...
CHI (TIK)
CHI
IT'S NOT FAIR!
ZUGAGA (SLIIDE)
!
チリ…
CHIRI (TRICKLE)
......!

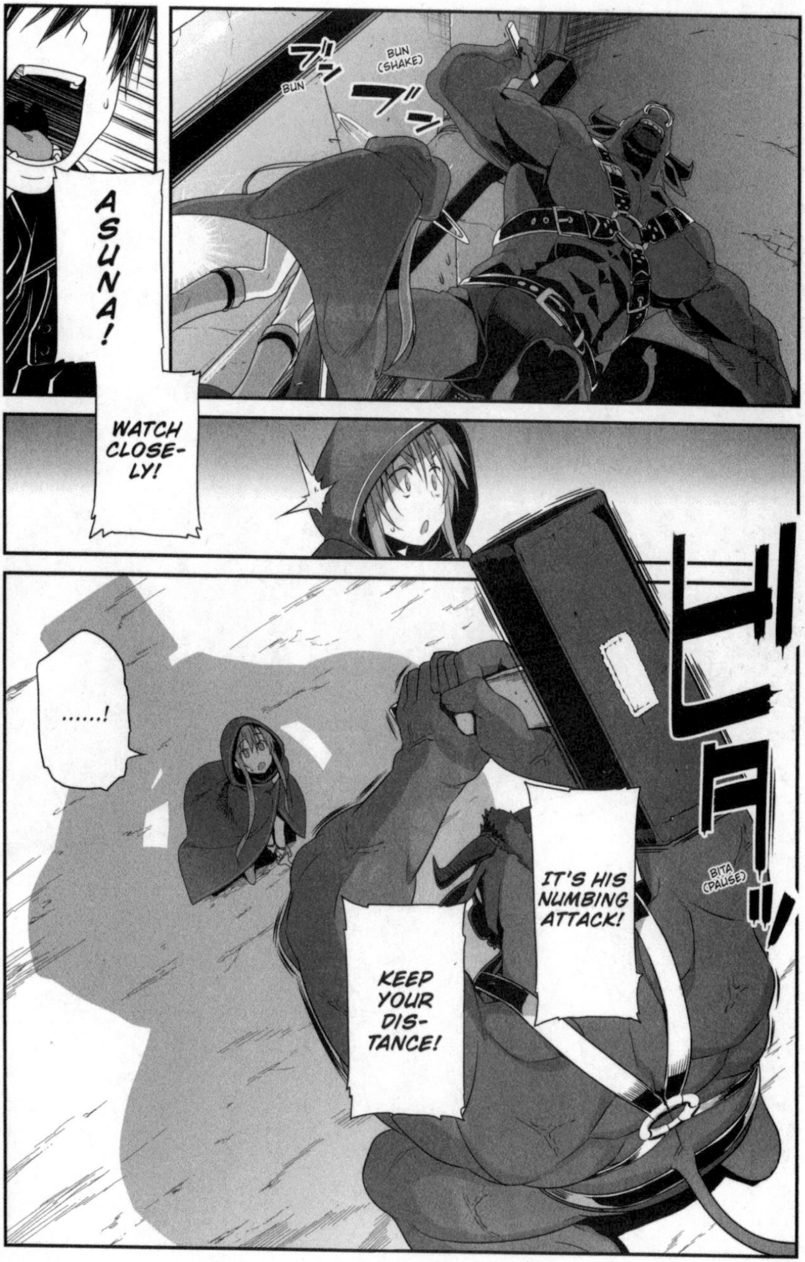
BUN (SHAKE)
BUN
ASUNA!
WATCH CLOSE-LY!
BITA (PAUSE)
IT'S HIS NUMBING ATTACK!
KEEP YOUR DIS-TANCE!
......!

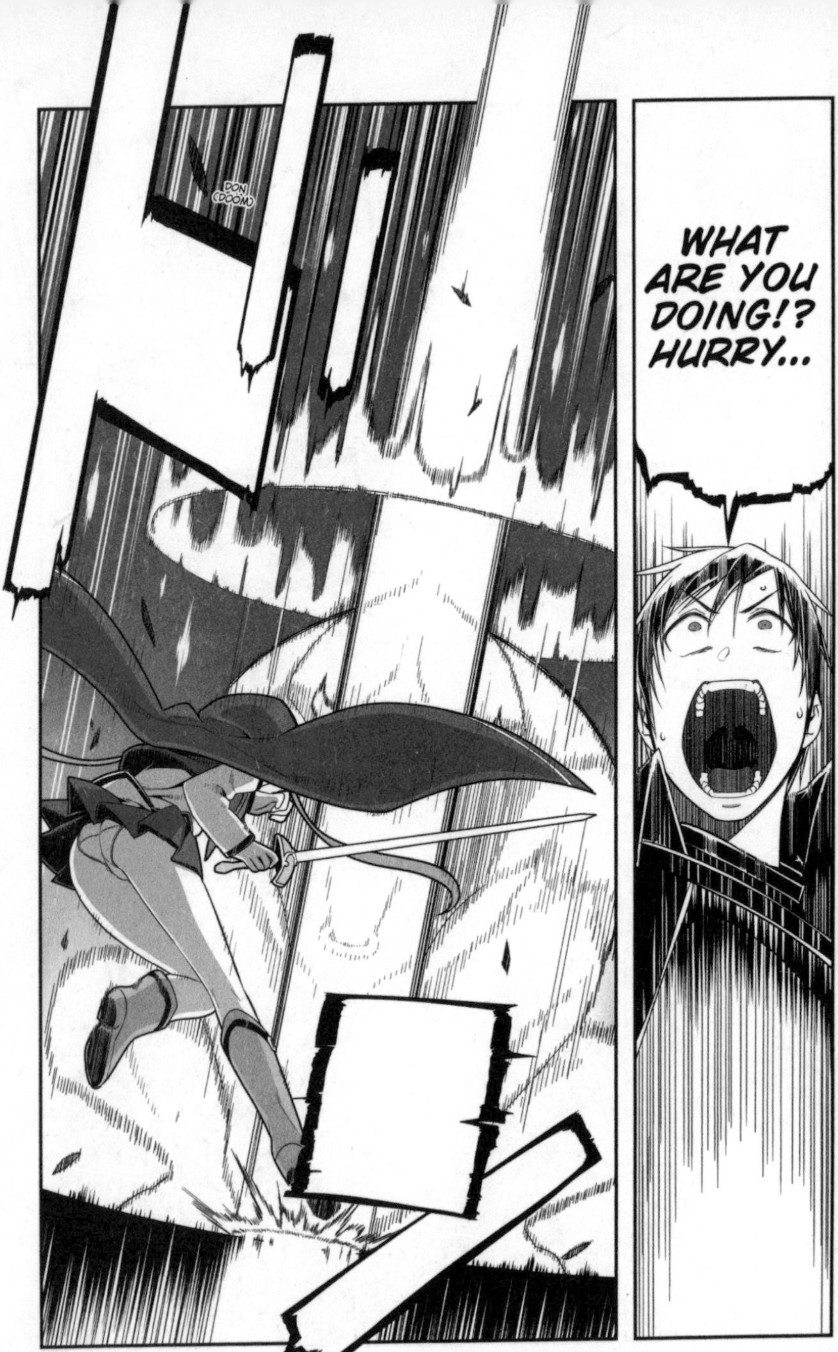
WHAT ARE YOU DOING!? HURRY...
DON (DOOM)

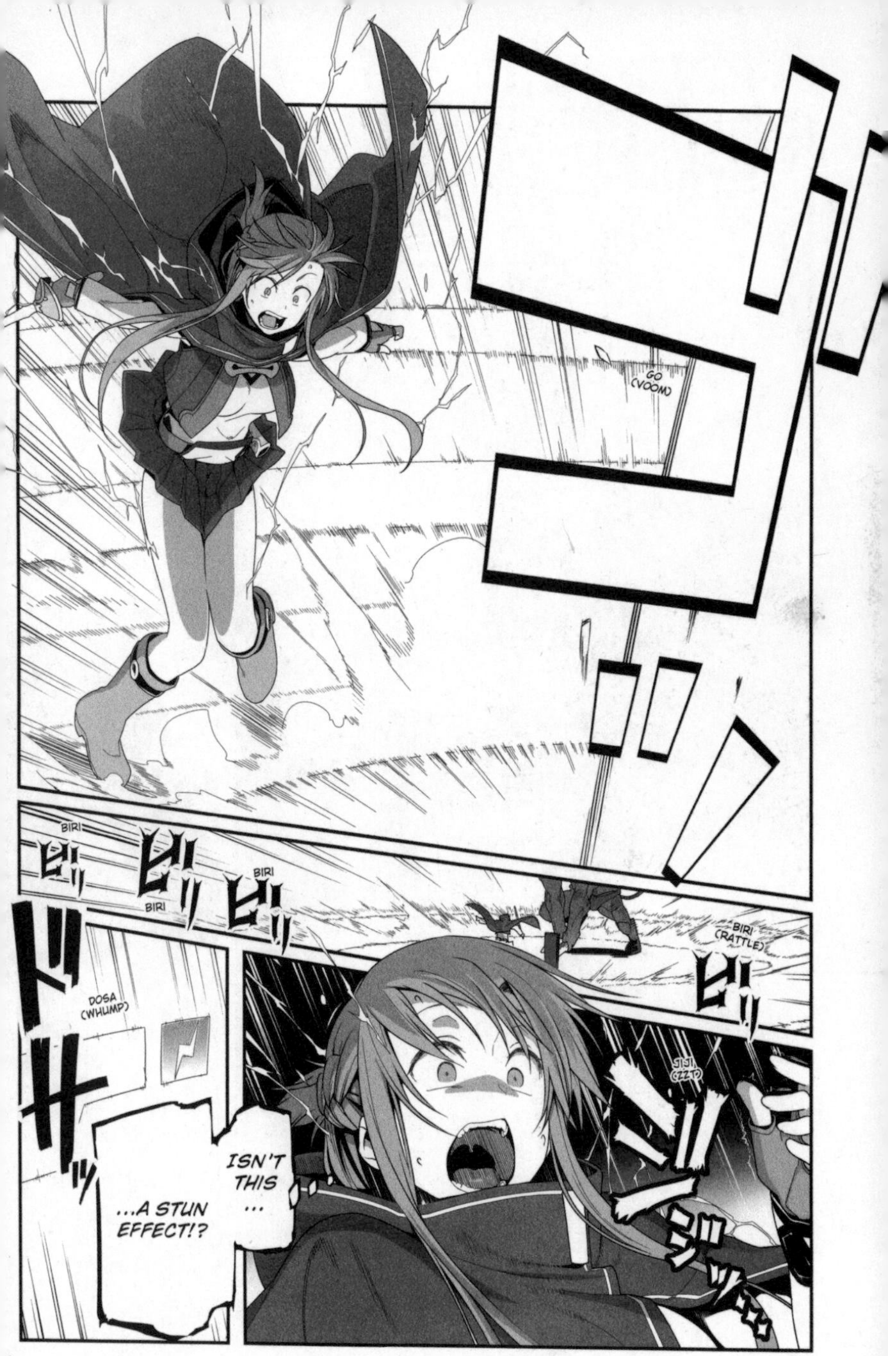
GO (VOOM)
BIRI (RATTLE)
BIRI
BIRI
BIRI
JIJI (ZZT)
ISN'T THIS...
...A STUN EFFECT!?
DOSA (WHUMP)

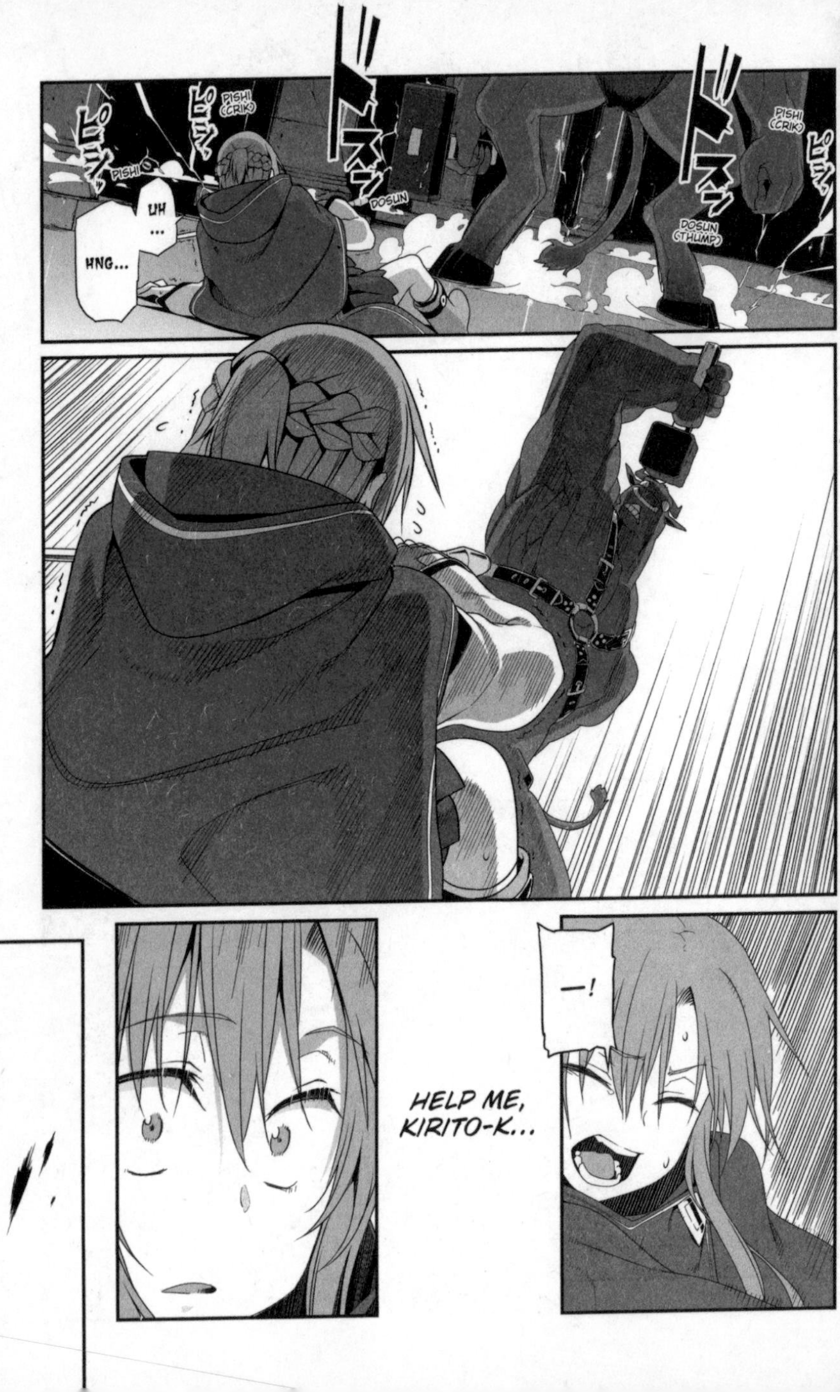
PISHI (CRIK)
DOSUN (THUMP)
DOSUN
PISHI (CRIK)
PISHI
UH ...
HNG...
—!
HELP ME, KIRITO-K...

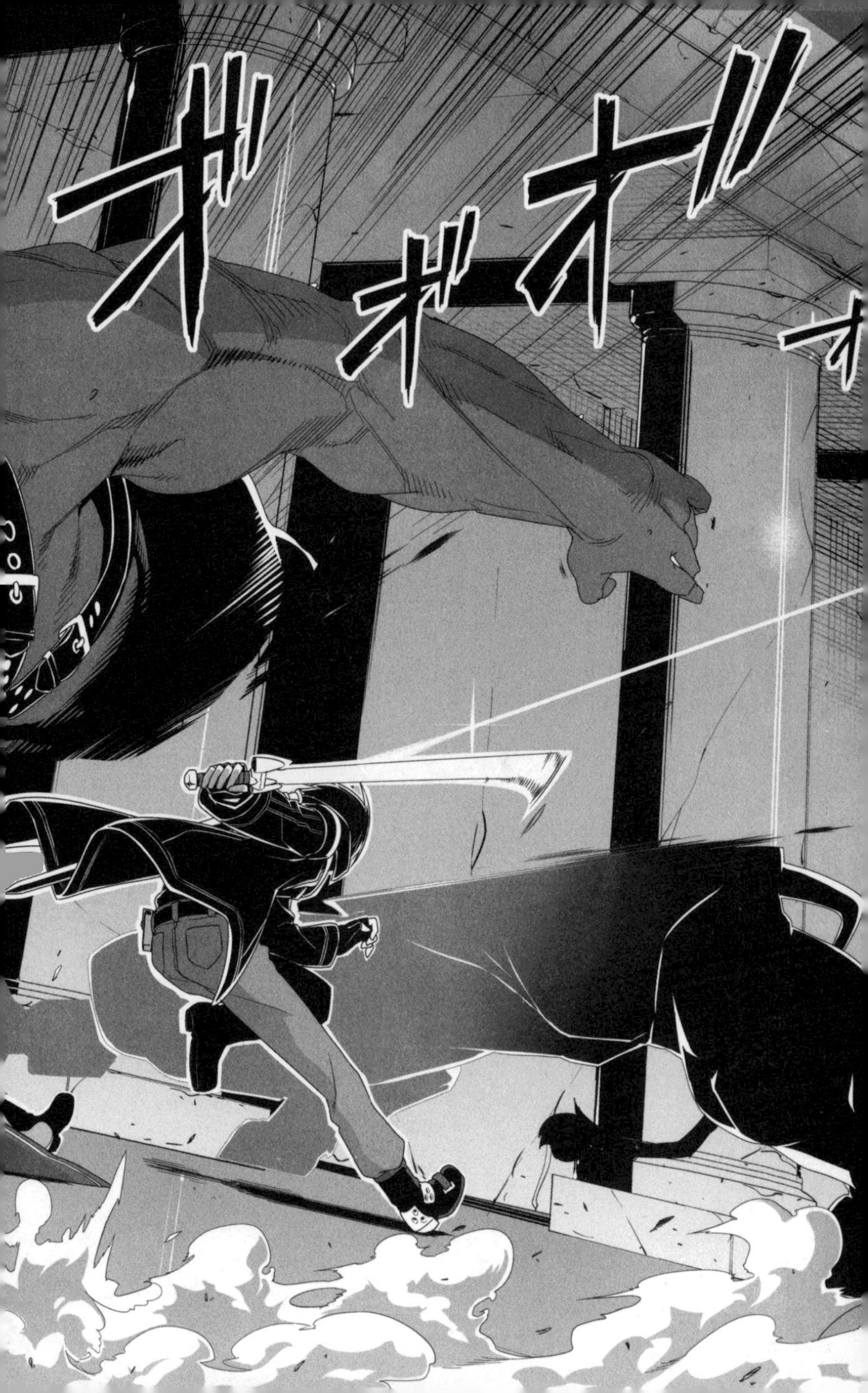
ザオオオォ

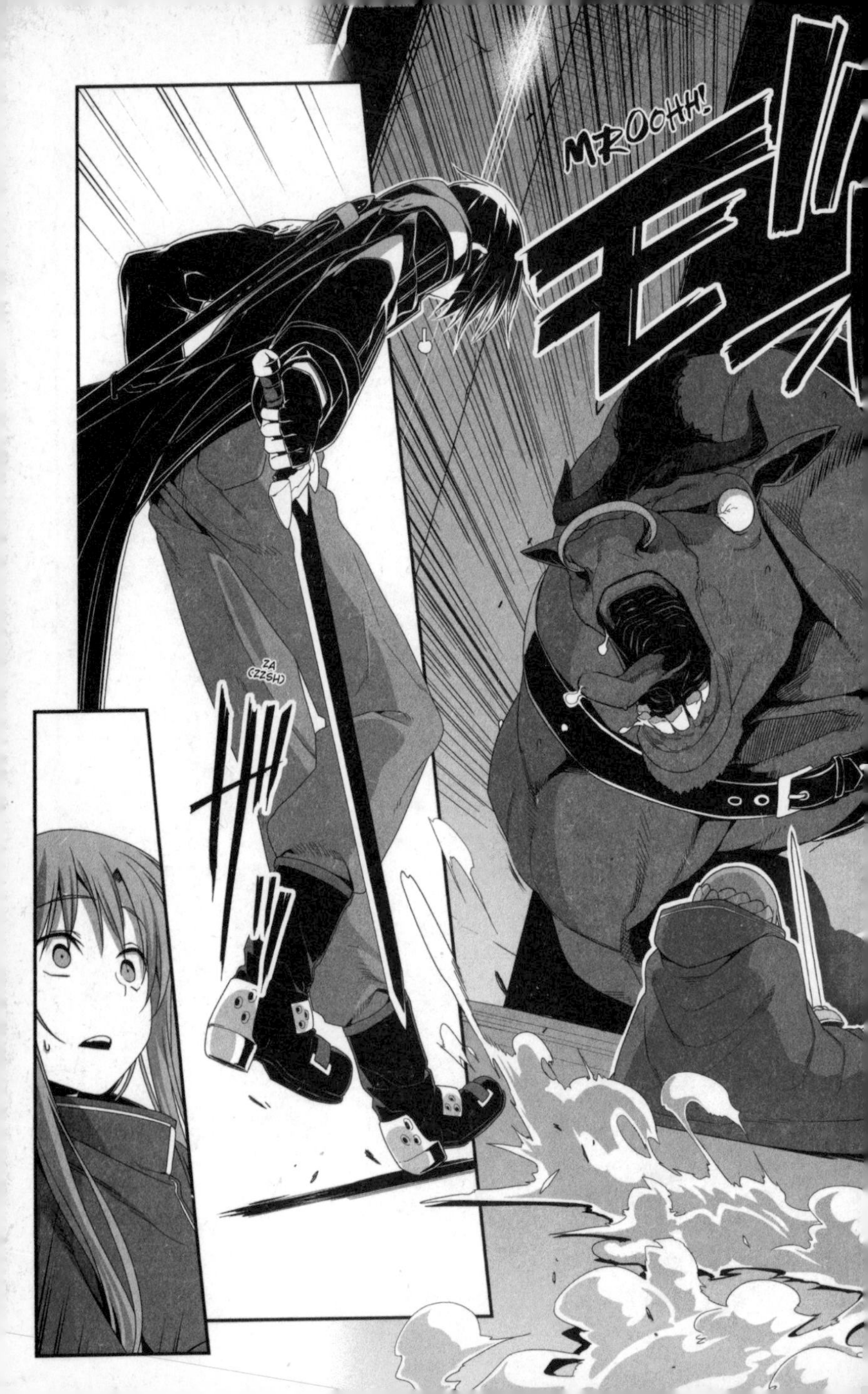
MROOHH!
ZA
(ZZSH)

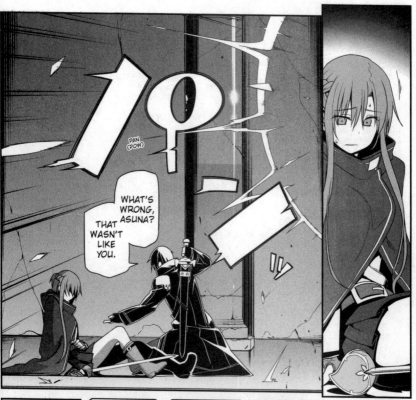

PAN
(POW)

WHAT'S WRONG, ASUNA? THAT WASN'T LIKE YOU.

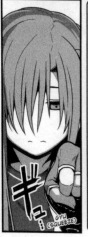

GYU
(SQUEEZE)

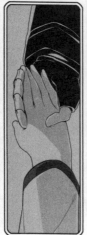

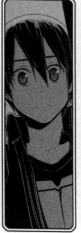

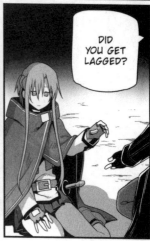

DID YOU GET LAGGED?

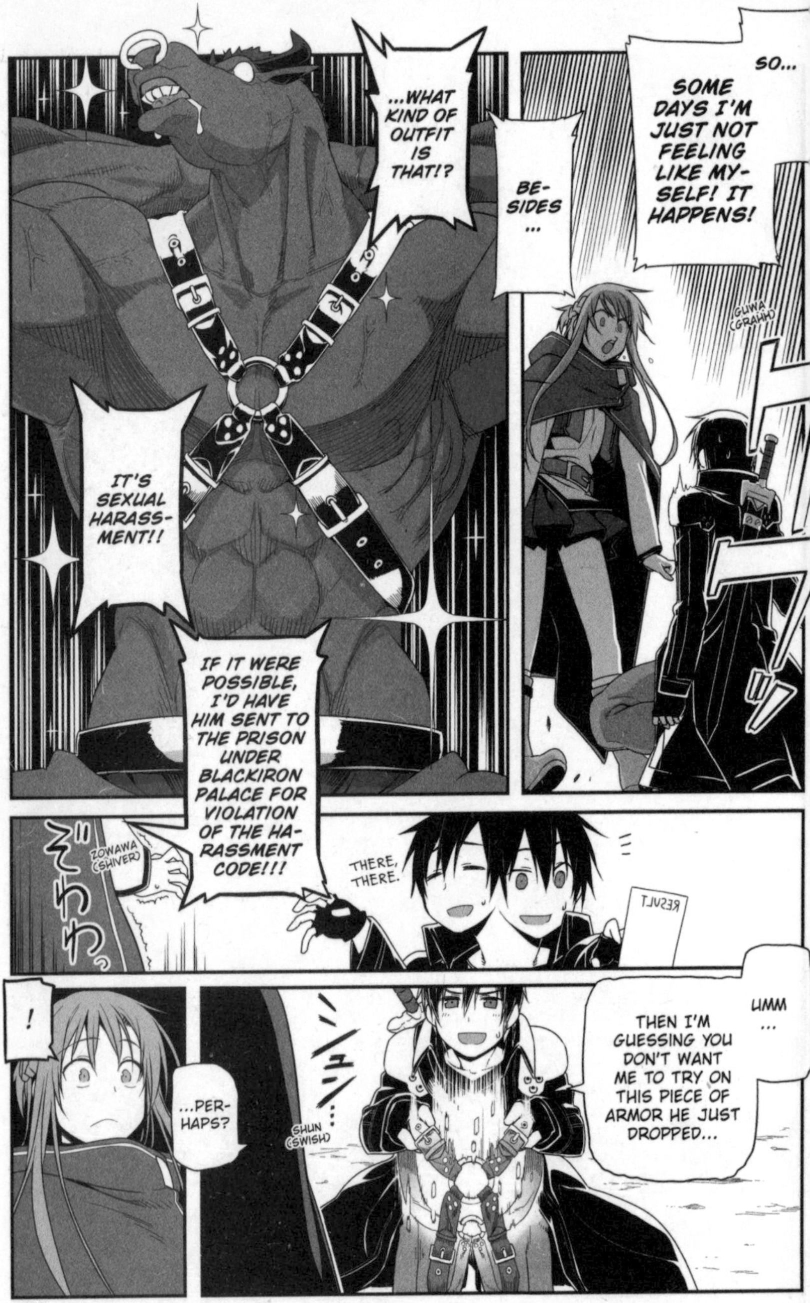
SO...
SOME DAYS I'M JUST NOT FEELING LIKE MY-SELF! IT HAPPENS!
GUWA (GRAHH)
BE-SIDES ...
...WHAT KIND OF OUTFIT IS THAT!?
IT'S SEXUAL HARASS-MENT!!
IF IT WERE POSSIBLE, I'D HAVE HIM SENT TO THE PRISON UNDER BLACKIRON PALACE FOR VIOLATION OF THE HA-RASSMENT CODE!!!
RESULT
THERE, THERE.
ZOWAWA (SHIVER)
UMM ...
THEN I'M GUESSING YOU DON'T WANT ME TO TRY ON THIS PIECE OF ARMOR HE JUST DROPPED...
SHUN (SWISH)
!
...PER-HAPS?

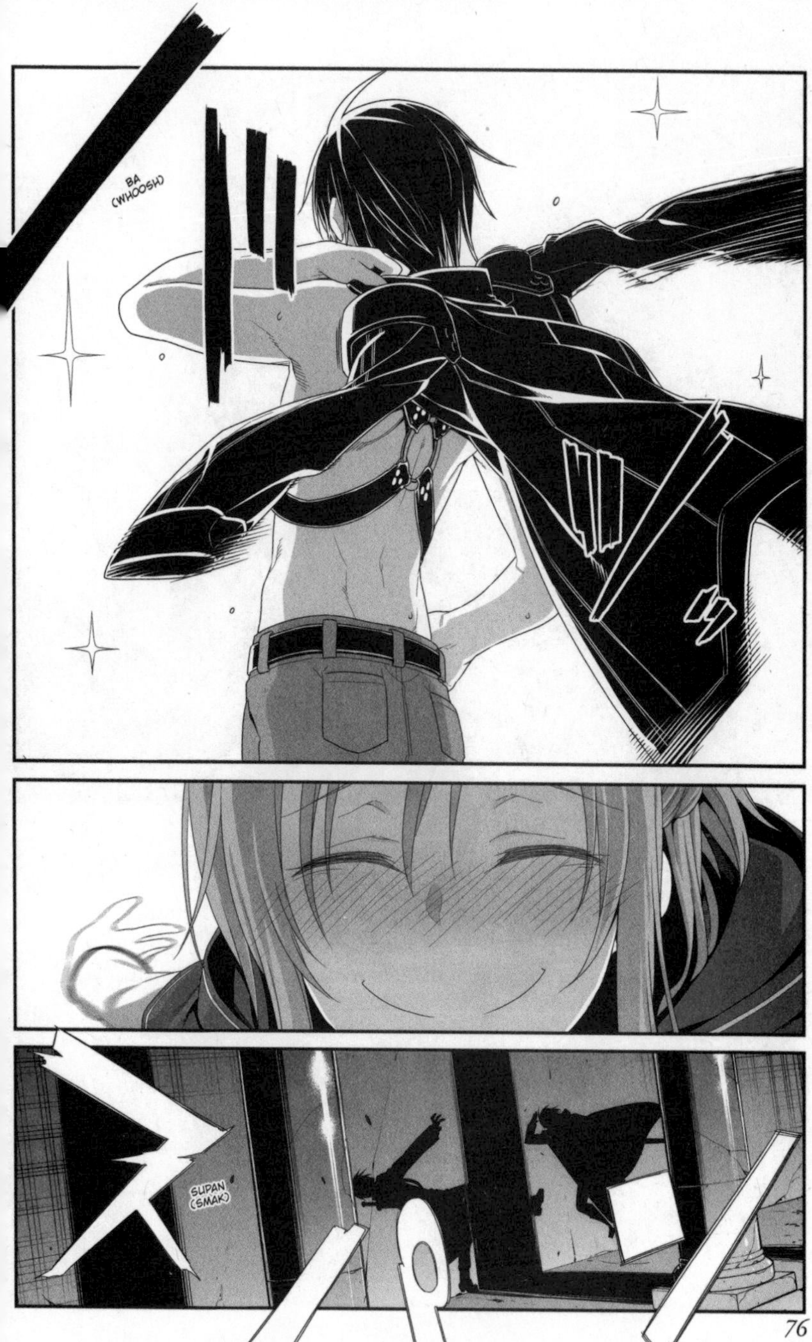
BA
(WHOOSH)
SUPAN
(SMAK)

#013: Pitfall

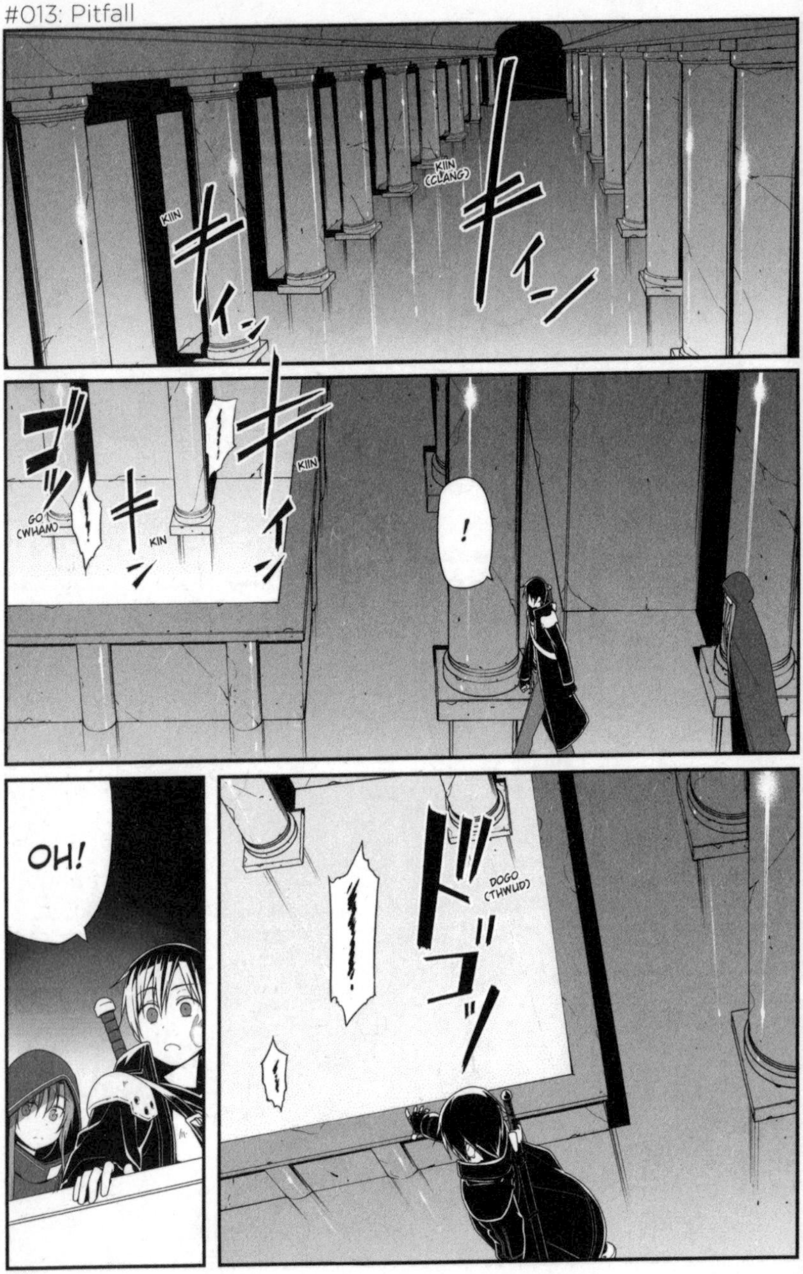
KIIN (CLANG)
KIIN
KIIN
!
KIN
GO (WHAM)
DOGO (THWUD)
OH!

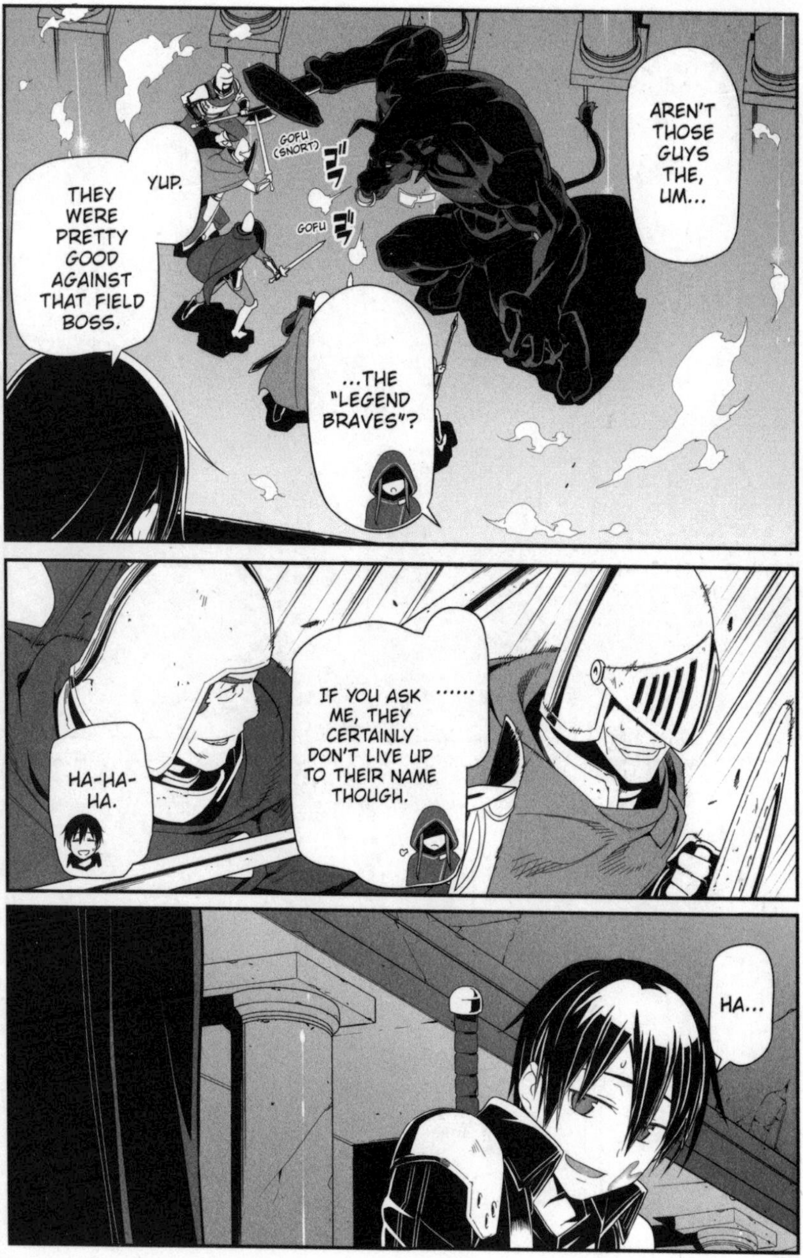
AREN'T THOSE GUYS THE, UM...
...THE "LEGEND BRAVES"?
GOFU (SNORT)
GOFU
YUP.
THEY WERE PRETTY GOOD AGAINST THAT FIELD BOSS.
......
IF YOU ASK ME, THEY CERTAINLY DON'T LIVE UP TO THEIR NAME THOUGH.
HA-HA-HA.
HA...

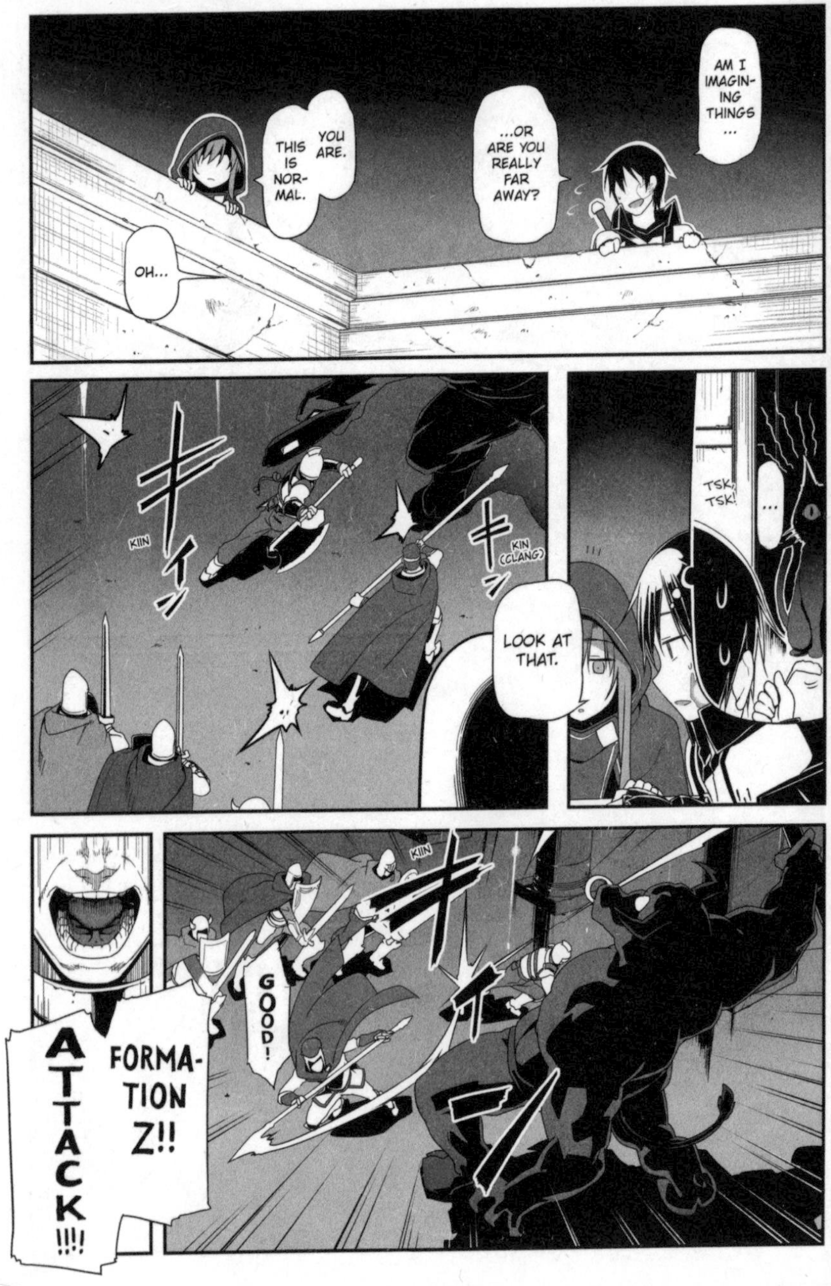
AM I IMAGINING THINGS...
...OR ARE YOU REALLY FAR AWAY?
YOU ARE.
THIS IS NORMAL.
OH...
TSK, TSK!
...
LOOK AT THAT.
KIN (CLANG)
KIIN
KIIN
GOOD!
FORMATION Z!!
ATTACK!!!!

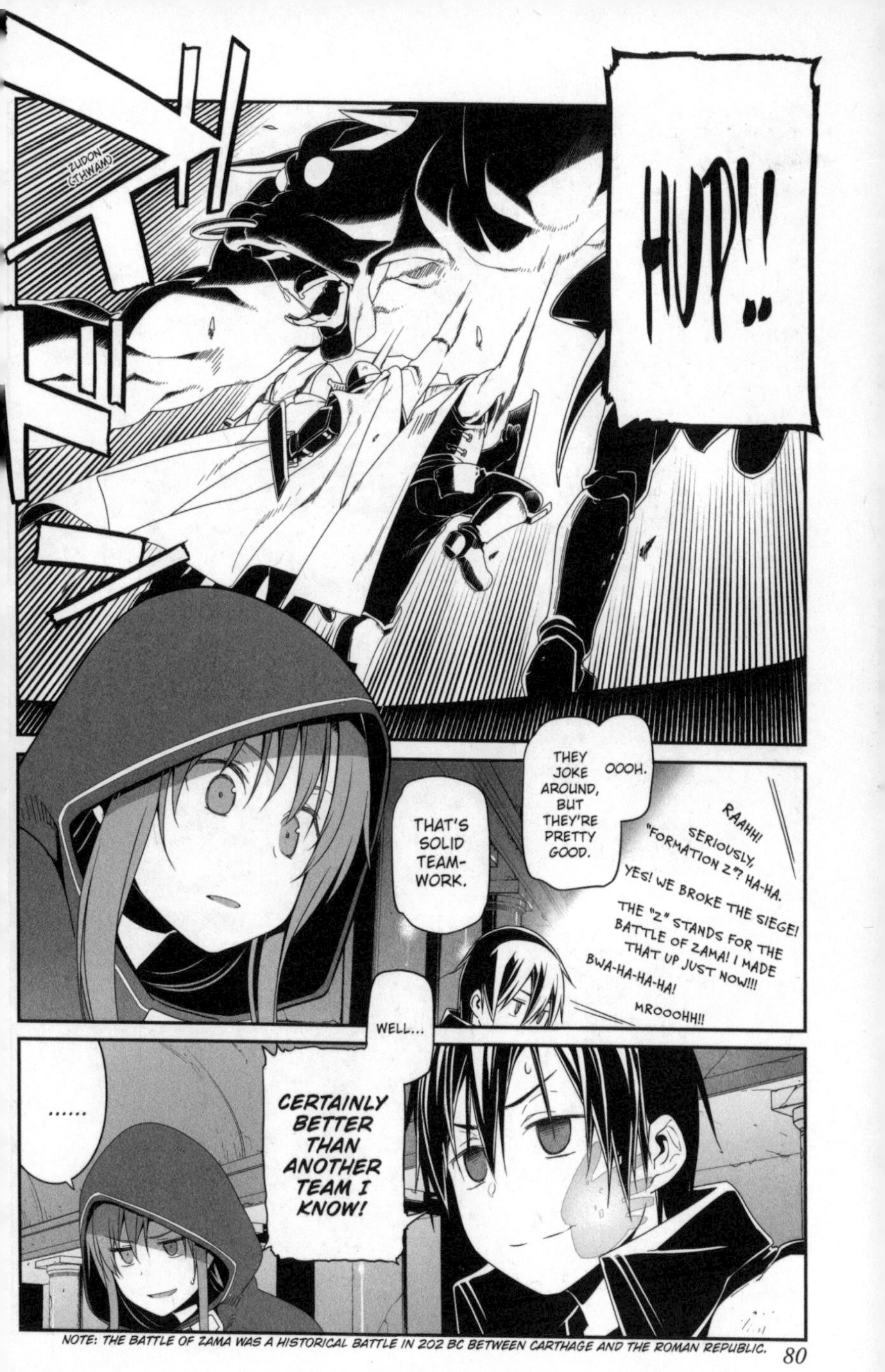
HUP!!
ZUDON (THWAM)
RAAHH!
SERIOUSLY, "FORMATION Z"? HA-HA.
YES! WE BROKE THE SIEGE!
THE "Z" STANDS FOR THE BATTLE OF ZAMA! I MADE THAT UP JUST NOW!!!
BWA-HA-HA-HA!
MROOOHH!!
OOOH.
THEY JOKE AROUND, BUT THEY'RE PRETTY GOOD.
THAT'S SOLID TEAM-WORK.
WELL...
CERTAINLY BETTER THAN ANOTHER TEAM I KNOW!
......

NOTE: THE BATTLE OF ZAMA WAS A HISTORICAL BATTLE IN 202 BC BETWEEN CARTHAGE AND THE ROMAN REPUBLIC.

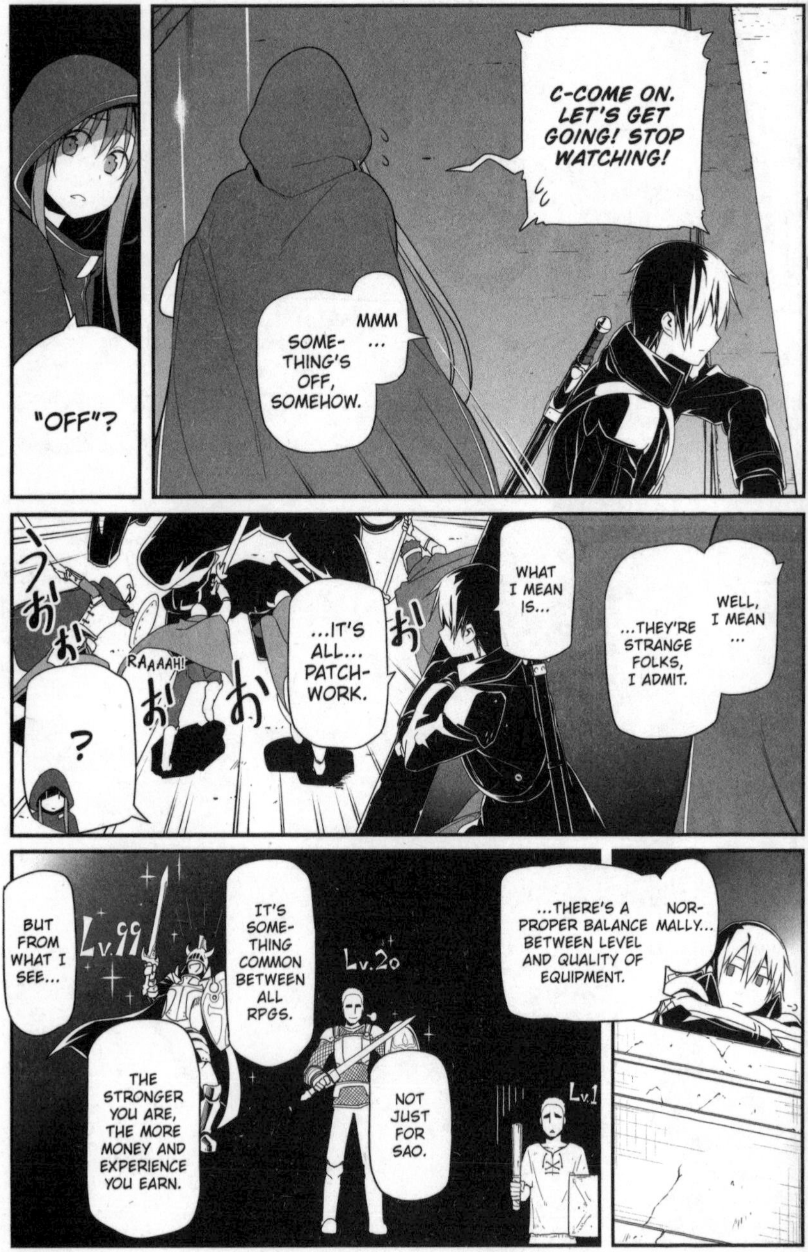
C-COME ON. LET'S GET GOING! STOP WATCHING!
MMM... SOMETHING'S OFF, SOMEHOW.
"OFF"?
WELL, I MEAN...
...THEY'RE STRANGE FOLKS, I ADMIT.
WHAT I MEAN IS...
...IT'S ALL... PATCHWORK.
うおおおお
RAAAAH!
?
NORMALLY...
...THERE'S A PROPER BALANCE BETWEEN LEVEL AND QUALITY OF EQUIPMENT.
Lv.1
IT'S SOMETHING COMMON BETWEEN ALL RPGS.
NOT JUST FOR SAO.
Lv.20
THE STRONGER YOU ARE, THE MORE MONEY AND EXPERIENCE YOU EARN.
Lv.99
BUT FROM WHAT I SEE...

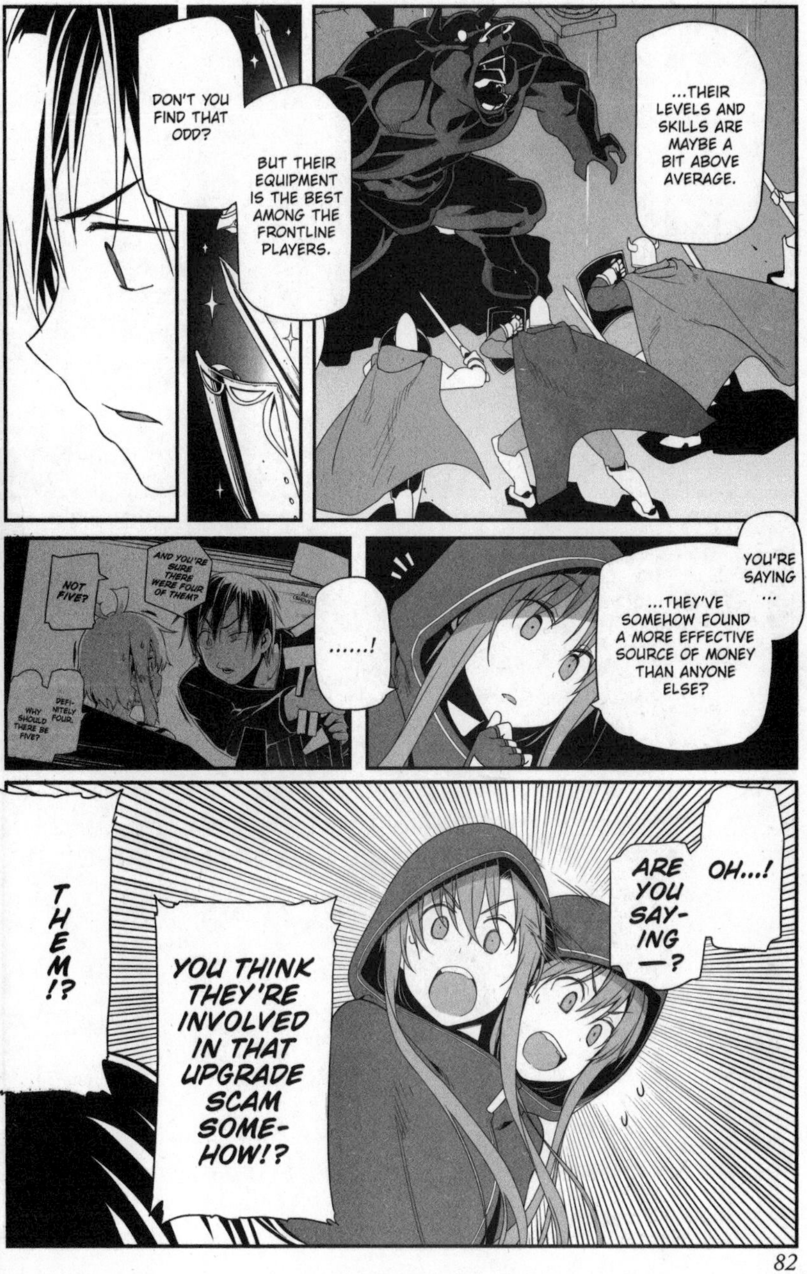
...THEIR LEVELS AND SKILLS ARE MAYBE A BIT ABOVE AVERAGE.
BUT THEIR EQUIPMENT IS THE BEST AMONG THE FRONTLINE PLAYERS.
DON'T YOU FIND THAT ODD?
YOU'RE SAYING ...
...THEY'VE SOMEHOW FOUND A MORE EFFECTIVE SOURCE OF MONEY THAN ANYONE ELSE?
......!
AND YOU'RE SURE THERE WERE FOUR OF THEM?
NOT FIVE?
DEFI-NITELY FOUR.
WHY SHOULD THERE BE FIVE?
OH...!
ARE YOU SAY-ING—?
YOU THINK THEY'RE INVOLVED IN THAT UPGRADE SCAM SOME-HOW!?
THEM!?

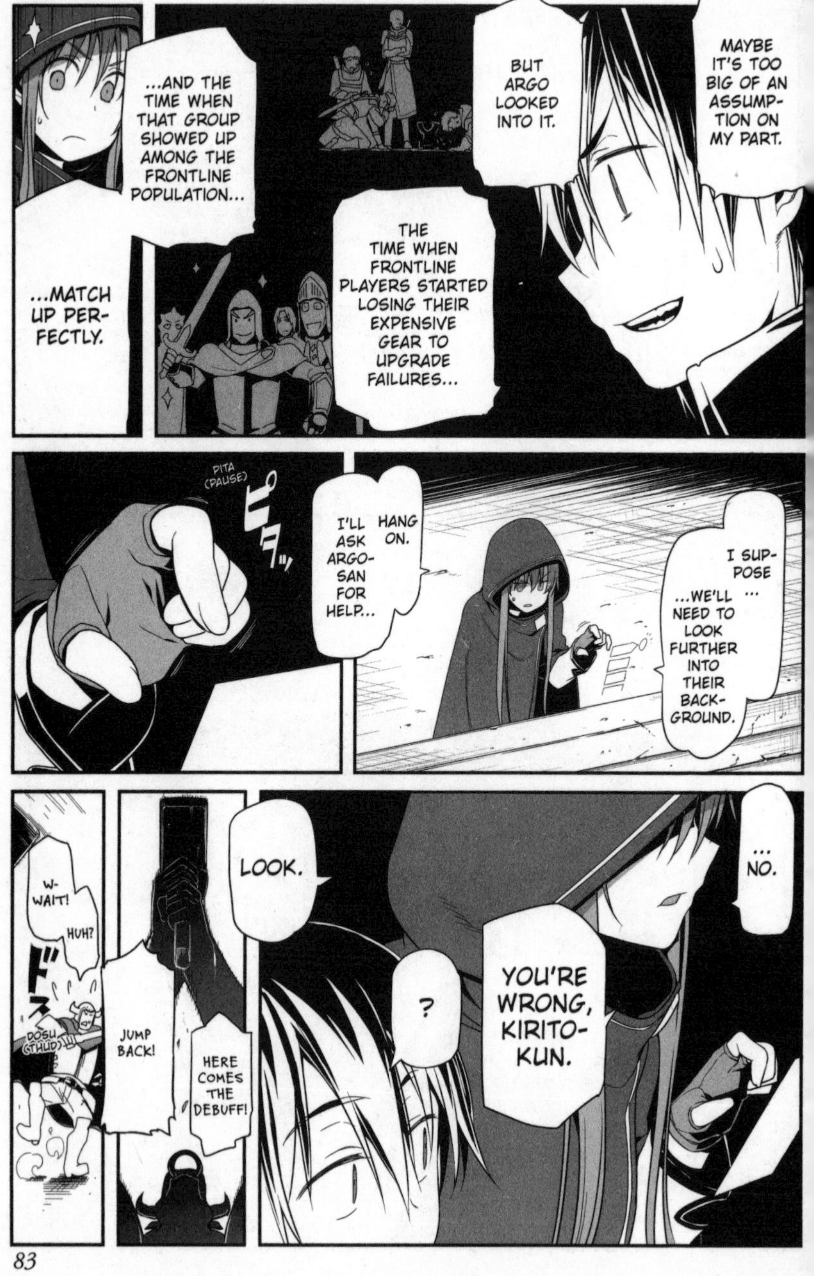
MAYBE IT'S TOO BIG OF AN ASSUMPTION ON MY PART.
BUT ARGO LOOKED INTO IT.
THE TIME WHEN FRONTLINE PLAYERS STARTED LOSING THEIR EXPENSIVE GEAR TO UPGRADE FAILURES...
...AND THE TIME WHEN THAT GROUP SHOWED UP AMONG THE FRONTLINE POPULATION...
...MATCH UP PERFECTLY.
I SUPPOSE...
...WE'LL NEED TO LOOK FURTHER INTO THEIR BACKGROUND.
HANG ON.
I'LL ASK ARGO-SAN FOR HELP...
PITA (PAUSE)
...NO.
YOU'RE WRONG, KIRITO-KUN.
?
LOOK.
HERE COMES THE DEBUFF!
JUMP BACK!
W-WAIT!
HUH?
DOSU (THUD)

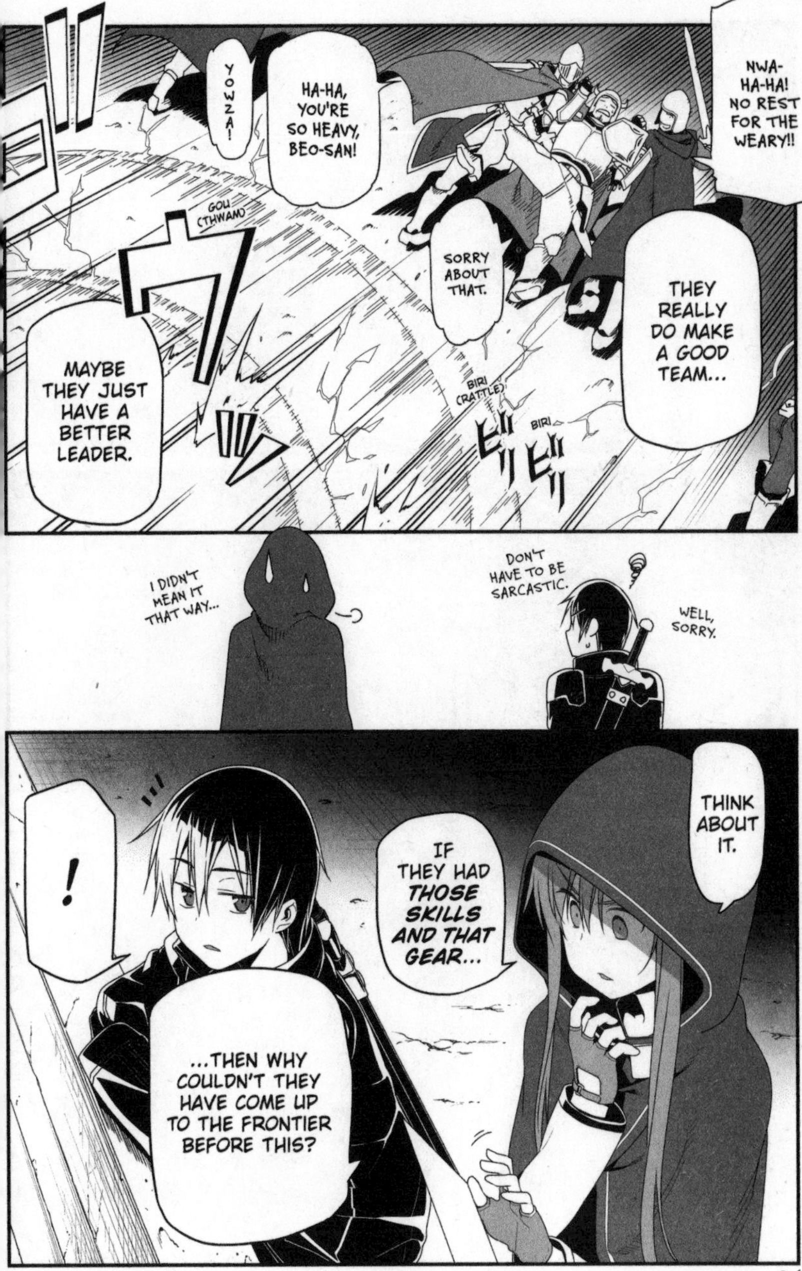
NWA-HA-HA! NO REST FOR THE WEARY!!
HA-HA, YOU'RE SO HEAVY, BEO-SAN!
YOWZA!
THEY REALLY DO MAKE A GOOD TEAM...
SORRY ABOUT THAT.
GOU (THWAM)
BIRI (RATTLE)
BIRI
MAYBE THEY JUST HAVE A BETTER LEADER.
WELL, SORRY.
DON'T HAVE TO BE SARCASTIC.
I DIDN'T MEAN IT THAT WAY...
THINK ABOUT IT.
IF THEY HAD *THOSE SKILLS AND THAT GEAR*...
!
...THEN WHY COULDN'T THEY HAVE COME UP TO THE FRONTIER BEFORE THIS?

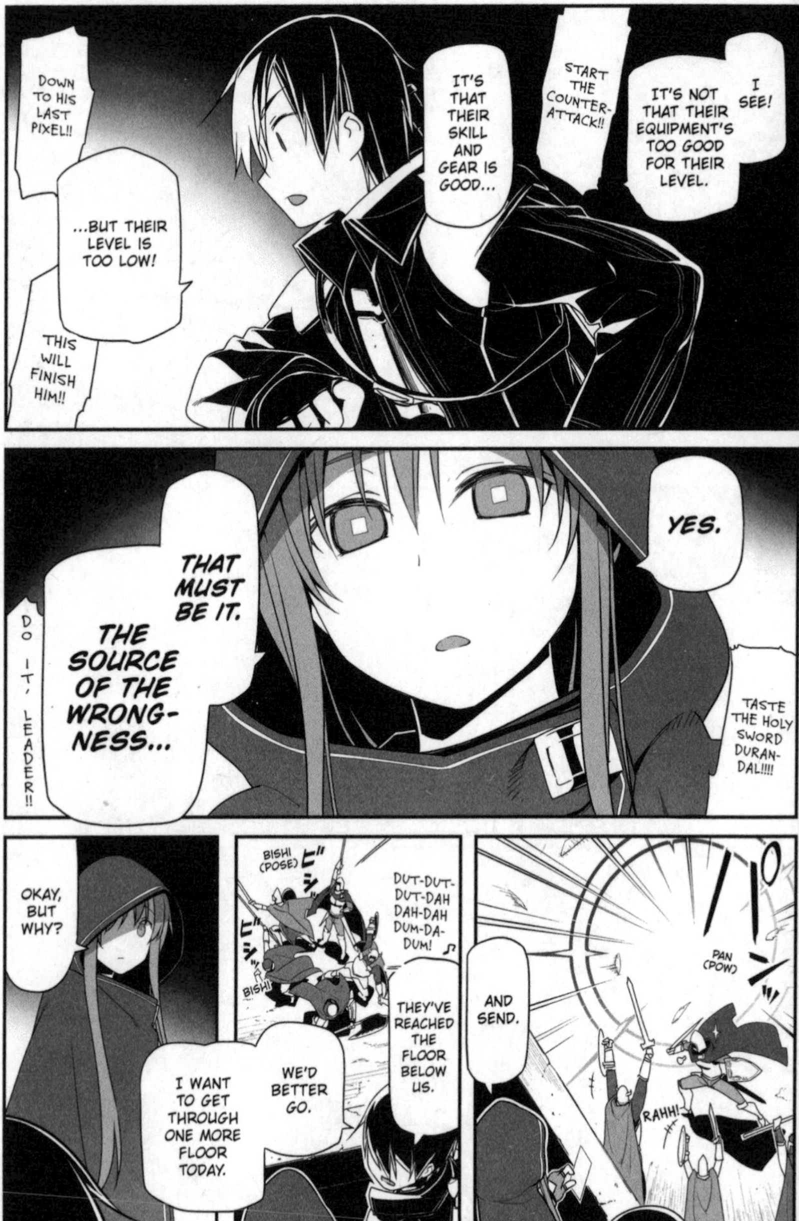
I SEE!
IT'S NOT THAT THEIR EQUIPMENT'S TOO GOOD FOR THEIR LEVEL.
START THE COUNTER-ATTACK!!
IT'S THAT THEIR SKILL AND GEAR IS GOOD...
DOWN TO HIS LAST PIXEL!!
...BUT THEIR LEVEL IS TOO LOW!
THIS WILL FINISH HIM!!
YES.
TASTE THE HOLY SWORD DURAN-DAL!!!!
THAT MUST BE IT.
THE SOURCE OF THE WRONG-NESS...
DO IT, LEADER!!
PAN (POW)
AND SEND.
RAHH!
BISHI (POSE)
DUT-DUT-DUT-DAH DAH-DAH DUM-DA-DUM!
BISHI
THEY'VE REACHED THE FLOOR BELOW US.
WE'D BETTER GO.
I WANT TO GET THROUGH ONE MORE FLOOR TODAY.
OKAY, BUT WHY?

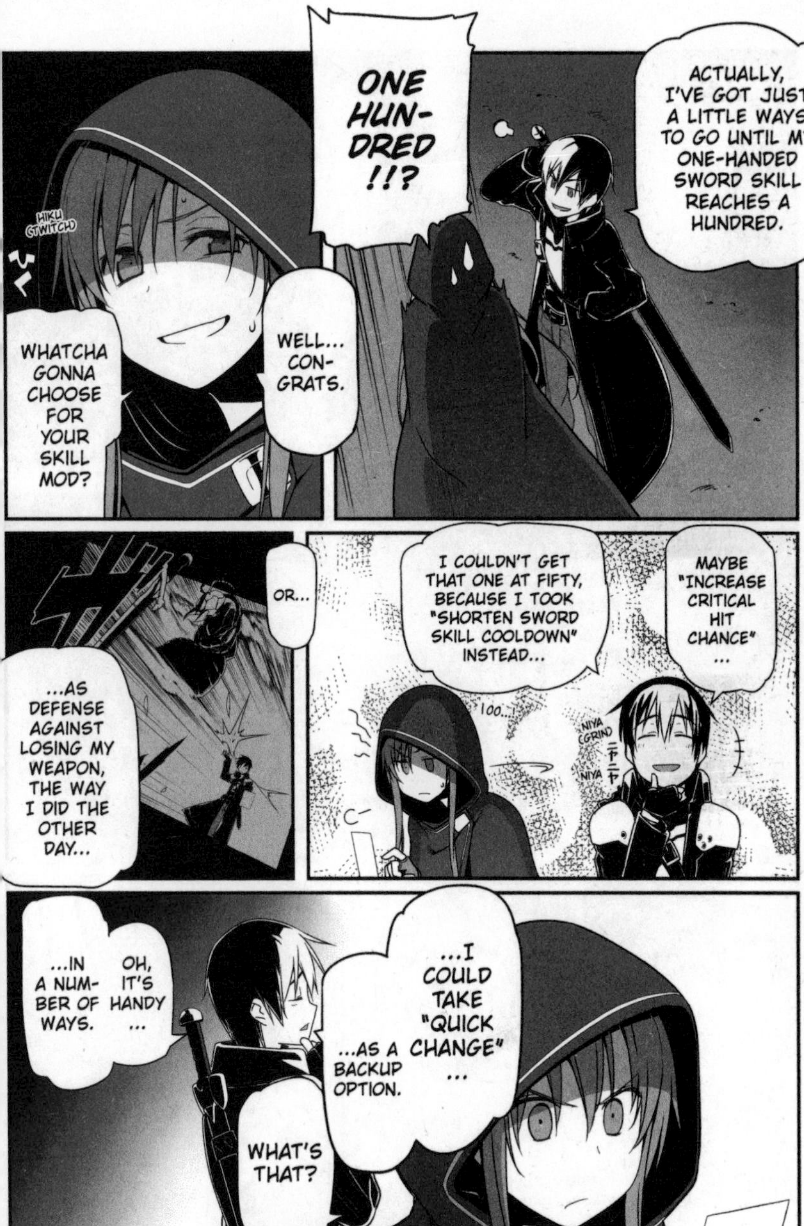
ACTUALLY, I'VE GOT JUST A LITTLE WAYS TO GO UNTIL MY ONE-HANDED SWORD SKILL REACHES A HUNDRED.
ONE HUNDRED!!?
HIKU (TWITCH)
WELL... CONGRATS.
WHATCHA GONNA CHOOSE FOR YOUR SKILL MOD?
MAYBE "INCREASE CRITICAL HIT CHANCE"...
I COULDN'T GET THAT ONE AT FIFTY, BECAUSE I TOOK "SHORTEN SWORD SKILL COOLDOWN" INSTEAD...
NIYA (GRIN) NIYA
100...
OR...
...AS DEFENSE AGAINST LOSING MY WEAPON, THE WAY I DID THE OTHER DAY...
...I COULD TAKE "QUICK CHANGE"...
...AS A BACKUP OPTION.
OH, IT'S HANDY...
...IN A NUMBER OF WAYS.
WHAT'S THAT?

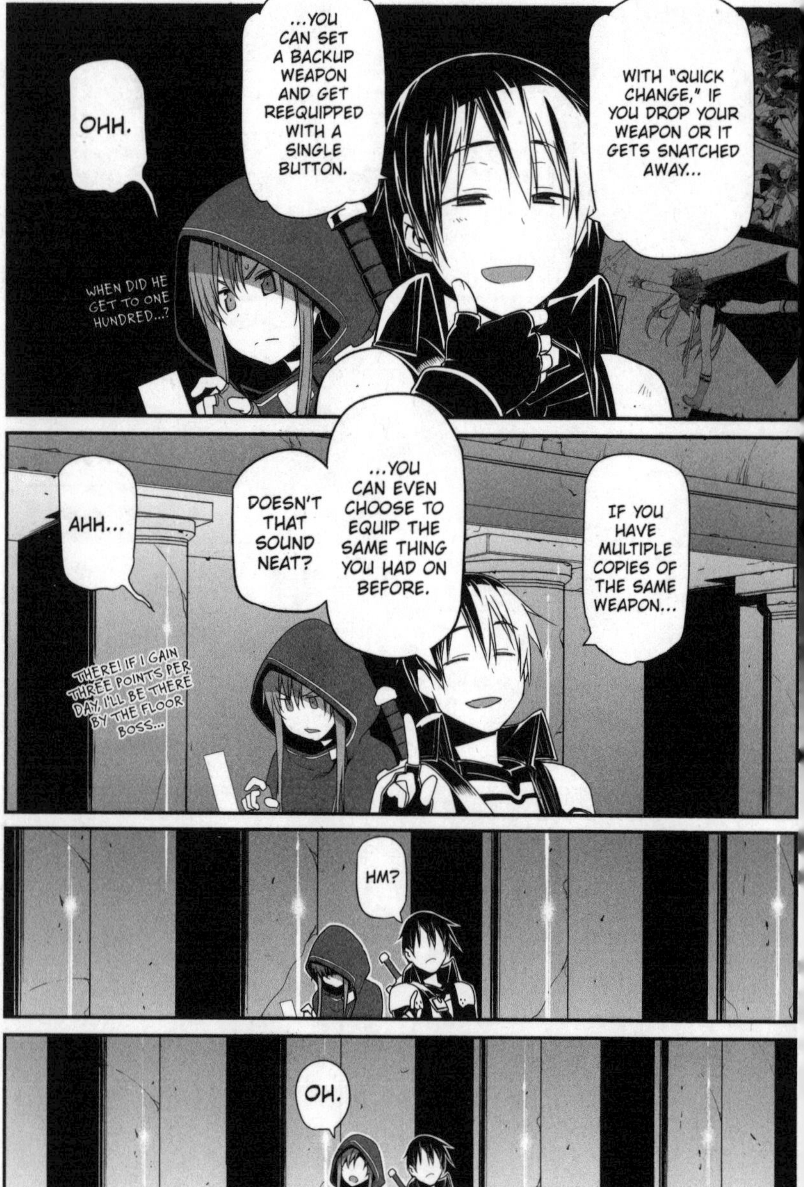
WITH "QUICK CHANGE," IF YOU DROP YOUR WEAPON OR IT GETS SNATCHED AWAY...
...YOU CAN SET A BACKUP WEAPON AND GET REEQUIPPED WITH A SINGLE BUTTON.
OHH.
WHEN DID HE GET TO ONE HUNDRED...?
IF YOU HAVE MULTIPLE COPIES OF THE SAME WEAPON...
...YOU CAN EVEN CHOOSE TO EQUIP THE SAME THING YOU HAD ON BEFORE.
DOESN'T THAT SOUND NEAT?
AHH...
THERE! IF I GAIN THREE POINTS PER DAY, I'LL BE THERE BY THE FLOOR BOSS...
HM?
OH.

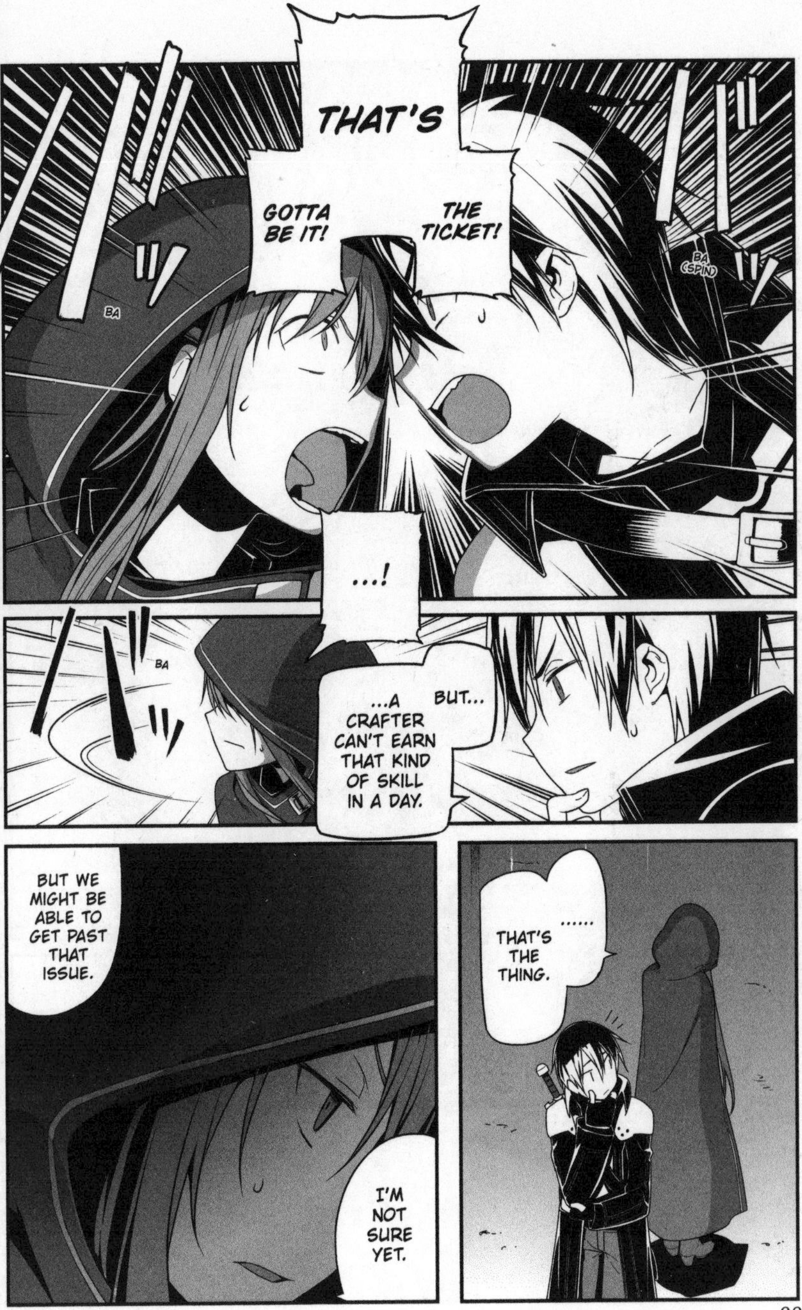
THAT'S
THE TICKET!
GOTTA BE IT!
BA (SPIN)
BA
...!
BUT...
...A CRAFTER CAN'T EARN THAT KIND OF SKILL IN A DAY.
BA
...... THAT'S THE THING.
BUT WE MIGHT BE ABLE TO GET PAST THAT ISSUE.
I'M NOT SURE YET.

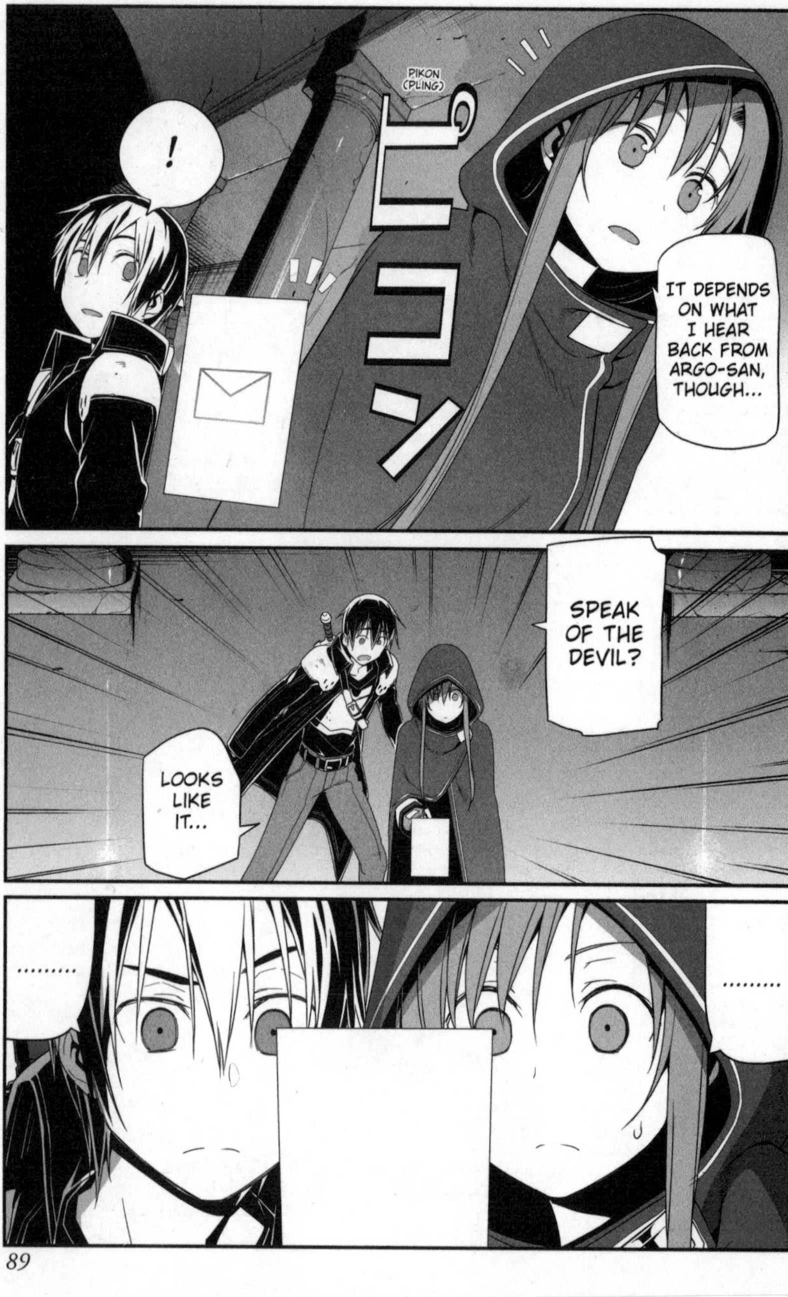
IT DEPENDS ON WHAT I HEAR BACK FROM ARGO-SAN, THOUGH...
PIKON (PLING)
ピコン
!
SPEAK OF THE DEVIL?
LOOKS LIKE IT...
....
....

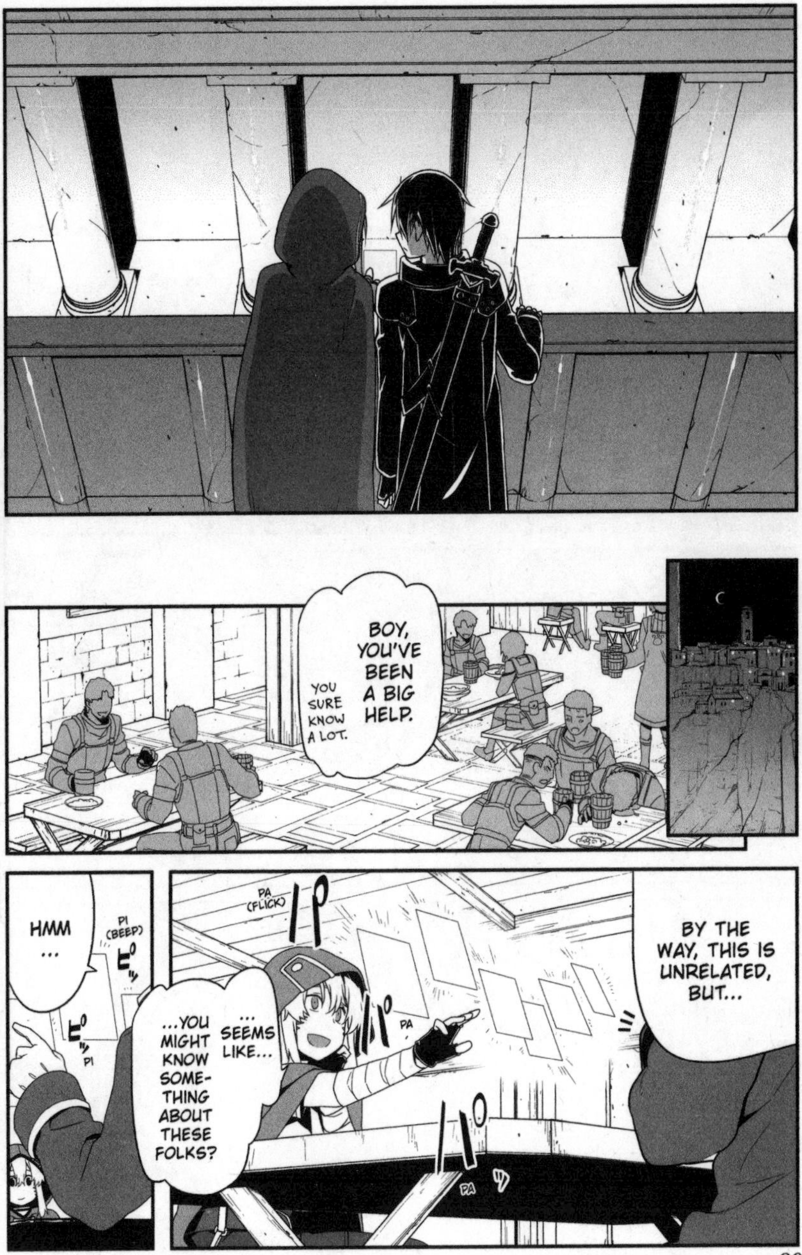
BOY, YOU'VE BEEN A BIG HELP.
YOU SURE KNOW A LOT.
BY THE WAY, THIS IS UNRELATED, BUT...
PA (FLICK)
PA
PA
... SEEMS LIKE...
...YOU MIGHT KNOW SOMETHING ABOUT THESE FOLKS?
PI (BEEP)
PI
HMM ...

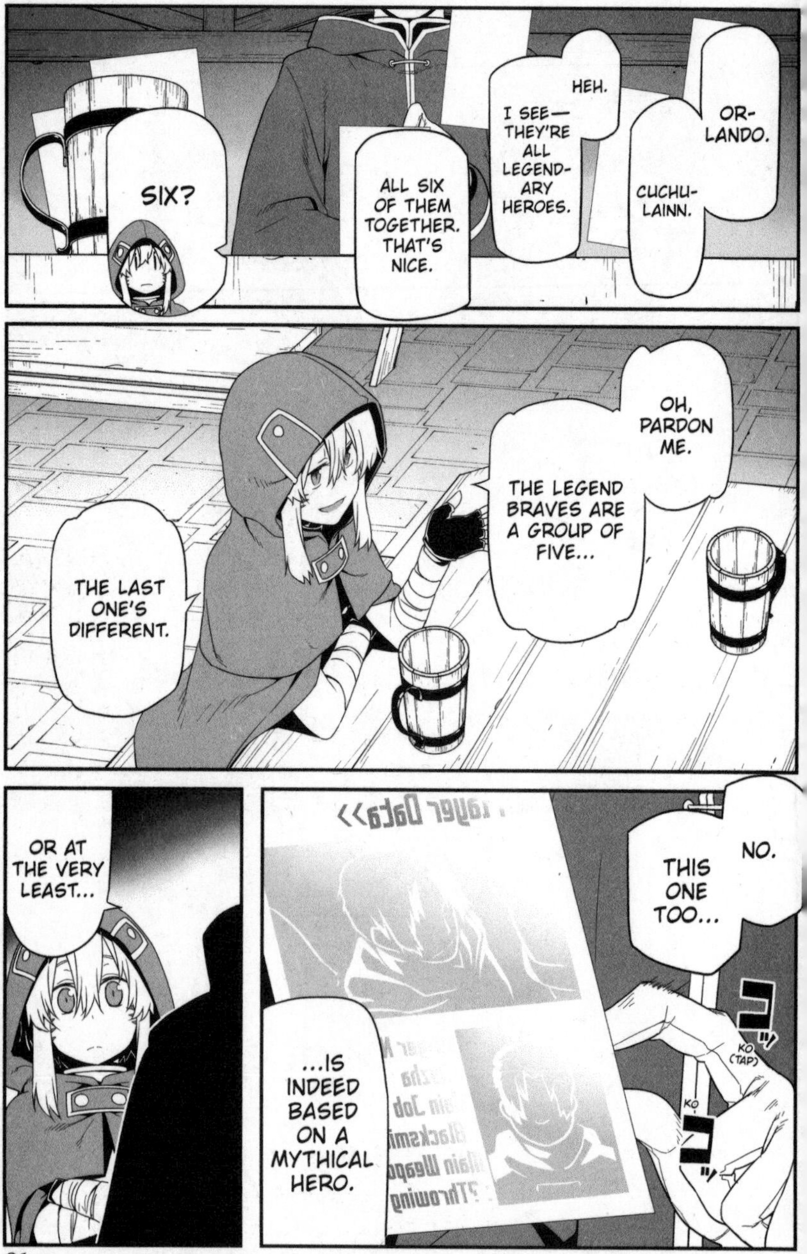
OR-LANDO.
CUCHU-LAINN.
HEH. I SEE— THEY'RE ALL LEGEND-ARY HEROES.
ALL SIX OF THEM TOGETHER. THAT'S NICE.
SIX?
OH, PARDON ME.
THE LEGEND BRAVES ARE A GROUP OF FIVE...
THE LAST ONE'S DIFFERENT.
NO.
THIS ONE TOO...
KO (TAP)
KO-
...IS INDEED BASED ON A MYTHICAL HERO.
OR AT THE VERY LEAST...

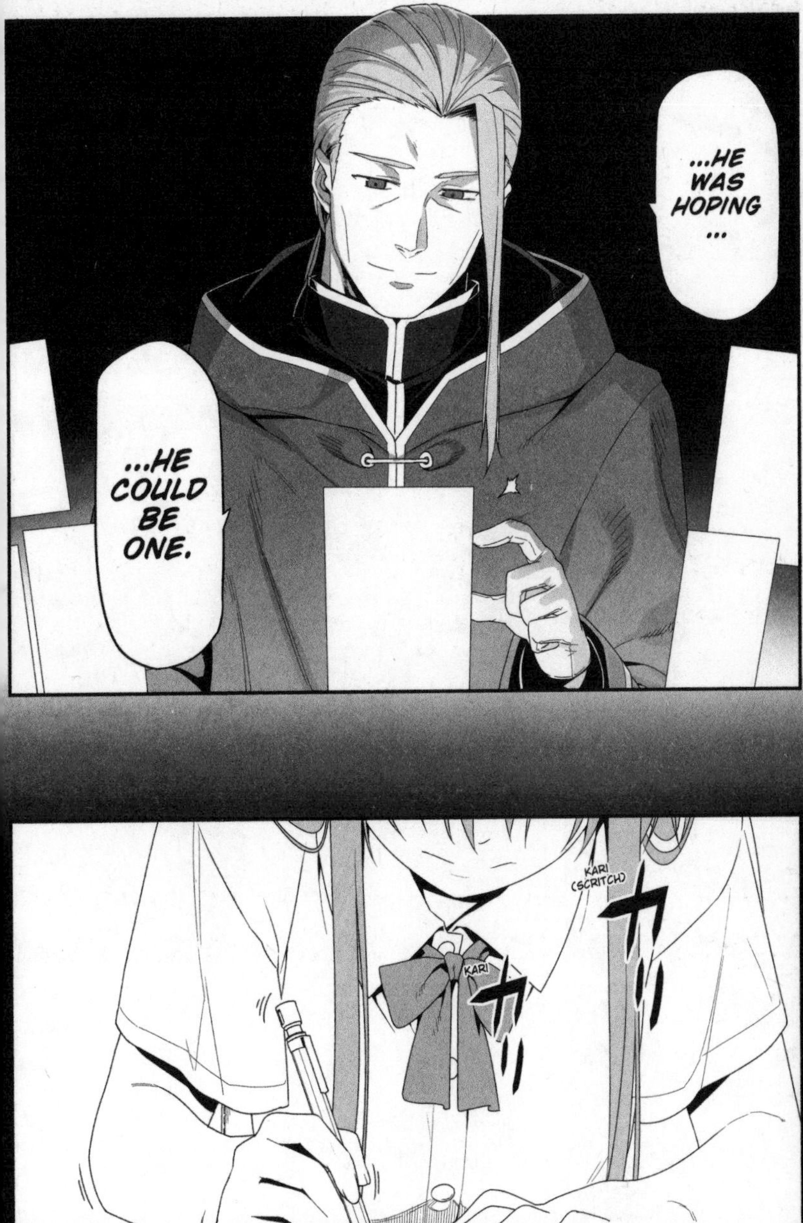
...HE WAS HOPING ...
...HE COULD BE ONE.
KARI (SCRITCH)
KARI

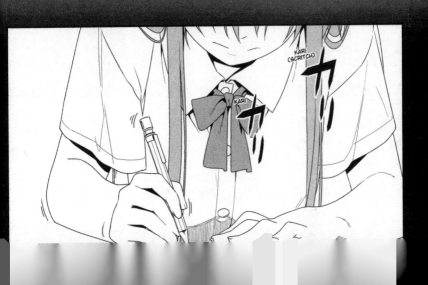

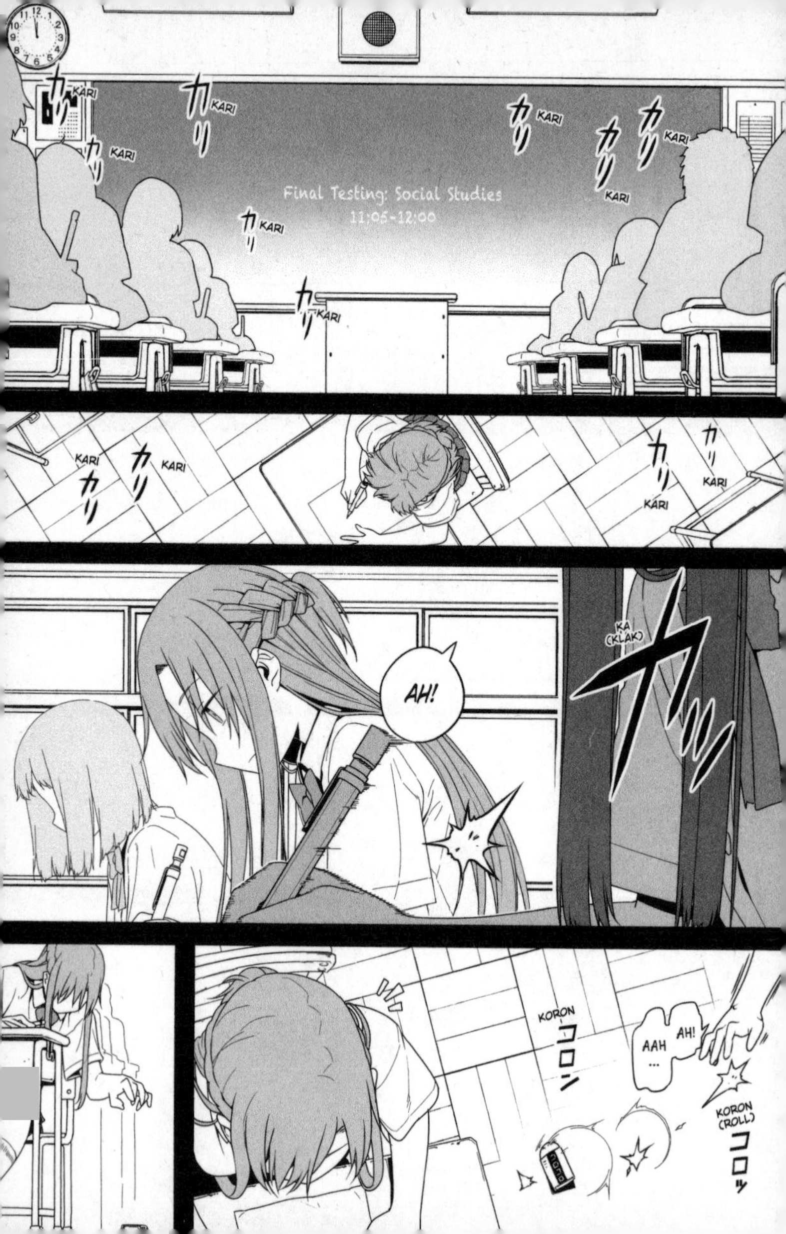

カリ KARI
カリ KARI
カリ KARI
Final Testing: Social Studies
11:05-12:00
カリ KARI
カリ KARI
カリ KARI
カリ KARI
カリ KARI
カリ KARI
カリ KARI
カリ KARI
カリ KARI
KA (KLAK)
AH!
AH!
AAH ...
KORON (ROLL)
KORON

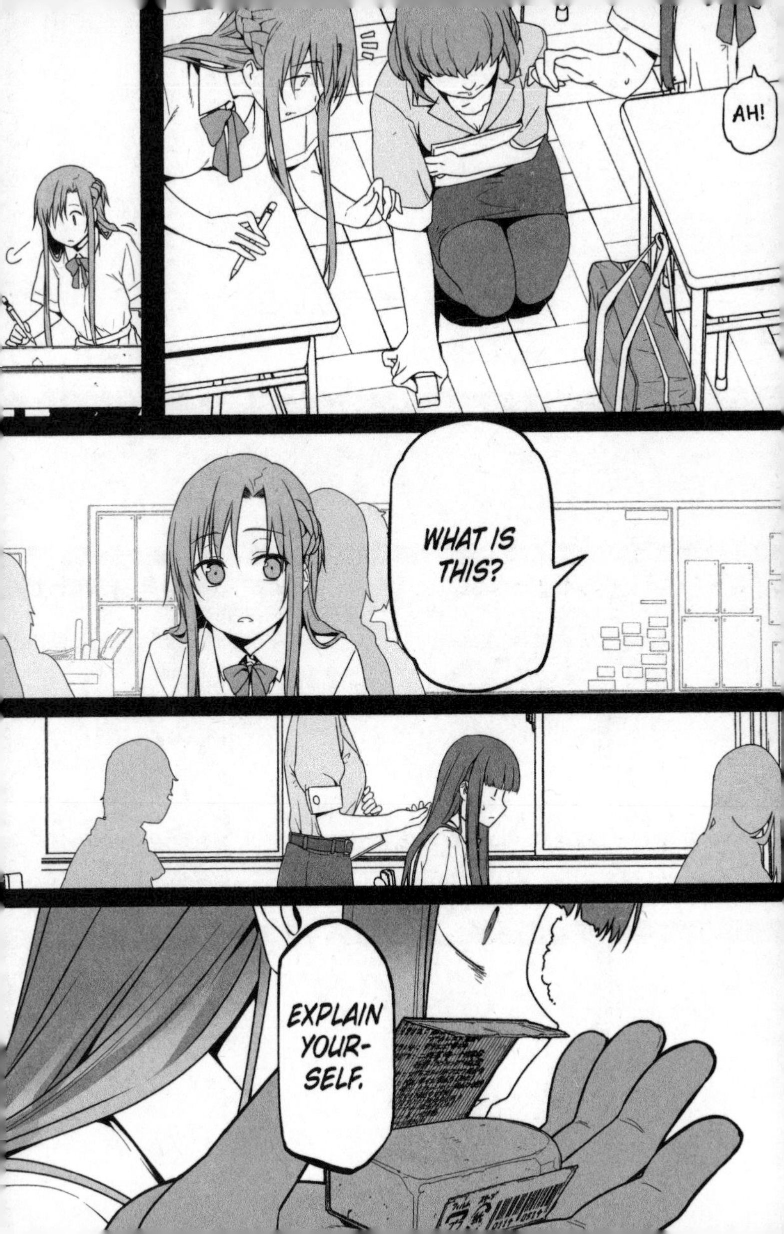
AH!
WHAT IS THIS?
EXPLAIN YOUR-SELF.

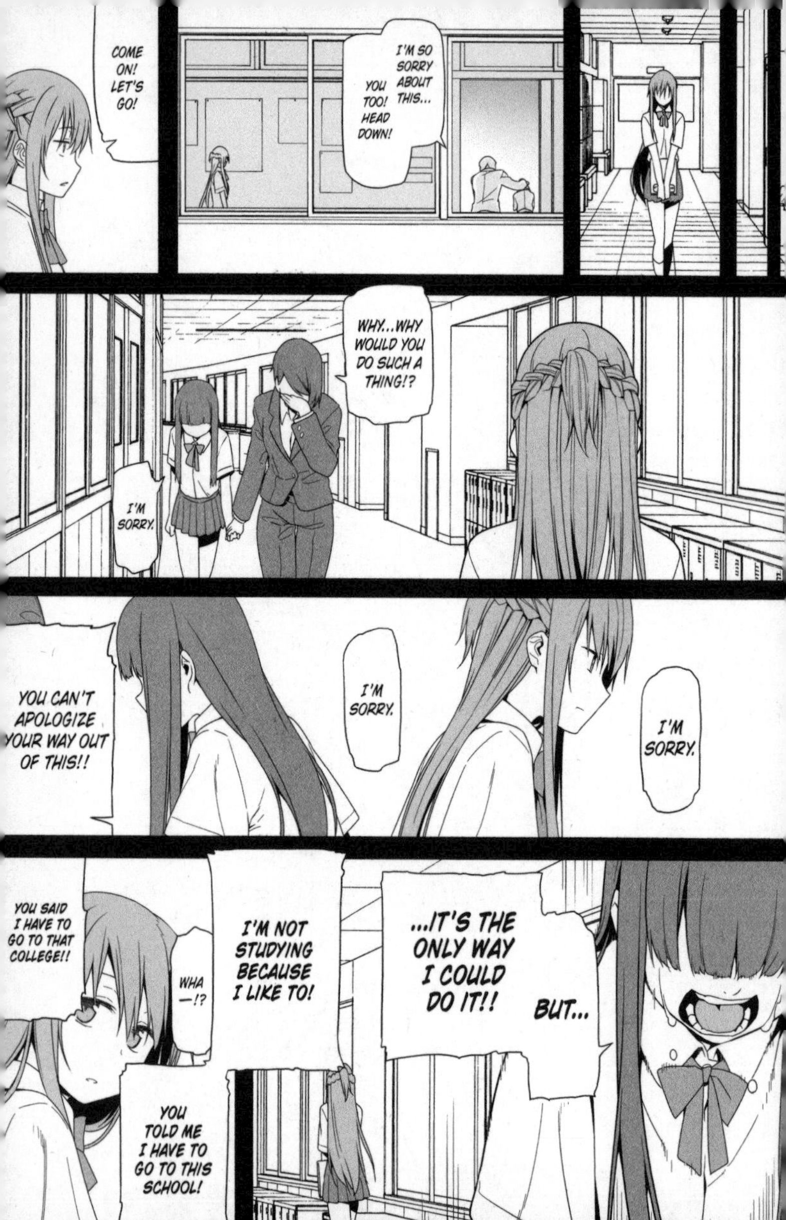
I'M SO SORRY ABOUT THIS...
YOU TOO! HEAD DOWN!
COME ON! LET'S GO!
WHY...WHY WOULD YOU DO SUCH A THING!?
I'M SORRY.
I'M SORRY.
I'M SORRY.
YOU CAN'T APOLOGIZE YOUR WAY OUT OF THIS!!
BUT...
...IT'S THE ONLY WAY I COULD DO IT!!
I'M NOT STUDYING BECAUSE I LIKE TO!
WHA—!?
YOU SAID I HAVE TO GO TO THAT COLLEGE!!
YOU TOLD ME I HAVE TO GO TO THIS SCHOOL!

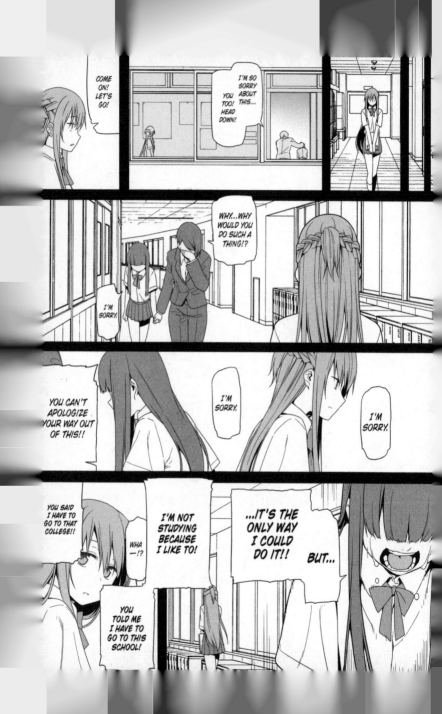

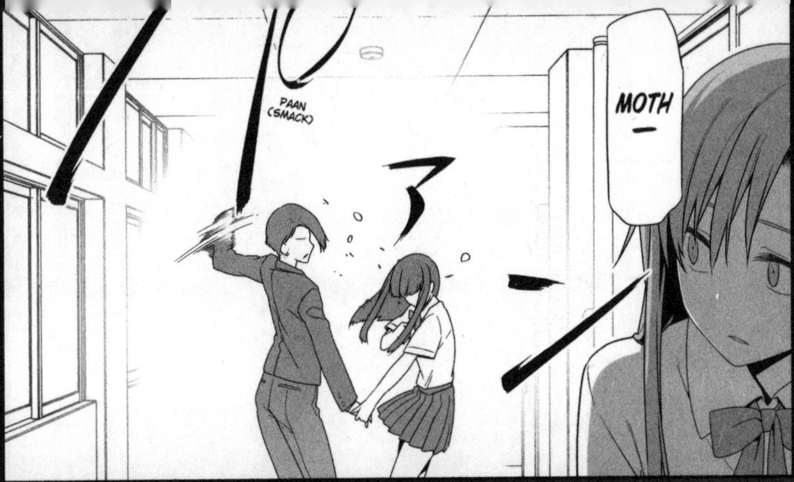
MOTH
—
PAAN
(SMACK)
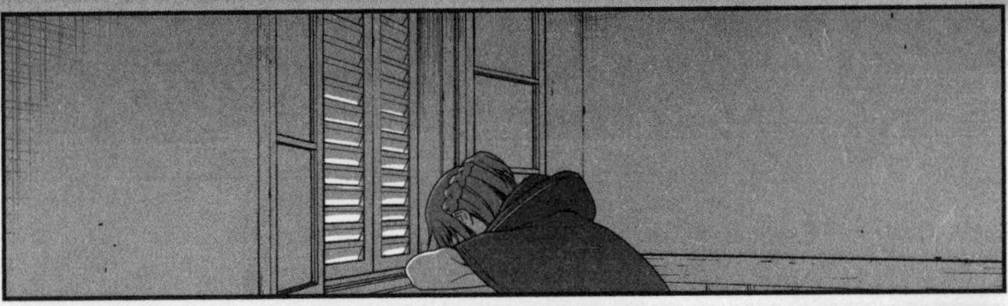
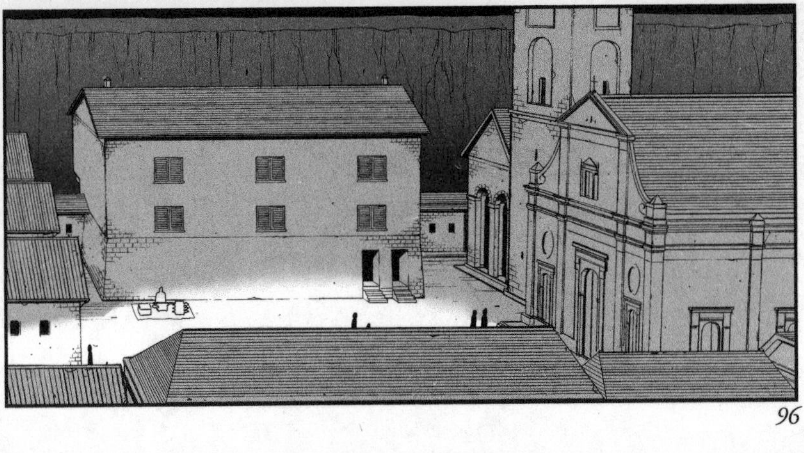

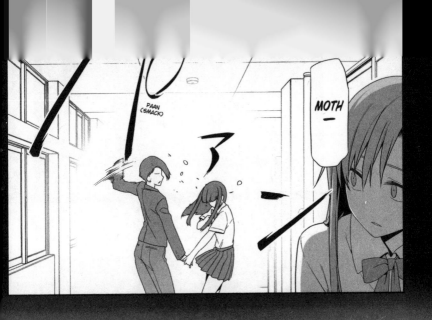

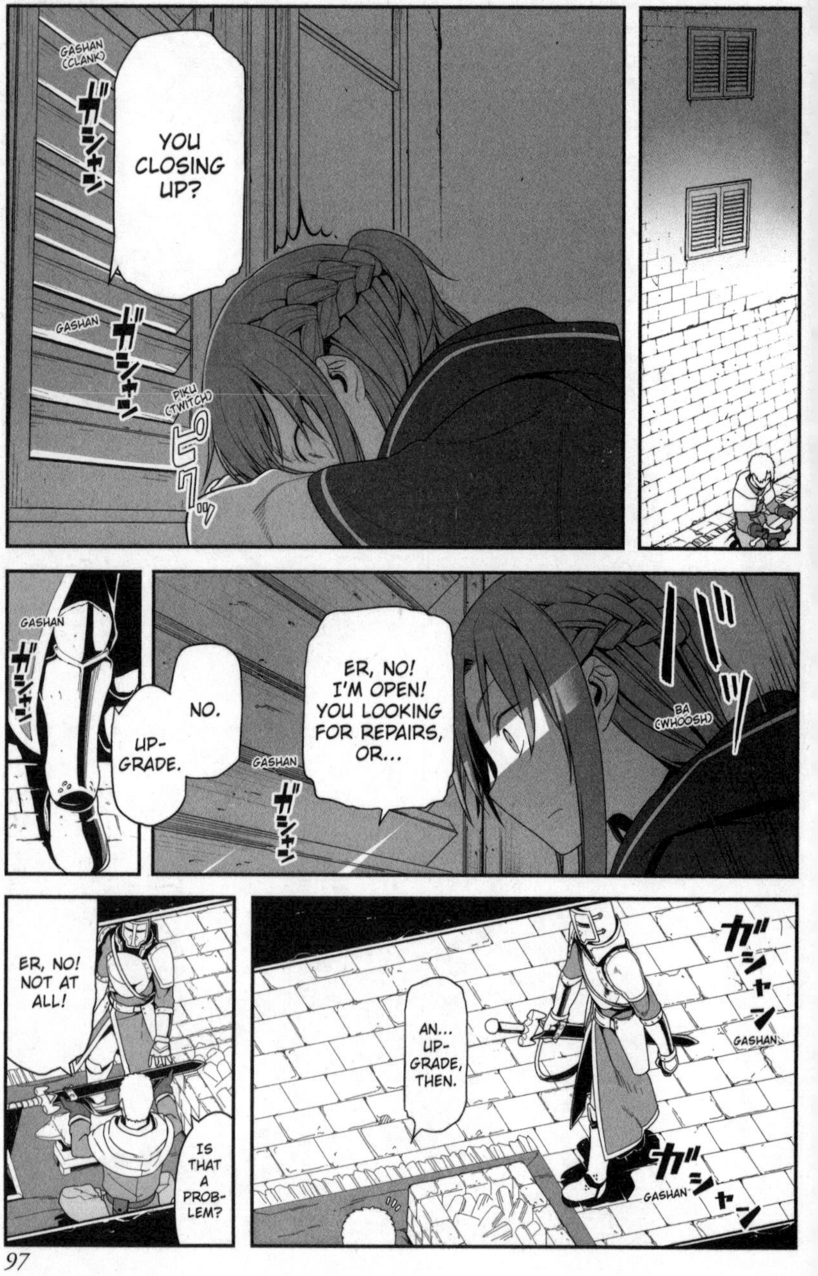
YOU CLOSING UP?
ガシャン
GASHAN (CLANK)
ガシャン
GASHAN
ピクッ
PIKU (TWITCH)
バッ
BA (WHOOSH)
ER, NO! I'M OPEN! YOU LOOKING FOR REPAIRS, OR...
ガシャン
GASHAN
NO.
UP-GRADE.
ガシャン
GASHAN
ガシャン
GASHAN
AN... UP-GRADE, THEN.
ガシャン
GASHAN
ER, NO! NOT AT ALL!
IS THAT A PROB-LEM?

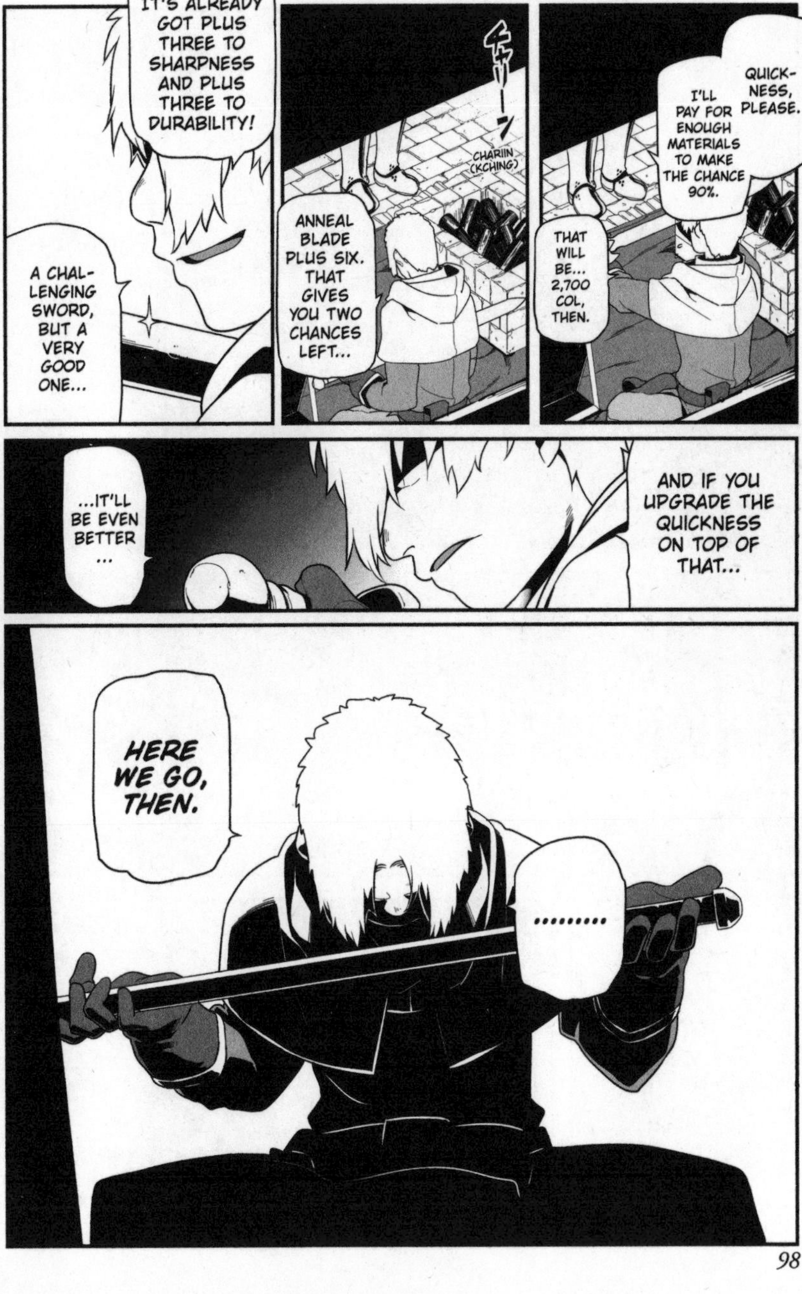
QUICK-NESS, PLEASE.
I'LL PAY FOR ENOUGH MATERIALS TO MAKE THE CHANCE 90%.
THAT WILL BE... 2,700 COL, THEN.
チャリーン
CHARIIN (KCHING)
ANNEAL BLADE PLUS SIX. THAT GIVES YOU TWO CHANCES LEFT...
IT'S ALREADY GOT PLUS THREE TO SHARPNESS AND PLUS THREE TO DURABILITY!
A CHAL-LENGING SWORD, BUT A VERY GOOD ONE...
AND IF YOU UPGRADE THE QUICKNESS ON TOP OF THAT...
...IT'LL BE EVEN BETTER ...
HERE WE GO, THEN.
....

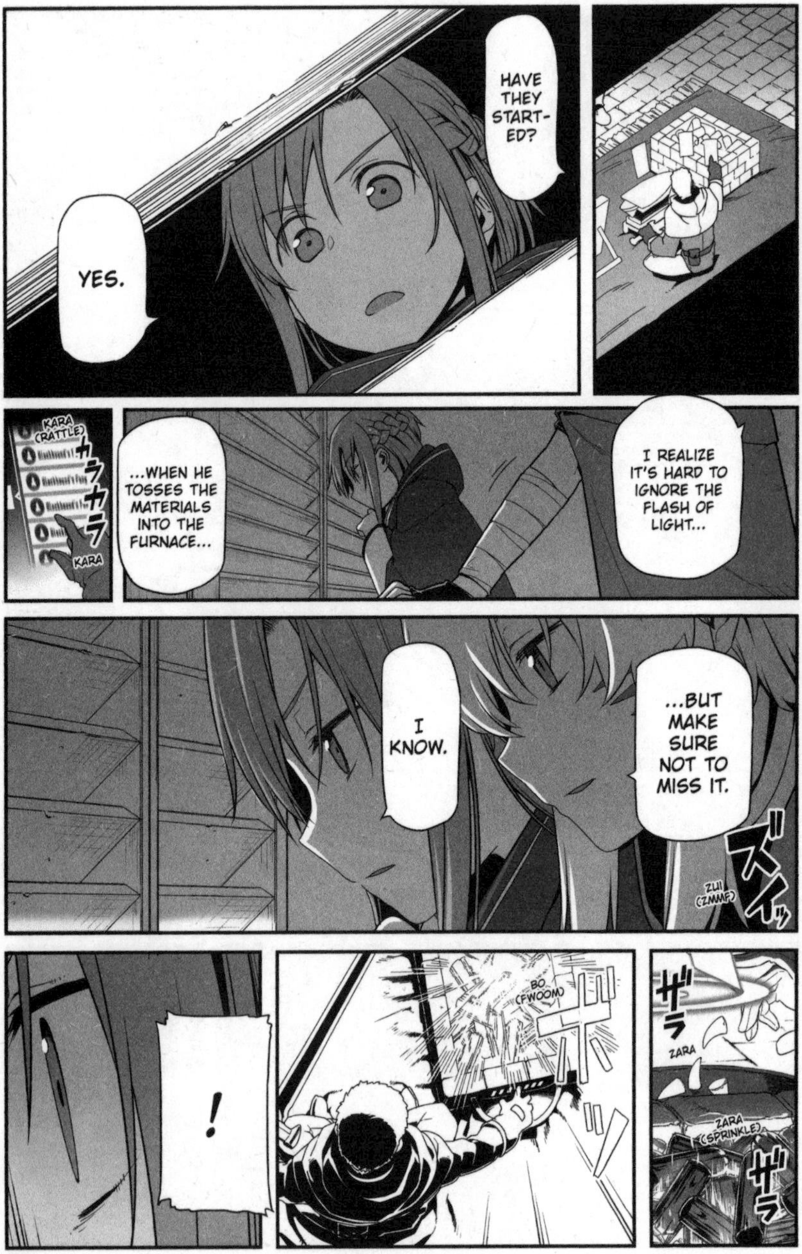
HAVE THEY START-ED?
YES.
I REALIZE IT'S HARD TO IGNORE THE FLASH OF LIGHT...
...WHEN HE TOSSES THE MATERIALS INTO THE FURNACE...
KARA (RATTLE)
カラカラ
KARA
...BUT MAKE SURE NOT TO MISS IT.
ズイッ
ZUI (ZMMF)
I KNOW.
ザラ
ZARA
ZARA (SPRINKLE)
ザラ
BO (FWOOM)
!

A... ARGO-SAN, I SAW IT!!

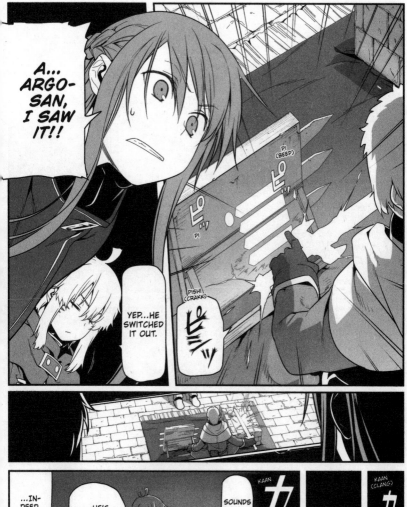

PI (BEEP)

PI

PISHI (CRAKK)

YEP...HE SWITCHED IT OUT.

...IN-DEED.

...HE'S REALLY PUTTIN' HIS HEART INTO THOSE STROKES.

SOUNDS LIKE...

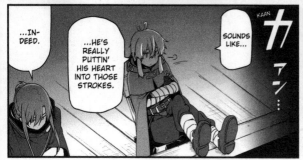

KAAN

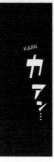

KAAN

KAAN (CLANG)

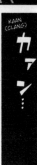

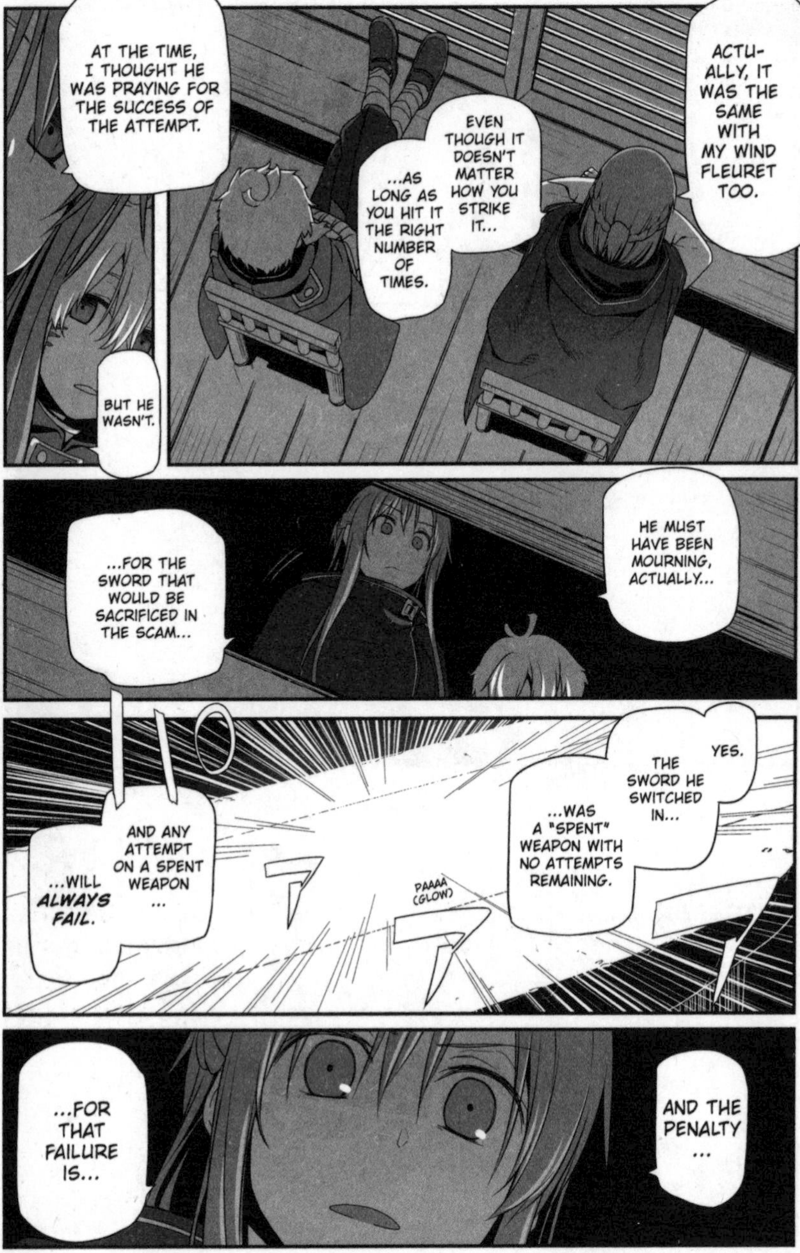
ACTUALLY, IT WAS THE SAME WITH MY WIND FLEURET TOO.
EVEN THOUGH IT DOESN'T MATTER HOW YOU STRIKE IT...
...AS LONG AS YOU HIT IT THE RIGHT NUMBER OF TIMES.
AT THE TIME, I THOUGHT HE WAS PRAYING FOR THE SUCCESS OF THE ATTEMPT.
BUT HE WASN'T.
HE MUST HAVE BEEN MOURNING, ACTUALLY...
...FOR THE SWORD THAT WOULD BE SACRIFICED IN THE SCAM...
YES.
THE SWORD HE SWITCHED IN...
...WAS A "SPENT" WEAPON WITH NO ATTEMPTS REMAINING.
PAAAA (GLOW)
AND ANY ATTEMPT ON A SPENT WEAPON ...
...WILL **ALWAYS FAIL**.
AND THE PENALTY ...
...FOR THAT FAILURE IS...

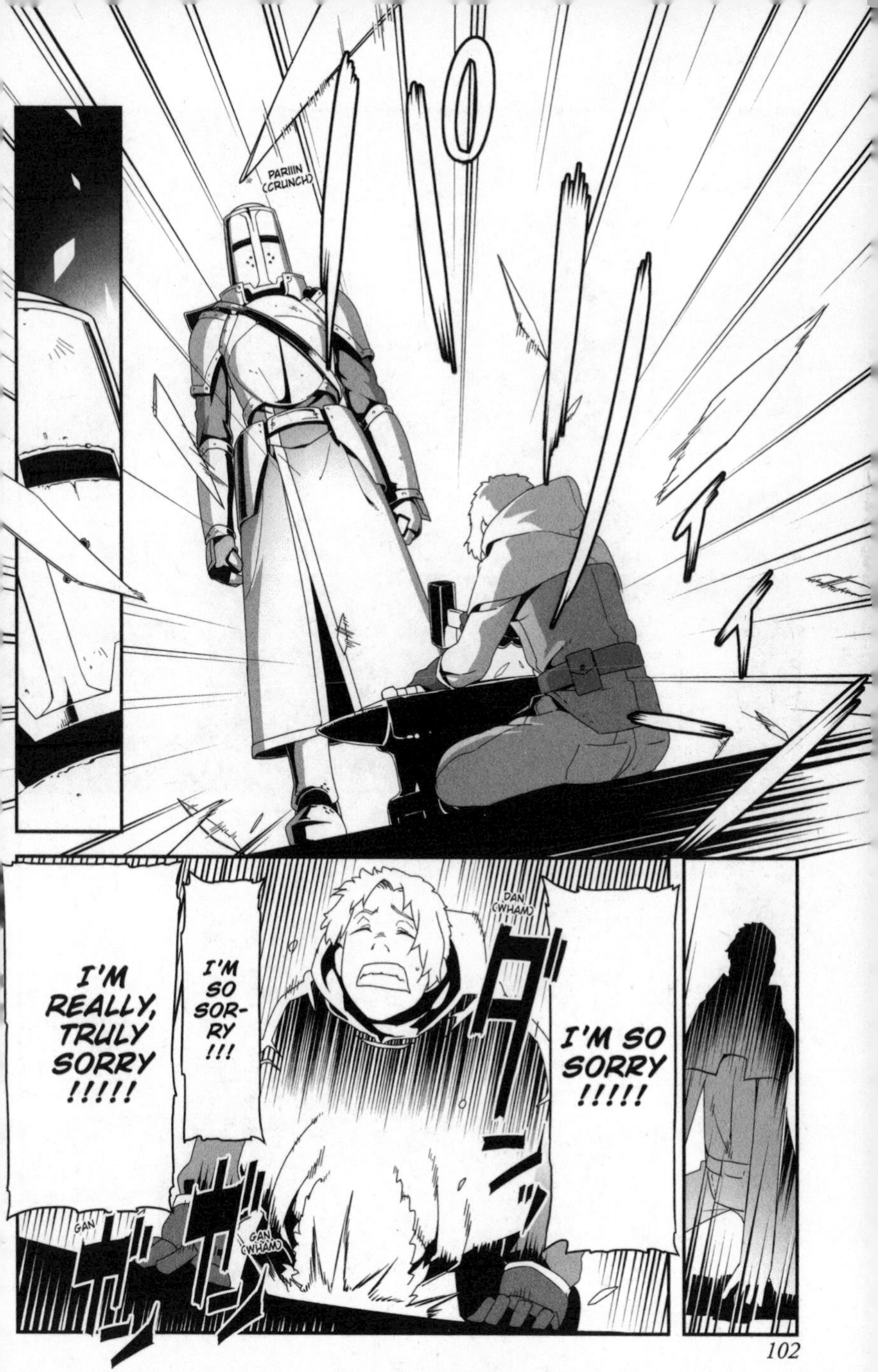
PARIIIN (CRUNCH)
DAN (WHAM)
I'M SO SORRY!!!!!
I'M SO SOR-RY!!!
GAN (WHAM)
GAN
I'M REALLY, TRULY SORRY!!!!!

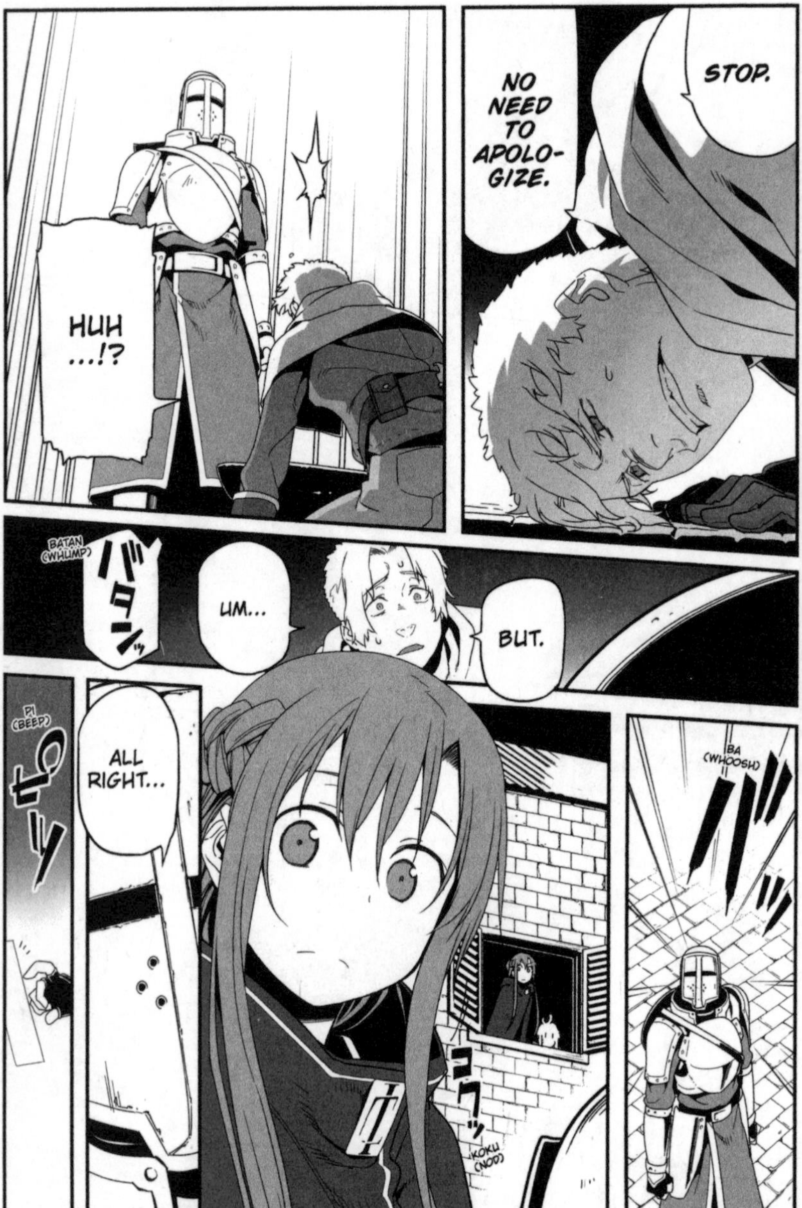
STOP.
NO NEED TO APOLOGIZE.
HUH ...!?
BUT.
UM...
BATAN (WHUMP)
BA (WHOOSH)
KOKU (NOD)
ALL RIGHT...
PI (BEEP)

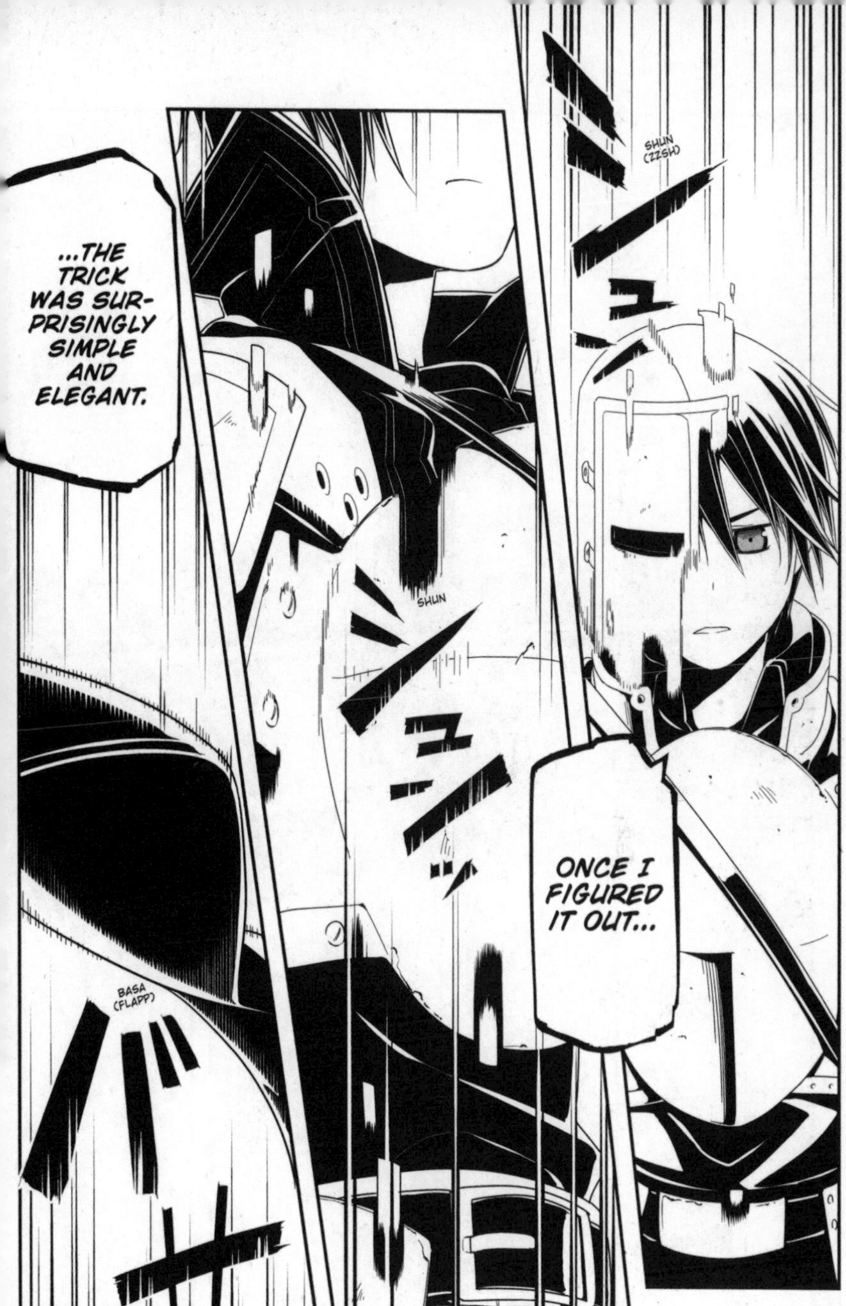
SHUN (ZZSH)
ONCE I FIGURED IT OUT...
SHUN
...THE TRICK WAS SUR-PRISINGLY SIMPLE AND ELEGANT.
BASA (FLAPP)

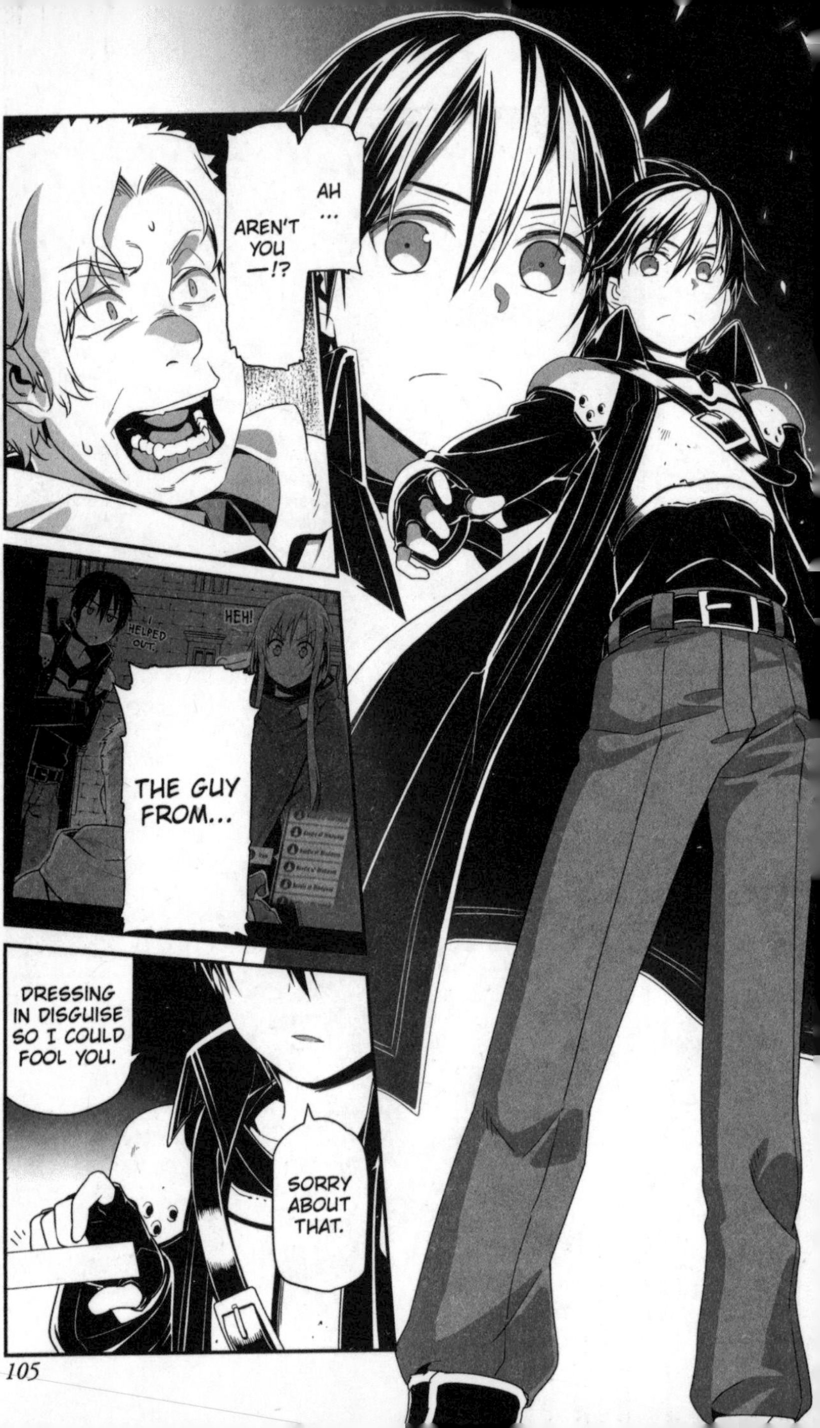
AH ... AREN'T YOU —!?
HEH!
I HELPED OUT.
THE GUY FROM...
DRESSING IN DISGUISE SO I COULD FOOL YOU.
SORRY ABOUT THAT.

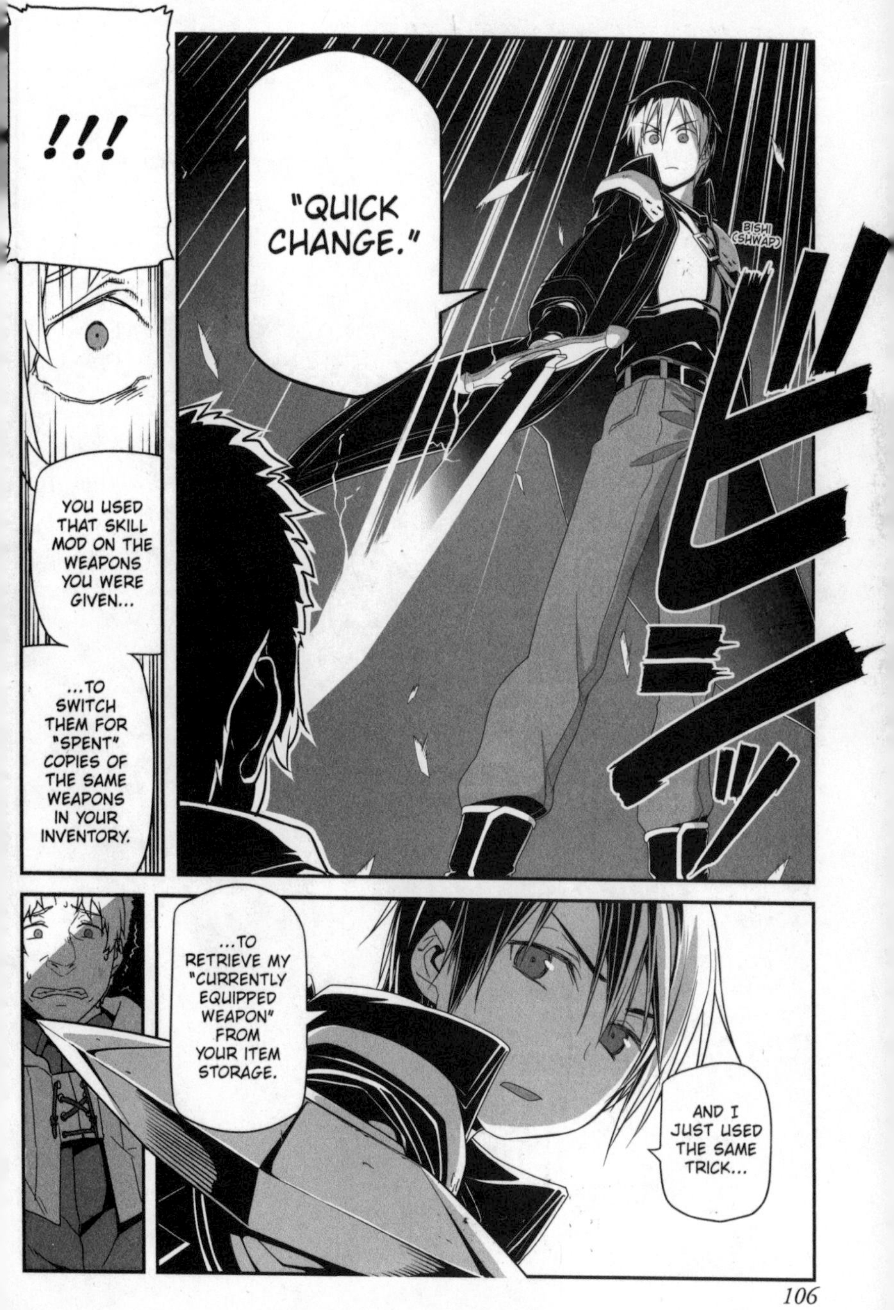
"QUICK CHANGE."
BISHI (SHWAP)
!!!
YOU USED THAT SKILL MOD ON THE WEAPONS YOU WERE GIVEN...
...TO SWITCH THEM FOR "SPENT" COPIES OF THE SAME WEAPONS IN YOUR INVENTORY.
...TO RETRIEVE MY "CURRENTLY EQUIPPED WEAPON" FROM YOUR ITEM STORAGE.
AND I JUST USED THE SAME TRICK...

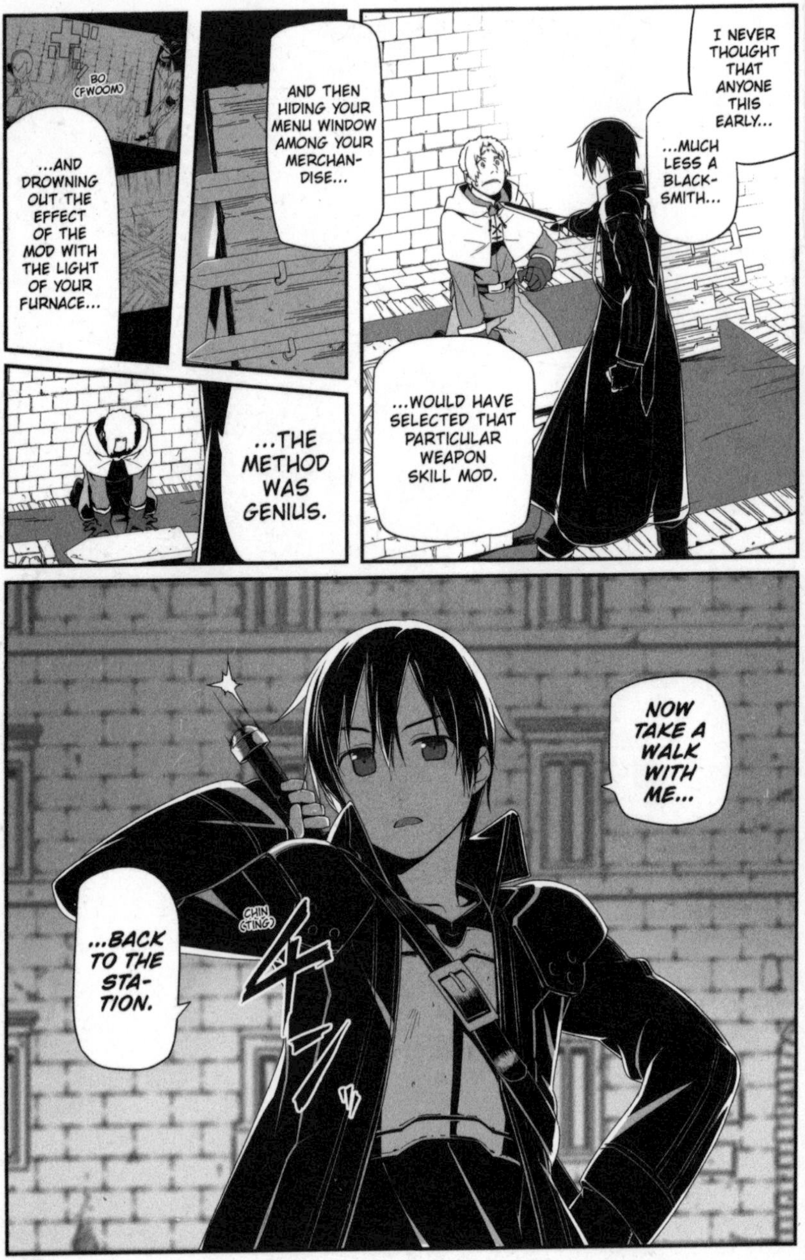
I NEVER THOUGHT THAT ANYONE THIS EARLY...
...MUCH LESS A BLACKSMITH...
...WOULD HAVE SELECTED THAT PARTICULAR WEAPON SKILL MOD.
AND THEN HIDING YOUR MENU WINDOW AMONG YOUR MERCHANDISE...
BO (FWOOM)
...AND DROWNING OUT THE EFFECT OF THE MOD WITH THE LIGHT OF YOUR FURNACE...
...THE METHOD WAS GENIUS.
NOW TAKE A WALK WITH ME...
CHIN (TING)
...BACK TO THE STATION.

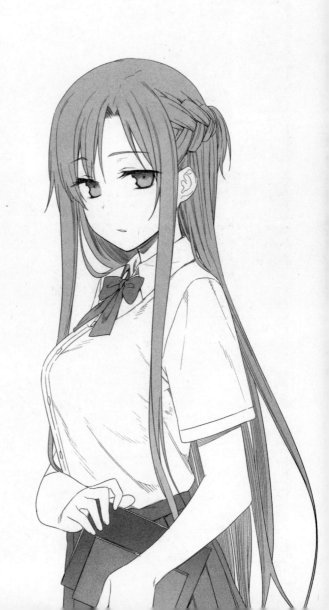

#014: Dawn

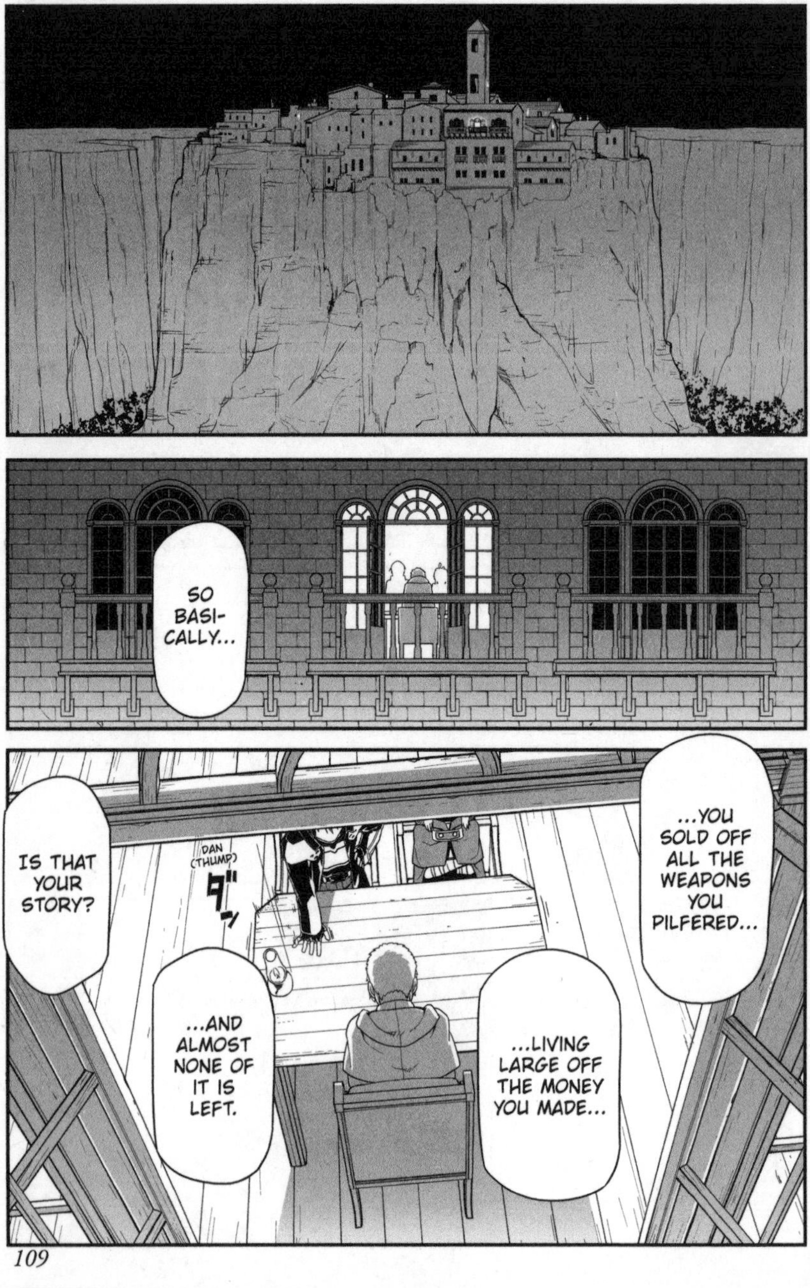
SO BASI-CALLY...
...YOU SOLD OFF ALL THE WEAPONS YOU PILFERED...
...LIVING LARGE OFF THE MONEY YOU MADE...
...AND ALMOST NONE OF IT IS LEFT.
DAN (THUMP)
IS THAT YOUR STORY?

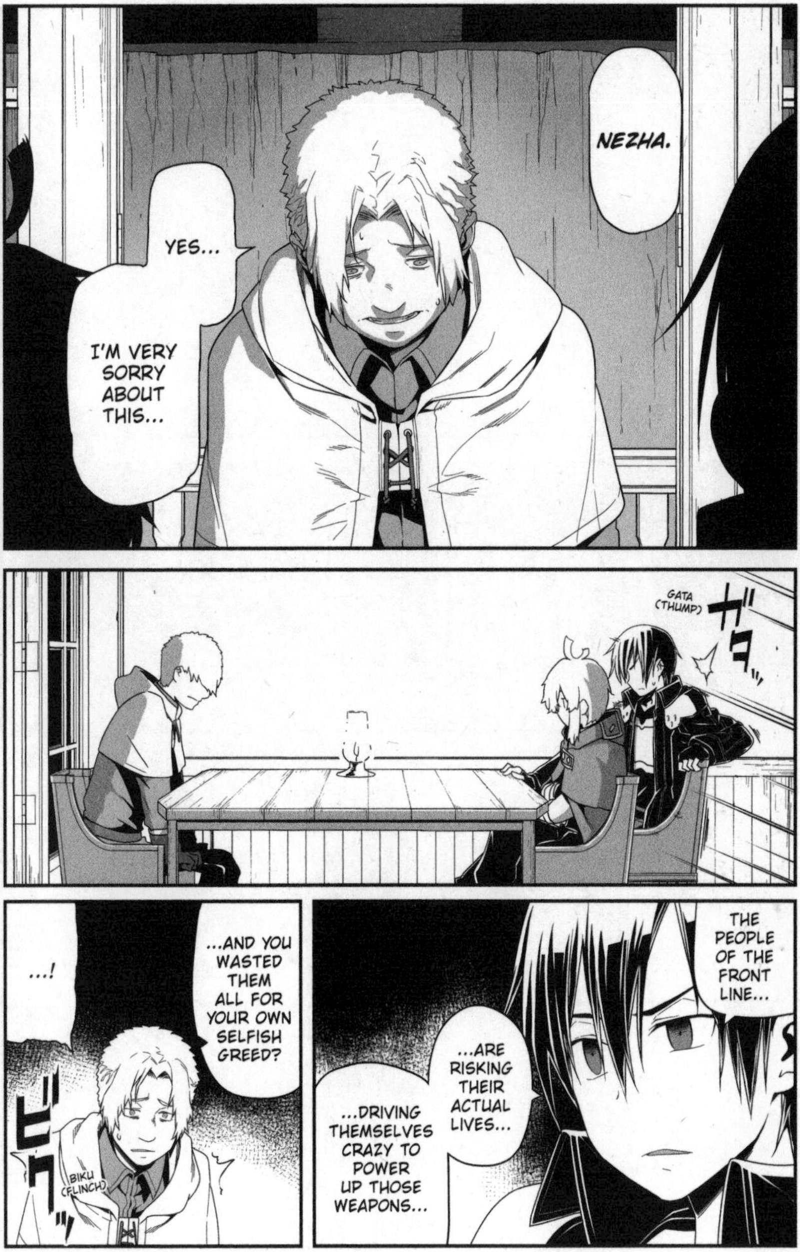
NEZHA.
YES...
I'M VERY SORRY ABOUT THIS...
GATA (THUMP)
THE PEOPLE OF THE FRONT LINE...
...ARE RISKING THEIR ACTUAL LIVES...
...DRIVING THEMSELVES CRAZY TO POWER UP THOSE WEAPONS...
...AND YOU WASTED THEM ALL FOR YOUR OWN SELFISH GREED?
...!
BIKU (FLINCH)

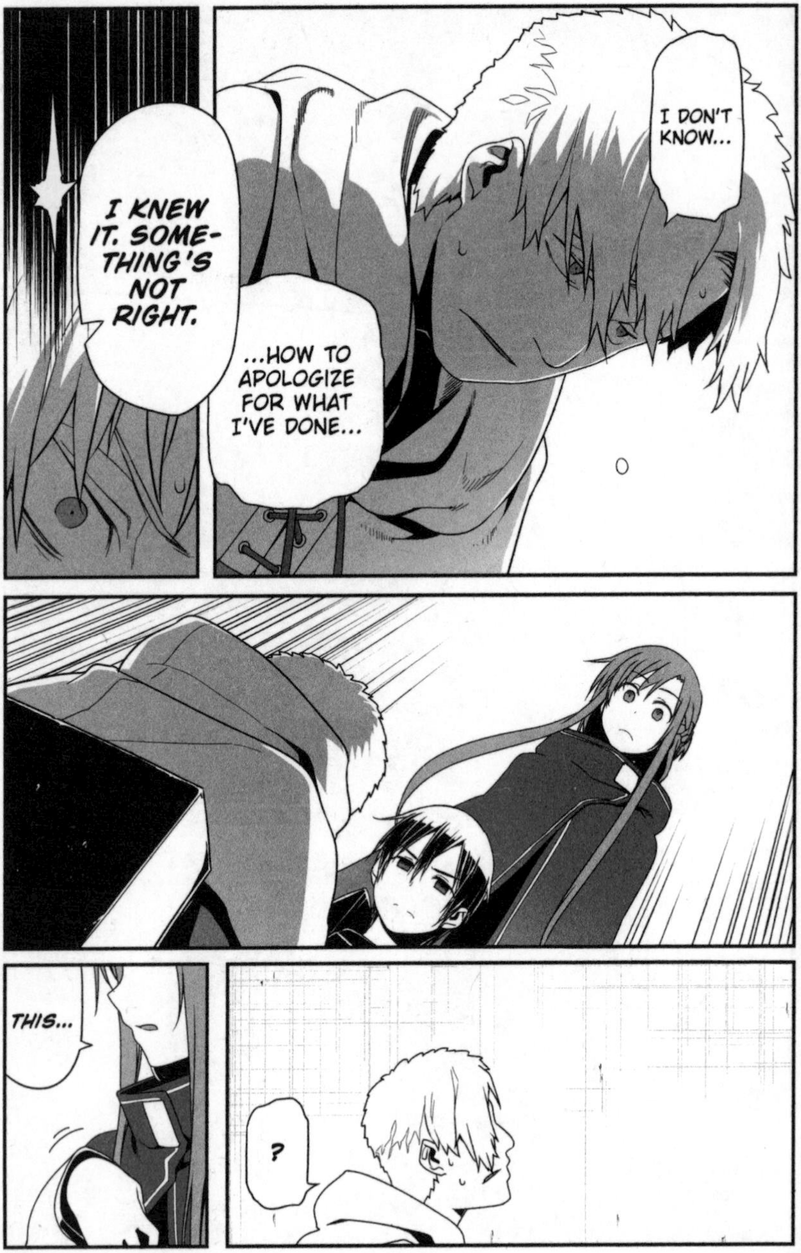
I DON'T KNOW...
...HOW TO APOLOGIZE FOR WHAT I'VE DONE...
I KNEW IT. SOME-THING'S NOT RIGHT.
?
THIS...

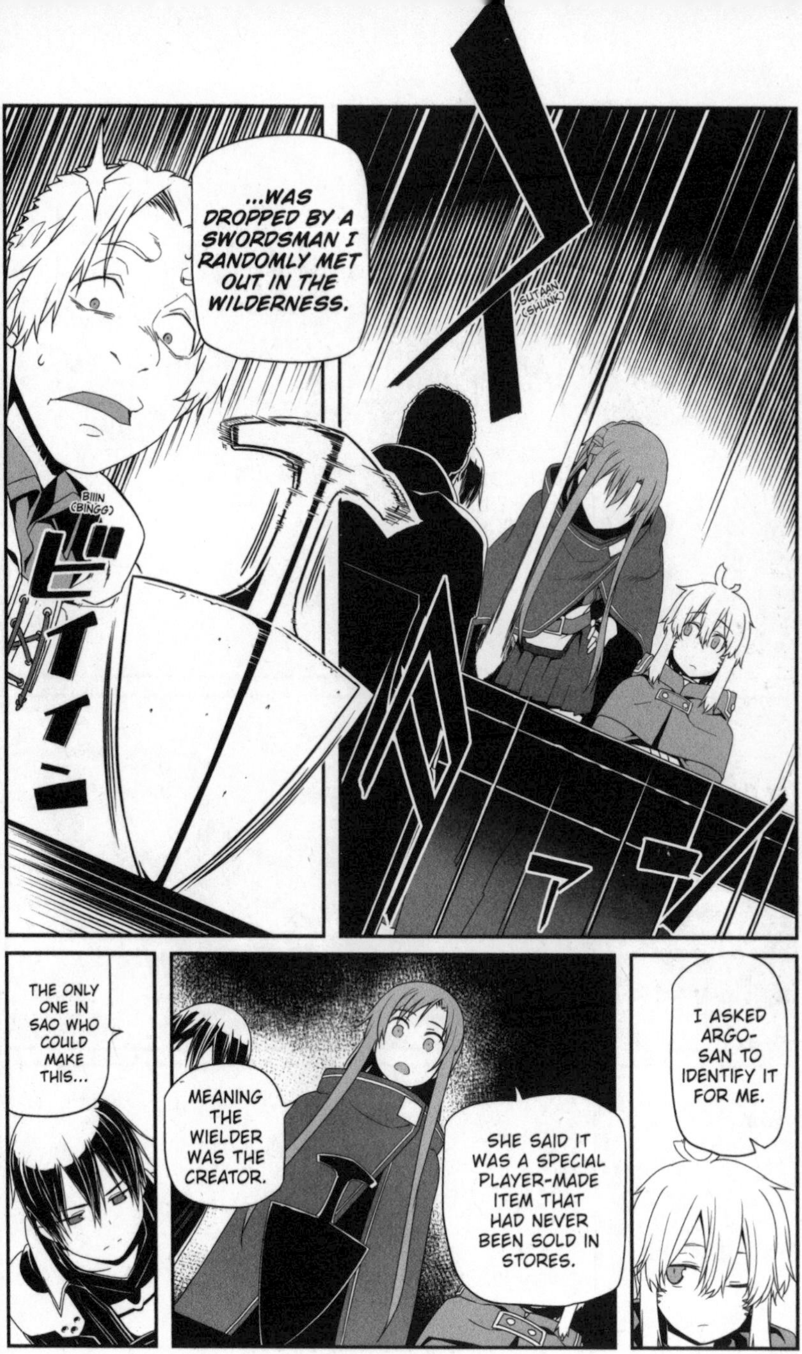
SUTAAN (SHUNK)
...WAS DROPPED BY A SWORDSMAN I RANDOMLY MET OUT IN THE WILDERNESS.
BIIN (BINGG)
I ASKED ARGO-SAN TO IDENTIFY IT FOR ME.
SHE SAID IT WAS A SPECIAL PLAYER-MADE ITEM THAT HAD NEVER BEEN SOLD IN STORES.
MEANING THE WIELDER WAS THE CREATOR.
THE ONLY ONE IN SAO WHO COULD MAKE THIS...

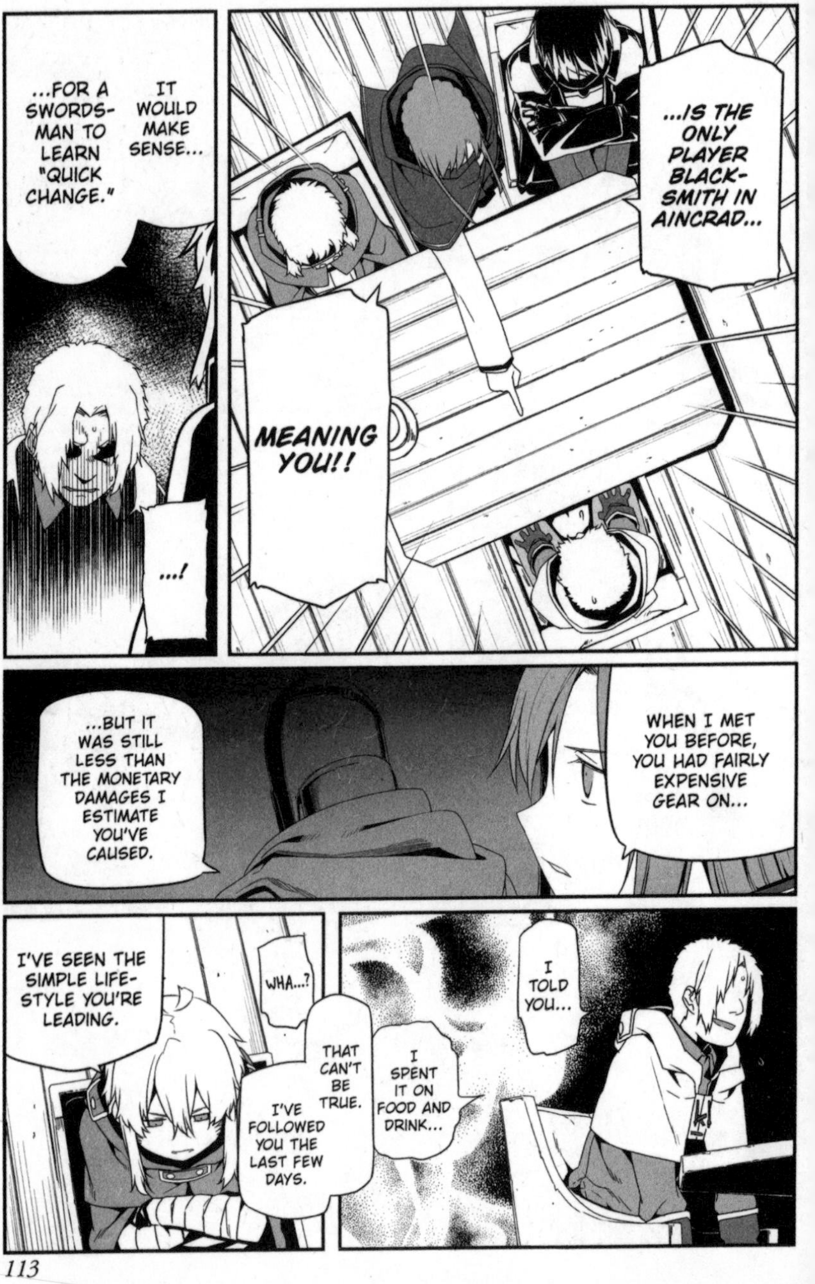
...IS THE ONLY PLAYER BLACKSMITH IN AINCRAD...
MEANING YOU!!
IT WOULD MAKE SENSE...
...FOR A SWORDSMAN TO LEARN "QUICK CHANGE."
...!
WHEN I MET YOU BEFORE, YOU HAD FAIRLY EXPENSIVE GEAR ON...
...BUT IT WAS STILL LESS THAN THE MONETARY DAMAGES I ESTIMATE YOU'VE CAUSED.
I TOLD YOU...
I SPENT IT ON FOOD AND DRINK...
WHA...?
I'VE SEEN THE SIMPLE LIFESTYLE YOU'RE LEADING.
THAT CAN'T BE TRUE.
I'VE FOLLOWED YOU THE LAST FEW DAYS.

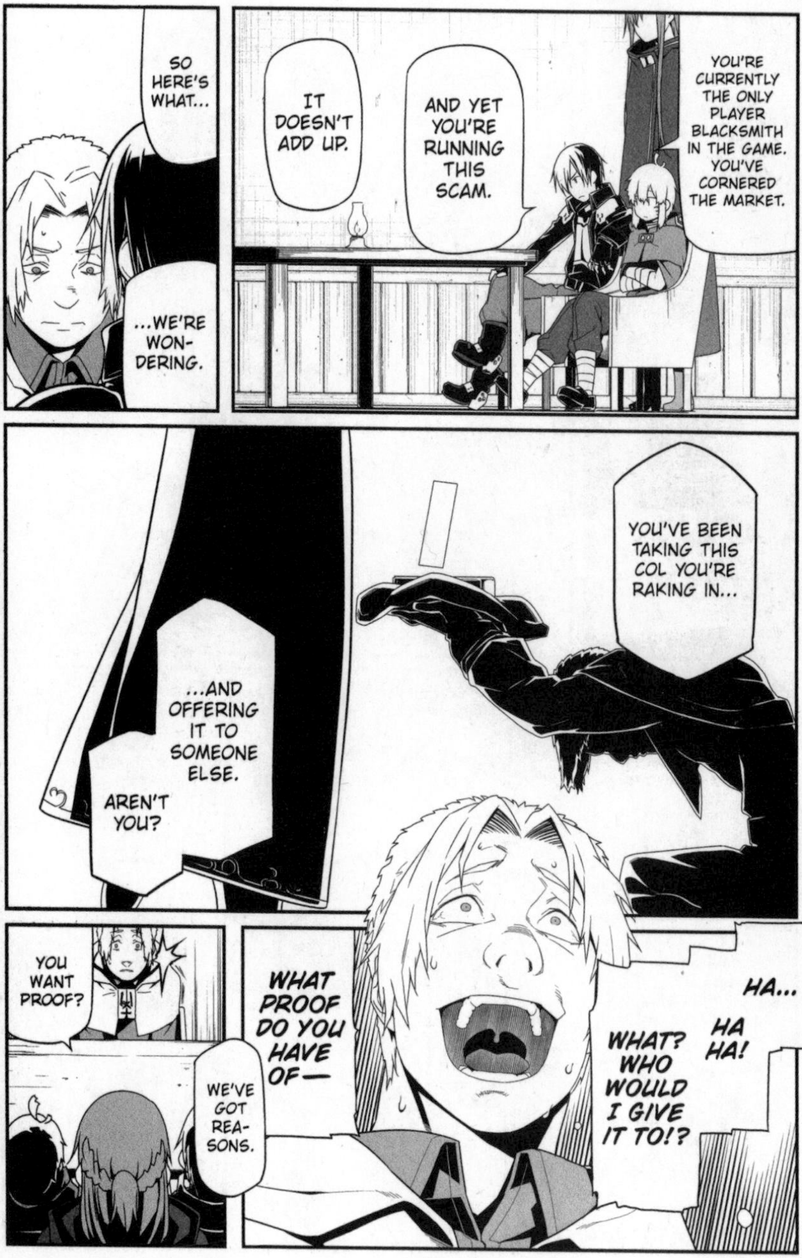
YOU'RE CURRENTLY THE ONLY PLAYER BLACKSMITH IN THE GAME. YOU'VE CORNERED THE MARKET.
AND YET YOU'RE RUNNING THIS SCAM.
IT DOESN'T ADD UP.
SO HERE'S WHAT...
...WE'RE WON-DERING.
YOU'VE BEEN TAKING THIS COL YOU'RE RAKING IN...
...AND OFFERING IT TO SOMEONE ELSE.
AREN'T YOU?
HA...
HA HA!
WHAT? WHO WOULD I GIVE IT TO!?
WHAT PROOF DO YOU HAVE OF—
YOU WANT PROOF?
WE'VE GOT REA-SONS.

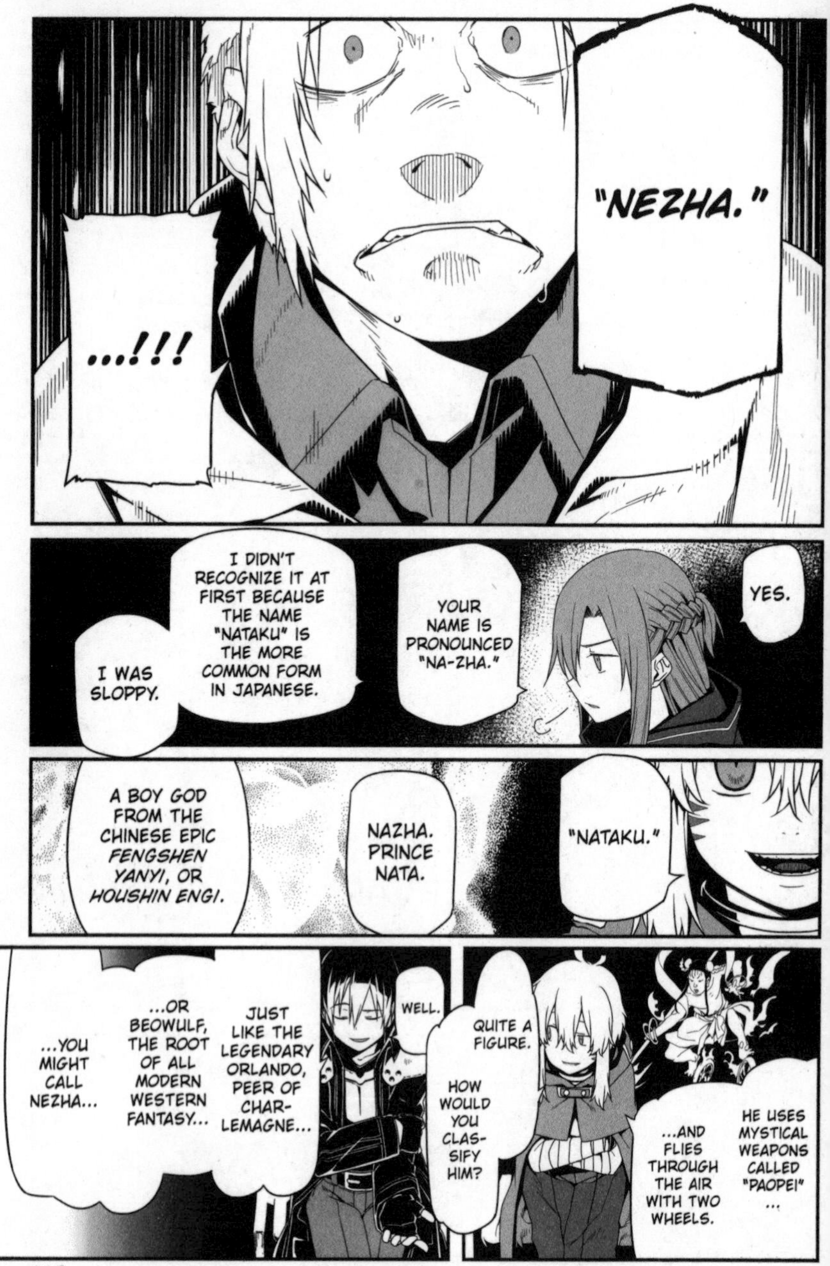
"NEZHA."
...!!!
YES.
YOUR NAME IS PRONOUNCED "NA-ZHA."
I DIDN'T RECOGNIZE IT AT FIRST BECAUSE THE NAME "NATAKU" IS THE MORE COMMON FORM IN JAPANESE.
I WAS SLOPPY.
"NATAKU."
NAZHA. PRINCE NATA.
A BOY GOD FROM THE CHINESE EPIC *FENGSHEN YANYI*, OR *HOUSHIN ENGI*.
HE USES MYSTICAL WEAPONS CALLED "PAOPEI" ...
...AND FLIES THROUGH THE AIR WITH TWO WHEELS.
QUITE A FIGURE.
HOW WOULD YOU CLAS-SIFY HIM?
WELL.
JUST LIKE THE LEGENDARY ORLANDO, PEER OF CHAR-LEMAGNE...
...OR BEOWULF, THE ROOT OF ALL MODERN WESTERN FANTASY...
...YOU MIGHT CALL NEZHA...

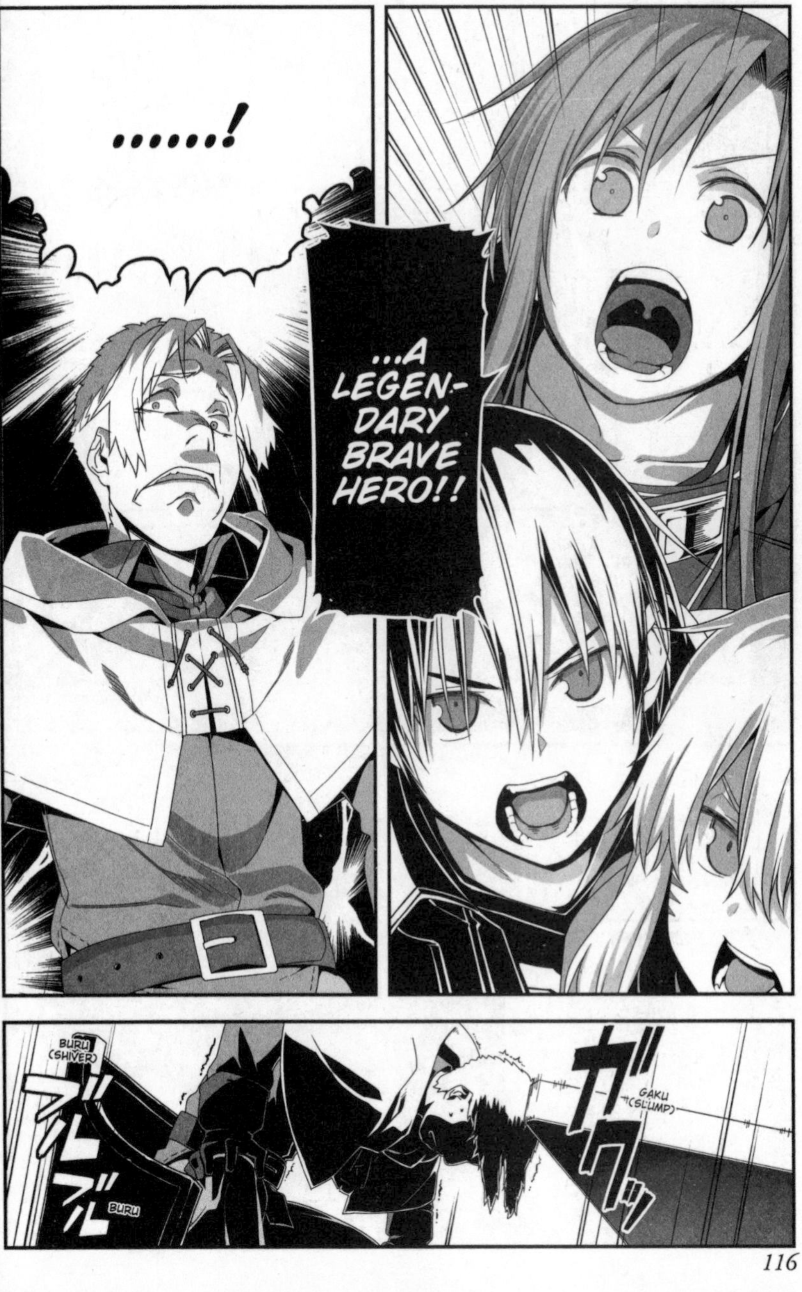
...A LEGEN-DARY BRAVE HERO!!
......!
ガクッ
GAKU (SLUMP)
ブルブル
BURU (SHIVER)
BURU

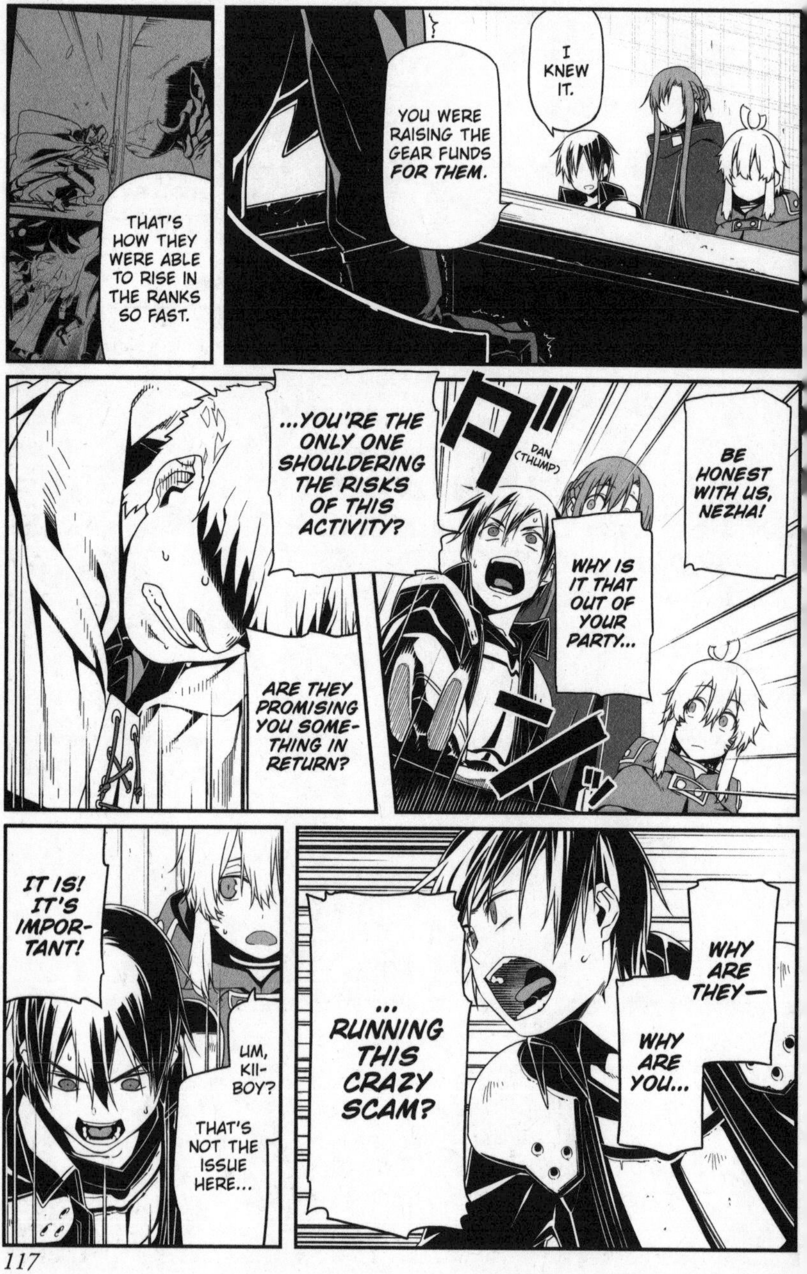
I KNEW IT.
YOU WERE RAISING THE GEAR FUNDS FOR THEM.
THAT'S HOW THEY WERE ABLE TO RISE IN THE RANKS SO FAST.
BE HONEST WITH US, NEZHA!
DAN (THUMP)
WHY IS IT THAT OUT OF YOUR PARTY...
...YOU'RE THE ONLY ONE SHOULDERING THE RISKS OF THIS ACTIVITY?
ARE THEY PROMISING YOU SOMETHING IN RETURN?
WHY ARE THEY—
WHY ARE YOU...
... RUNNING THIS CRAZY SCAM?
UM, KII-BOY?
THAT'S NOT THE ISSUE HERE...
IT IS! IT'S IMPORTANT!

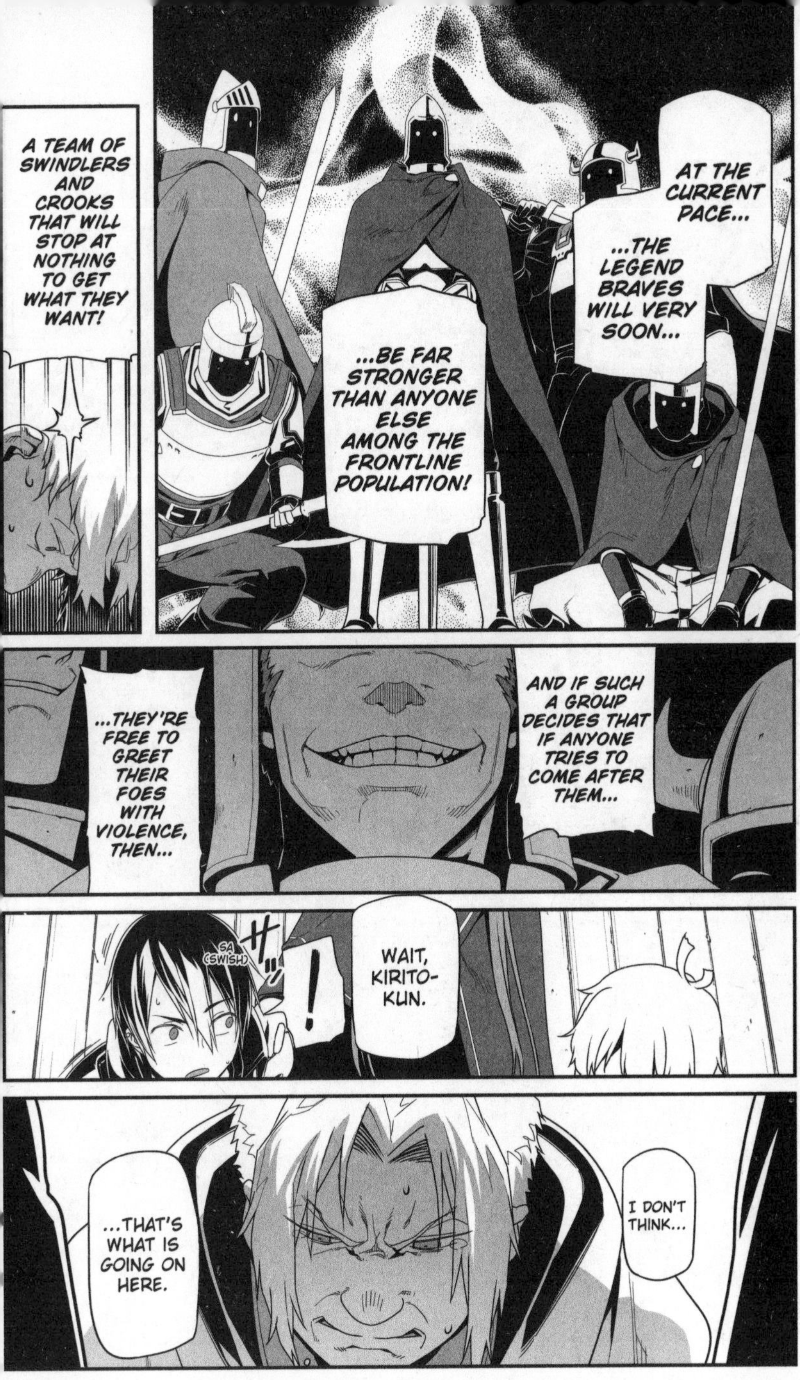
AT THE CURRENT PACE...
...THE LEGEND BRAVES WILL VERY SOON...
...BE FAR STRONGER THAN ANYONE ELSE AMONG THE FRONTLINE POPULATION!
A TEAM OF SWINDLERS AND CROOKS THAT WILL STOP AT NOTHING TO GET WHAT THEY WANT!
AND IF SUCH A GROUP DECIDES THAT IF ANYONE TRIES TO COME AFTER THEM...
...THEY'RE FREE TO GREET THEIR FOES WITH VIOLENCE, THEN...
WAIT, KIRITO-KUN.
!
SA (SWISH)
I DON'T THINK...
...THAT'S WHAT IS GOING ON HERE.

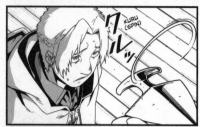

KURU
(SPIN)

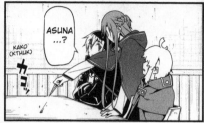

ASUNA
...?

KAKO
(KTHUK)

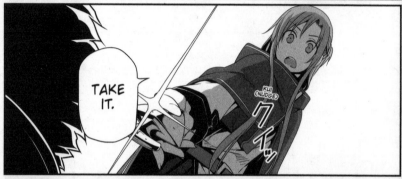

TAKE IT.

KUI
(NUDGE)

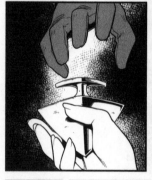

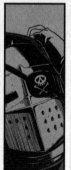

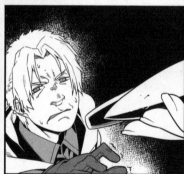

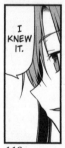

I KNEW IT.

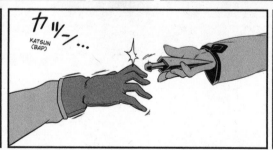

カッ-/...

KATSUN
(BAP)

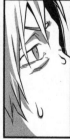

119

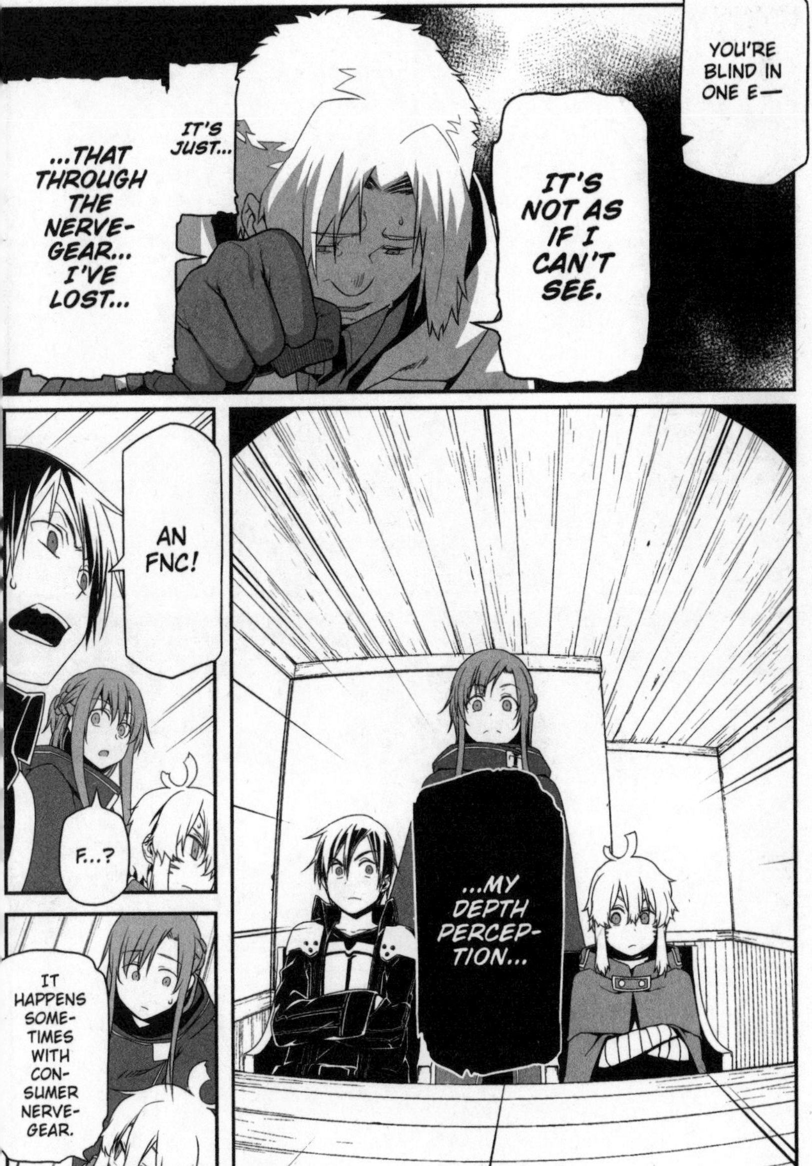
YOU'RE BLIND IN ONE E—
IT'S NOT AS IF I CAN'T SEE.
IT'S JUST...
...THAT THROUGH THE NERVEGEAR... I'VE LOST...
...MY DEPTH PERCEPTION...
AN FNC!
F...?
IT HAPPENS SOMETIMES WITH CONSUMER NERVEGEAR.

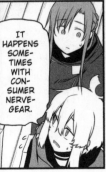

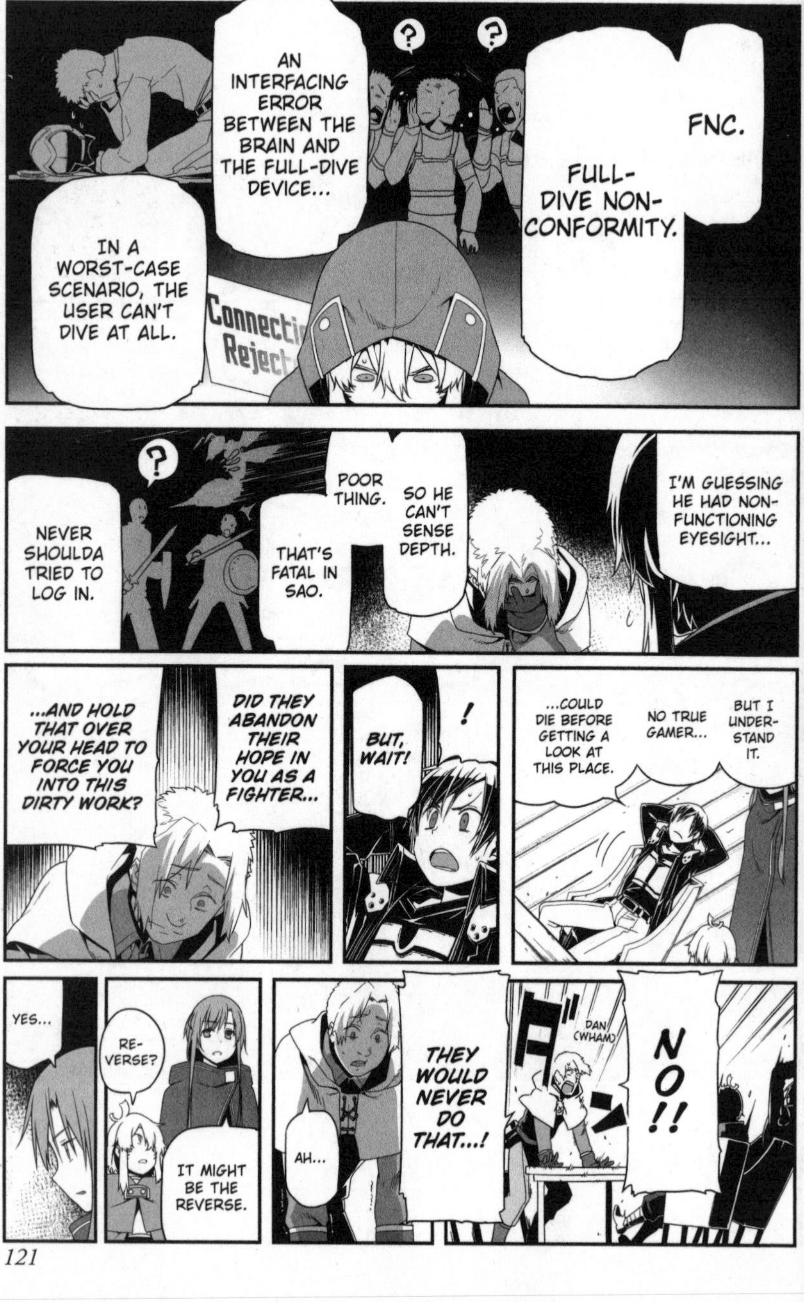
FNC.
FULL-DIVE NON-CONFORMITY.
AN INTERFACING ERROR BETWEEN THE BRAIN AND THE FULL-DIVE DEVICE...
IN A WORST-CASE SCENARIO, THE USER CAN'T DIVE AT ALL.
I'M GUESSING HE HAD NON-FUNCTIONING EYESIGHT...
SO HE CAN'T SENSE DEPTH.
POOR THING.
THAT'S FATAL IN SAO.
NEVER SHOULDA TRIED TO LOG IN.
BUT I UNDER-STAND IT.
NO TRUE GAMER...
...COULD DIE BEFORE GETTING A LOOK AT THIS PLACE.
!
BUT, WAIT!
DID THEY ABANDON THEIR HOPE IN YOU AS A FIGHTER...
...AND HOLD THAT OVER YOUR HEAD TO FORCE YOU INTO THIS DIRTY WORK?
NO!!
DAN (WHAM)
THEY WOULD NEVER DO THAT...!
AH...
IT MIGHT BE THE REVERSE.
RE-VERSE?
YES...

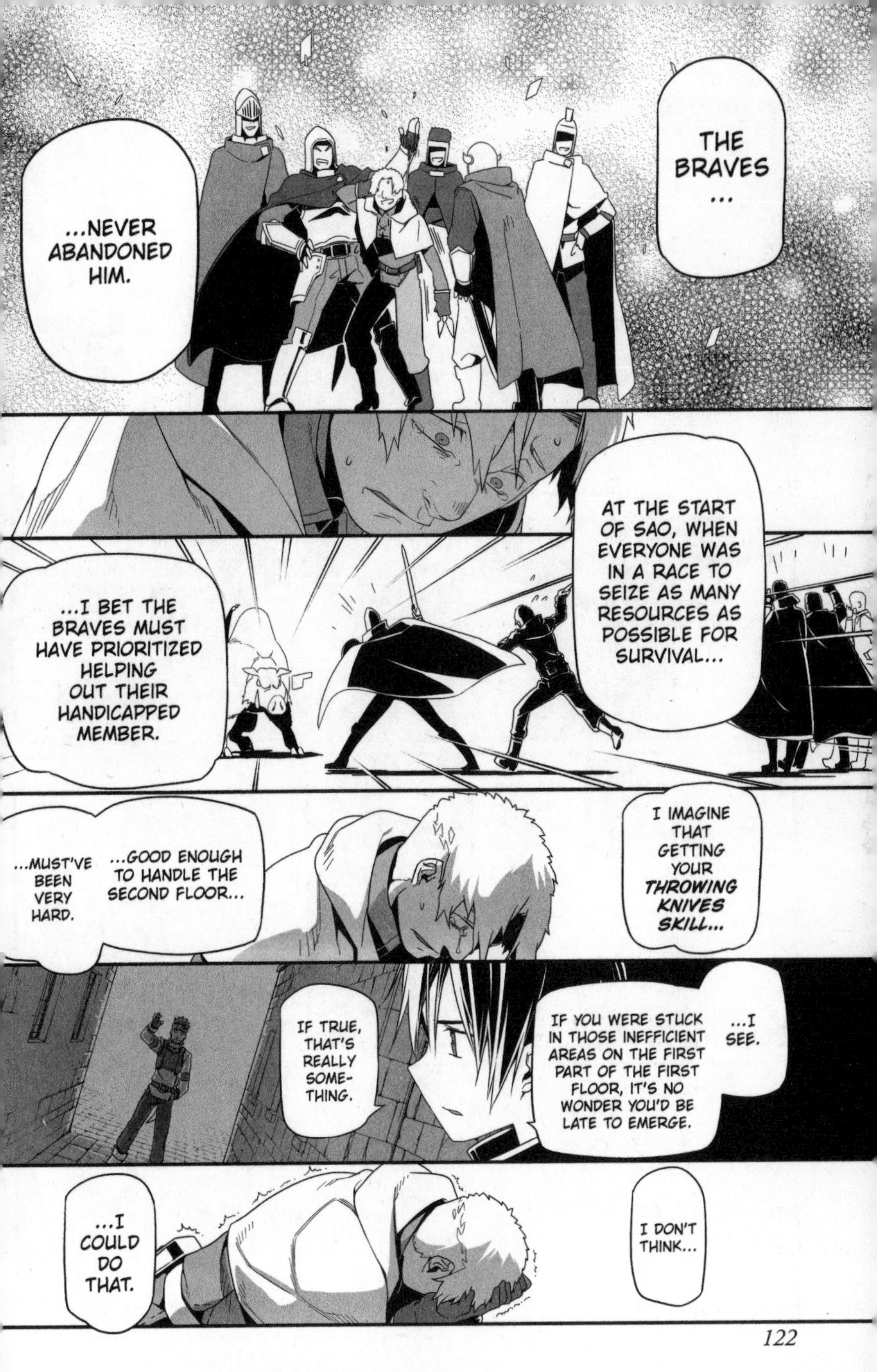
THE BRAVES...
...NEVER ABANDONED HIM.
AT THE START OF SAO, WHEN EVERYONE WAS IN A RACE TO SEIZE AS MANY RESOURCES AS POSSIBLE FOR SURVIVAL...
...I BET THE BRAVES MUST HAVE PRIORITIZED HELPING OUT THEIR HANDICAPPED MEMBER.
I IMAGINE THAT GETTING YOUR *THROWING KNIVES SKILL*...
...GOOD ENOUGH TO HANDLE THE SECOND FLOOR...
...MUST'VE BEEN VERY HARD.
...I SEE.
IF YOU WERE STUCK IN THOSE INEFFICIENT AREAS ON THE FIRST PART OF THE FIRST FLOOR, IT'S NO WONDER YOU'D BE LATE TO EMERGE.
IF TRUE, THAT'S REALLY SOME-THING.
I DON'T THINK...
...I COULD DO THAT.

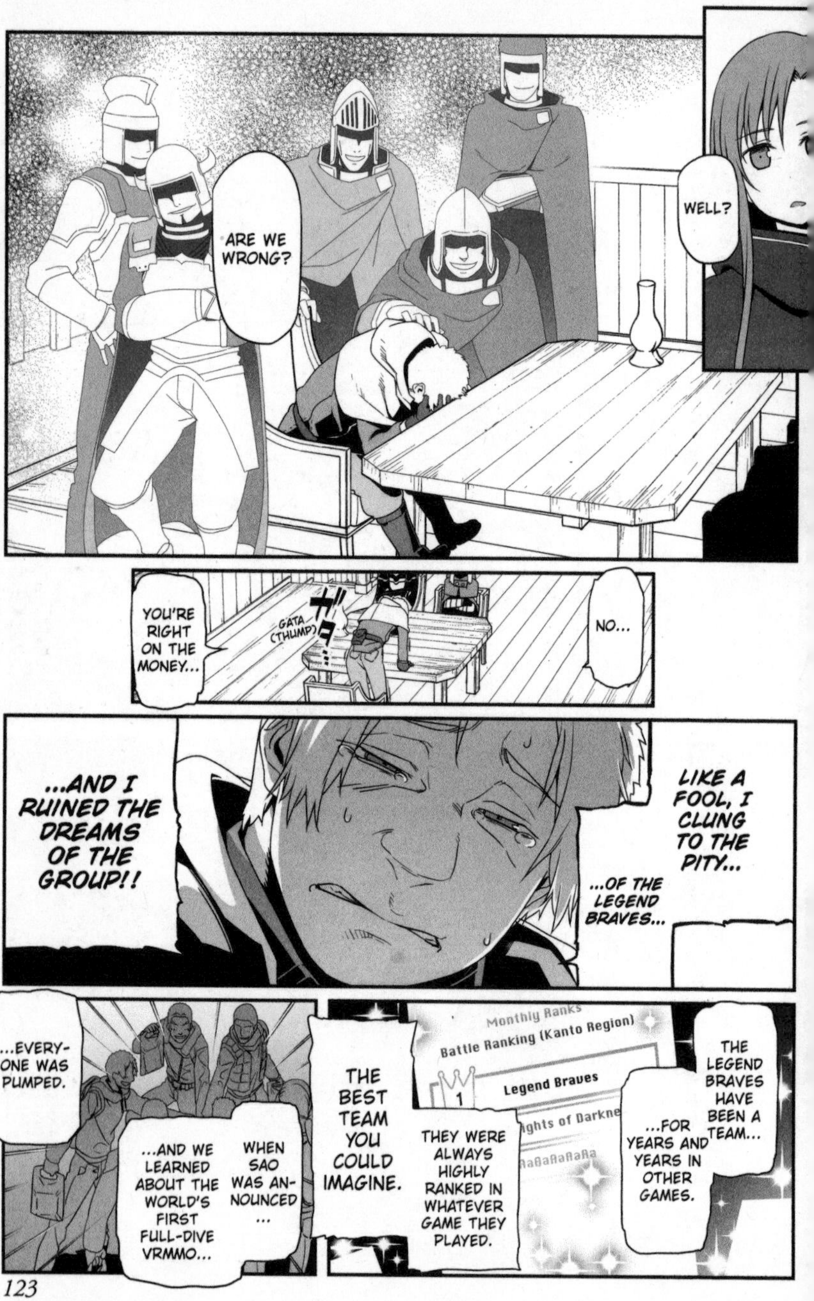
WELL?
ARE WE WRONG?
NO...
GATA (THUMP)
YOU'RE RIGHT ON THE MONEY...
LIKE A FOOL, I CLUNG TO THE PITY...
...OF THE LEGEND BRAVES...
...AND I RUINED THE DREAMS OF THE GROUP!!
THE LEGEND BRAVES HAVE BEEN A TEAM...
...FOR YEARS AND YEARS IN OTHER GAMES.
Monthly Ranks
Battle Ranking (Kanto Region)
1
Legend Braves
THEY WERE ALWAYS HIGHLY RANKED IN WHATEVER GAME THEY PLAYED.
THE BEST TEAM YOU COULD IMAGINE.
WHEN SAO WAS ANNOUNCED...
...AND WE LEARNED ABOUT THE WORLD'S FIRST FULL-DIVE VRMMO...
...EVERY-ONE WAS PUMPED.

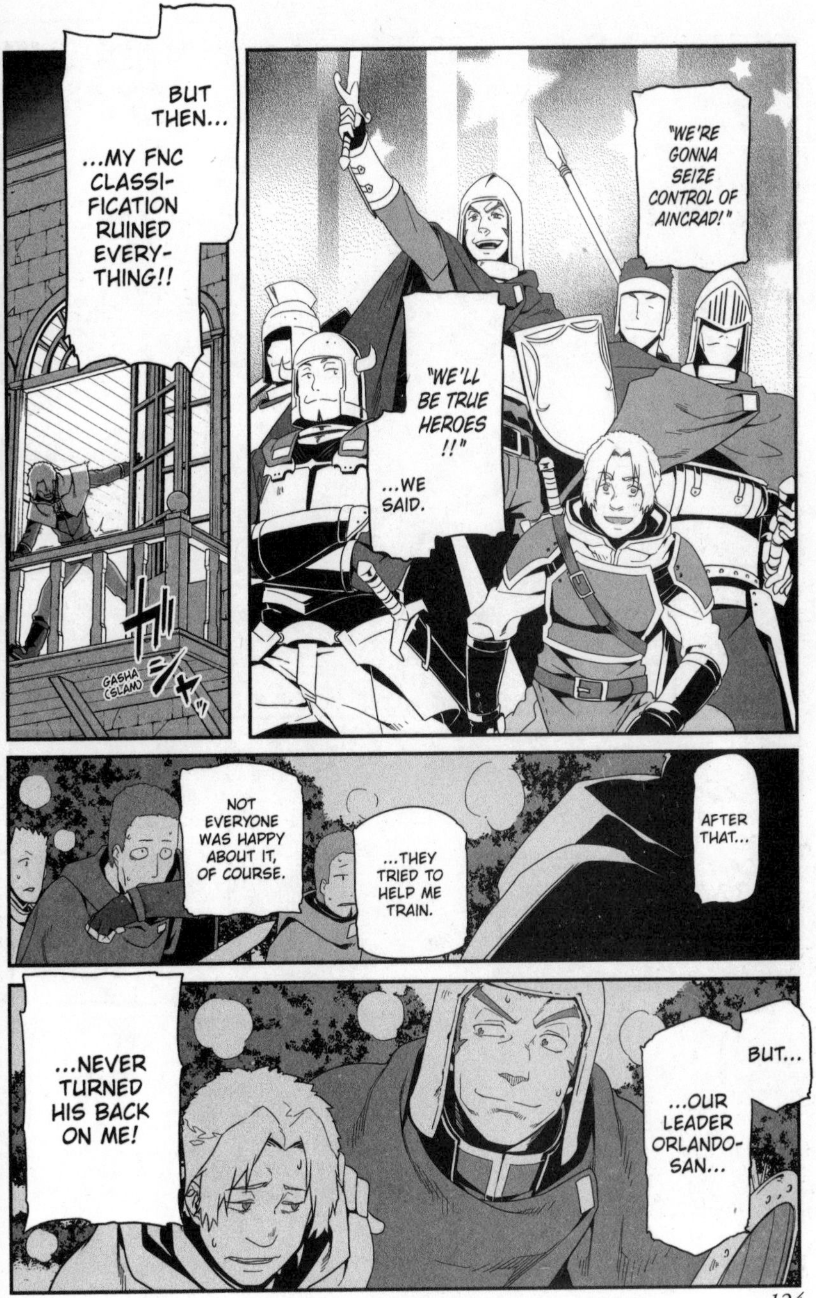
"WE'RE GONNA SEIZE CONTROL OF AINCRAD!"
"WE'LL BE TRUE HEROES!!"
...WE SAID.
BUT THEN...
...MY FNC CLASSIFICATION RUINED EVERYTHING!!
GASHA (SLAM)
AFTER THAT...
...THEY TRIED TO HELP ME TRAIN.
NOT EVERYONE WAS HAPPY ABOUT IT, OF COURSE.
BUT...
...OUR LEADER ORLANDO-SAN...
...NEVER TURNED HIS BACK ON ME!

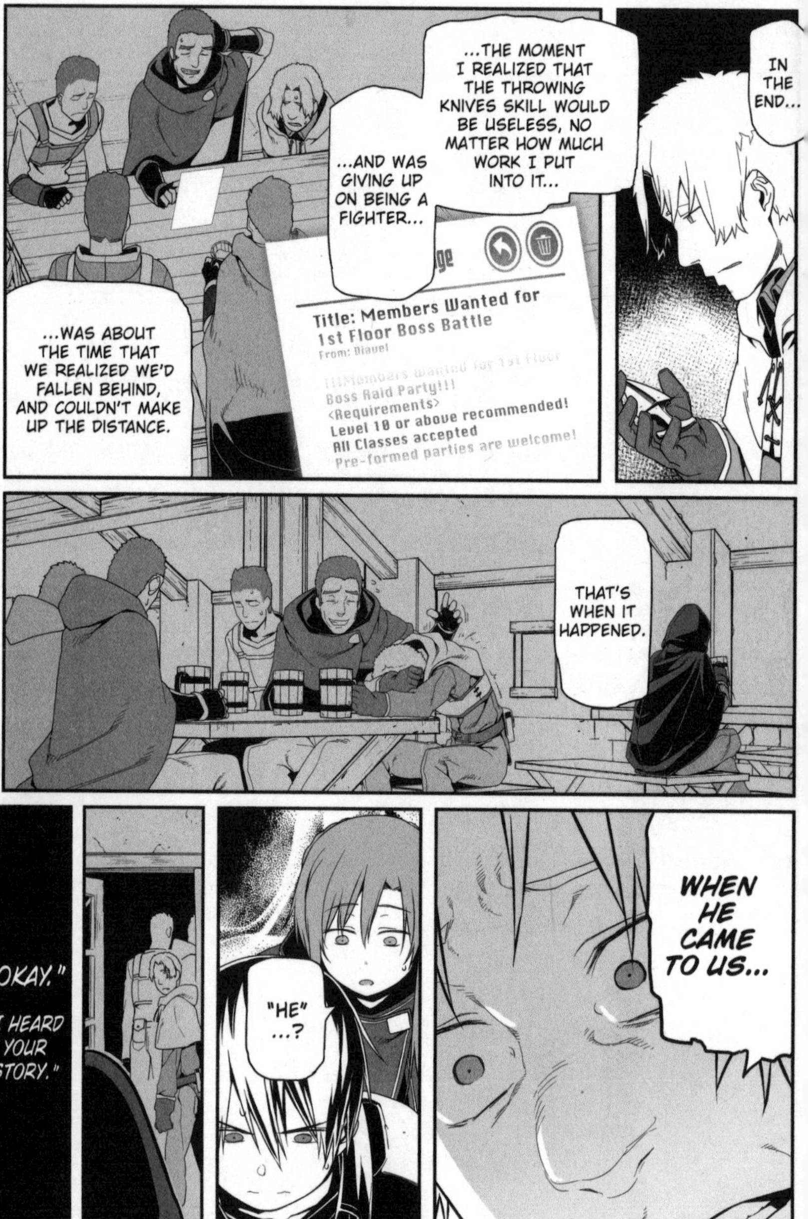
IN THE END...
...THE MOMENT I REALIZED THAT THE THROWING KNIVES SKILL WOULD BE USELESS, NO MATTER HOW MUCH WORK I PUT INTO IT...
...AND WAS GIVING UP ON BEING A FIGHTER...
Title: Members Wanted for 1st Floor Boss Battle
From: Diavel
!!!Members Wanted for 1st Floor Boss Raid Party!!!
<Requirements>
Level 10 or above recommended!
All Classes accepted
Pre-formed parties are welcome!
...WAS ABOUT THE TIME THAT WE REALIZED WE'D FALLEN BEHIND, AND COULDN'T MAKE UP THE DISTANCE.
THAT'S WHEN IT HAPPENED.
WHEN HE CAME TO US...
"HE" ...?
"OKAY."
"I HEARD YOUR STORY."

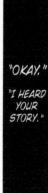

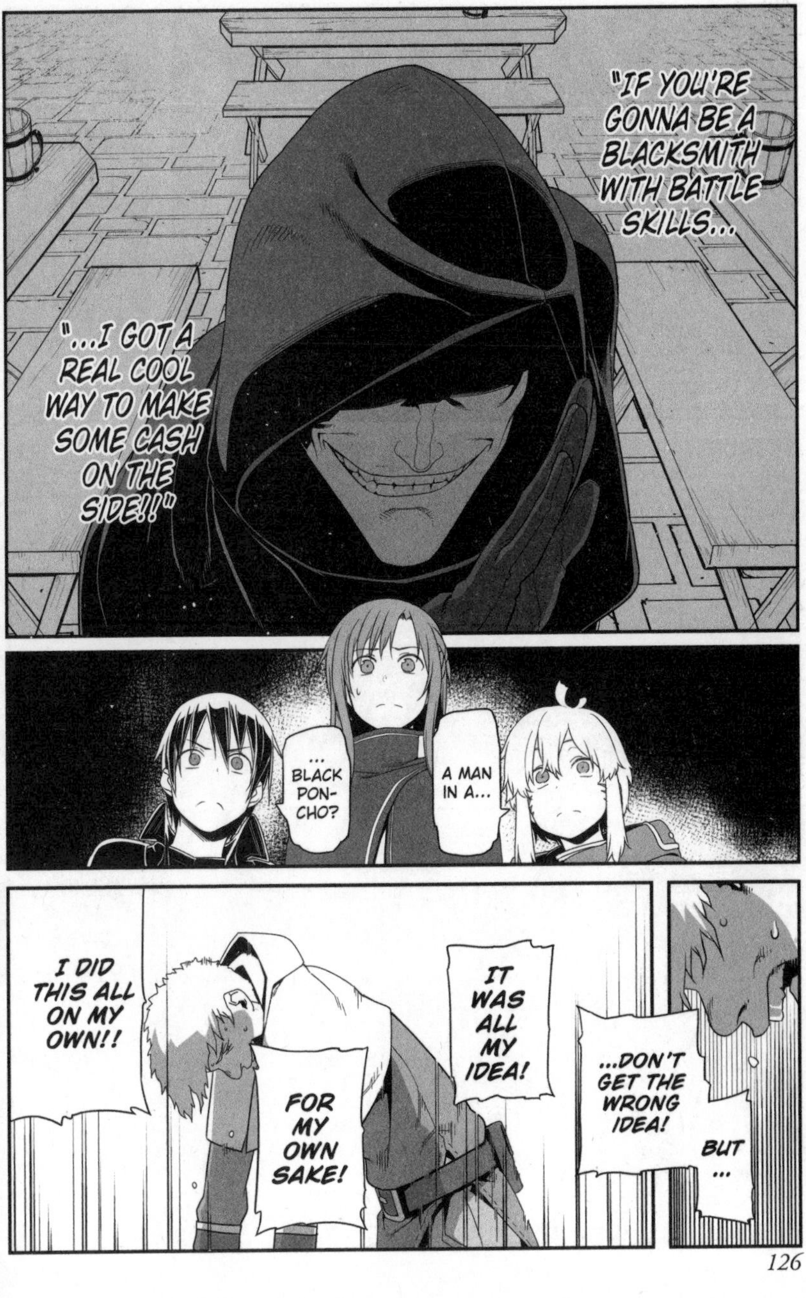
"IF YOU'RE GONNA BE A BLACKSMITH WITH BATTLE SKILLS...
"...I GOT A REAL COOL WAY TO MAKE SOME CASH ON THE SIDE!!"
A MAN IN A...
...BLACK PON-CHO?
...DON'T GET THE WRONG IDEA!
BUT ...
IT WAS ALL MY IDEA!
FOR MY OWN SAKE!
I DID THIS ALL ON MY OWN!!

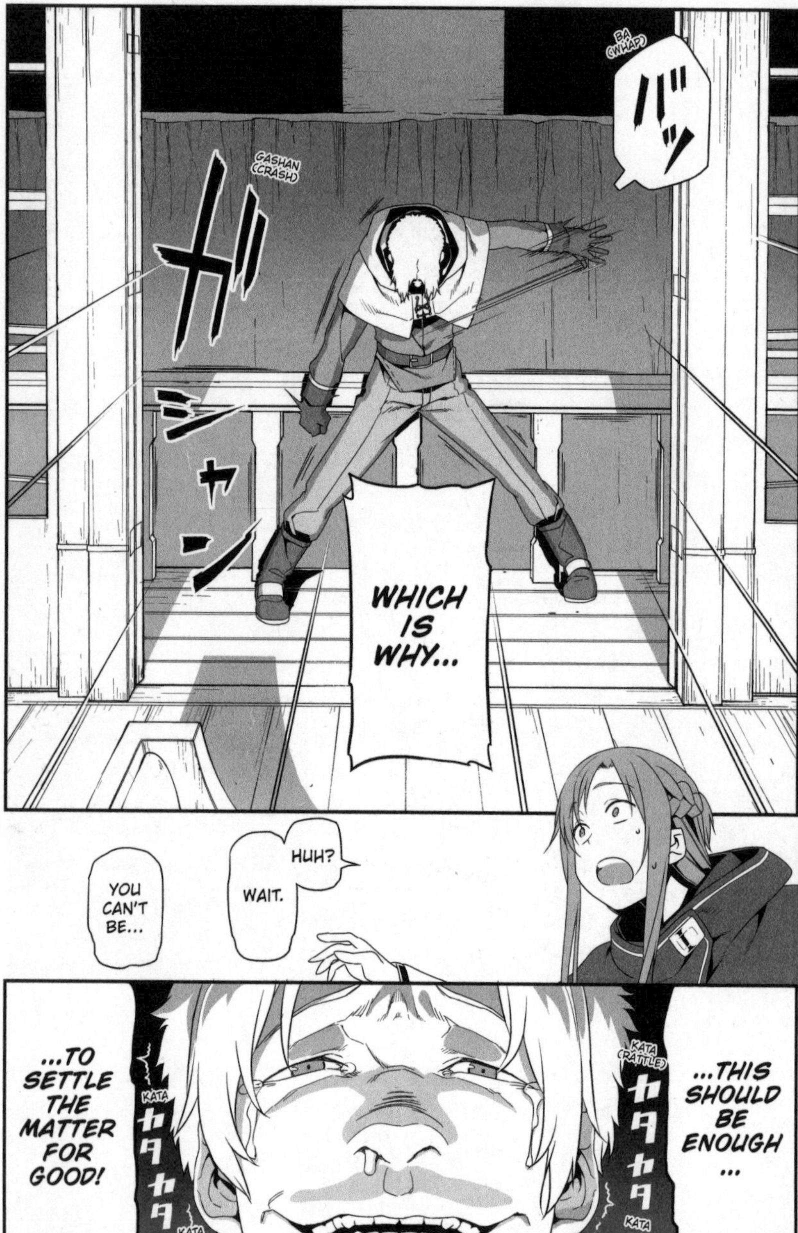
BA (WHAP)
バッ
GASHAN (CRASH)
ガシャン
WHICH IS WHY...
HUH?
WAIT.
YOU CAN'T BE...
...THIS SHOULD BE ENOUGH...
KATA (RATTLE)
カタカタ
KATA
KATA
カタカタ
KATA
...TO SETTLE THE MATTER FOR GOOD!

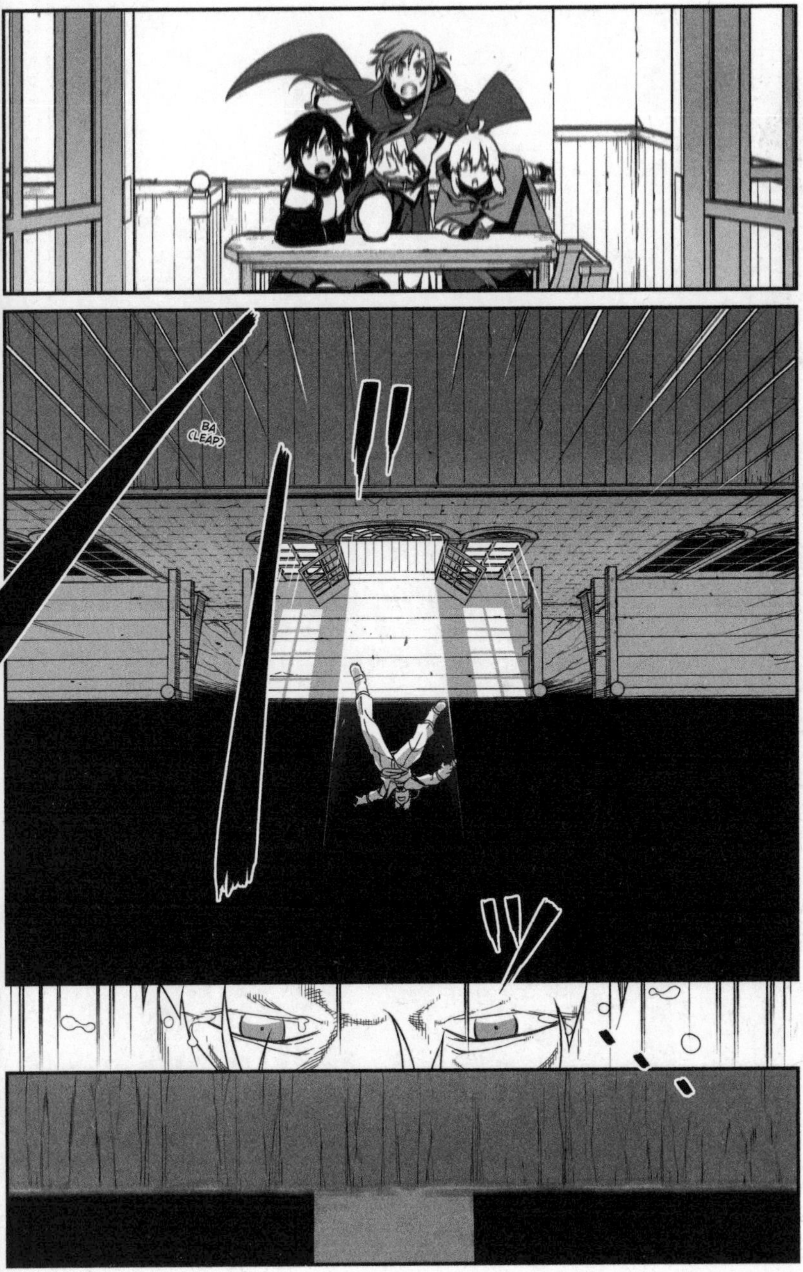
BA
(LEAP)

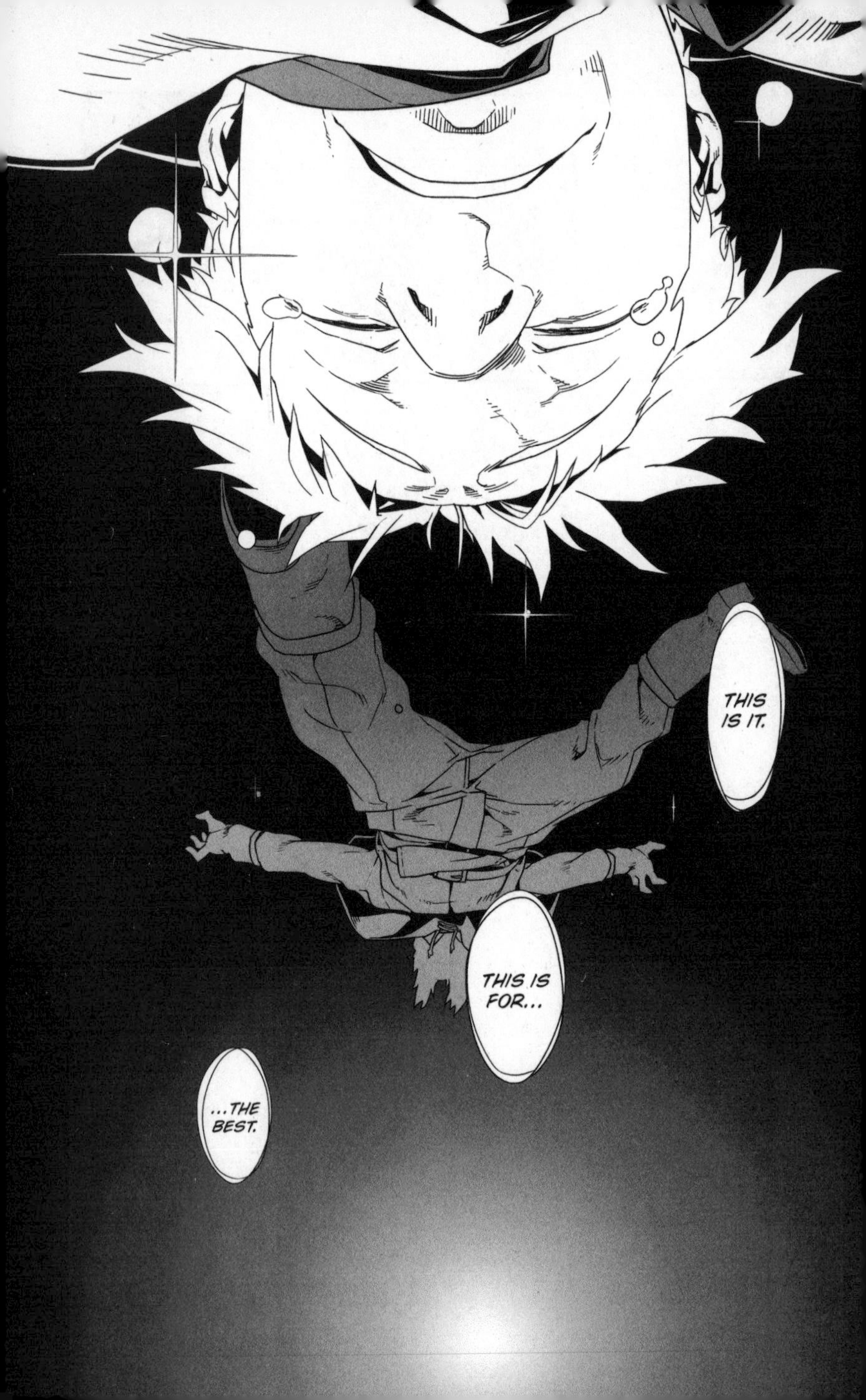
THIS IS IT.
THIS IS FOR...
...THE BEST.

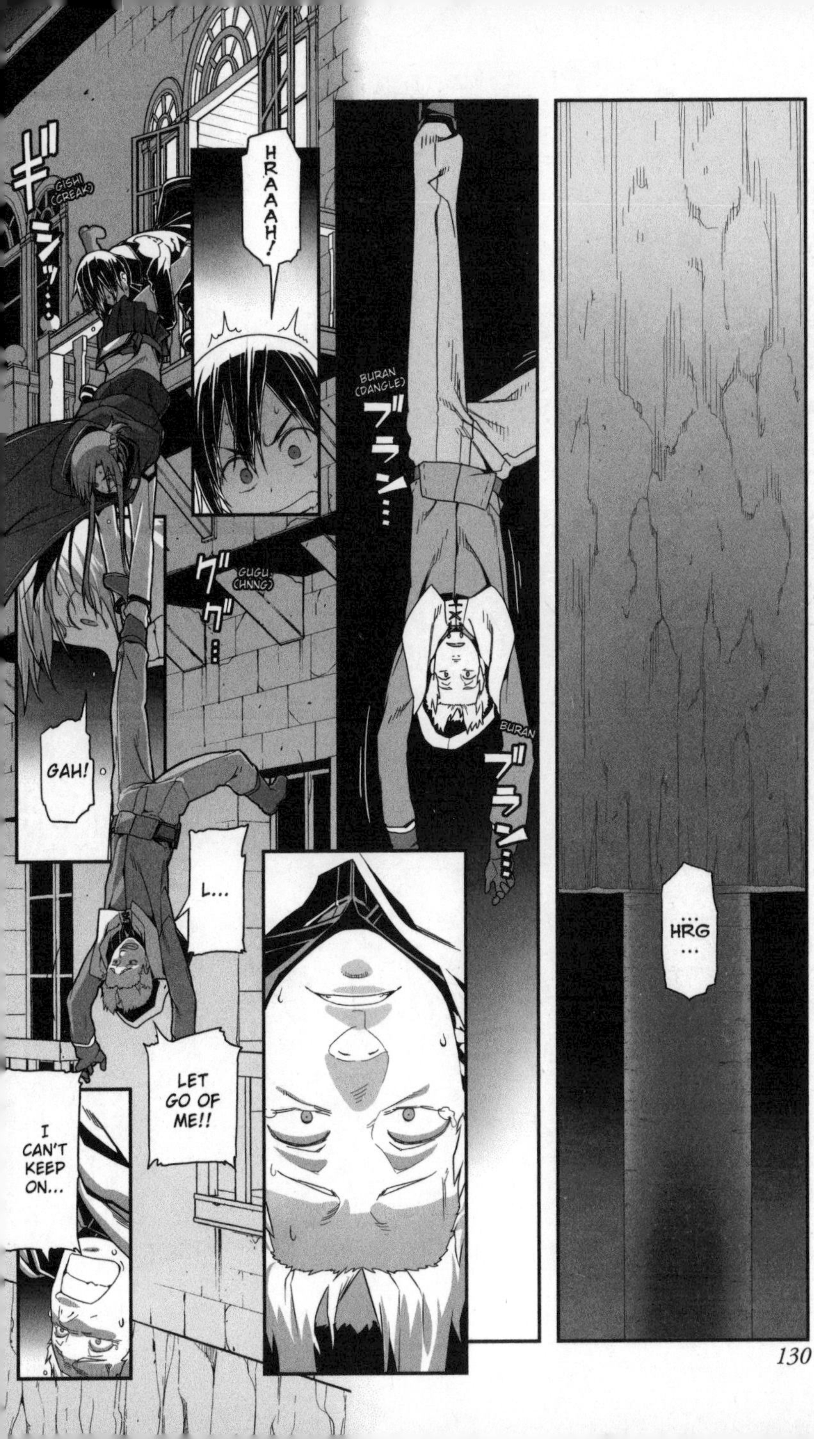
...HRG...
BURAN (DANGLE)
ブラン…
BURAN
ブラン…
HRAAAH!
ギシッ…
GISHI (CREAK)
ググ…
GUGU (HNNG)
GAH!
L...
LET GO OF ME!!
I CAN'T KEEP ON...

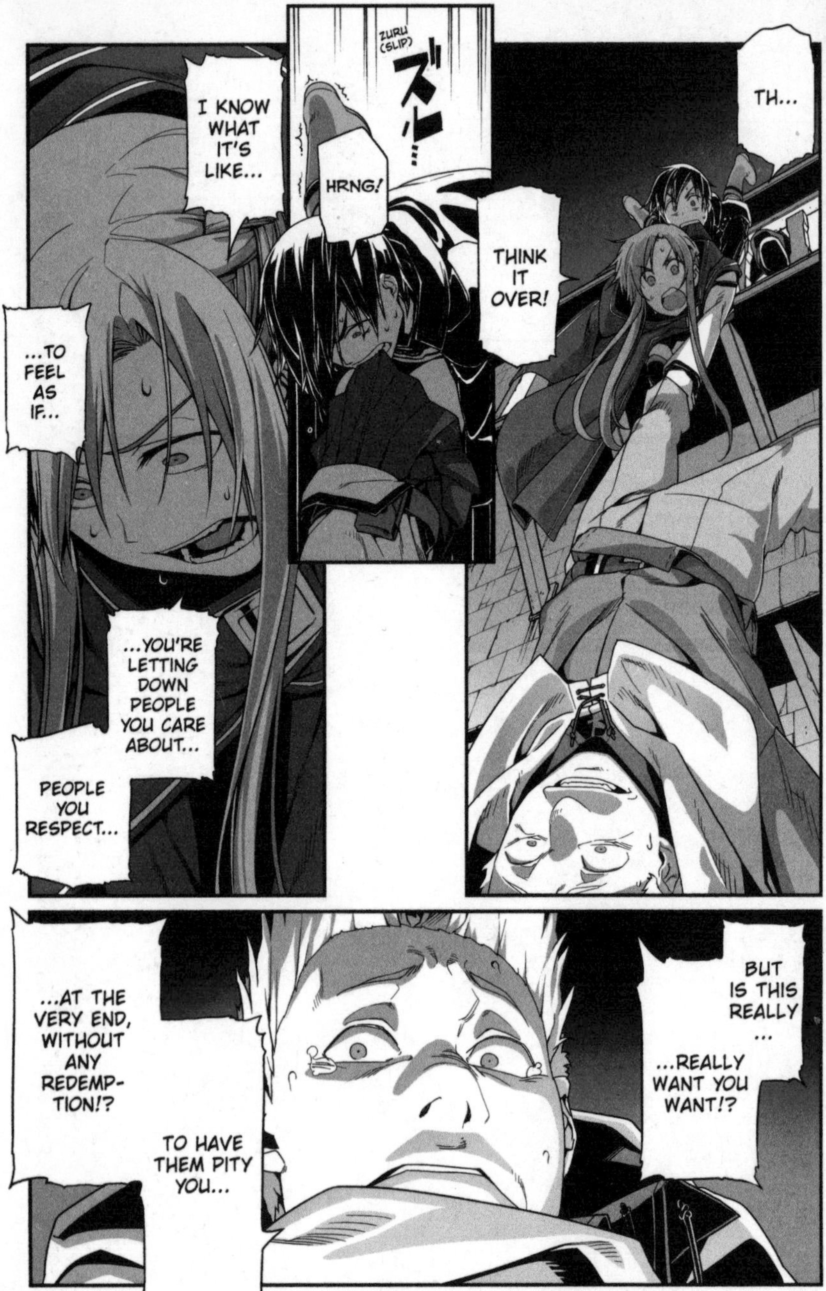
TH...
THINK IT OVER!
ZURU (SLIP)
ズル...
HRNG!
I KNOW WHAT IT'S LIKE...
...TO FEEL AS IF...
...YOU'RE LETTING DOWN PEOPLE YOU CARE ABOUT...
PEOPLE YOU RESPECT...
BUT IS THIS REALLY...
...REALLY WANT YOU WANT!?
TO HAVE THEM PITY YOU...
...AT THE VERY END, WITHOUT ANY REDEMPTION!?

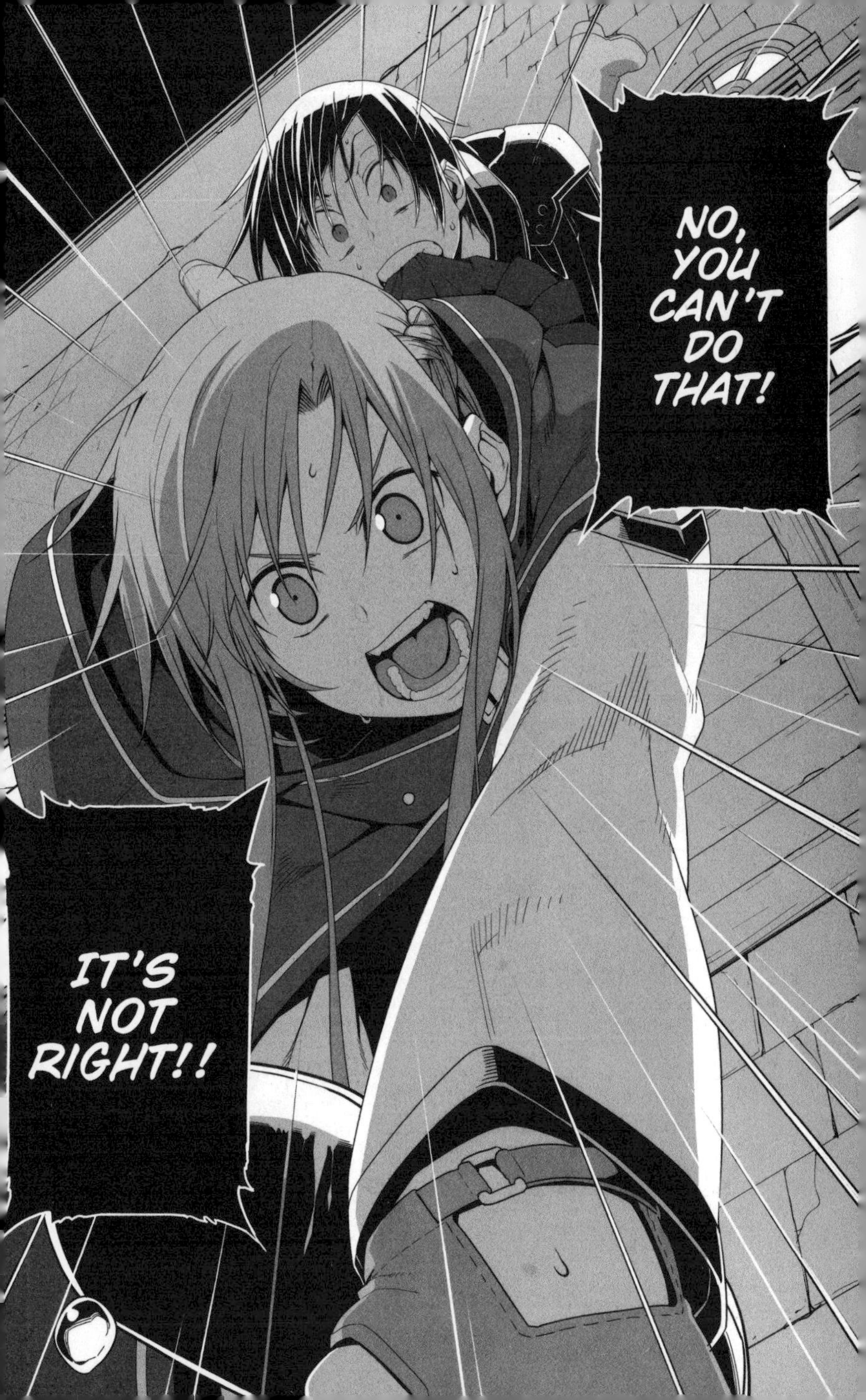
NO, YOU CAN'T DO THAT!
IT'S NOT RIGHT!!

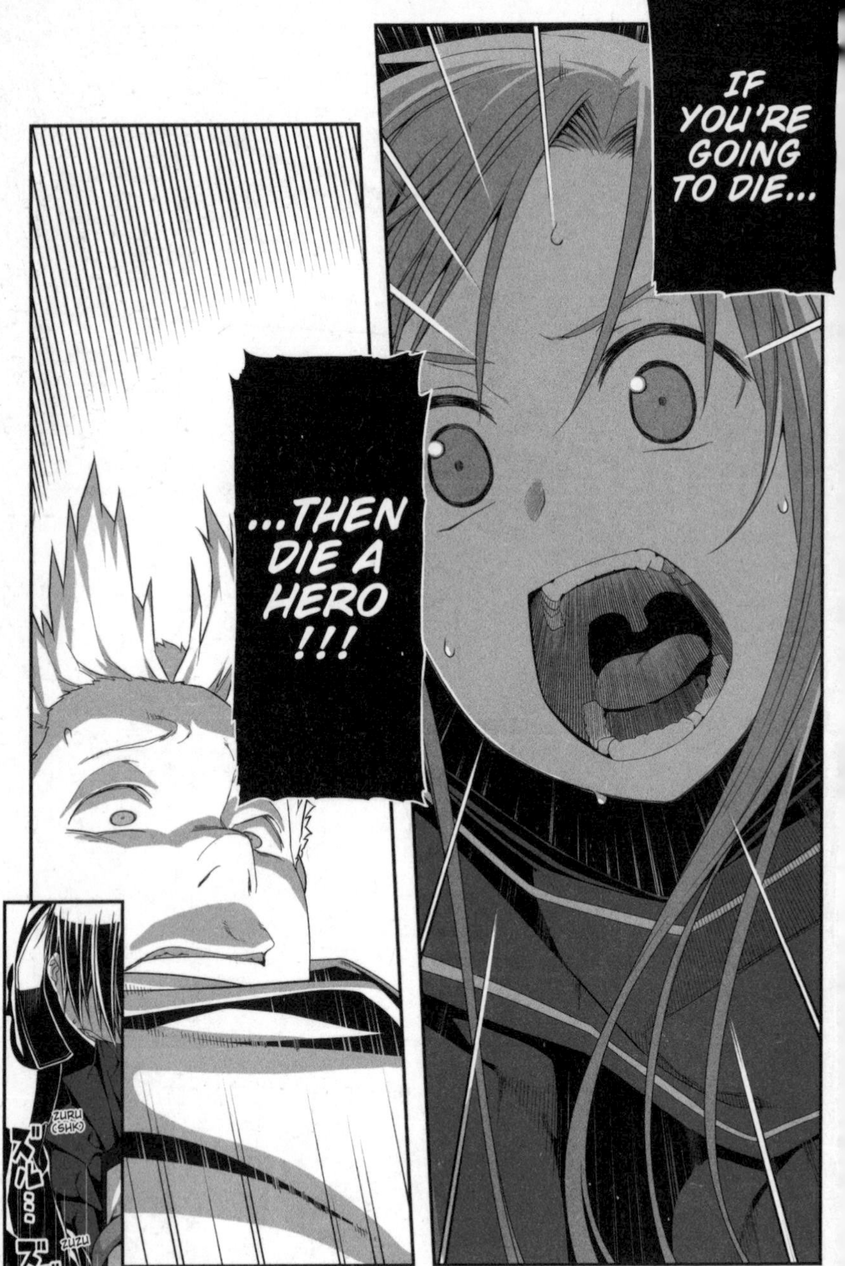
IF YOU'RE GOING TO DIE...
...THEN DIE A HERO!!!
ズル…
ZURU (SHK)
ズズ
ZUZU

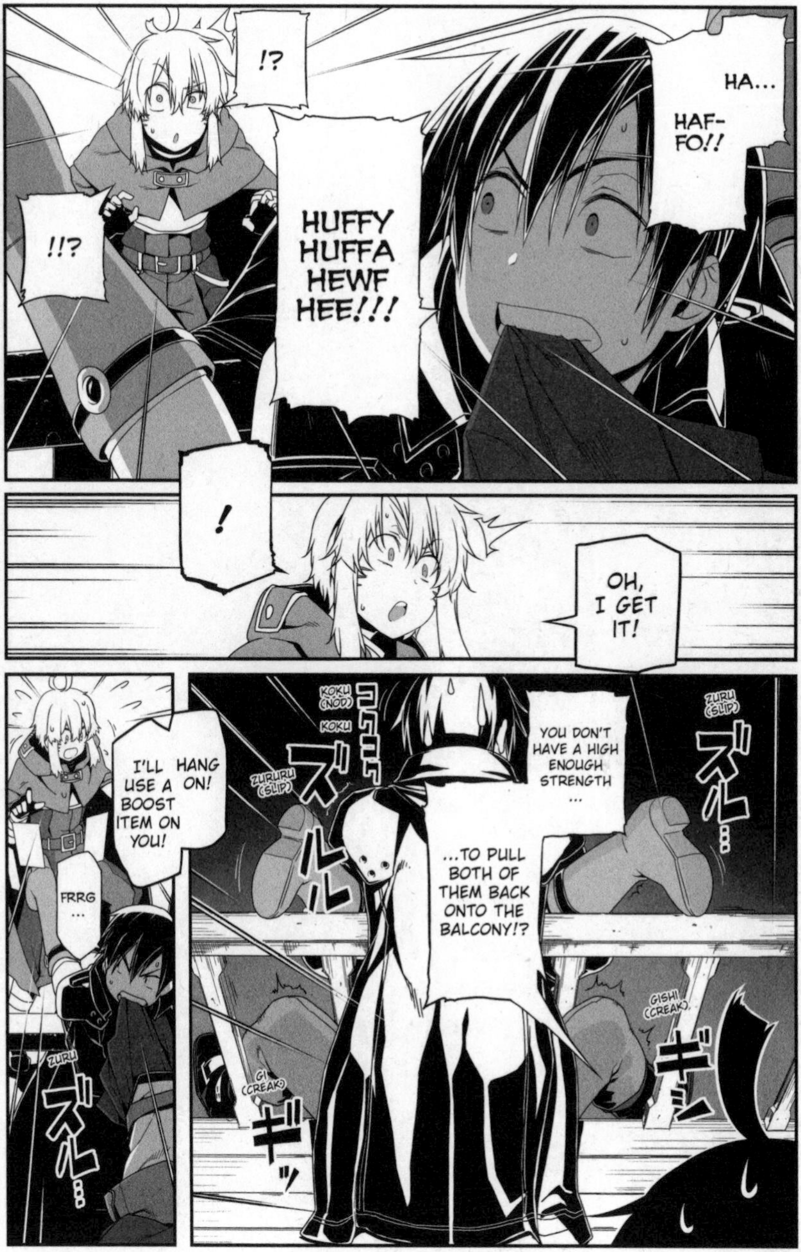
HA...
HAF-
FO!!
!?
HUFFY
HUFFA
HEWF
HEE!!!
!!?
OH, I GET IT!
!
ZURU (SLIP)
YOU DON'T HAVE A HIGH ENOUGH STRENGTH...
KOKU (NOD) KOKU
ZURURU (SLIP)
...TO PULL BOTH OF THEM BACK ONTO THE BALCONY!?
GISHI (CREAK)
GI (CREAK)
HANG ON!
I'LL USE A BOOST ITEM ON YOU!
FRRG...
ZURU

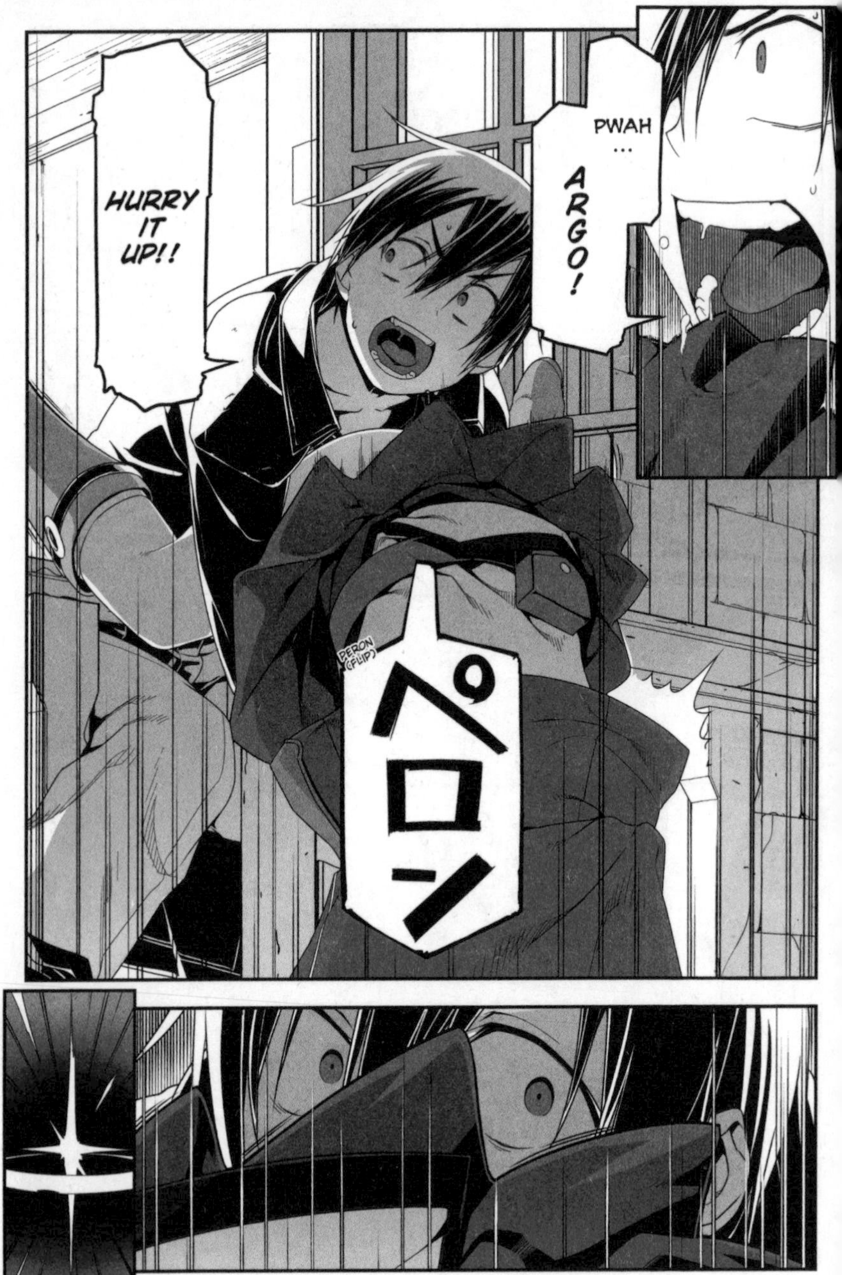
PWAH ... ARGO!
HURRY IT UP!!
ペロン
PERON (FLIP)

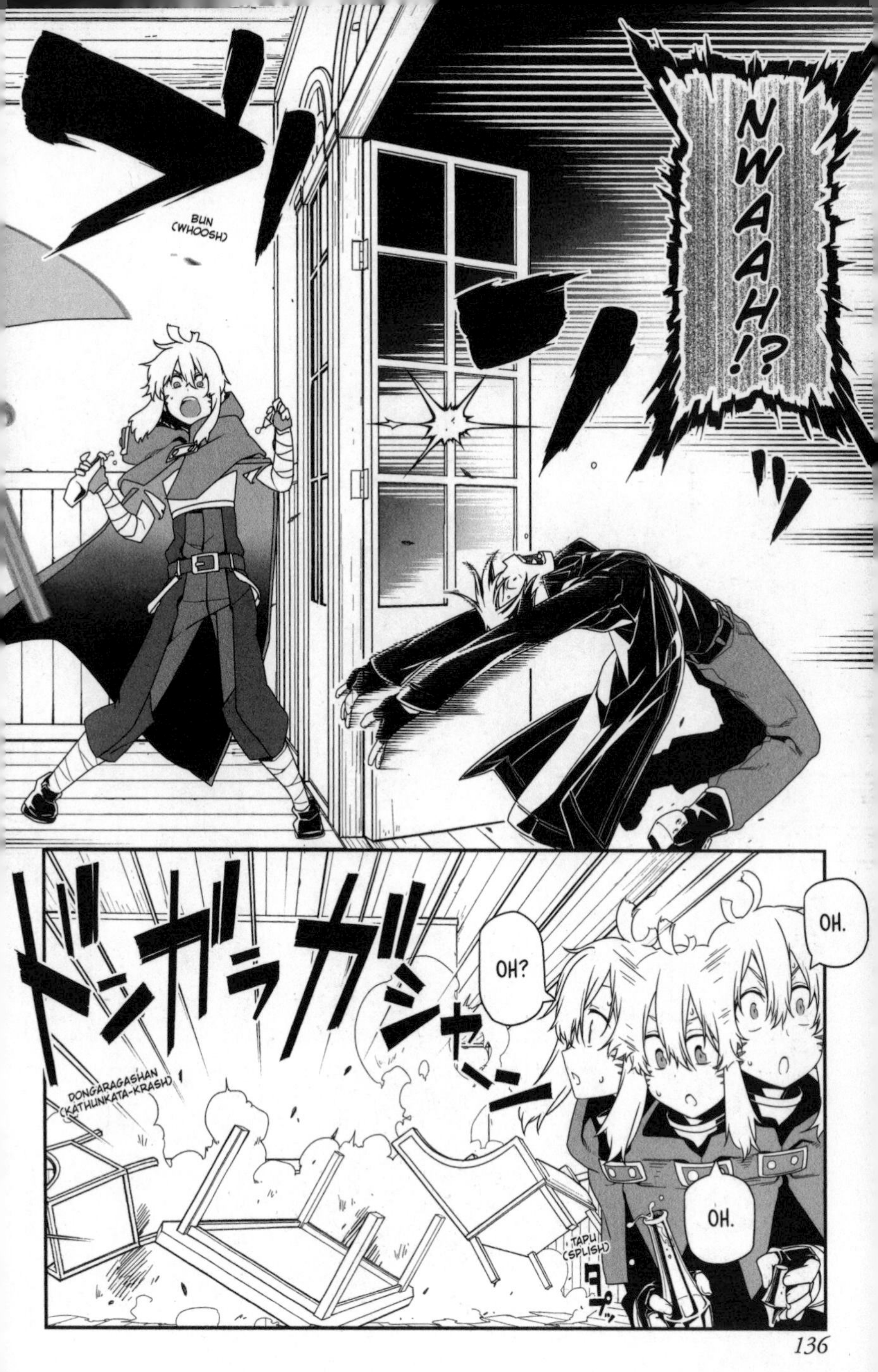
NWAAH!?
BUN
(WHOOSH)
OH.
OH?
OH.
DONGARAGASHAN
(KATHUNKATA-KRASH)
TAPU
(SPLISH)

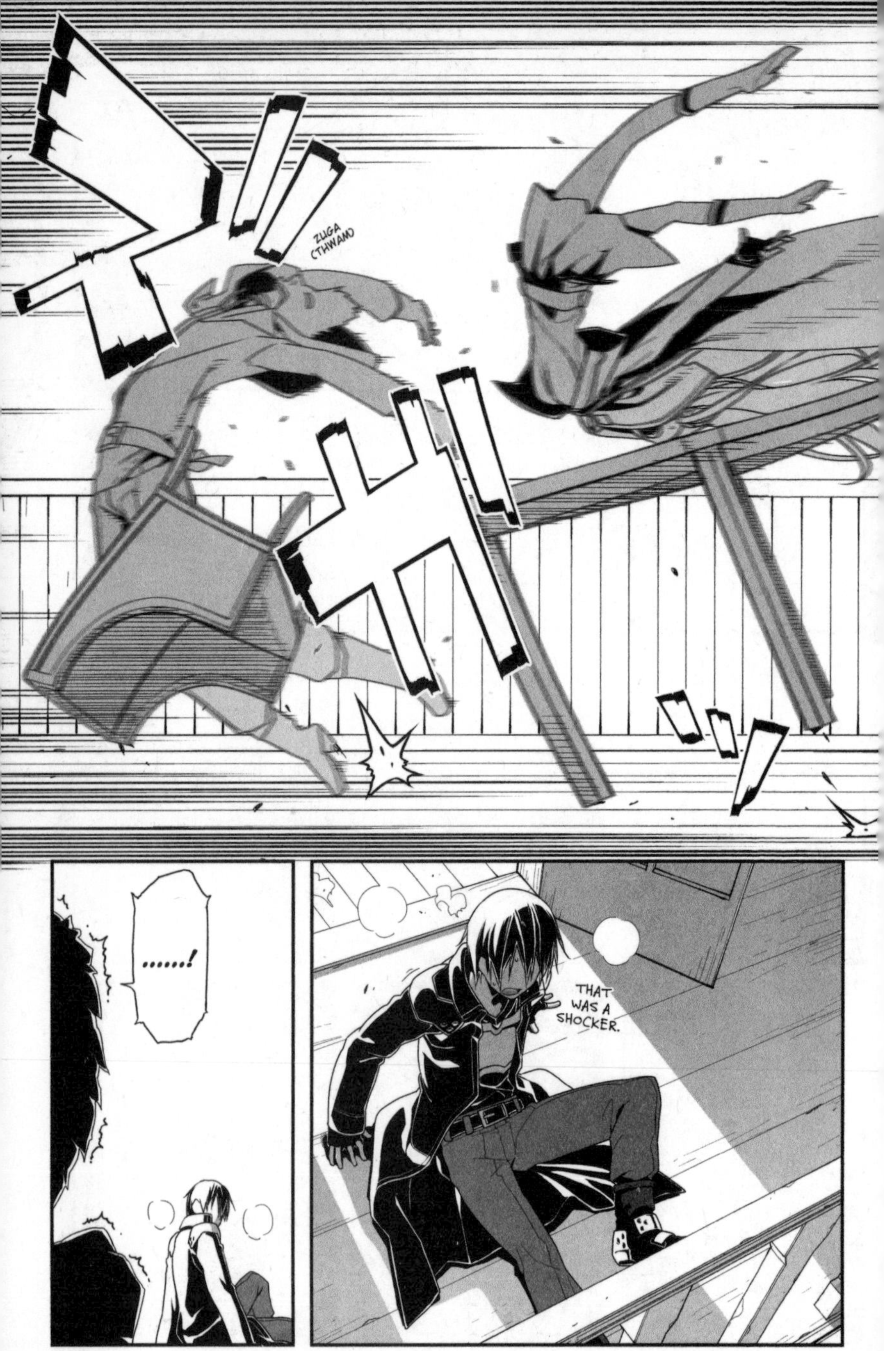
ZUGA (THWAM)
THAT WAS A SHOCKER.
......!

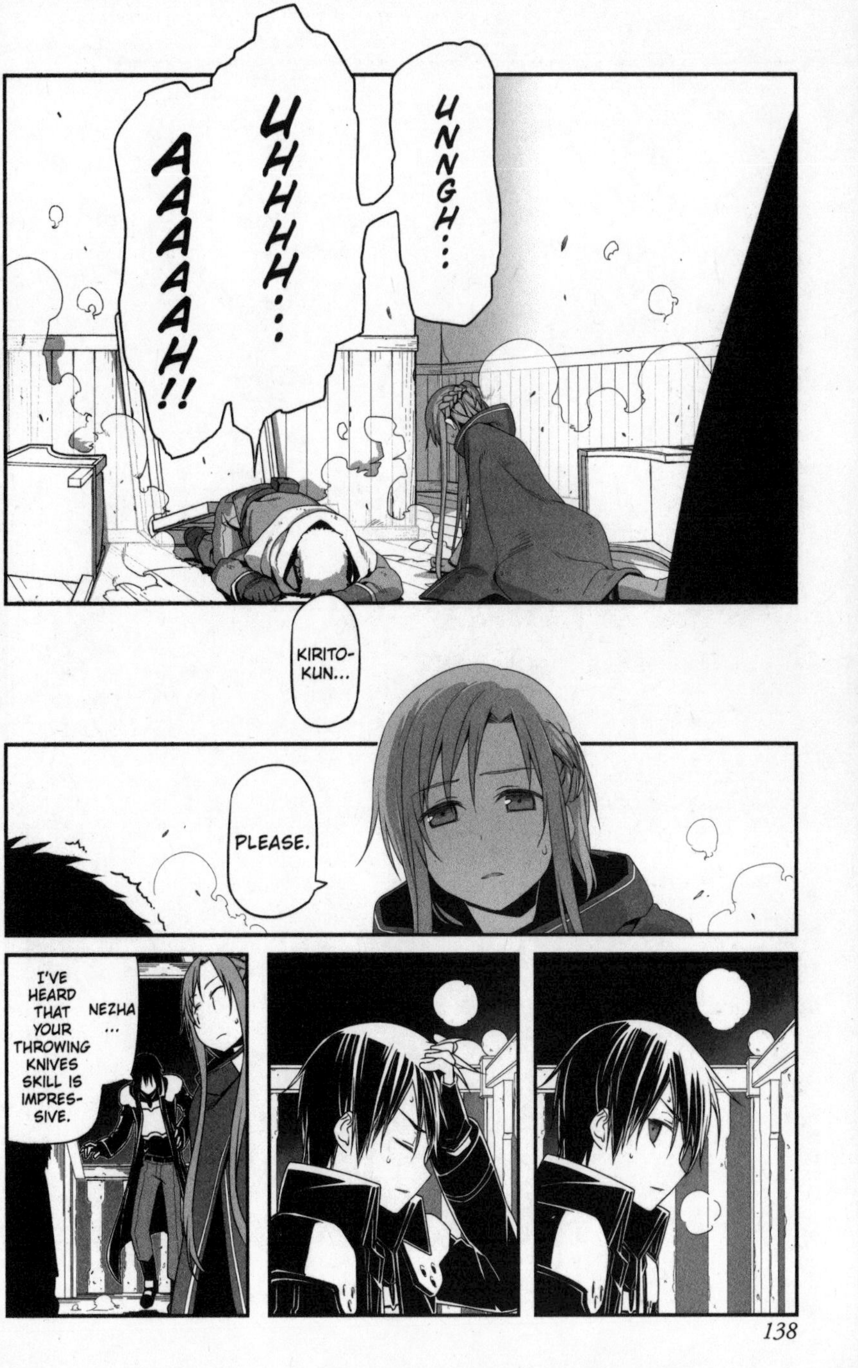
UNNGH...
UHHHH...
AAAAAAH!!
KIRITO-KUN...
PLEASE.
NEZHA...
I'VE HEARD THAT YOUR THROWING KNIVES SKILL IS IMPRESSIVE.

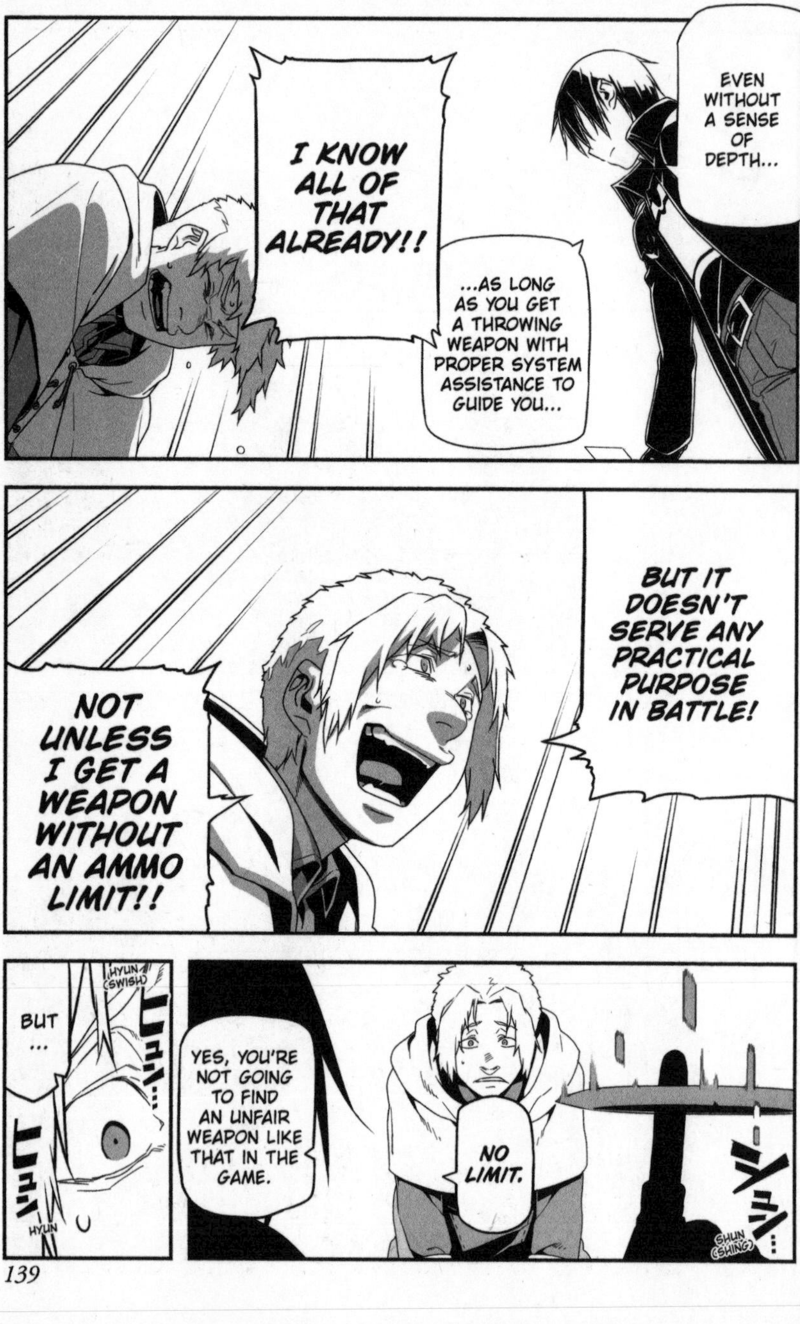
EVEN WITHOUT A SENSE OF DEPTH...
...AS LONG AS YOU GET A THROWING WEAPON WITH PROPER SYSTEM ASSISTANCE TO GUIDE YOU...
I KNOW ALL OF THAT ALREADY!!
BUT IT DOESN'T SERVE ANY PRACTICAL PURPOSE IN BATTLE!
NOT UNLESS I GET A WEAPON WITHOUT AN AMMO LIMIT!!
SHUN (SHING)
YES, YOU'RE NOT GOING TO FIND AN UNFAIR WEAPON LIKE THAT IN THE GAME.
NO LIMIT.
HYUN (SWISH)
BUT ...
HYUN

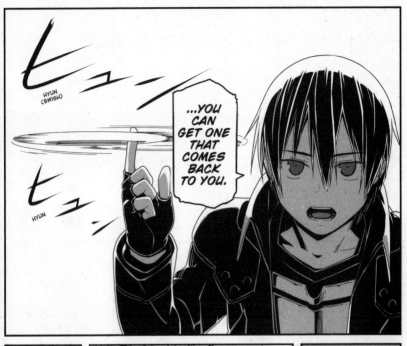

...YOU CAN GET ONE THAT COMES BACK TO YOU.

HYUN
(SWISH)

HYUN

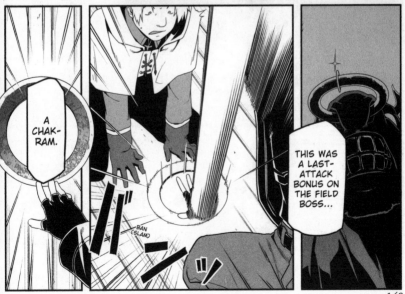

A CHAK-RAM.

BAN
(SLAM)

THIS WAS A LAST-ATTACK BONUS ON THE FIELD BOSS...

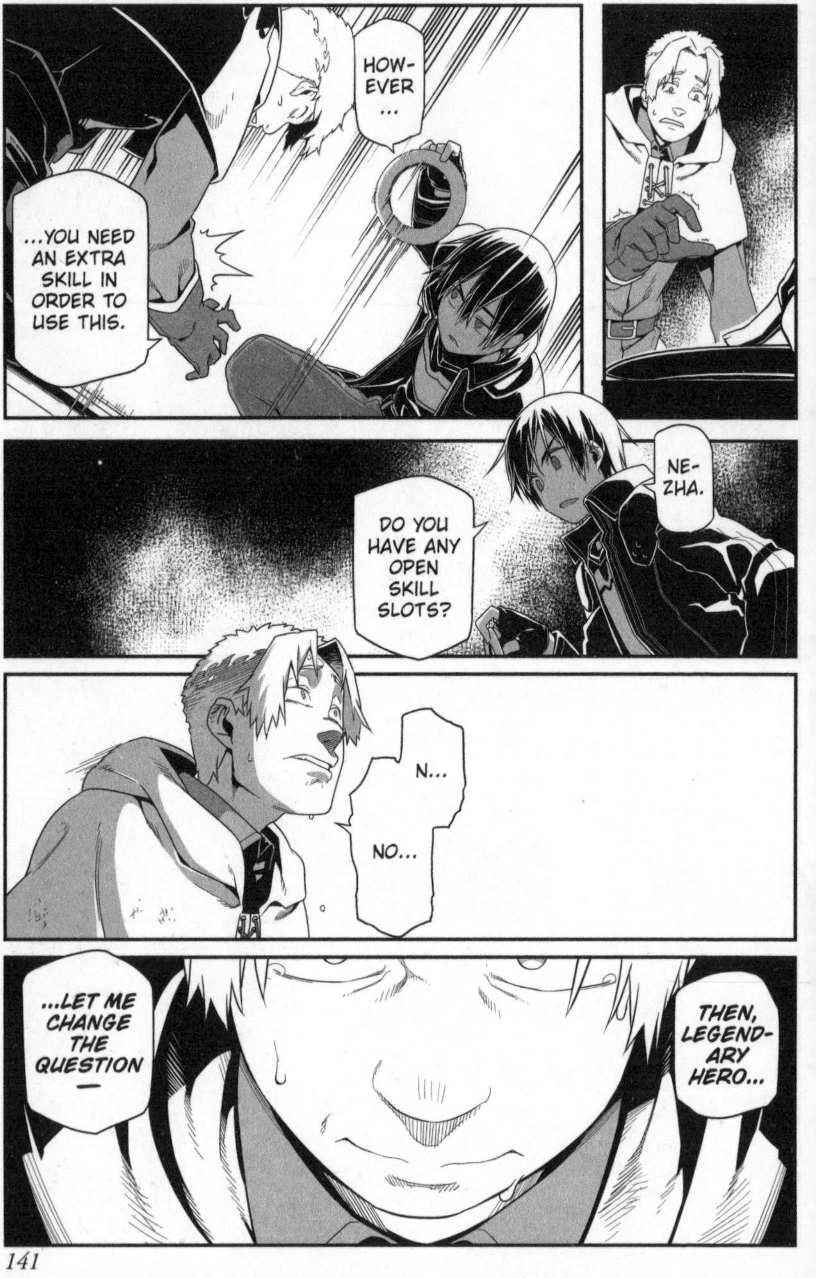
HOW-EVER...
...YOU NEED AN EXTRA SKILL IN ORDER TO USE THIS.
NE-ZHA.
DO YOU HAVE ANY OPEN SKILL SLOTS?
N...
NO...
THEN, LEGENDARY HERO...
...LET ME CHANGE THE QUESTION—

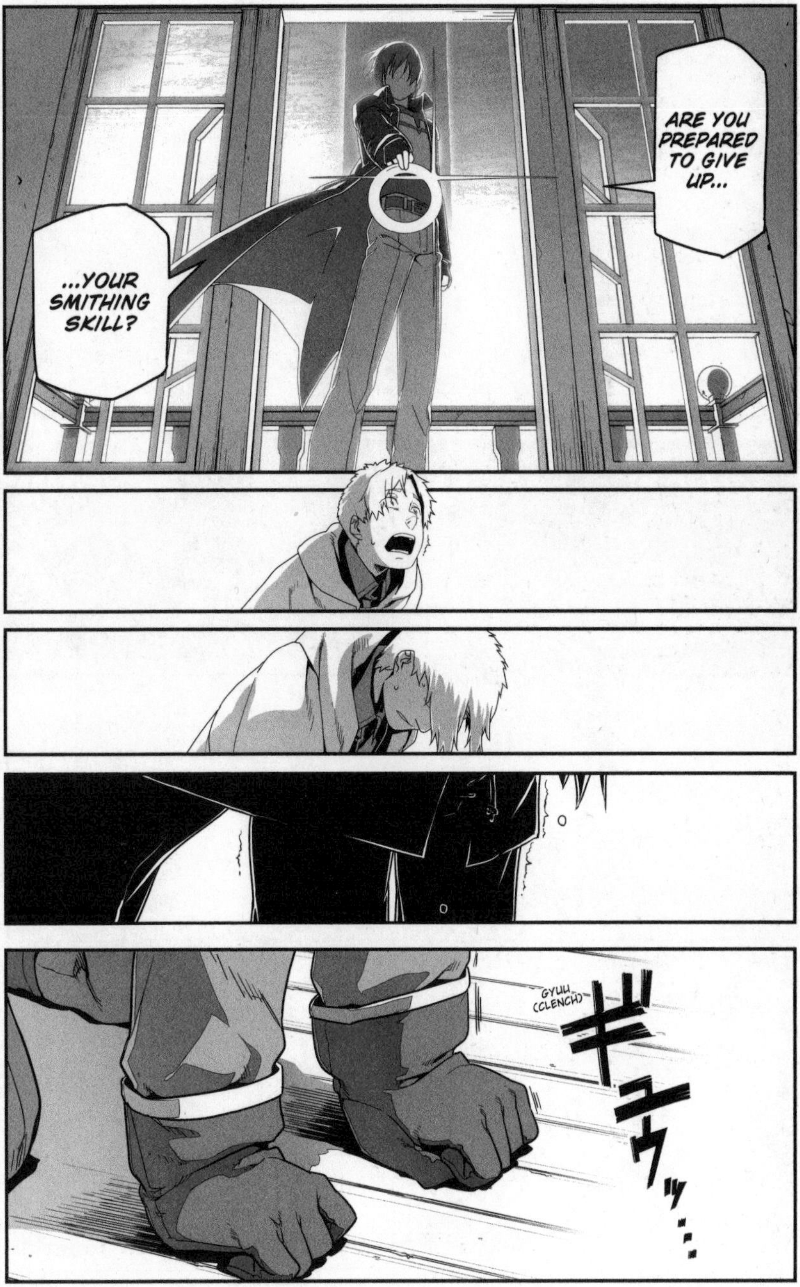
ARE YOU PREPARED TO GIVE UP...
...YOUR SMITHING SKILL?
GYUU (CLENCH)
ギュウッ…

#015: Training

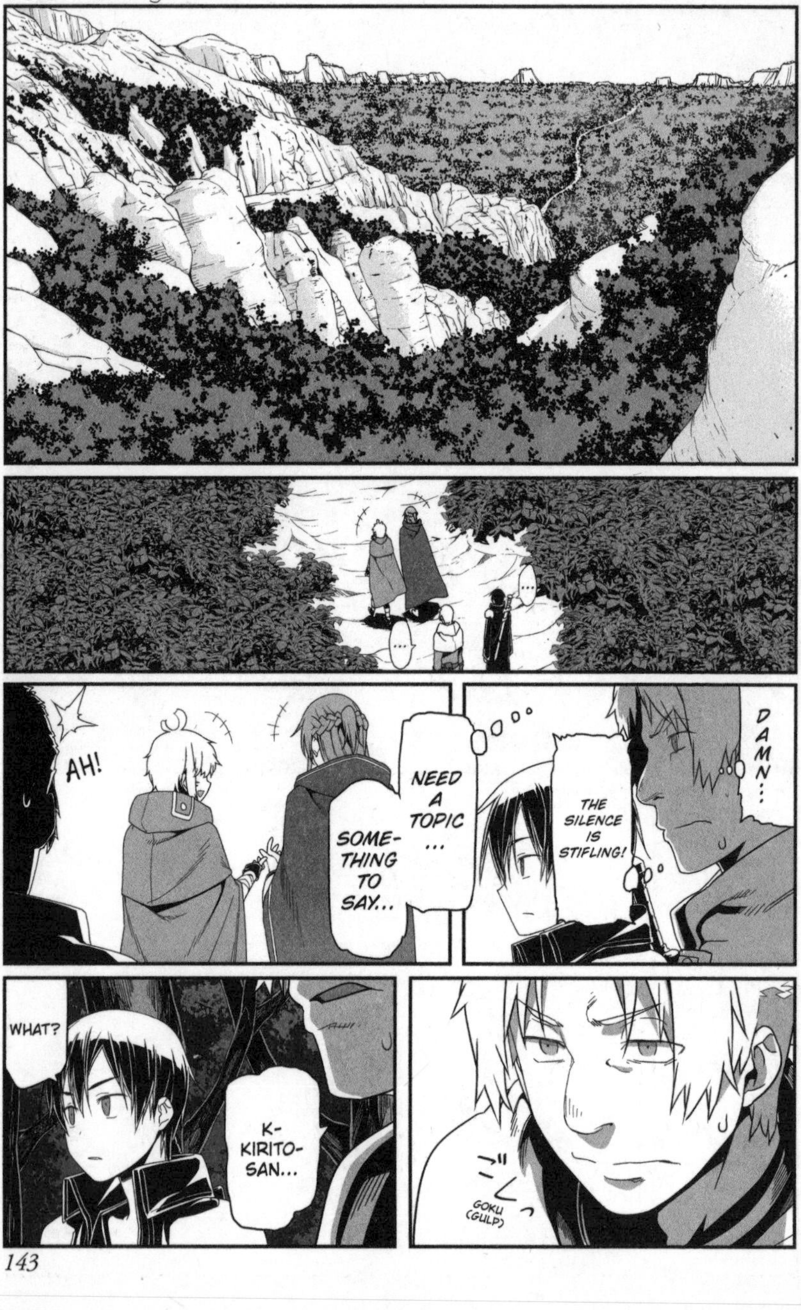
...
...
DAMN...
THE SILENCE IS STIFLING!
NEED A TOPIC...
SOME-THING TO SAY...
AH!
ごくっ
GOKU (GULP)
K-KIRITO-SAN...
WHAT?

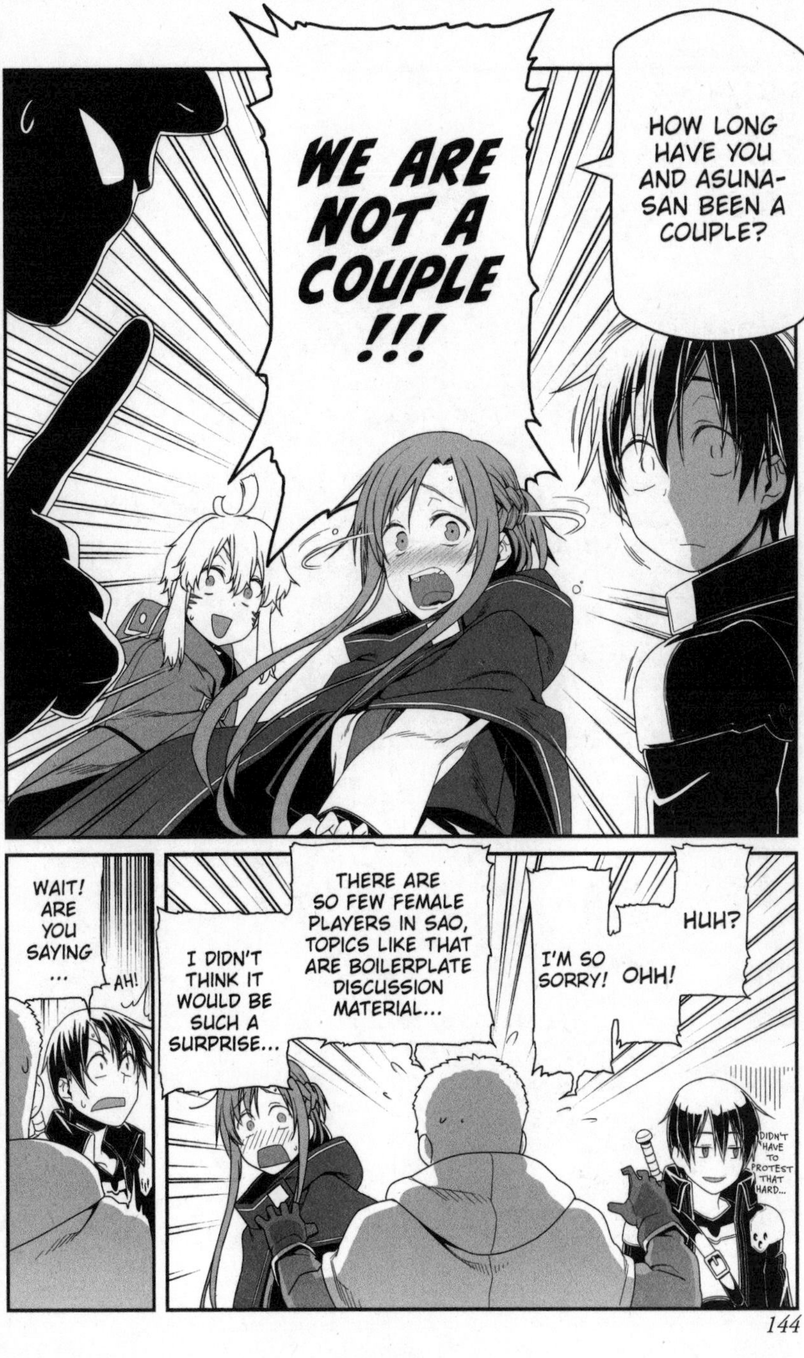
HOW LONG HAVE YOU AND ASUNA-SAN BEEN A COUPLE?
WE ARE NOT A COUPLE!!!
HUH?
OHH!
I'M SO SORRY!
THERE ARE SO FEW FEMALE PLAYERS IN SAO, TOPICS LIKE THAT ARE BOILERPLATE DISCUSSION MATERIAL...
I DIDN'T THINK IT WOULD BE SUCH A SURPRISE...
DIDN'T HAVE TO PROTEST THAT HARD...
WAIT! ARE YOU SAYING ...
AH!

SIGN: REST (4H) 4,500 COL
NIGHT (14H) 10,000 COL

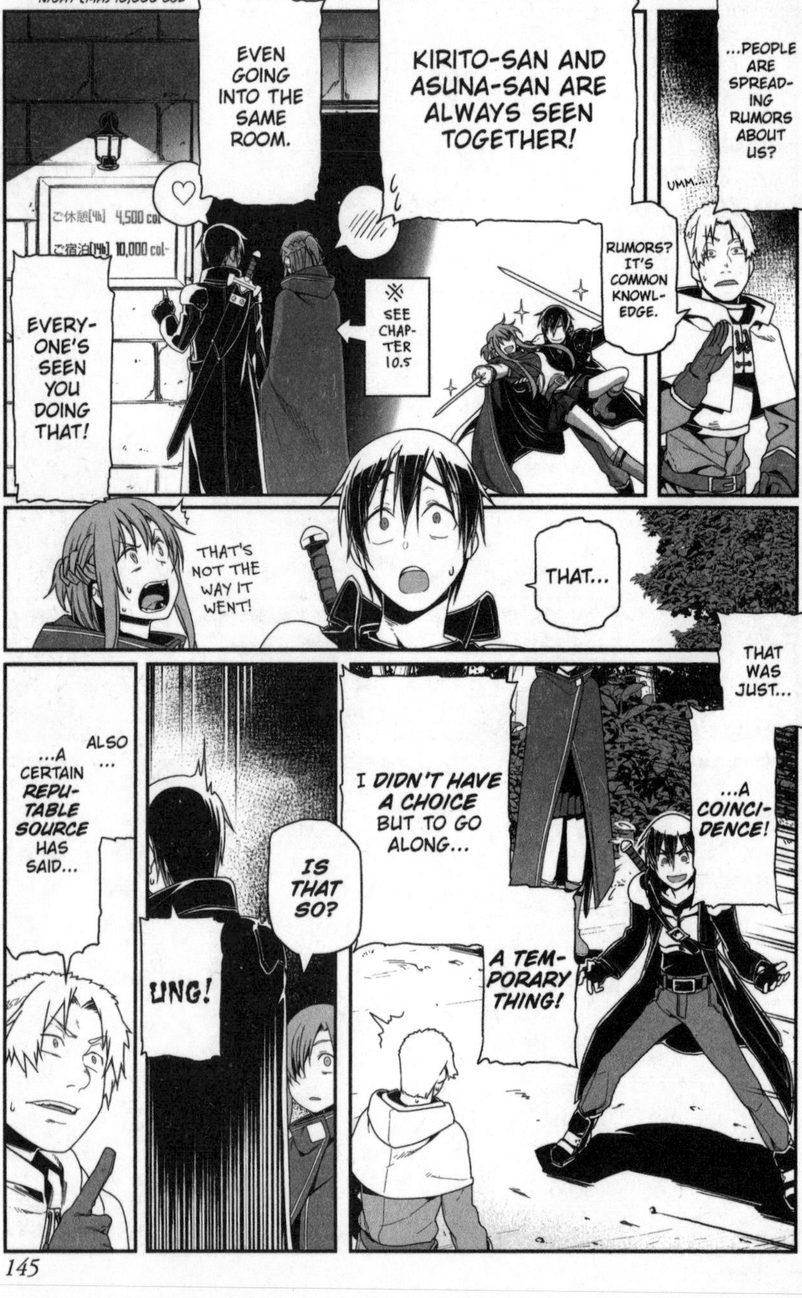

...PEOPLE ARE SPREADING RUMORS ABOUT US?
UMM...
RUMORS? IT'S COMMON KNOWLEDGE.
KIRITO-SAN AND ASUNA-SAN ARE ALWAYS SEEN TOGETHER!
EVEN GOING INTO THE SAME ROOM.
ご休憩[4h] 4,500 col
ご宿泊[14h] 10,000 col-
※ SEE CHAPTER 10.5
EVERYONE'S SEEN YOU DOING THAT!
THAT...
THAT'S NOT THE WAY IT WENT!
THAT WAS JUST...
...A COINCIDENCE!
A TEMPORARY THING!
I DIDN'T HAVE A CHOICE BUT TO GO ALONG...
IS THAT SO?
UNG!
ALSO...
...A CERTAIN REPUTABLE SOURCE HAS SAID...

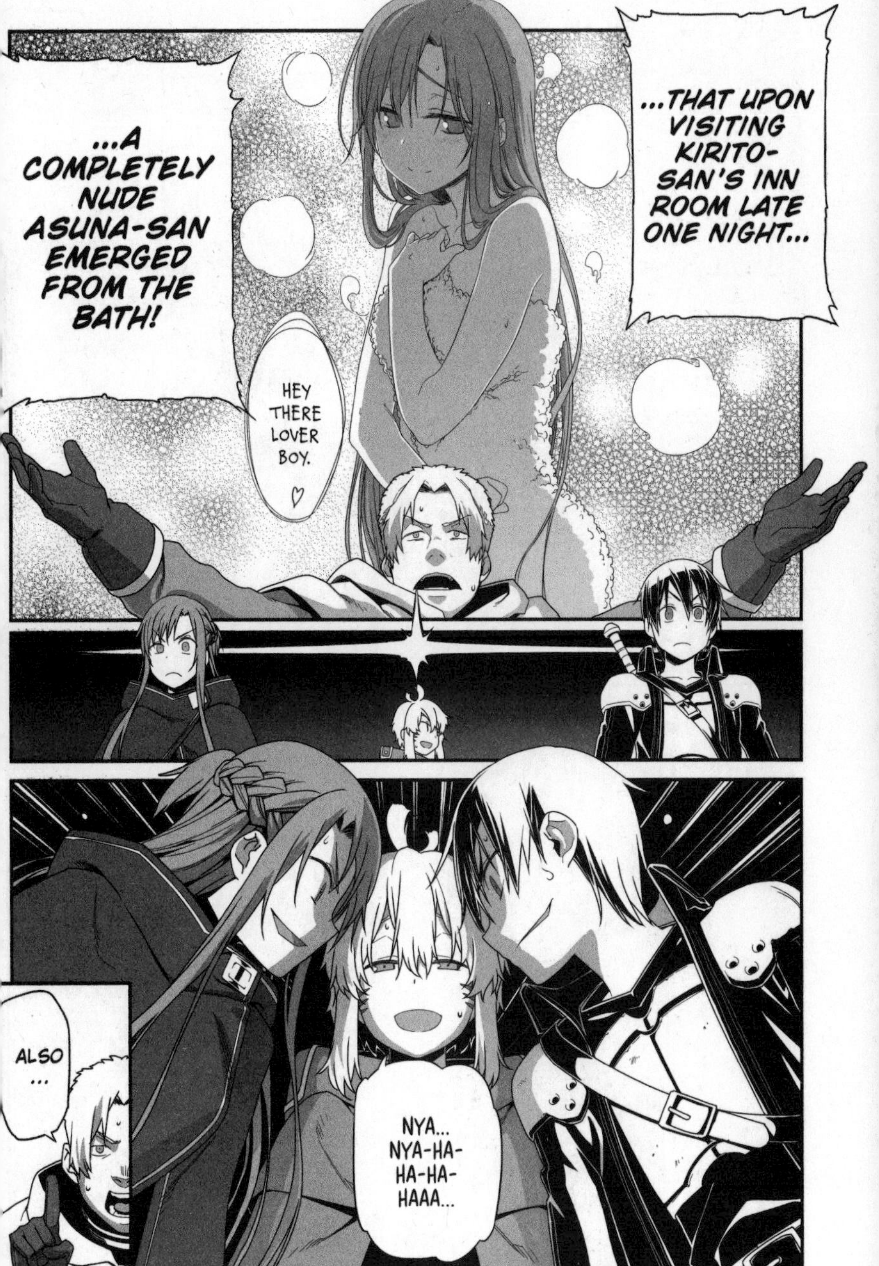
...THAT UPON VISITING KIRITO-SAN'S INN ROOM LATE ONE NIGHT...
...A COMPLETELY NUDE ASUNA-SAN EMERGED FROM THE BATH!
HEY THERE LOVER BOY. ♡
NYA... NYA-HA-HA-HA-HAAA...
ALSO ...

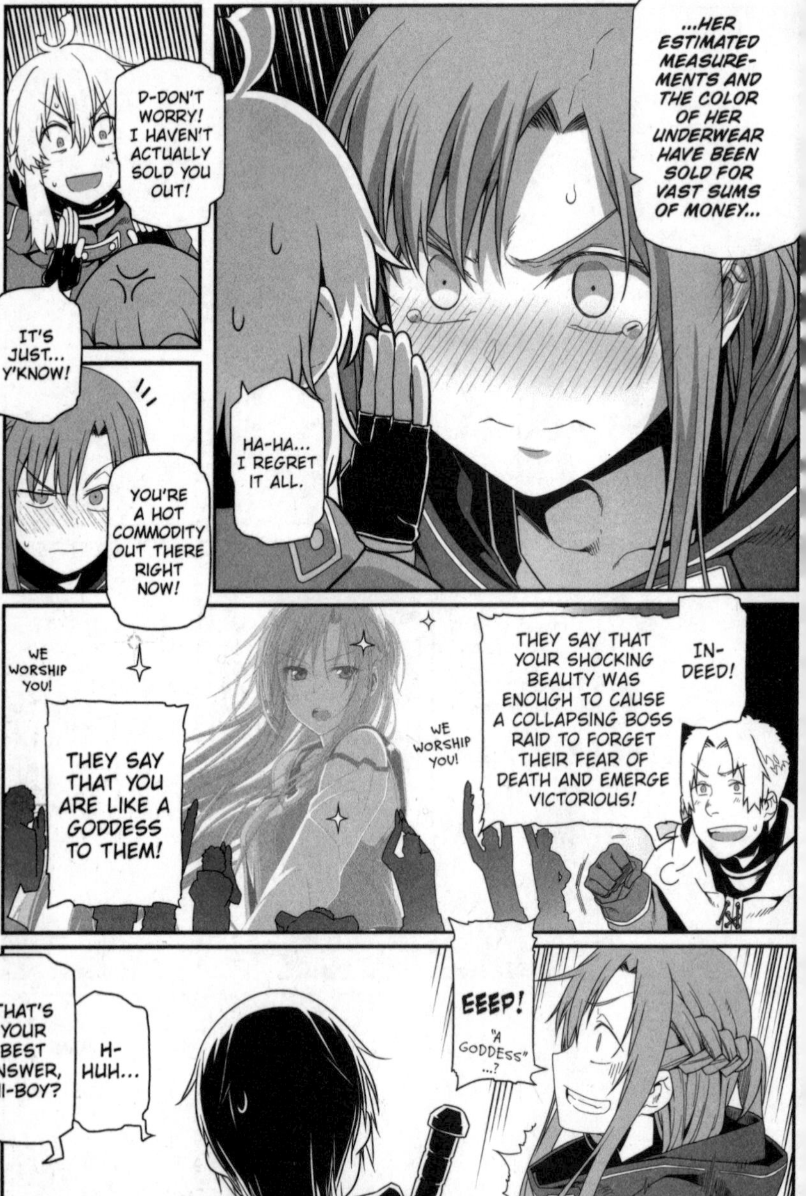
...HER ESTIMATED MEASUREMENTS AND THE COLOR OF HER UNDERWEAR HAVE BEEN SOLD FOR VAST SUMS OF MONEY...
HA-HA... I REGRET IT ALL.
D-DON'T WORRY! I HAVEN'T ACTUALLY SOLD YOU OUT!
IT'S JUST... Y'KNOW!
YOU'RE A HOT COMMODITY OUT THERE RIGHT NOW!
IN-DEED!
THEY SAY THAT YOUR SHOCKING BEAUTY WAS ENOUGH TO CAUSE A COLLAPSING BOSS RAID TO FORGET THEIR FEAR OF DEATH AND EMERGE VICTORIOUS!
WE WORSHIP YOU!
THEY SAY THAT YOU ARE LIKE A GODDESS TO THEM!
WE WORSHIP YOU!
EEEP!
"A GODDESS" ...?
H-HUH...
THAT'S YOUR BEST ANSWER, KII-BOY?

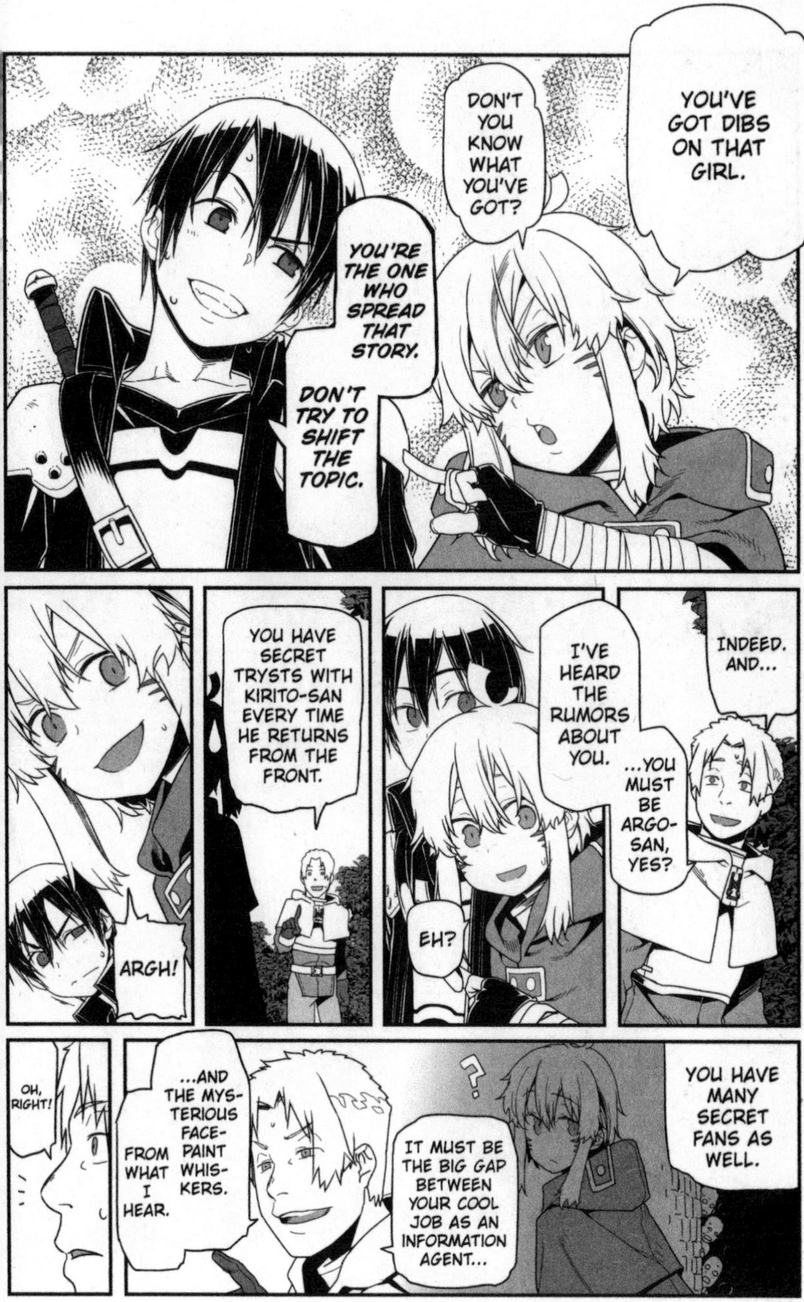
YOU'VE GOT DIBS ON THAT GIRL.
DON'T YOU KNOW WHAT YOU'VE GOT?
YOU'RE THE ONE WHO SPREAD THAT STORY.
DON'T TRY TO SHIFT THE TOPIC.
INDEED. AND...
I'VE HEARD THE RUMORS ABOUT YOU.
...YOU MUST BE ARGO-SAN, YES?
EH?
YOU HAVE SECRET TRYSTS WITH KIRITO-SAN EVERY TIME HE RETURNS FROM THE FRONT.
ARGH!
YOU HAVE MANY SECRET FANS AS WELL.
?
IT MUST BE THE BIG GAP BETWEEN YOUR COOL JOB AS AN INFORMATION AGENT...
...AND THE MYS-TERIOUS FACE-PAINT WHIS-KERS.
FROM WHAT I HEAR.
OH, RIGHT!

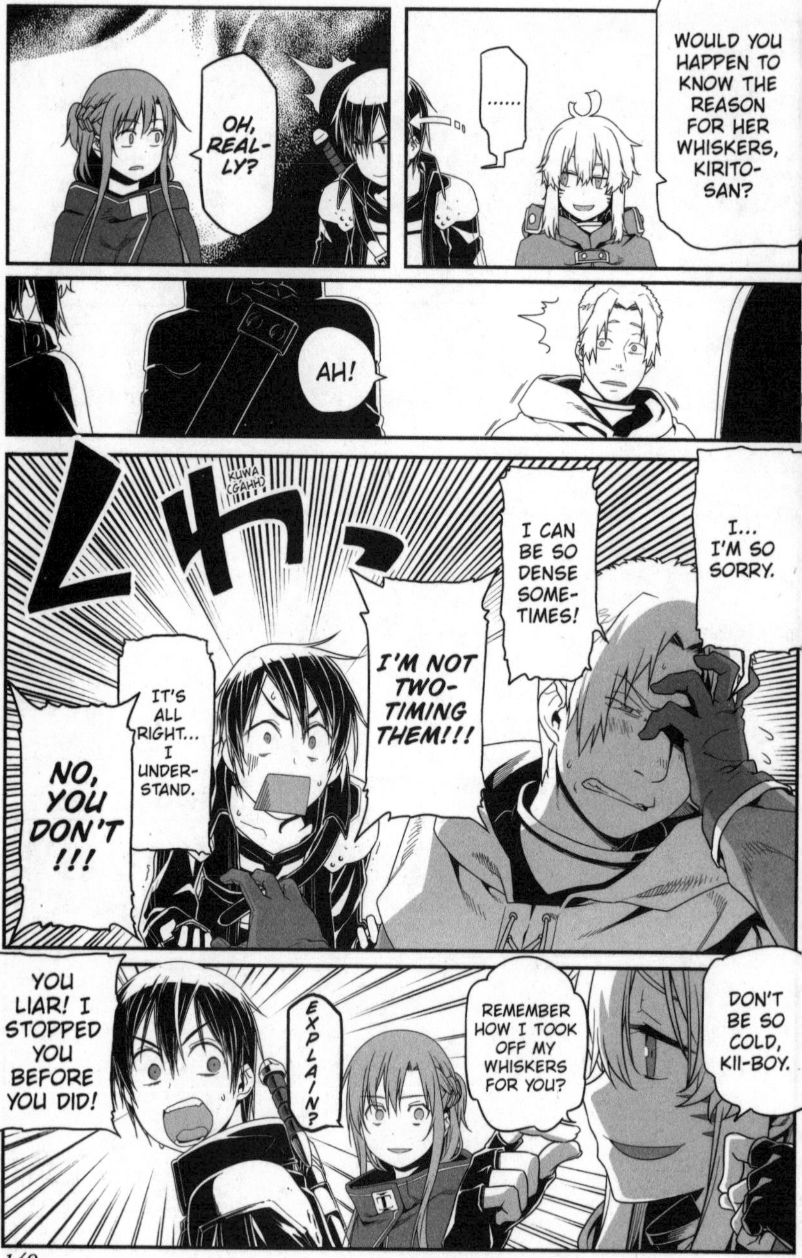
WOULD YOU HAPPEN TO KNOW THE REASON FOR HER WHISKERS, KIRITO-SAN?
......
OH, REALLY?
AH!
I... I'M SO SORRY.
I CAN BE SO DENSE SOMETIMES!
KUWA (GAHH)
I'M NOT TWO-TIMING THEM!!!
IT'S ALL RIGHT... I UNDERSTAND.
NO, YOU DON'T!!!
DON'T BE SO COLD, KII-BOY.
REMEMBER HOW I TOOK OFF MY WHISKERS FOR YOU?
EXPLAIN?
YOU LIAR! I STOPPED YOU BEFORE YOU DID!

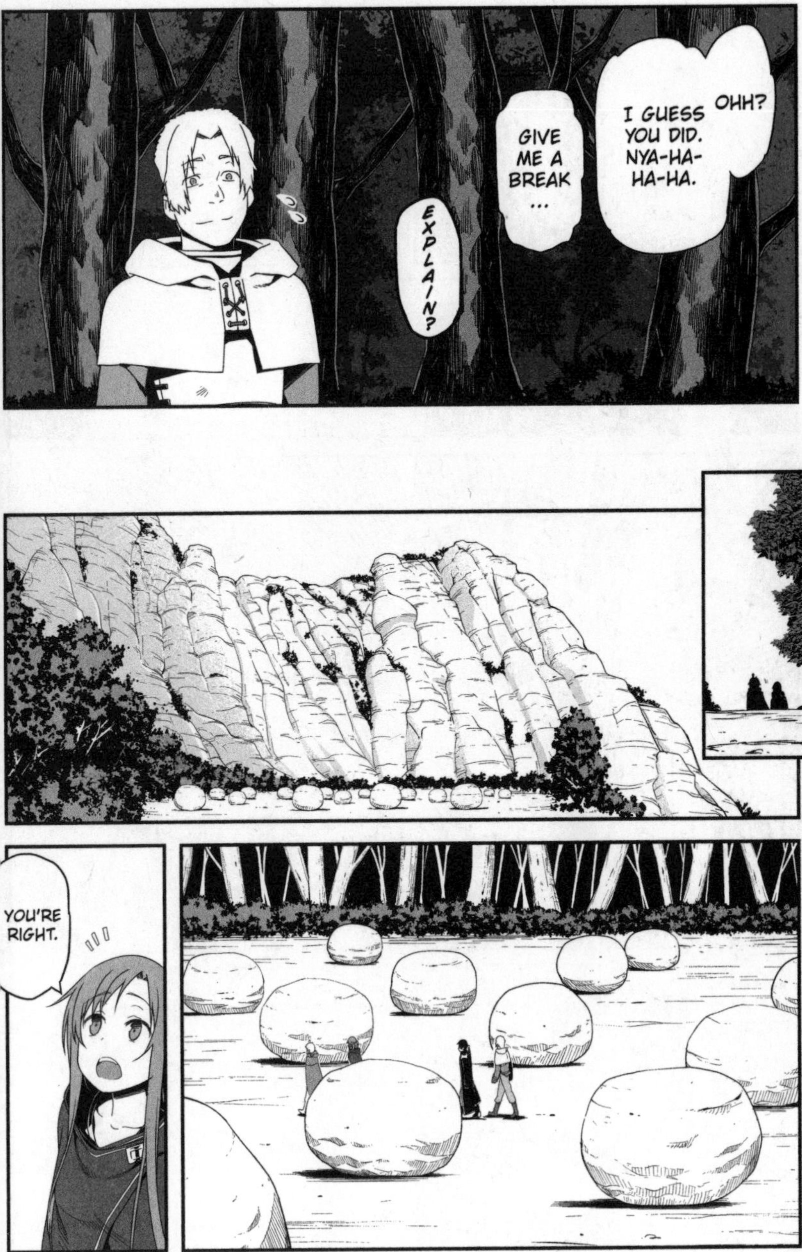
OHH?
I GUESS YOU DID. NYA-HA-HA-HA.
GIVE ME A BREAK...
EXPLAIN?
YOU'RE RIGHT.

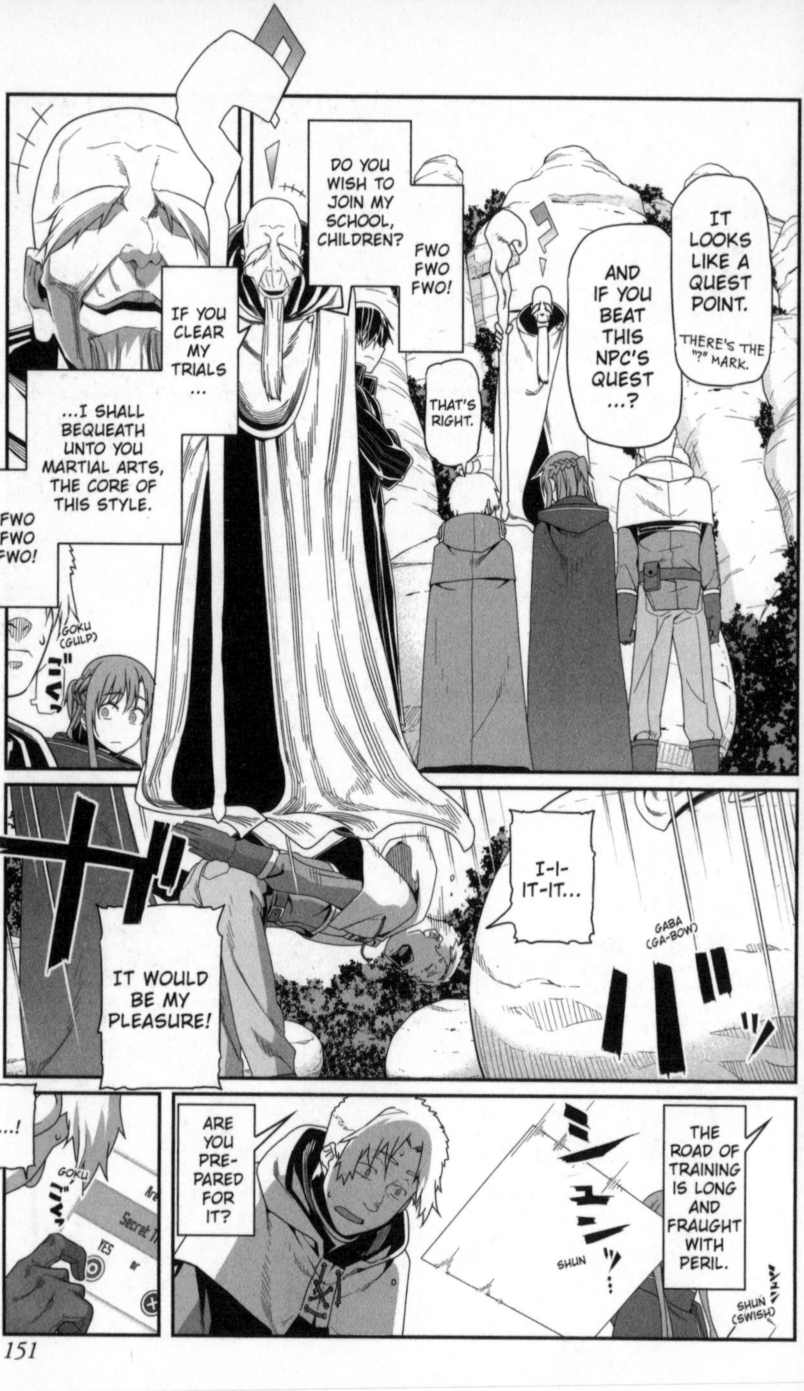
IT LOOKS LIKE A QUEST POINT.
THERE'S THE "?" MARK.
AND IF YOU BEAT THIS NPC'S QUEST ...?
THAT'S RIGHT.
DO YOU WISH TO JOIN MY SCHOOL, CHILDREN?
FWO FWO FWO!
IF YOU CLEAR MY TRIALS ...
...I SHALL BEQUEATH UNTO YOU MARTIAL ARTS, THE CORE OF THIS STYLE.
FWO FWO FWO!
GOKU (GULP)
GABA (GA-BOW)
I-I-IT-IT...
IT WOULD BE MY PLEASURE!
THE ROAD OF TRAINING IS LONG AND FRAUGHT WITH PERIL.
SHUN (SWISH)
SHUN
ARE YOU PREPARED FOR IT?
...!
GOKU
YES
or

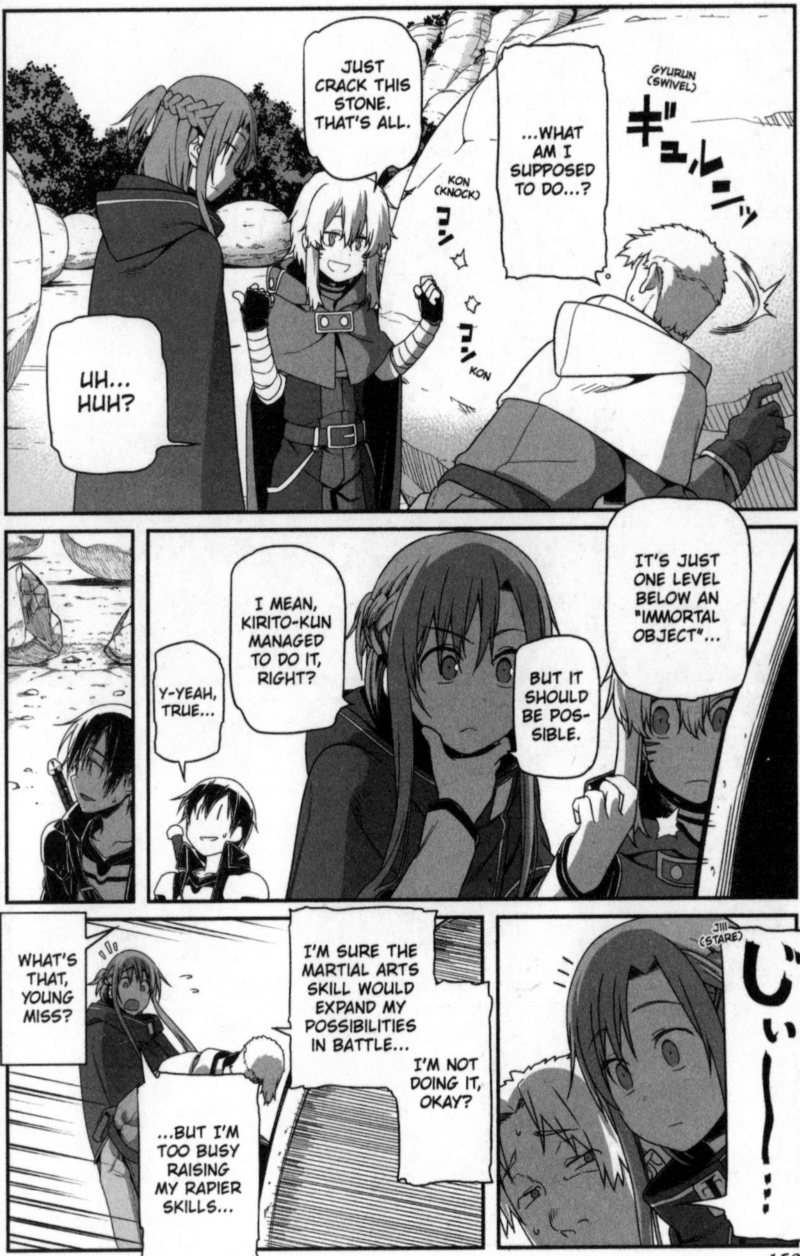
GYURUN (SWIVEL)
ギュルンッ
...WHAT AM I SUPPOSED TO DO...?
JUST CRACK THIS STONE. THAT'S ALL.
KON (KNOCK)
コン
コン
KON
UH... HUH?
IT'S JUST ONE LEVEL BELOW AN "IMMORTAL OBJECT"...
BUT IT SHOULD BE POS-SIBLE.
I MEAN, KIRITO-KUN MANAGED TO DO IT, RIGHT?
Y-YEAH, TRUE...
JIII (STARE)
じぃ〜〜…
I'M SURE THE MARTIAL ARTS SKILL WOULD EXPAND MY POSSIBILITIES IN BATTLE...
...BUT I'M TOO BUSY RAISING MY RAPIER SKILLS...
I'M NOT DOING IT, OKAY?
WHAT'S THAT, YOUNG MISS?

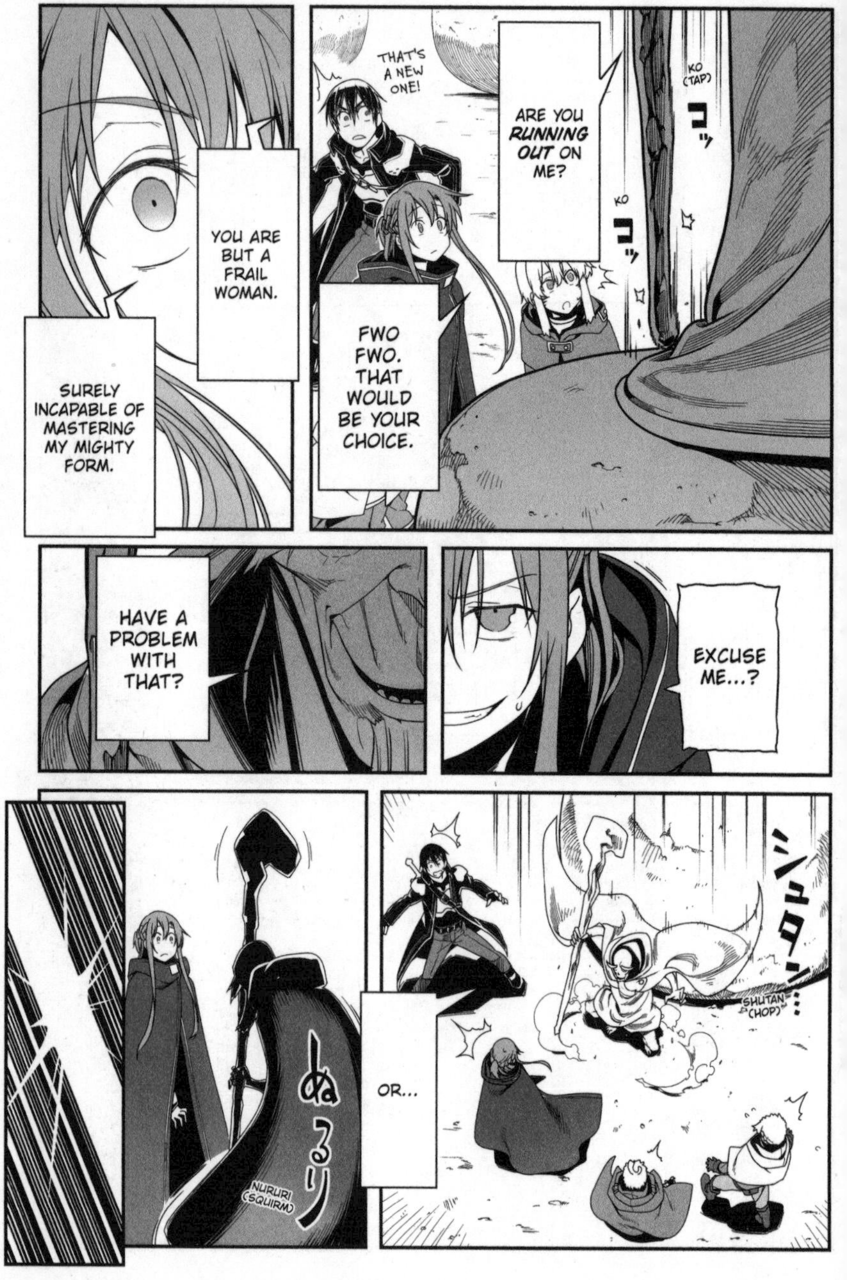

KO (TAP)
コッ
ARE YOU *RUNNING OUT* ON ME?
KO
コッ
THAT'S A NEW ONE!
FWO FWO. THAT WOULD BE YOUR CHOICE.
YOU ARE BUT A FRAIL WOMAN.
SURELY INCAPABLE OF MASTERING MY MIGHTY FORM.
EXCUSE ME...?
HAVE A PROBLEM WITH THAT?
シュタン
SHUTAN (HOP)
OR...
ぬるり
NURURI (SQUIRM)

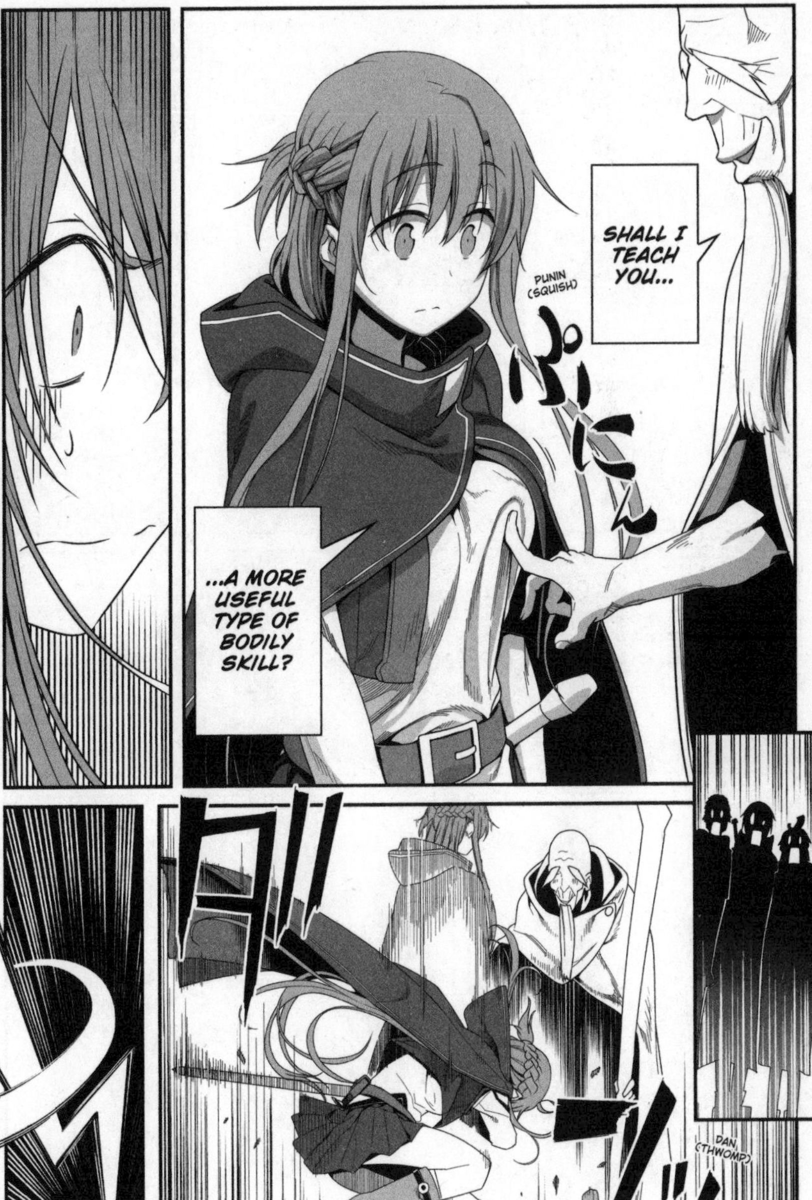
SHALL I TEACH YOU...
PUNIN (SQUISH)
ぷにん
...A MORE USEFUL TYPE OF BODILY SKILL?
DAN (THWOMP)

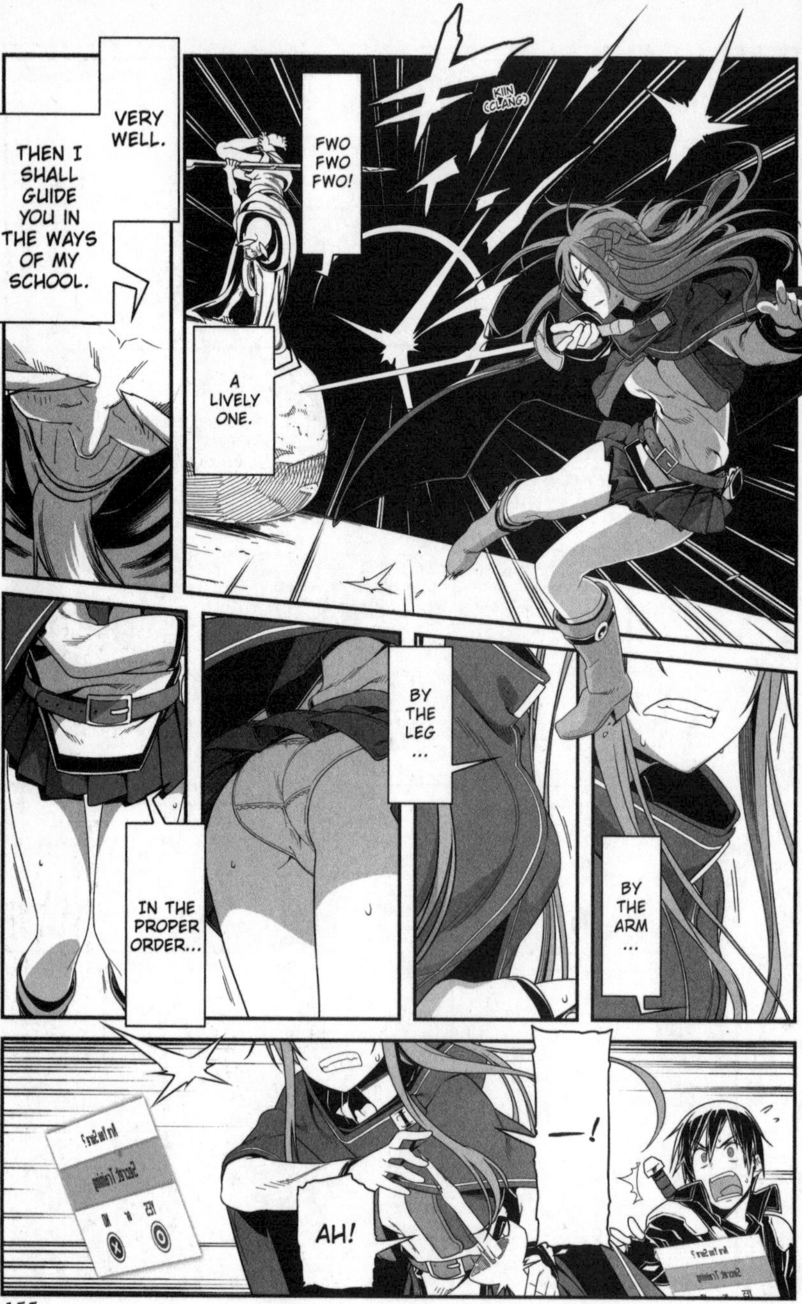
KIIN (CLANG)
FWO FWO FWO!
A LIVELY ONE.
VERY WELL.
THEN I SHALL GUIDE YOU IN THE WAYS OF MY SCHOOL.
BY THE ARM...
BY THE LEG...
IN THE PROPER ORDER...
—!
AH!

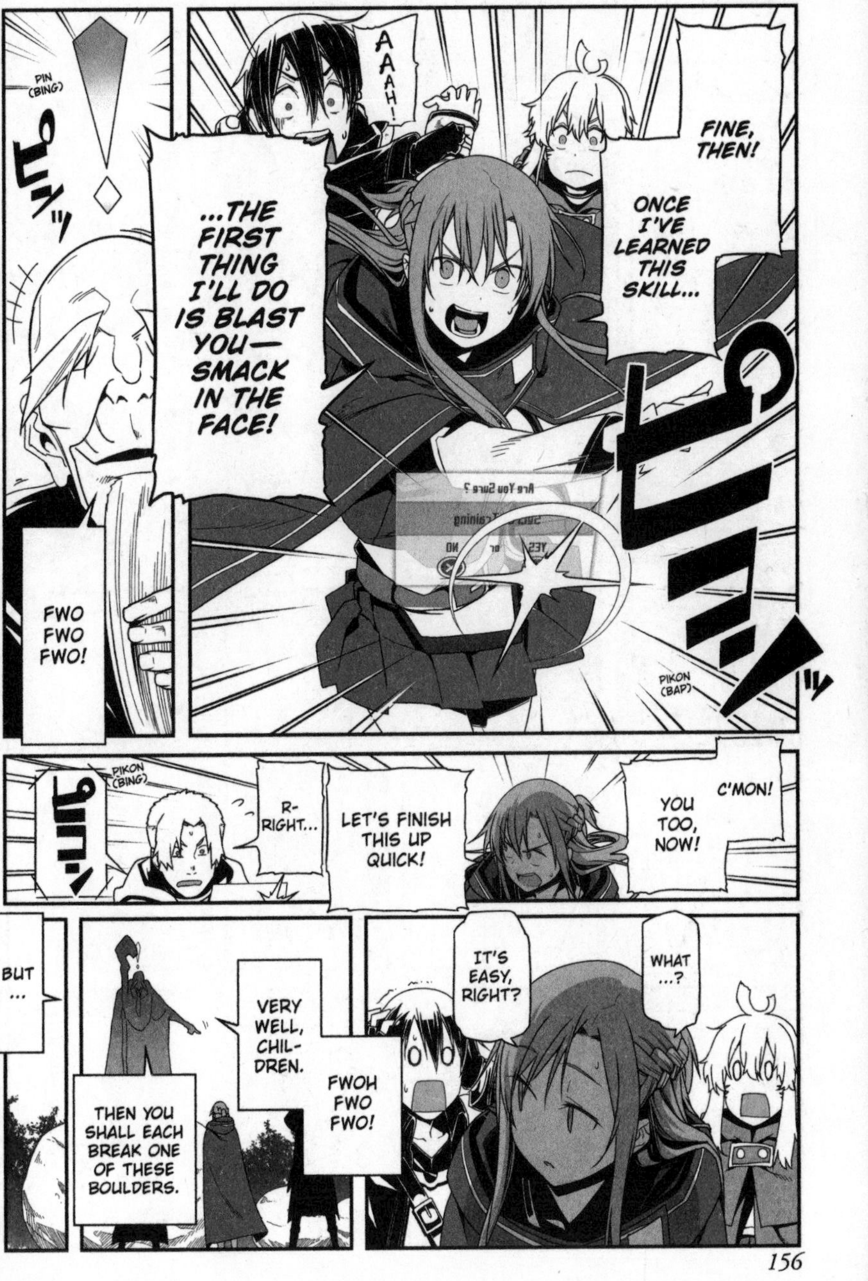

AAAH!
FINE, THEN!
ONCE I'VE LEARNED THIS SKILL...
...THE FIRST THING I'LL DO IS BLAST YOU—SMACK IN THE FACE!
PIKON (BAP)
PIN (BING)
FWO FWO FWO!
C'MON!
YOU TOO, NOW!
LET'S FINISH THIS UP QUICK!
R-RIGHT...
PIKON (BING)
WHAT ...?
IT'S EASY, RIGHT?
VERY WELL, CHILDREN.
FWOH FWO FWO!
THEN YOU SHALL EACH BREAK ONE OF THESE BOULDERS.
BUT ...

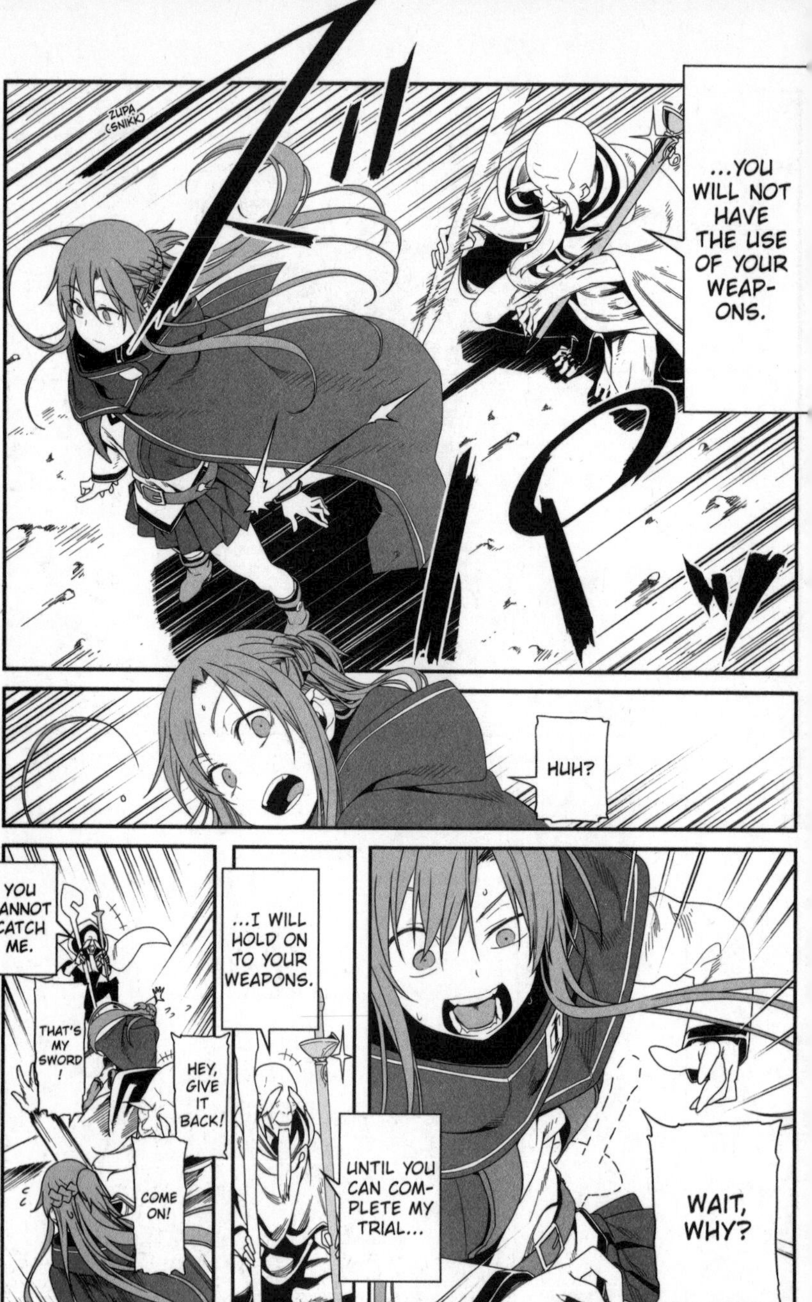
...YOU WILL NOT HAVE THE USE OF YOUR WEAPONS.
ZUPA (SNIKK)
HUH?
WAIT, WHY?
...I WILL HOLD ON TO YOUR WEAPONS.
UNTIL YOU CAN COMPLETE MY TRIAL...
YOU CANNOT CATCH ME.
HEY, GIVE IT BACK!
THAT'S MY SWORD!
COME ON!

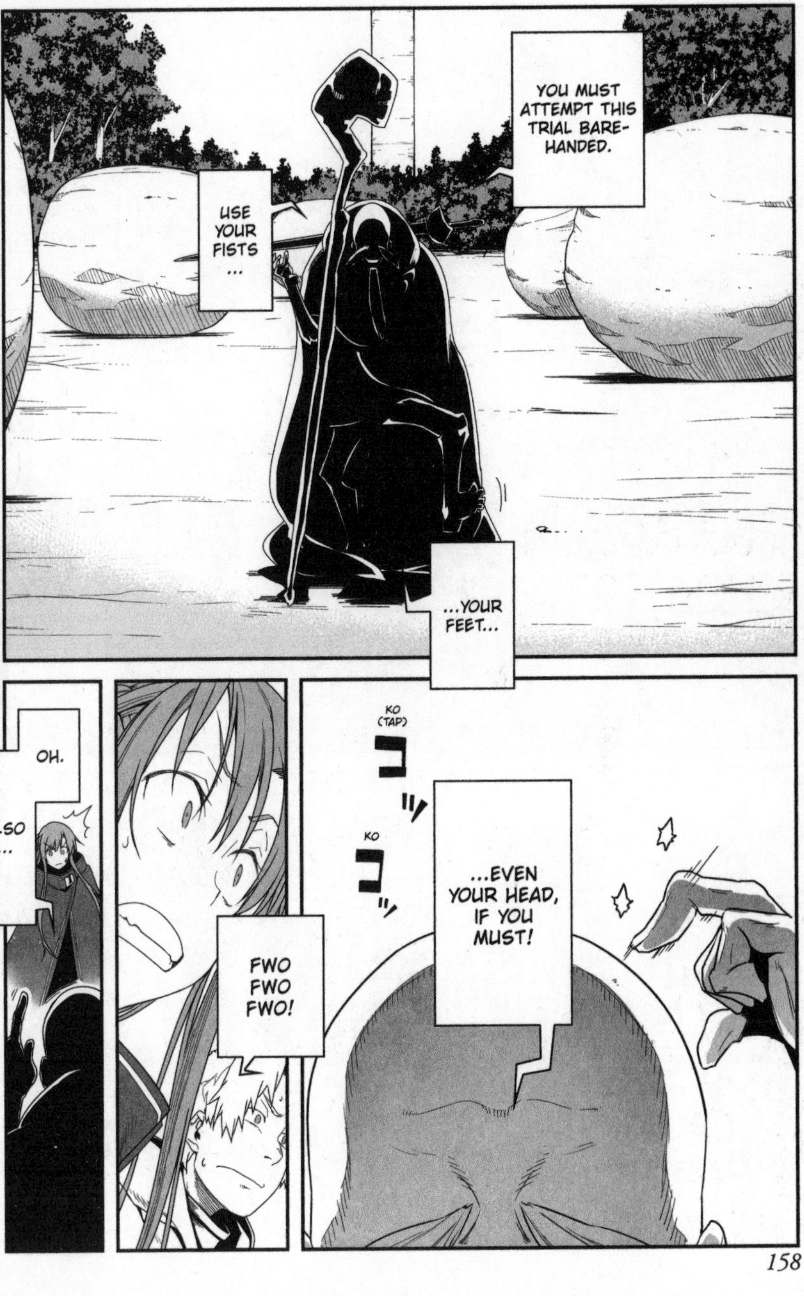

YOU MUST ATTEMPT THIS TRIAL BARE-HANDED.
USE YOUR FISTS ...
...YOUR FEET...
KO (TAP)
KO
...EVEN YOUR HEAD, IF YOU MUST!
FWO FWO FWO!
OH.
LSO ...

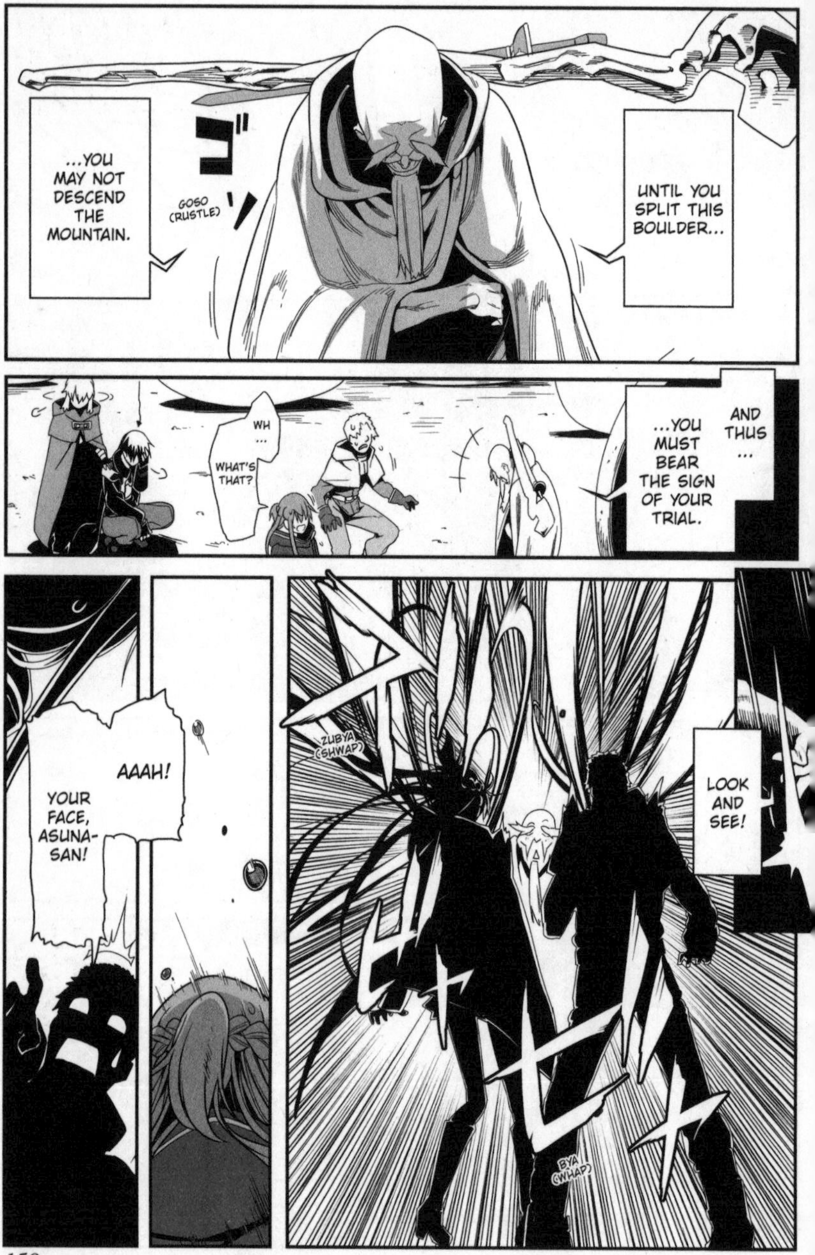
UNTIL YOU SPLIT THIS BOULDER...
GOSO (RUSTLE)
...YOU MAY NOT DESCEND THE MOUNTAIN.
AND THUS...
...YOU MUST BEAR THE SIGN OF YOUR TRIAL.
WH... WHAT'S THAT?
LOOK AND SEE!
ZUBYA (SHWAP)
BYA (WHAP)
AAAH!
YOUR FACE, ASUNA-SAN!

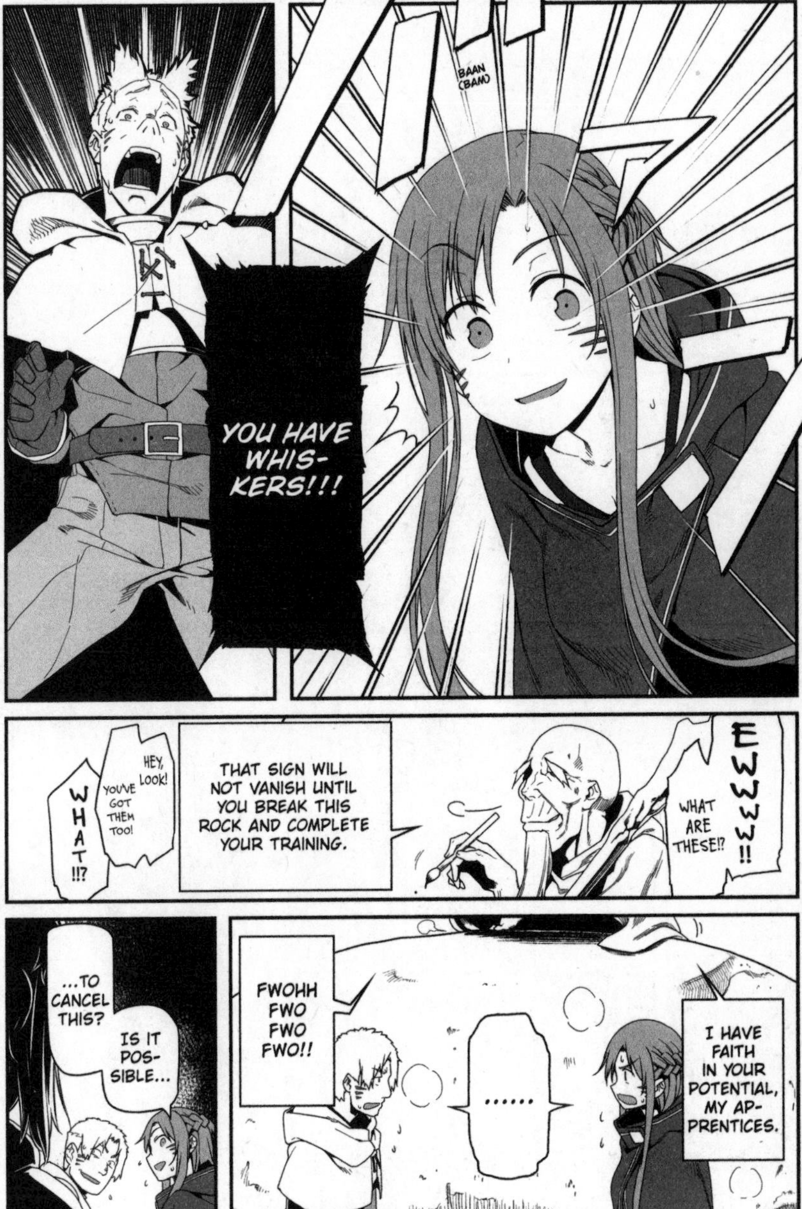
BAAN (BAM)
YOU HAVE WHIS-KERS!!!
EWWWWW!!
WHAT ARE THESE!?
THAT SIGN WILL NOT VANISH UNTIL YOU BREAK THIS ROCK AND COMPLETE YOUR TRAINING.
HEY, LOOK!
YOU'VE GOT THEM TOO!
WHAT!!?
I HAVE FAITH IN YOUR POTENTIAL, MY AP-PRENTICES.
......
FWOHH FWO FWO FWO!!
IS IT POS-SIBLE...
...TO CANCEL THIS?

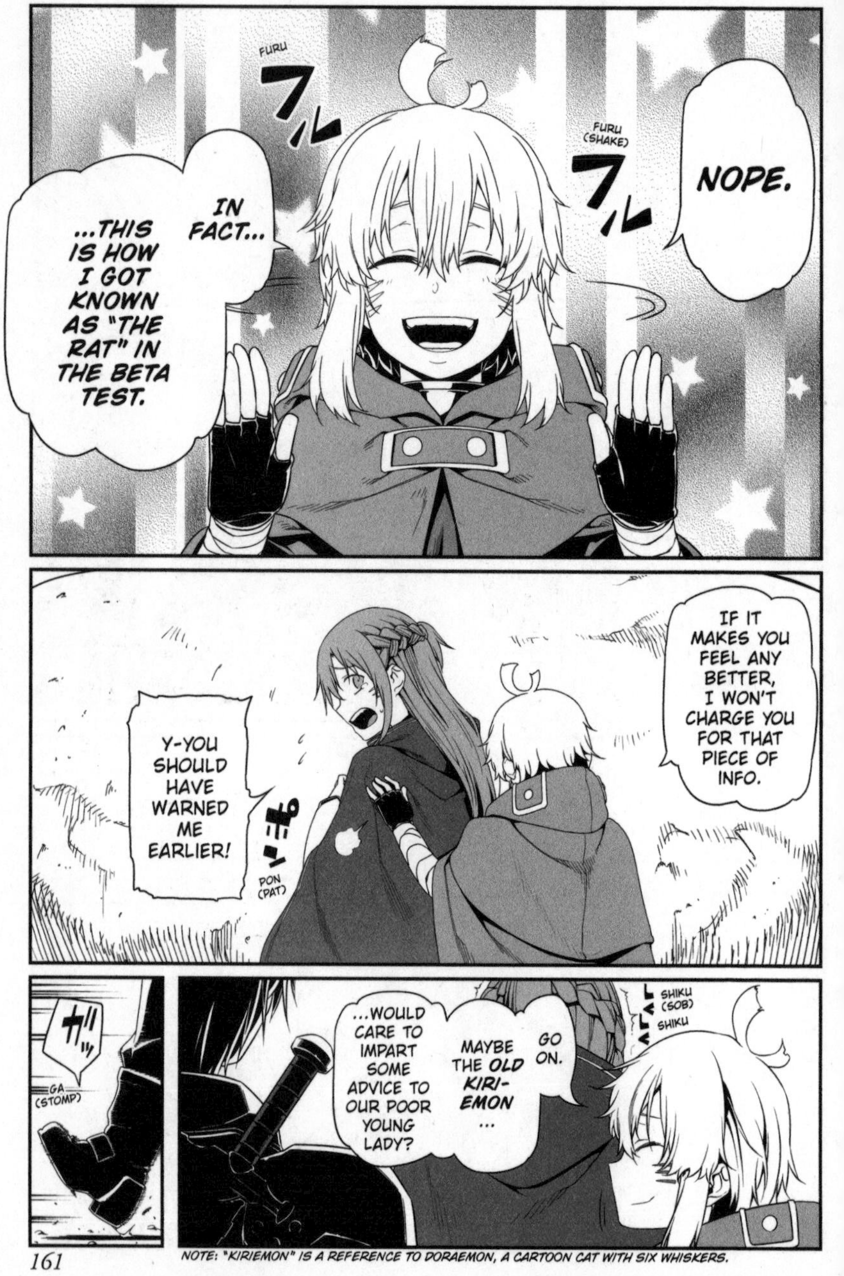
FURU (SHAKE)
NOPE.
FURU
IN FACT...
...THIS IS HOW I GOT KNOWN AS "THE RAT" IN THE BETA TEST.
IF IT MAKES YOU FEEL ANY BETTER, I WON'T CHARGE YOU FOR THAT PIECE OF INFO.
PON (PAT)
Y-YOU SHOULD HAVE WARNED ME EARLIER!
SHIKU (SOB) SHIKU
GO ON.
MAYBE THE OLD KIRIEMON...
...WOULD CARE TO IMPART SOME ADVICE TO OUR POOR YOUNG LADY?
GA (STOMP)

NOTE: "KIRIEMON" IS A REFERENCE TO DORAEMON, A CARTOON CAT WITH SIX WHISKERS.

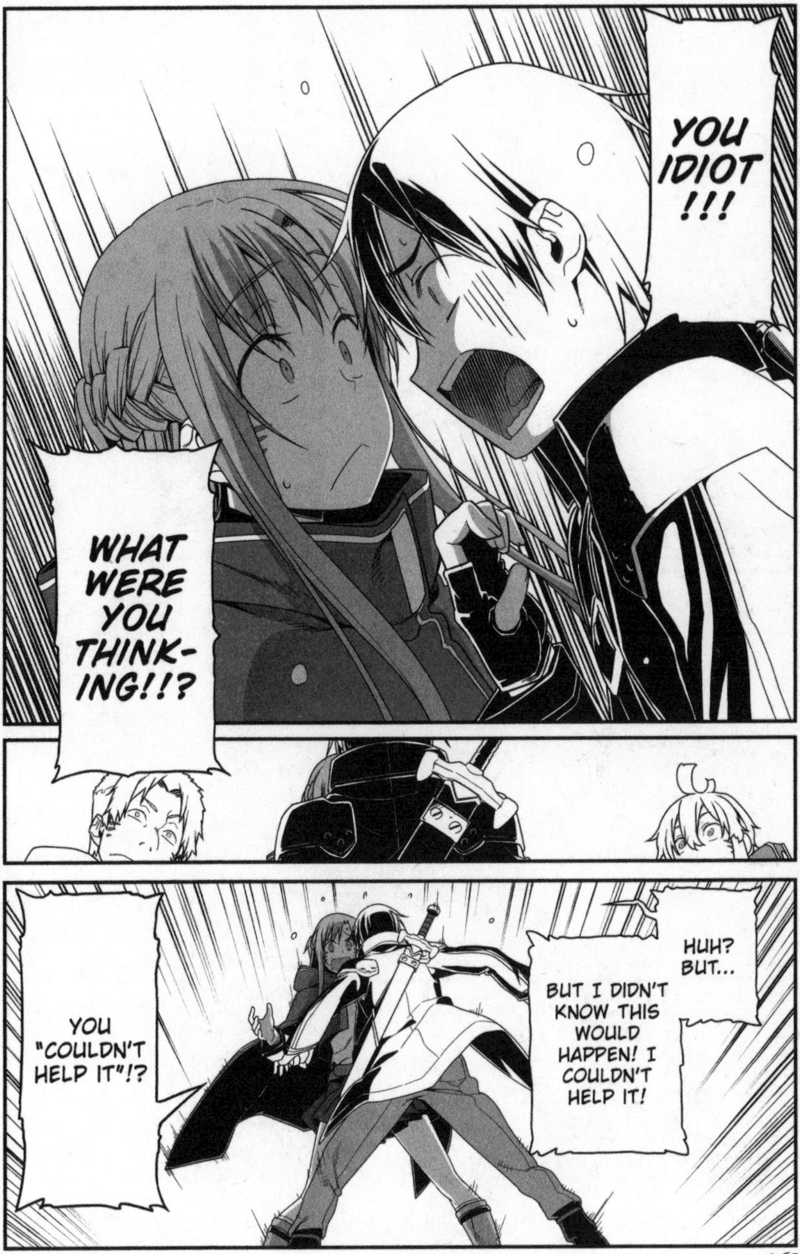
YOU IDIOT!!!
WHAT WERE YOU THINKING!!?
HUH? BUT...
BUT I DIDN'T KNOW THIS WOULD HAPPEN! I COULDN'T HELP IT!
YOU "COULDN'T HELP IT"!?

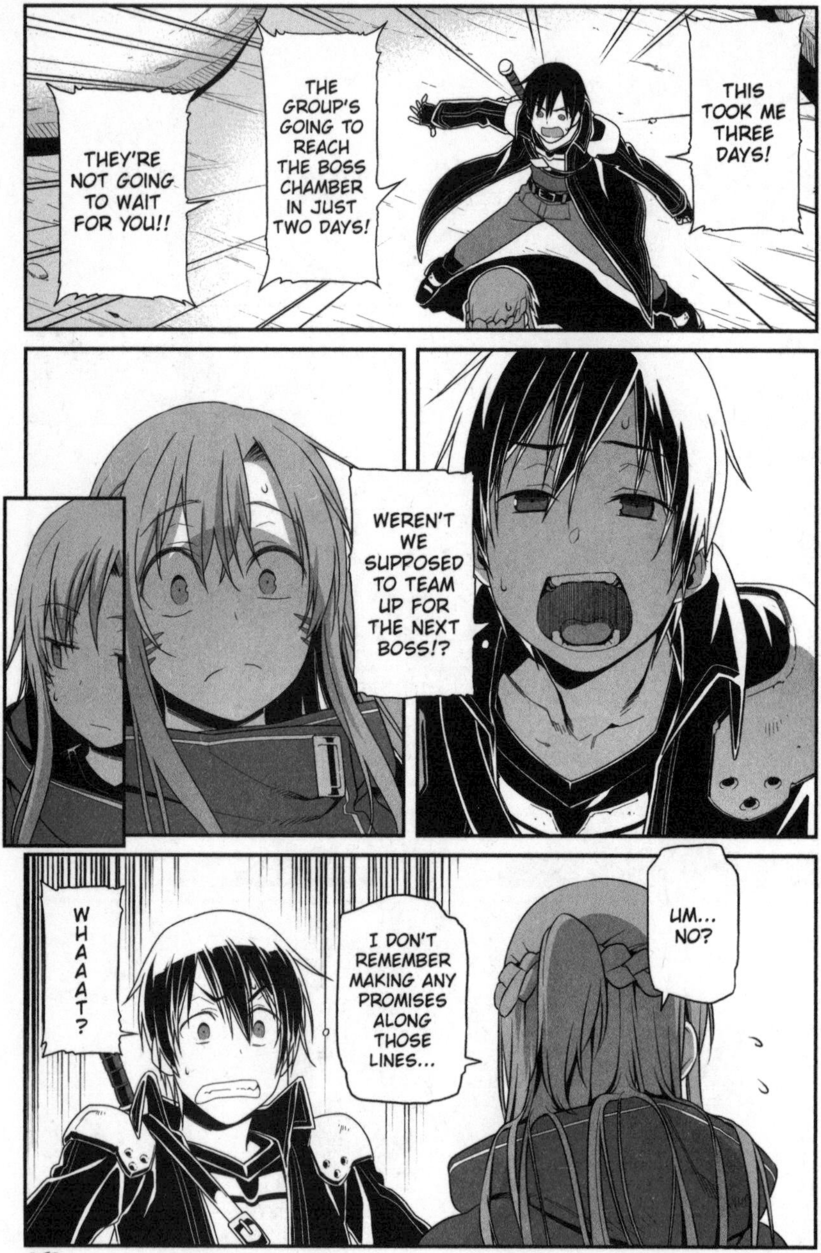
THIS TOOK ME THREE DAYS!
THE GROUP'S GOING TO REACH THE BOSS CHAMBER IN JUST TWO DAYS!
THEY'RE NOT GOING TO WAIT FOR YOU!!
WEREN'T WE SUPPOSED TO TEAM UP FOR THE NEXT BOSS!?
UM... NO?
I DON'T REMEMBER MAKING ANY PROMISES ALONG THOSE LINES...
WHAAAAT?

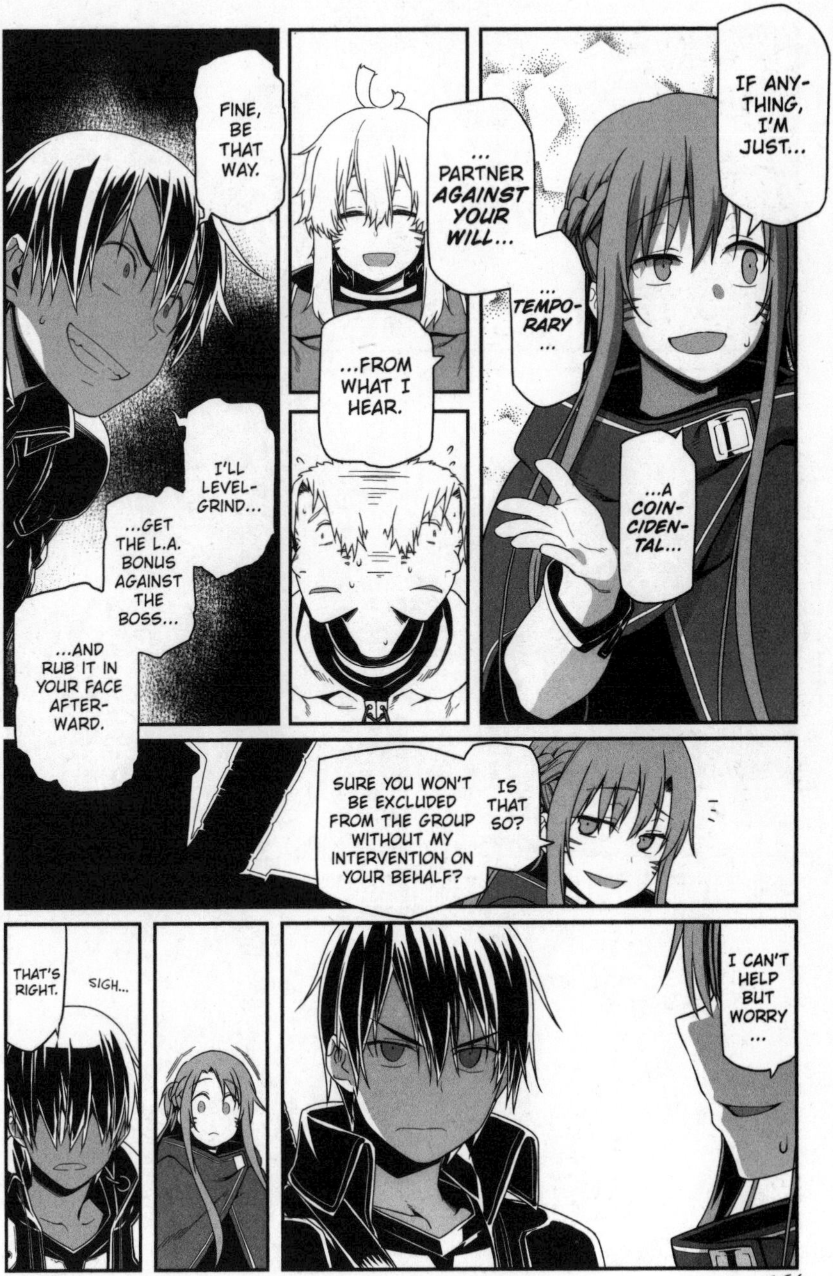

IF ANY-THING, I'M JUST...
...TEMPO-RARY...
...A COIN-CIDEN-TAL...
...PARTNER AGAINST YOUR WILL...
...FROM WHAT I HEAR.
FINE, BE THAT WAY.
I'LL LEVEL-GRIND...
...GET THE L.A. BONUS AGAINST THE BOSS...
...AND RUB IT IN YOUR FACE AFTER-WARD.
IS THAT SO?
SURE YOU WON'T BE EXCLUDED FROM THE GROUP WITHOUT MY INTERVENTION ON YOUR BEHALF?
I CAN'T HELP BUT WORRY...
SIGH...
THAT'S RIGHT.

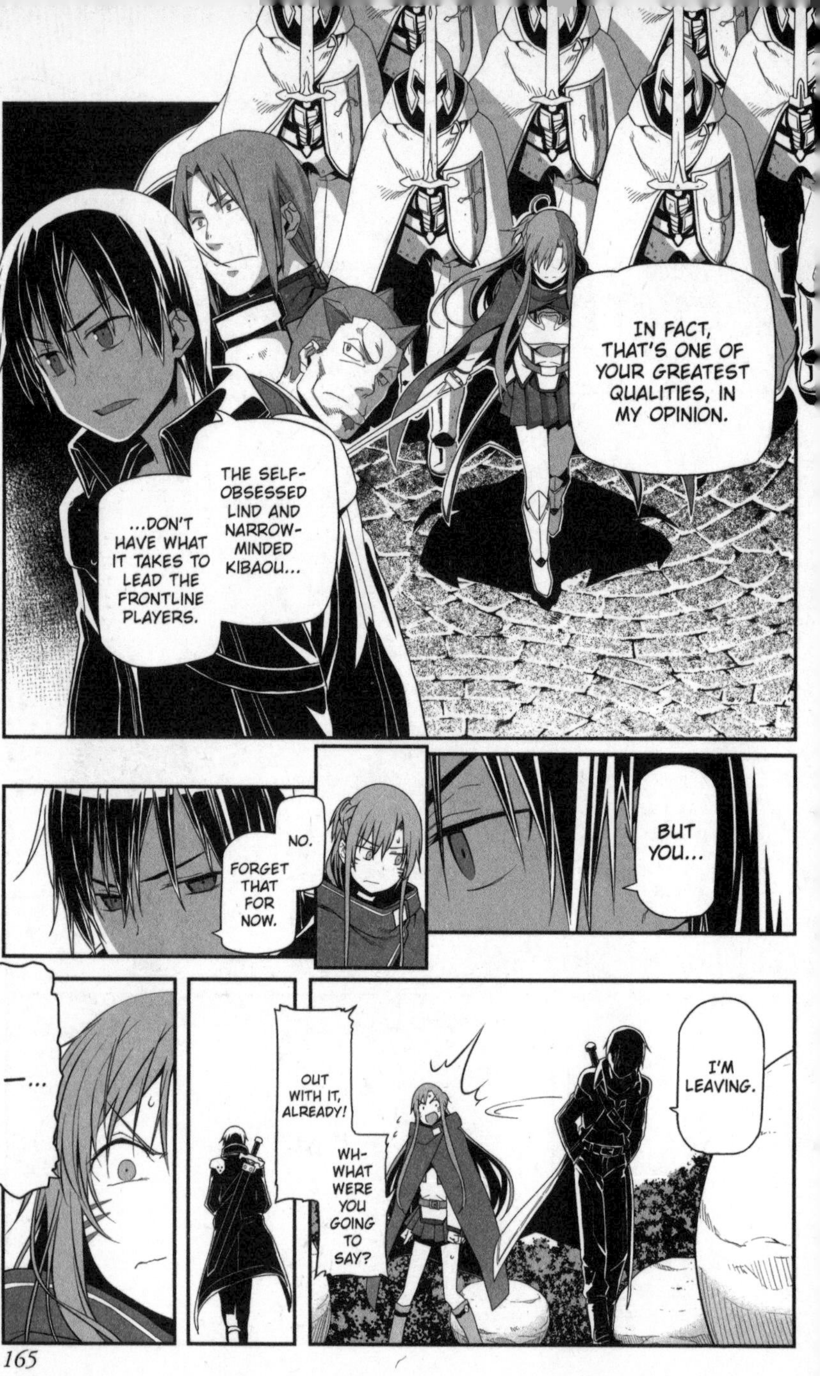
IN FACT, THAT'S ONE OF YOUR GREATEST QUALITIES, IN MY OPINION.
THE SELF-OBSESSED LIND AND NARROW-MINDED KIBAOU...
...DON'T HAVE WHAT IT TAKES TO LEAD THE FRONTLINE PLAYERS.
BUT YOU...
NO.
FORGET THAT FOR NOW.
I'M LEAVING.
WH-WHAT WERE YOU GOING TO SAY?
OUT WITH IT, ALREADY!
—...

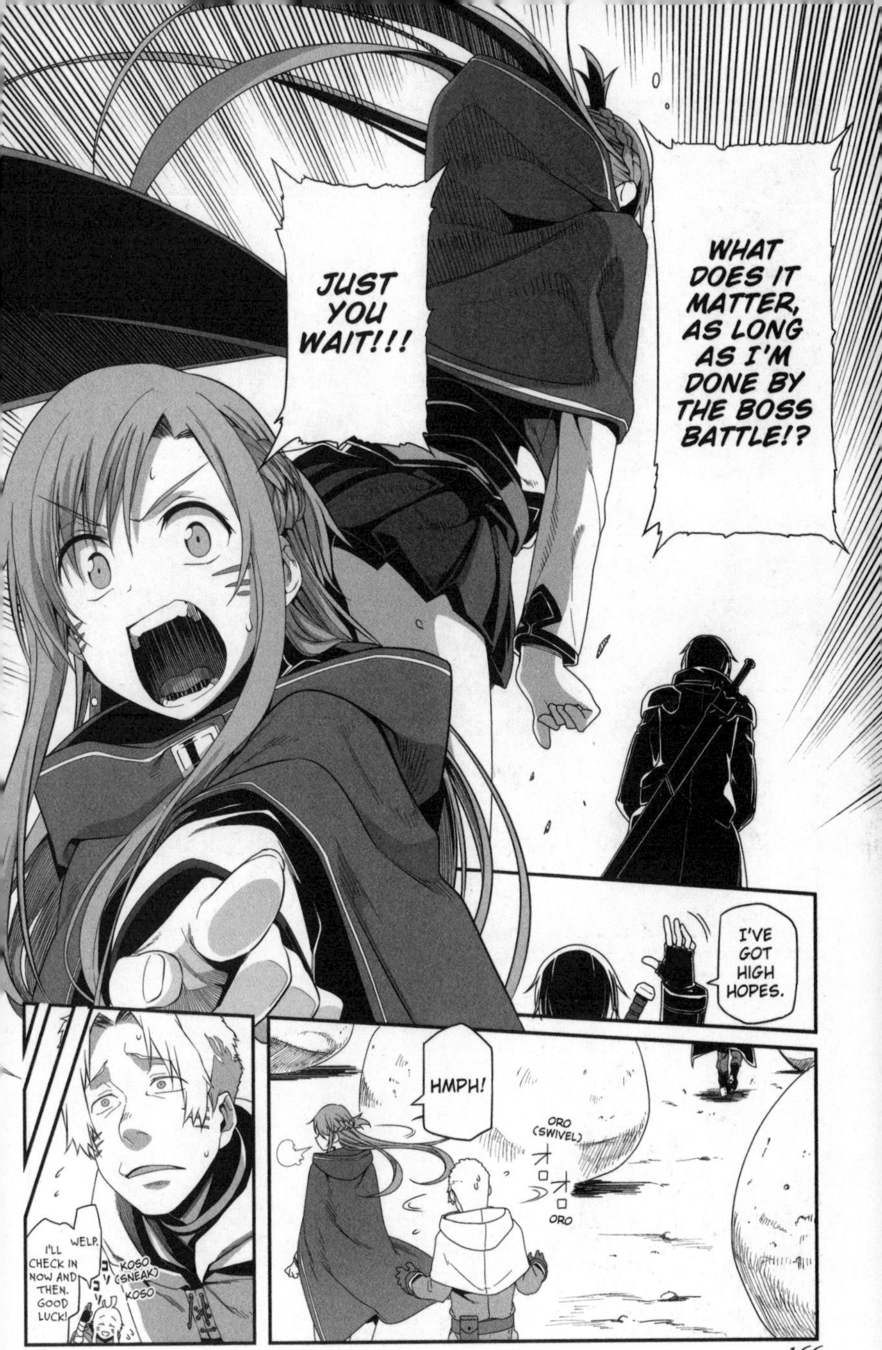
WHAT DOES IT MATTER, AS LONG AS I'M DONE BY THE BOSS BATTLE!?
JUST YOU WAIT!!!
I'VE GOT HIGH HOPES.
HMPH!
ORO (SWIVEL)
ORO
WELP.
I'LL CHECK IN NOW AND THEN. GOOD LUCK!
KOSO (SNEAK)
KOSO

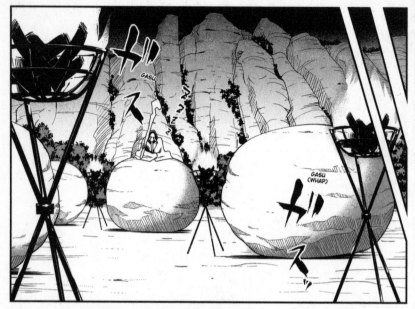

GASU

GASU
(WHAP)

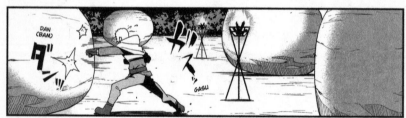

DAN
(BAM)

GASU

HOW
LONG HAS IT
BEEN SINCE
I SLEPT
OUTDOORS?

GOOD
GRIEF
...

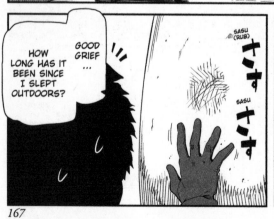

SASU
(RUB)

SASU

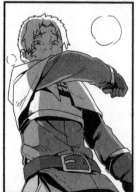

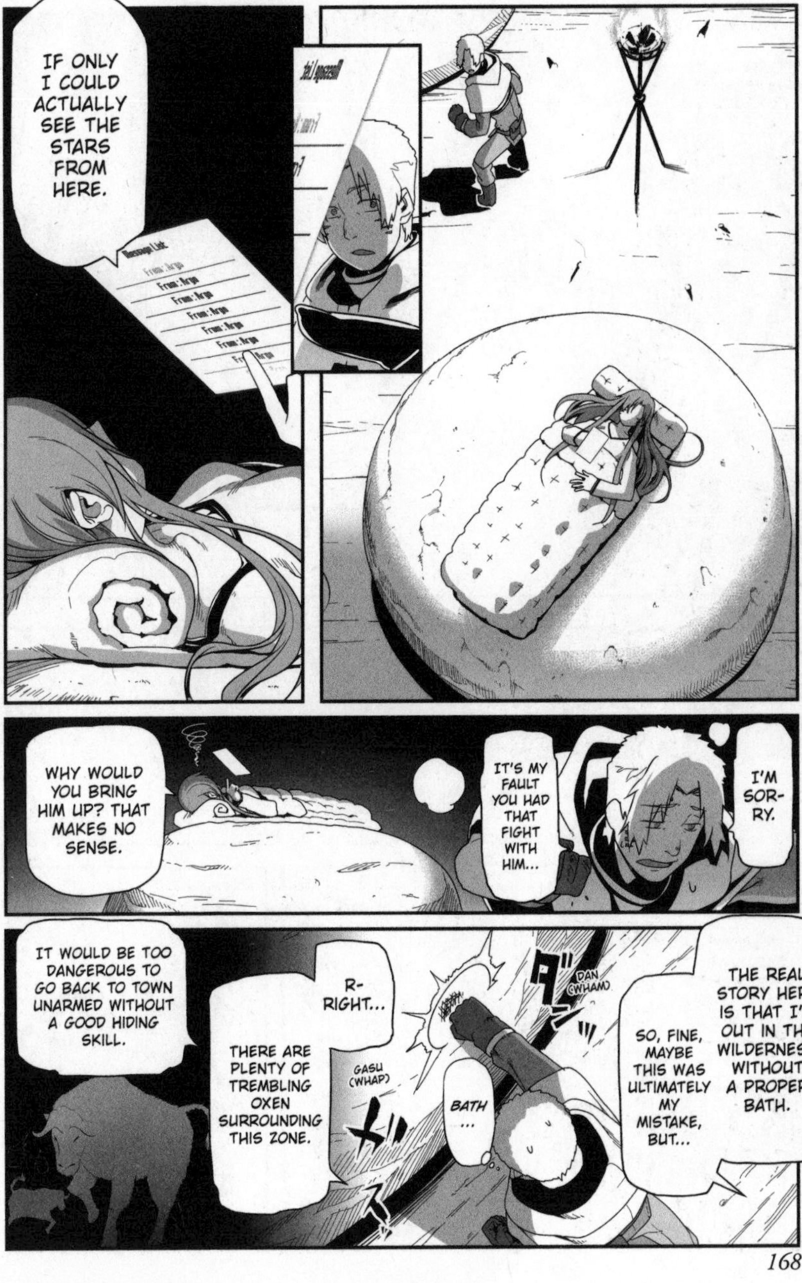
IF ONLY I COULD ACTUALLY SEE THE STARS FROM HERE.
I'M SORRY.
IT'S MY FAULT YOU HAD THAT FIGHT WITH HIM...
WHY WOULD YOU BRING HIM UP? THAT MAKES NO SENSE.
THE REAL STORY HERE IS THAT I'M OUT IN THE WILDERNESS WITHOUT A PROPER BATH.
SO, FINE, MAYBE THIS WAS ULTIMATELY MY MISTAKE, BUT...
DAN (WHAM)
BATH...
GASU (WHAP)
R- RIGHT...
THERE ARE PLENTY OF TREMBLING OXEN SURROUNDING THIS ZONE.
IT WOULD BE TOO DANGEROUS TO GO BACK TO TOWN UNARMED WITHOUT A GOOD HIDING SKILL.

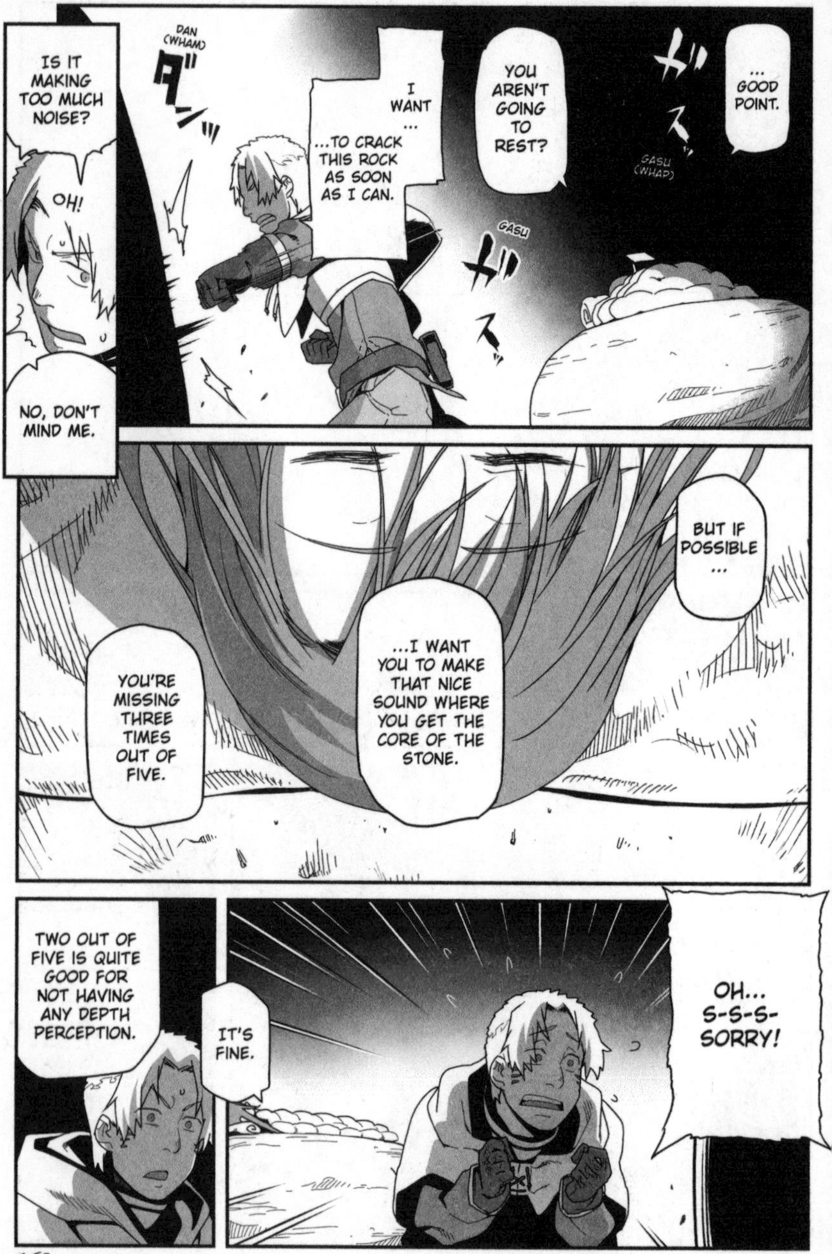

... GOOD POINT.
GASU (WHAP)
YOU AREN'T GOING TO REST?
I WANT ...
...TO CRACK THIS ROCK AS SOON AS I CAN.
DAN (WHAM)
GASU
IS IT MAKING TOO MUCH NOISE?
OH!
NO, DON'T MIND ME.
BUT IF POSSIBLE ...
...I WANT YOU TO MAKE THAT NICE SOUND WHERE YOU GET THE CORE OF THE STONE.
YOU'RE MISSING THREE TIMES OUT OF FIVE.
OH... S-S-S-SORRY!
IT'S FINE.
TWO OUT OF FIVE IS QUITE GOOD FOR NOT HAVING ANY DEPTH PERCEPTION.

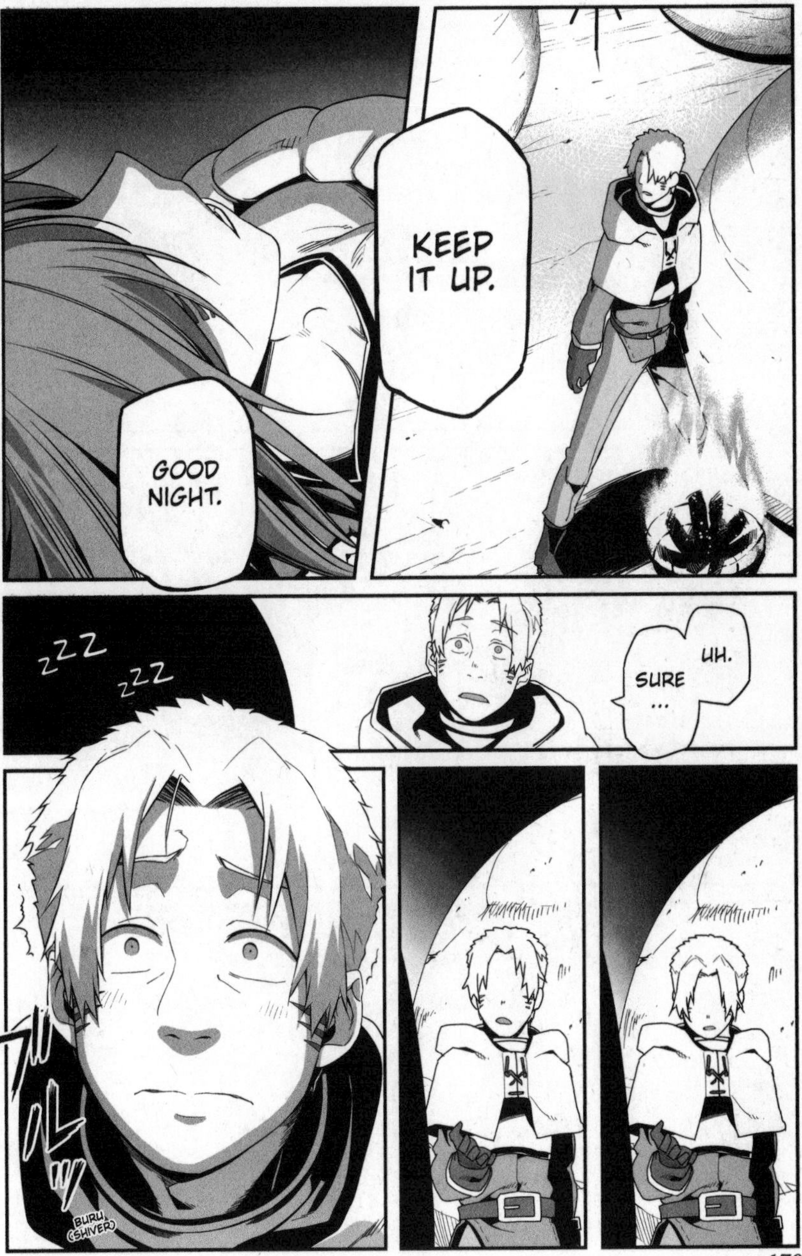
KEEP IT UP.
GOOD NIGHT.
UH.
SURE ...
zZZ zZZ
BURU (SHIVER)

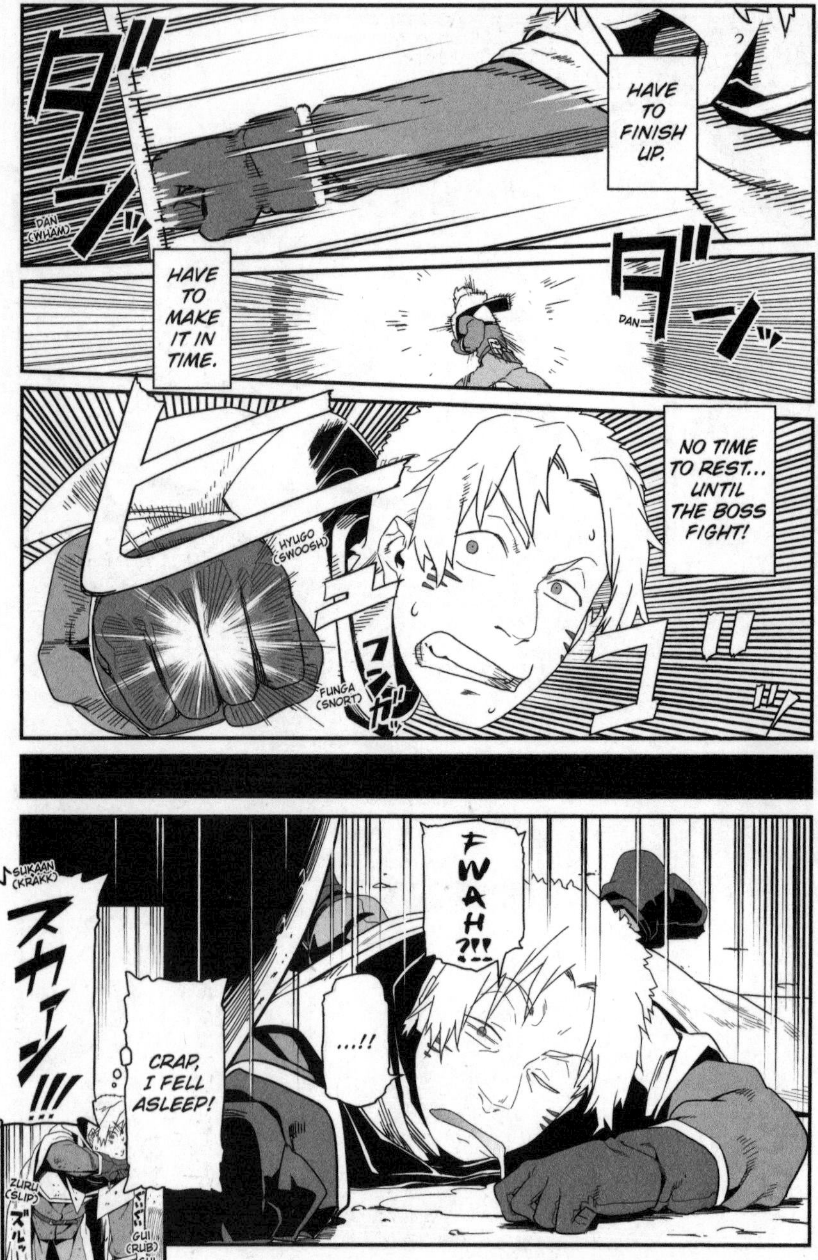
HAVE TO FINISH UP.
DAN (WHAM)
DAN
HAVE TO MAKE IT IN TIME.
NO TIME TO REST... UNTIL THE BOSS FIGHT!
HYUGO (SWOOSH)
FUNGA (SNORT)
FWAH?!!
...!!
CRAP, I FELL ASLEEP!
SUKAAN (KRAKK)
ZURU (SLIP)
GUI (RUB) GUI

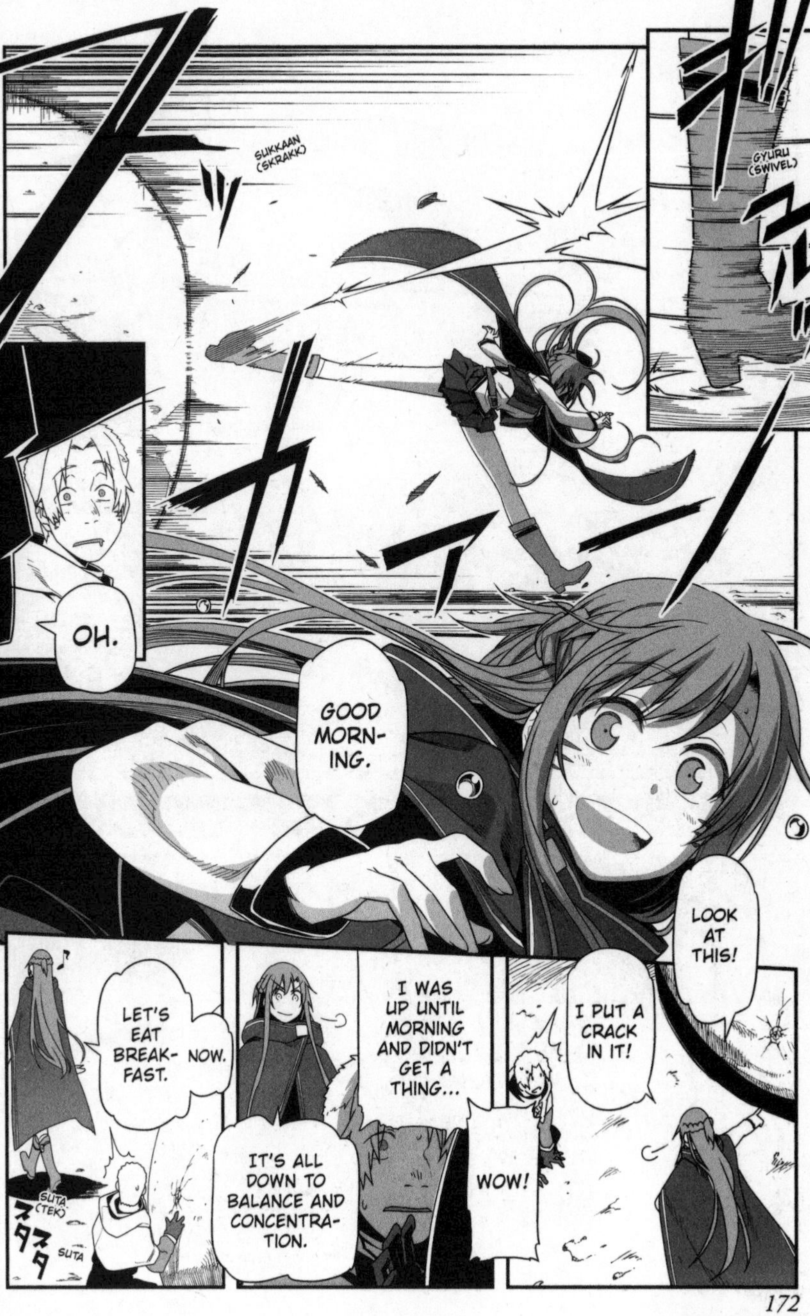
GYURU (SWIVEL)
SUKKAAN (SKRAKK)
OH.
GOOD MORNING.
LOOK AT THIS!
I PUT A CRACK IN IT!
WOW!
I WAS UP UNTIL MORNING AND DIDN'T GET A THING...
IT'S ALL DOWN TO BALANCE AND CONCENTRATION.
LET'S EAT BREAKFAST.
NOW.
SUTA (TEK)
SUTA

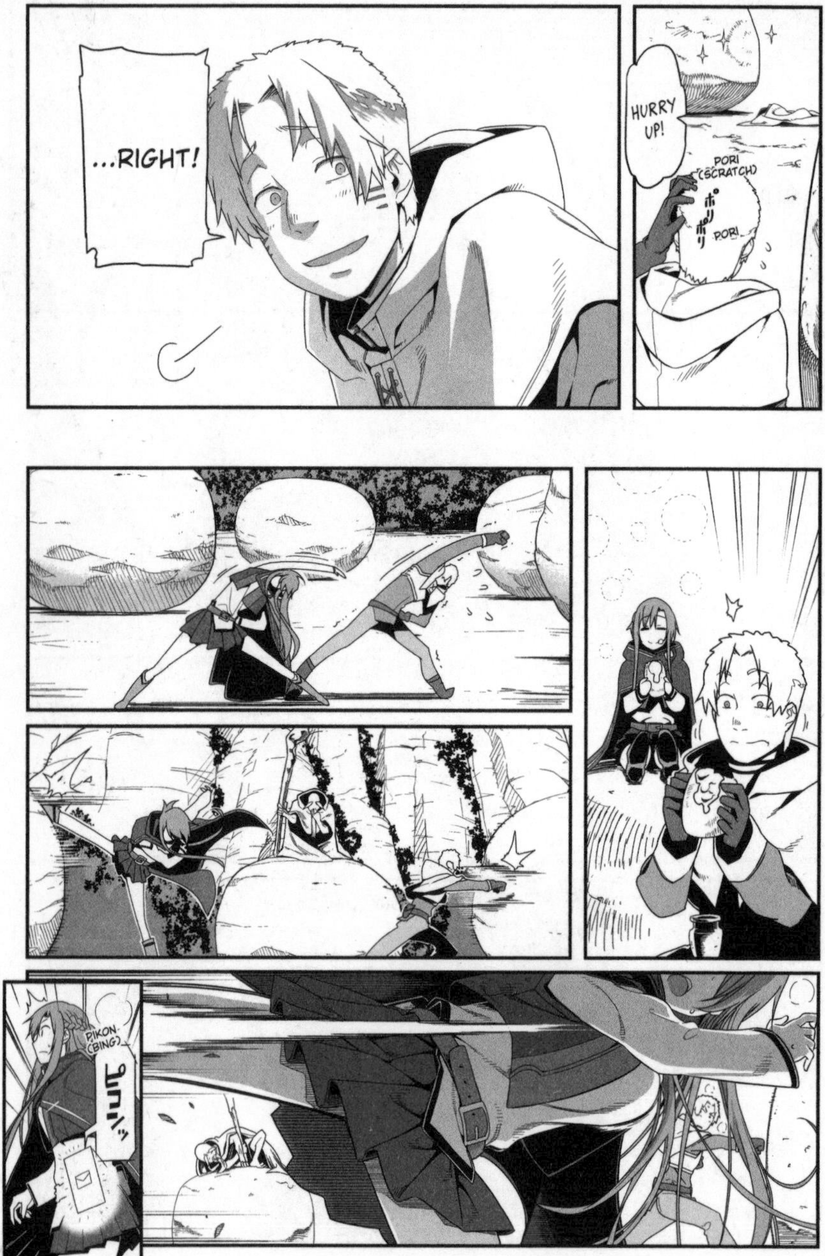
HURRY UP!
PORI (SCRATCH)
ポリポリ
PORI
...RIGHT!
PIKON (BING)
ピコンッ

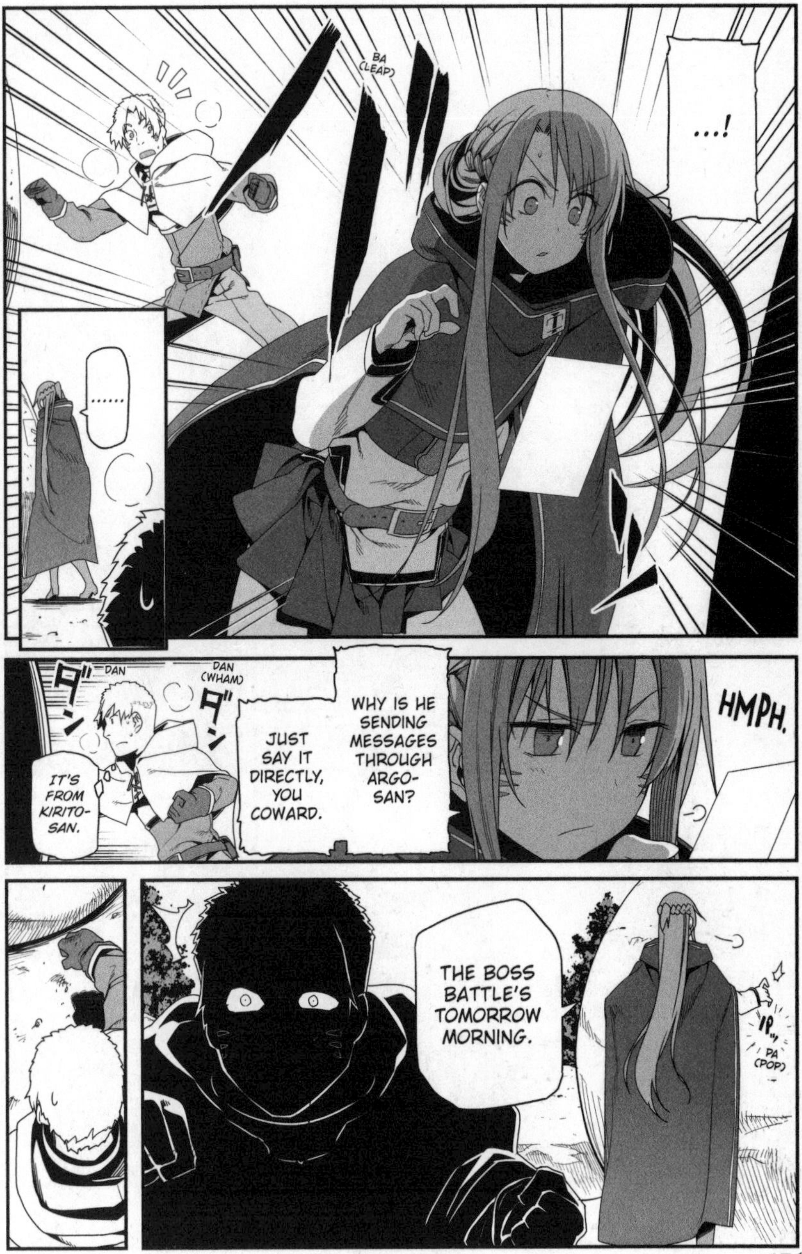
...!
BA (LEAP)
......
HMPH.
WHY IS HE SENDING MESSAGES THROUGH ARGO-SAN?
JUST SAY IT DIRECTLY, YOU COWARD.
DAN (WHAM)
DAN
IT'S FROM KIRITO-SAN.
PA (POP)
THE BOSS BATTLE'S TOMORROW MORNING.

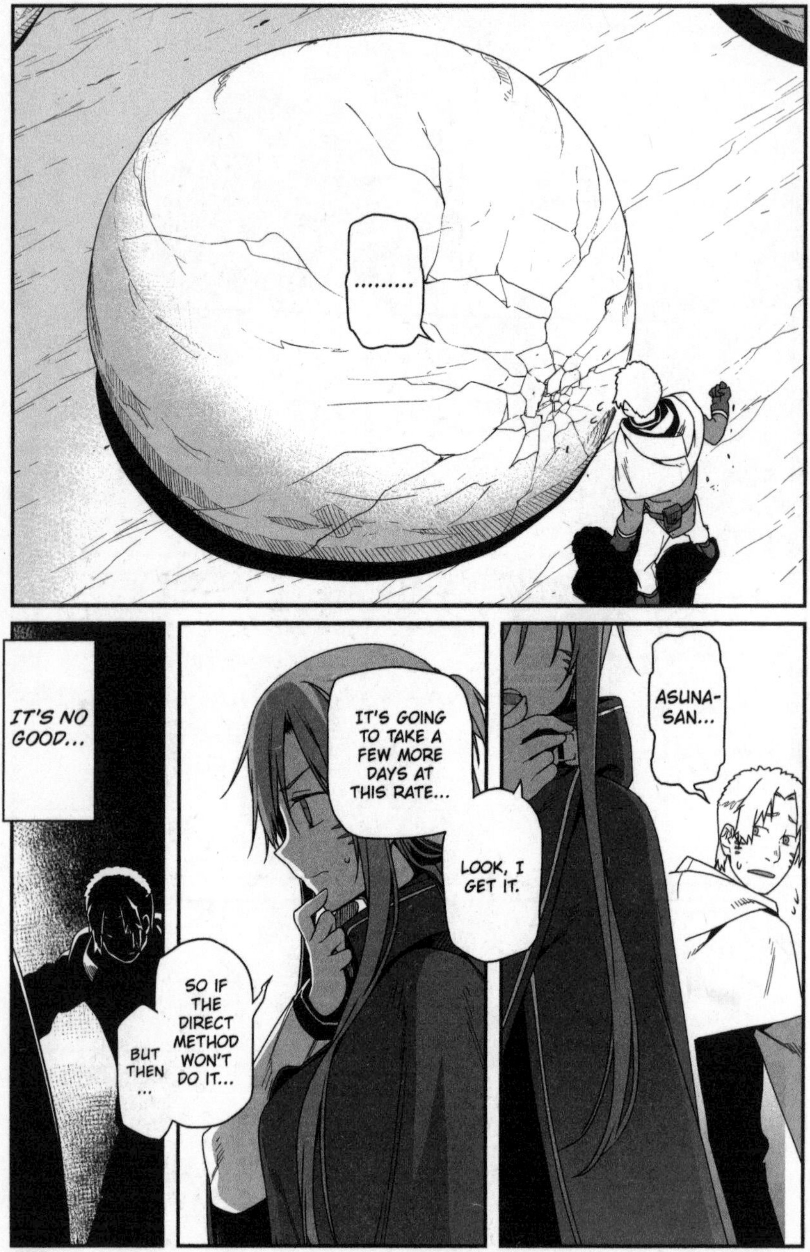
....
ASUNA-SAN...
IT'S GOING TO TAKE A FEW MORE DAYS AT THIS RATE...
LOOK, I GET IT.
SO IF THE DIRECT METHOD WON'T DO IT...
BUT THEN ...
IT'S NO GOOD...

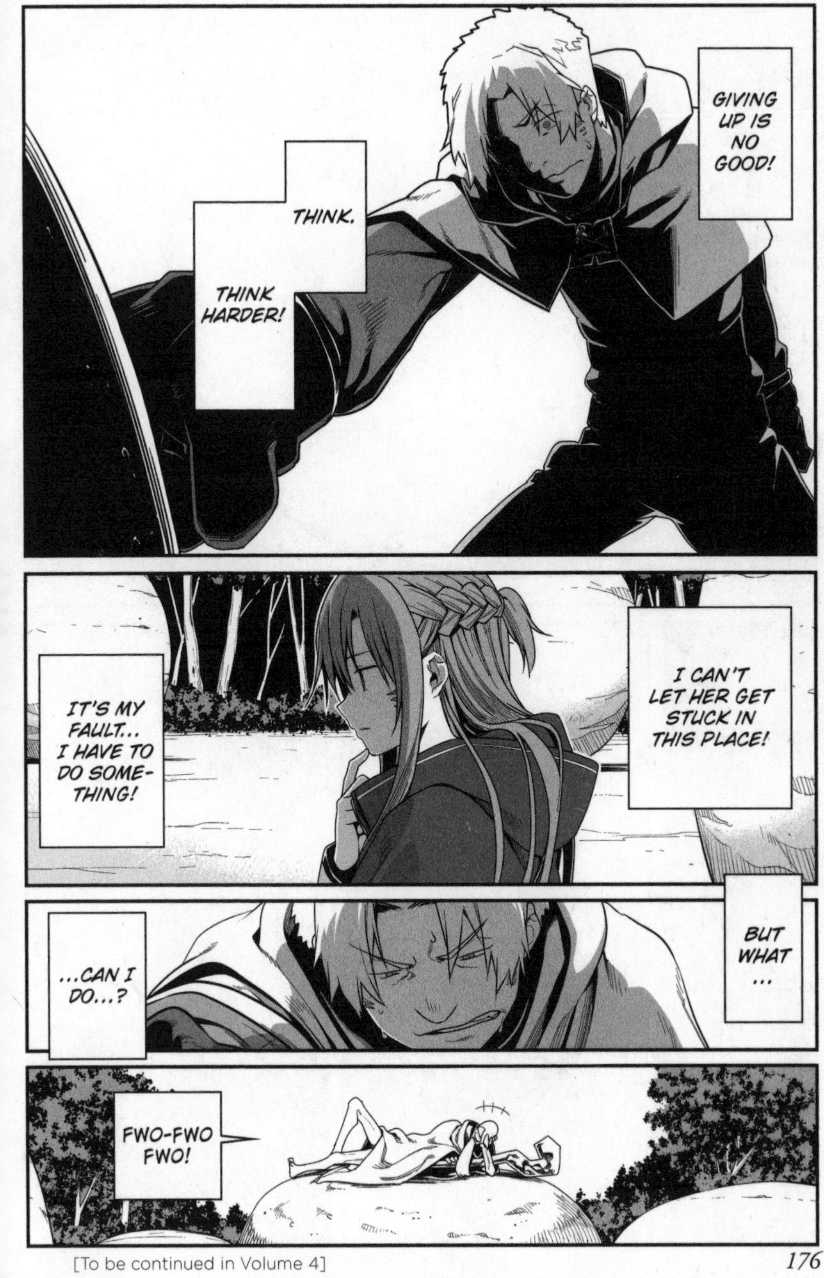
GIVING UP IS NO GOOD!
THINK.
THINK HARDER!
I CAN'T LET HER GET STUCK IN THIS PLACE!
IT'S MY FAULT... I HAVE TO DO SOME-THING!
BUT WHAT...
...CAN I DO...?
FWO-FWO FWO!

[To be continued in Volume 4]

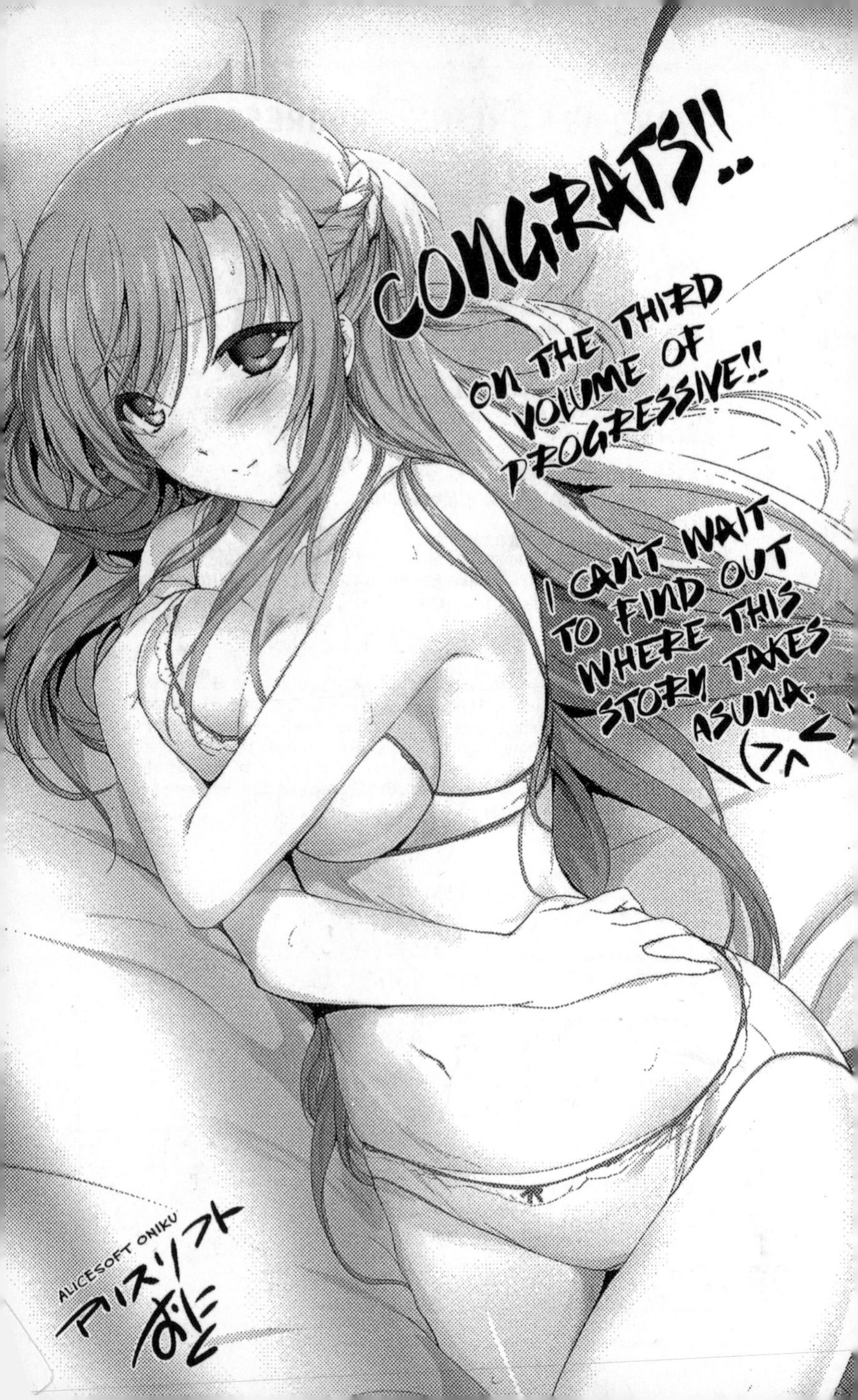
CONGRATS!!
ON THE THIRD VOLUME OF PROGRESSIVE!!
I CAN'T WAIT TO FIND OUT WHERE THIS STORY TAKES ASUNA.
ALICESOFT ONIKU
アリスソフト おにく

SWORD ART ONLINE: P

ORIGINAL STORY: REKI KAWAHARA
CHARACTER DESIGN: abec

Translation: Stephen Paul
Lettering: Brndn Blakeslee & Lys Blakeslee

This book is a work of fiction. Names, characters, places, and incidents are the product of the author's imagination or are used fictitiously. Any resemblance to actual events, locales, or persons, living or dead, is coincidental.

SWORD ART ONLINE: PROGRESSIVE
© REKI KAWAHARA/KISEKI HIMURA 2014
All rights reserved.
Edited by ASCII MEDIA WORKS
First published in Japan in 2014 by KADOKAWA CORPORATION, Tokyo.
English translation rights arranged with KADOKAWA CORPORATION, Tokyo, through Tuttle-Mori Agency, Inc., Tokyo.

English translation © 2015 by Hachette Book Group, Inc.

All rights reserved. In accordance with the U.S. Copyright Act of 1976, the scanning, uploading, and electronic sharing of any part of this book without the permission of the publisher is unlawful piracy and theft of the author's intellectual property. If you would like to use material from the book (other than for review purposes), prior written permission must be obtained by contacting the publisher at permissions@hbgusa.com. Thank you for your support of the author's rights.

Yen Press
Hachette Book Group
1290 Avenue of the Americas
New York, NY 10104

www.HachetteBookGroup.com
www.YenPress.com

Yen Press is an imprint of Hachette Book Group, Inc. The Yen Press name and logo are trademarks of Hachette Book Group, Inc.

The publisher is not responsible for websites (or their content) that are not owned by the publisher.

First Yen Press Edition: September 2015

ISBN: 978-0-316-34875-1

10 9 8 7 6 5 4 3 2 1

BVG

Printed in the United States of America